Delusional Saints

A Novel

S. C. CARPENTER

ISBN: 978-09863687-0-7

Library of Congress Control Number: 2014922787

Requests for information and special discounts orders should be addressed to: Carpenter's Press Sales department at 770-885-3186 or please visit www.carpenterspress.com

Carpenter's Press & Media, Inc.
4575 Webb Bridge Road, #3386
Alpharetta, GA
30005-9998

Manufactured in the United States of America

Preface

"Stay sober, stay alert! Your enemy, the Adversary, stalks about like a roaring lion looking for someone to devour."

(1Peter 5:8).

Acknowledgments

I give all thanks and praise to God, my Heavenly Father, to Jesus Christ my Personal Savior and to the guidance of the Holy Spirit who dwells inside of me. Without them, I could not have accomplished this goal.

To the loves of my life my sons:

Forest W. Carpenter
Hunter E. Carpenter

Delusional Saints

1

The Beginning

On October 5, 2009, Pastor Juan Cortez knew that his life would never be the same. It was a day that started out as any other day. He got up, had his morning devotion with the Lord, ate his breakfast with his wife Joyce—all the usual. Later on in the afternoon, as he sat on his living room sofa preparing for Wednesday night service at the church where he had been the senior pastor for over 35 years, he heard a loud sound outside. He jumped from the sofa and moved his tall, husky body toward the living room window. With his little pot belly lightly touching the cool glass of the window, Juan looked outside and noticed that the sky had an array of blue, white, purple and red. It wasn't a rainbow. It hadn't rained, so he had no idea what this peculiar event going on in the sky was.

Continuing to stare into the sky, Juan said, "Lord, what are you guys doing up there?" As a man who feared God and preached God's unadulterated Gospel, Juan was not concerned that God was doing something wrong, but he was extremely curious about what God, the Father, Son, Holy Spirit, angels, and saints were doing up in the heavenlies.

All he could do was wonder and ask questions. He really didn't need to ask any questions at all. He was so fixated with the scene in the sky. He'd seen different colors in the sky before, but it was just something unusual about it on this particular day.

Juan stared so long and so hard at the sky that he eventually worked himself up. There was no way he could focus on the evening service because he began to get a splitting headache. With no answers to the colorful event occurring in the sky, he decided to lie down and take a nap, hoping he would forget the noise he heard that made him look outside in the first place.

In Heaven, God was surrounded by angels, and in the far distance the saints of God praised and worshipped the Great I Am. The seraphim angels made sure that Heaven was clean at all times. Angels flew around, the sweet savory smell of incense floating all around the Throne of Grace. All it took was God's presence to light up Heaven. The cherubim's surrounded the Throne of God. Before the throne there was a sea of glass, like crystal. And in the midst of the throne, and around the throne, were four living creatures full of eyes in front and in back.

The first living creature was like a lion, the second living creature like a calf, the third living creature had a face like a man, and the fourth living creature was like a flying eagle. And the four living creatures, each having six wings, were full of eyes around and within. And they did not rest day or night as they said, "Holy, holy, holy, Lord God

Almighty, Who was and is and is to come!" Jesus sat on the right hand side of the throne of the Heavenly Father.

God summoned the angels: Ashshod, Alexander, Deoriel, Enu, Ethan, EL, Gabe, Hunter, Mickel, Rafael, Sebastian, Wade and Zaso.

"I need for you to oversee a project for me," God said.

Ashshod and the host of angels listened to God's voice while He gave them His orders.

"Ashshod," God continued, "I am putting you in charge of this mission."

"Yes, holy and righteous Yahweh," Ashshod responded.

"The rest of my angels...you are to follow."

The host of angels replied, "We will, almighty Elohim. We praise your name, Adonai."

Shortly after this, all 13 angels kneeled and started worshipping their Lord God.

"I will send more angels down in time of need," God added.

As the host of angels stood, Jesus looked at them and nodded.

This mission required strength from the saints, and it would show other characteristics of how they would handle a storm.

"I want you all to be assertive and quick," God said. "Watch and wait at all times. I also need for all of you to be prepared because Satan will try to manipulate my plan at any cost. Watch very carefully when it comes to his imps. They will stop at nothing to try to prove their point that they can defeat me. It's Satan and his imps' job to try to destroy me, and they will keep trying to take me down."

"We will be prepared, Yahweh," they all said.

Then the angels flew down to earth as they passed by the many different galaxies.

In Hell, Satan and his imps plotted their schemes. Satan yelled and screamed because the unbelievers were loud, screaming as they were being tormented. As his imps laughed at the sinners crying like little children, fire and brimstone covered the whole room as the sinners begged for mercy.

"God has a wonderful plan in the works," Satan said, "And I am going to do everything in my power to stop it. As you can tell, we need more people down here with us. I need more souls. I love when individuals who called themselves saints are in Hell screaming and hollering. Asking themselves, *why did I just go through the formalities. Why didn't I believe?* Listen to them they're screaming get me out of here, Lord. We believe now. Please come and get us."

Satan laughed before yelling, "Shut up, you whimpering fools. God will not hear your cries. You did this to yourselves. I did this to you. You paid sole attention to me and see where that got you, in this lovely burning inferno separated from The Great Almighty Himself. You have me to look over you. I'm watching you burn in your sins, and watching the worms fester inside and outside of your wretched pathetic bodies."

Satan looked around at the billions of souls. The smell of sulfur and rotten eggs reeked up Hell in its entirety.

"Imps, get over here." They all came rushing over. "Listen, I'm only sending the ones I really need to hold strong positions and the rest of you I will just send for assisting them."

They all started to drool and hiss.

Satan looked over at Greed and said, "Greed, I am putting you in charge of this project."

"I will make you proud, my lord!" Greed said.

Satan turned to Greed with an evil look and said, "You better do just that. And the rest of you better not fail me. Now go and do your jobs or I will destroy you. Be gone my little characters of greatness."

Solid Rock Missionary Baptist Church, a Multicultural congregation in Westlake, Ohio was having Wednesday night service. The imps arrived at the church and several circled around the building while others walked around hissing and drooling.

Greed looked around and let out a big roar. He summoned many of the imps to go on top of the church and he pointed to six imps and told them to go inside of the place of worship.

The six imps went inside the sanctuary, two were flying in the air and two were walking up and down the aisle just hissing, the parishioners were unaware of their presence because they were only visible in the spirit realm. The last two were jumping from pew to pew. After they saw what was going on, they all looked at each other, met in the air, and reported back to Greed.

"What did you see?" Greed asked.

"We saw individuals that seemed sincere and loyal to God and saved through the precious Blood of Jesus Christ," said one imp.

"Then we saw some that just came to do what we need for them to do," another imp replied.

The imp False Doctrine said, "We will exceed expectations in getting our mission accomplished."

Greed started to grin and hiss very loudly before summoning all the imps to follow him; they all left the area of the church grounds.

Ashshod and the host of angels arrived to earth, circling the sky. He looked around and moved swiftly across the sky, looking at their surroundings. Ashshod called all the angels and told them they were going to Solid Rock. While they flew to their destination, he and the other angels smelled the sulfur in the air. Ashshod's eyes began to glow. He stopped in mid-air and the other angels noticed. They stopped and circled around him.

"What's wrong, Ashshod?" Zaso asked.

"I see that Satan's imps have been around," Ashshod replied.

"We know. We smell the sulfur in the air."

"We need to head to the church right away."

They all moved like lightning. When they arrived at the church, there were no visible signs of the imps. They all knew that they had been there. Ashshod told Zaso and three other angels to go inside the sanctuary, and he and the rest looked around the area to see what was going on.

As Ashshod flew around, he kept running into marked territory; the powerful stench covered several blocks of the city. His eyes were glowing in the mist of the night; the other angels' eyes glowed, looking like airplanes flying in the night sky. Ashshod showed a great deal of concern because normally the imps just marked a small area. This time, he knew they were out to create havoc to a larger part of the town.

Ashshod and the host of angels regrouped at the top of the church, and he asked Zaso what he saw.

"You can see the imps' footprints all over the walls and on the pews," Zaso replied. "They walked up and down the aisles and it reeks of sulfur all over the building. They marked their territory. Ashshod, I can tell you this, this mission that they are on has me thinking they want to take everyone down who gets in their way.”

“Well,” Ashshod began, “We need to go and get ourselves ready to deal with the tasks that are in front of us. Let's go.”

Greed and the imps were gathered in an old abandoned building; they wanted to be around something familiar, a place where no one would go and if someone wanted help nobody could receive it—like Hell.

“I can feel it,” Greed said.

“We feel it, too,” the imps said in unison.

“It's God's angels, they are here in full force,” Hatred said.

“It angers me that they're here in the midst of our plans,” Greed said.

Hatred blew smoke out of his nostrils.

“Calm down, Hatred,” Greed said. “We will not let them get to us. They will not mess up our project.” They all started to hiss and drool.

“Greed, when do we put our plans into action?” Hatred asked.

“Soon, but first we must wait and continue to mark our territory.”

Ashshod and the angels were meeting at an abandoned church.

“So when do we make our move?” Gabe asked.

“We don't want to rush this because a lot of people will be dealing with a lot of hurt, pain, and suffering,” Ashshod replied.

“I know, but I just want to get rid of those malicious little imps.”

"Yes," Mickel said, "We want to get rid of them all."

"Let's settle down now," Ashshod said. "Just settle down. We must stay focused."

Thursday morning, while the parishioners had prayer service at the church, Greed and the imps were at the abandoned building discussing some of their plans.

"I am going to make sure these plans get accomplished," Greed said. "Hatred and Bully, come with me. I want to go by the church again. There is someone I want to see from a distance. The rest of you stay here. Those 'goody two shoes' angels might be lurking about, and I need to know if you see any of them around our turf."

Greed, Hatred, and Bully arrived at the church and at a distance looked at who was going inside the church.

"Stay here," Greed said before moving closer to the church. He circled around the building and went in. He looked around on the inside, noticing that the person he wanted to see was there at the service. Greed smiled and hissed, but he heard a noise that troubled him, so he fled from the church.

He went back to the other imps and said, "Fellas, I saw what I needed to see and let me just say I am going to enjoy this mission." He laughed hysterically. "We must get back to the others. The last thing I want to have happen now is to get into a confrontation with those irksome angels."

At the abandoned church, Ashshod told the angels, "It's time for me to give you your orders in which The Almighty has given to me. Zaso, you will watch over Rachael. You are to be by her side at all times. I will come by from time to time to see how you are coming along.

"Gabe, you will be at her property at all times, and the Lord has sent some more angels to help you, so you are fully in charge over there. Make sure they are where they need to be.

"Sebastian, Rafael and Deoriel, I need for you to stick with Forest. He is young and there is going to be a lot of ruckus going on, so I will need for you all to stay close and not allow anything to happen to him.

"Hunter, I just need you to be ready when I call you. I will need you to move swiftly."

Hunter nodded. "I understand."

"Alexander, Mickel and Wade," Ashshod continued, "You will come with me and I will give you your orders later. Just stay close. This will all be unfolding soon."

When Juan had arrived at Solid Rock Missionary Baptist Church, for prayer service he tried to shake off the bad vibes that roamed his body while he turned on the lights and unlocked all the doors. He walked around the sanctuary, frowning at the sour feeling that dropped into his belly. He looked up at the ceiling, then to the choir stand and began to walk up the aisle before stopping dead in his tracks. The feelings had washed over him like a tidal wave.

The feeling continued through service and traveled with him as he made his way to his appointment at Caldwell's Nursing Home where he was to meet up with his wife Joyce. The Nursing Home had asked him to come and speak a word of encouragement because the residents missed going to the place of worship. While there, he looked around and still, while in the midst of trying to provide comfort to those there, the strange feeling enveloped him. Even though he was preaching the gospel of Jesus Christ, he caught himself drifting into his own thoughts. As much as he told himself,

Get yourself together, Juan, he couldn't. He felt he was slowly losing control.

After speaking, he talked with the residents and the director of the nursing home, but his mind battled to stay in the moment and thwart the feelings that threatened to overwhelm him. Joyce was there as well because she was a part of the committee that sponsored this event. And more than once her eyes took in her husband with worry.

Juan knew his wife would ask him about his actions—especially considering they shared a quiet ride home. He couldn't tell her it was the only way he could insure they'd make it home in one piece. Without using his mind to hold a conversation, he could focus all of his attention on driving safely and still attempting to push the bad feelings from himself.

As soon as they made it home, Juan went into his den and went into prayer. His life, he felt, was so bizarre—as was his place of worship.

With amen barely off his lips, he exited the den and found Joyce there, staring. Although he knew questions were about to fly from her mouth, he couldn't help but to smile a little. He still found his wife so beautiful. At 57, she kept her slim build fit and well-groomed. He loved running his hand over her soft brown skin, kept so from her African-American heritage and her daily moisturizing regimen. God had definitely given favor when he placed Joyce in Juan's life.

"How was prayer service?" Joyce asked.

"It was okay," he responded with no sense of excitement in his voice.

"Was there a big turnout?"

"Nice size, not like usual though. I guess people were on vacation. You know when the weather is great people want to do what they want to do."

"Yes, I know."

They both laughed. He noticed that even though he was speaking to her, he could not stay focused; it was as if he had *(A.D.D.).* For two days, he had felt this—*something* infiltrated him.

Maybe I need more rest, he thought, smiling at his wife.

Joyce wandered off to busy herself, and Juan headed to their bedroom. He would sleep an hour and was sure that a long rest would cure him of what ailed him.

Not too long after, Joyce entered and stared at him, wide-eyed. "What are you doing in bed so early it's only 7:00 p.m.?" she asked.

"I just need to get more rest, that's all." The last thing Juan wanted to do was discuss this. He didn't even know what *this* was. He wouldn't talk that night—but was sure by morning he would be able to.

"Well I'm going to watch some more television and then I'll be ready for bed."

"Okay," he said, "Take your time."

When the door closed behind her, Juan took a breath, looked to the ceiling and whispered, "God, what's going on?"

Joyce stopped on the stairs hesitating to return back to the bedroom to demand an explanation from Juan because he had gone to bed early. She could see how distracted he was at the nursing home, and that episode, plus the silent ride home, and then the early to bed event. Joyce cupped her head in her hands.

Instead of heading back to the family room to watch television, she returned downstairs and went for her phone. Her dear friend Rachael would offer an encouraging word—this, she knew.

"Hey girl, what are you doing?" Joyce asked.

"Girl, I just got back from taking Forest and his girlfriend to the movies," Rachael replied.

"Forest has a girlfriend?"

"Yes girl, you know Piper Rodgers."

"Yes, she is a sweet girl."

"Yes, she is."

They both laughed.

"Oh, I'm sorry, Rachael, can you talk? I didn't ask if you could talk or not."

"Now Joyce, you know I always have time for you, what's going on?"

"Juan is in bed now."

"What, is he sick?"

"No, he just said he needed more rest."

"But you think it's something else?" Rachael asked.

Joyce sighed. "I don't know what to think, Rachael, but I can tell you I am concerned."

"I understand, but don't get yourself so worked up. If he said don't worry, then don't worry."

"I guess you're right. I just needed some words of encouragement, that's why I called."

"Girl, no problem, that's what friends are for."

After getting a word from Rachael, Joyce headed back upstairs; she opened the bedroom door and Juan was sound asleep. Joyce went back downstairs, but this time she headed into the kitchen and made her some tea. All the while, she thought about Juan. *This man is an ox*, she thought. *Something must be bothering him for him to be acting like this.*

Finishing up her tea, she shook her head and whispered. "Maybe I'm putting too much emphasis on this. Let me take my tired behind to bed."

Joyce had prayed that Friday morning would find Juan his happy, smiling self; but it didn't. Their morning ritual of breakfast, coffee, and chat was a silent affair and without asking for permission, she grabbed her phone while in front of Juan and called Dr. Writz's office. Juan's eyes widened as she set an appointment for that afternoon—for him. When she hung up, Joyce looked at Juan, concern etched in her eyes and said, "I'm worried. This will help me not be worried." Juan nodded and sipped his coffee.

"Pastor, what brings you both here today?" Dr. Writz asked. "Nice to see you, Mrs. Cortez."

"Young man, you look so great," Joyce said. "Juan, remember when he was a baby?"

Even through his smooth brown skin, Joyce and Juan could see Dr. Writz blush. It never got old, hearing the two go on and on about him. They had known him since he was born, and for 35 years he had been a member of the church along with his parents.

"Ah, come on now," Dr. Writz said.

"Look at him blushing."

"Why haven't we seen you at worship?" Juan asked.

"Well," Dr. Writz said, "The hospital is understaffed, and I do a lot of overtime."

Juan lifted an eyebrow; Joyce smirked. "Okay," they said in unison.

Dr. Writz smiled and shook his head.

"Dr. Writz," Joyce said, "I am concerned about my husband. He has been acting very awkward for the past couple of days. He doesn't think I've noticed, but I have. I want him to get the whole nine yards. Blood work and anything else. I don't think he needs an enema at this time."

Juan and Dr. Writz both looked at Joyce, and she began to laugh.

"I just wanted to see if you guys were paying attention to me," she said.

They all laughed.

"I had no choice but to hear what you said," Dr. Writz said, chuckling. "Rest assured, I will check him out and run all necessary tests to see what's going on."

He quickly assessed Juan's blood pressure and eyes and ears, and found them all normal.

"I will send in the nurse for some blood work," he said.

"As old as he is," Joyce said, "I still chuckle that he still does not like needles."

Juan grunted.

Dr. Writz grinned. "I'll let her know to be gentle."

The nurse came in and Juan acted like a big baby kicking and screaming.

"If you don't stop acting childish, I'm going to take off my belt and whip your tail," Joyce said, hiding her laughter.

The nurse, however, did not hide her laughter.

Juan feigned a pout. "Okay," he muttered. "Can you please just hold my hand? You know how I feel about needles."

Joyce grabbed his hand and gave him a look as if he was a child about to be disciplined. The needle journey was finally over. The nurse left the room.

"Don't you ever take me down that road ever again," Joyce said, scowling.

Juan just smiled, and she smacked her lips.

"I still love you," he said.

Joyce cut her eyes at him, and they both laughed.

An hour and a half later, Dr. Writz returned with test results.

"It appears," he said, "That you have a great bill of health. So you both need not to worry, your cholesterol is great, everything is fine. It was time for you to get a checkup anyway, so I'm glad you came in."

"Thank you," Joyce said.

"Yes, thank you," Juan said.

"No problem," Dr. Writz said.

"I hope we see you at worship service real soon," Juan added.

"Me too." He hugged Juan and Joyce and added, "I'll see you both soon."

On the way to the car, Joyce received a phone call from Rachael.

"Hey girl, what's going on?" Rachael asked.

"Just leaving the doctor's office."

"Is everything all right?'

"Yes, girl, thank God!"

"Yes, He is great."

"Yes," they said in agreement before breaking into laughter.

2

Marco and the Mega

Church

Friday morning, when Solid Rock was having prayer service, Marco was off work and on his way to service. He drove past the area mega church and noticed that the church parking lot was jammed pack and cars were lined up and down both sides of the street. Even from the street, the choir could be heard, sounding like singing angels. All he could do was shake his head because he could not believe how the mega church was doing so great and Solid Rock was stuck in the Stone Age.

Marco had spent much time either taking in the appearances of the nearby mega church; or watching the pomp and circumstances of those churches on TV. When he did, every time he closed his eyes, he saw himself as a pastor of a mega church. He saw his 6' athletic frame wrapped in an expensive suit; his beautiful Nubian queen of a wife, Lisa, by his side; and their children: Marion, Lanice, and Bryant in tow, painting the portrait of a successful black, God fearing family. *This is how an African-American family can show up and show out*, he would think. *For God, of course.*

Marco pulled up into Solid Rock parking lot, and there were maybe ten cars in the lot. He was so irritated and miserable he could not focus on anything. Marco stepped into the sanctuary and sat in the rear of the church, watching the nearly twenty people there. All he could do to keep from screaming was to say a prayer which he said immediately.

After he finished praying, Marco zeroed in on Pastor Cortez and became sick to his stomach.

Juan glanced at Marco and gave him a smile, but all Marco could think about was taking off his shoe and throwing it at the pastor's big apple head. Juan summoned him to come down to the altar. Marco was an associate minister at Solid Rock. Out of all the other associate ministers, Marco's services were used the most. Marco preached from time to time but not enough to satisfy himself. He visited the sick and taught the young adult Sunday school class.

Marco wanted to utilize his strengths in the church by becoming the new pastor. Although he knew that the parishioners thought he was a great young man, he also knew that only a few thought he was pastoral material. The majority of the congregation loved their pastor and they hoped that Juan Cortez would live forever.

Being an associate minister, Marco needed to be near the pastor during services. He knew this and wanted to refuse, but he went down anyway. Service lasted for an hour and a half, and the same faithful few were there. Everyone was so happy.

Marco must have had a look on his face because Juan said, "What's wrong?"

"Nothing," he said.

"You look as if you're somewhere else."

"Oh no, I'm all right."

"Are you sure, Minister Pablo?"

"Well there is something I would like to discuss with you."

"Okay, but we can't discuss it today. I have another engagement I must attend to. You can set up a time with the church secretary. We'll talk then."

He patted Marco on his arm and walked up the aisle and left the building. Marco felt that Pastor Cortez left him standing there as if he was a piece of crap. He kicked one of the pews then stormed out of the sanctuary without saying anything to anybody.

As Marco was driving home from prayer service, he noticed that the mega church was still crowded, so he decided to go in, and what a treat it was for him. When he walked inside the sanctuary, their hospitality committee greeted him and they wanted to seat him near the front. He asked to sit in the back so he could leave without making a scene.

As Marco looked around, all he could see was excited people. He caught himself smiling as the choir sang; he was in awe. What caught his undivided attention was Pastor Hummingbee. He was dressed to impress and he was received as if he was a god. Marco loved every moment of that and when he saw the good looking young women, he said, "Now this is what I'm talking about nice looking young women."

But when will this sort of opportunity come my way? He thought. How long would he only be an associate minister? Pastor Hummingbee was saying all the right things. He even spoke on prosperity and doing well.

Pastor Cortez always wants to preach about Jesus, Marco thought. *We all know who He is. Let's just talk about something new sometime.*

After Pastor Hummingbee finished his message, he did not extend an invitation to be saved because he didn't want to put any pressure on the people to accept Jesus Christ as their personal Savior. He wanted to give them time and to allow the people to accept Jesus at their own pace. The congregation was all in agreement. They sang a song and they said a chant "No Pressure, No Pressure Take Your Time," as they were dismissed.

When Marco walked out into the parking lot and saw all of the people interacting with one another, it did something to him. He felt as if he just left a social event. Needless to say, he left there on a high note.

When he returned home, his wife Lisa asked him where he'd been.

"I visited the new mega church and boy was it out of sight," he replied, excitedly. "It was so good it's hard for me to even describe it. The young people were excited, the choir was wonderful. The way the church was decorated…oh it's so sweet."

He could not take his mind off of what he had encountered. He could just feel the energy still.

Lisa peeked her head out from the kitchen and said, "Marco, dinner is ready."

"I'm not hungry. I'm just so high right now, Lisa, you just don't understand. You had to be there and you will understand why I can't eat. I'm not even sure I can sleep tonight."

"Marco, oh you will be going to sleep because you will not be keeping me up all night," Lisa said. "You will be taking your talkative spaced out thoughts to bed."

"Lisa, I am not going to allow you to rain on my parade. Do you hear me?"

"No Marco. Do you hear me? You will not be keeping me up all night. Better yet Marco, you will sleep on the sofa."

"Lisa, it's not necessary to take me through all of this."

"You think I want to keep hearing these dreams that you are not ready for? I don't think so."

"Lisa, sometimes you really get on my everlasting nerves. You just keep it up."

"And what Marco? You won't do nothing."

Marco just left the kitchen because he thought Lisa was being ignorant, and the last thing he wanted to deal with was an ignorant woman.

No matter what he tried that night, he couldn't sleep. He tried watching television and even listening to the radio. As the radio was on, the mega church commercial came on and it just gave him that high all over again. He started to wind down about 4:00 a.m. Lisa woke him up for work at six, and with less than two hours of sleep he was so refreshed; he just loved this feeling that he was experiencing. He got up and went to work without hesitation.

The Tanankas were in the kitchen having their morning coffee before they attended Sunday morning worship. Frisky, their German shepherd, laid at Mr. Tanankas feet.

They were also preparing for their dinner guests after service: the Cortezs, the Weinbergs, and the Pablos.

The Tanankas were a well-groomed couple, very well to do and just as sweet and generous as they could be. Mr. Tananka was a 60-year-old Japanese-American who loved and adored his wife, despite her almost obsessive need to indulge in plastic surgery. Years ago, when the two married, his parents were concerned for him—marrying a white woman with a penchant for changing her face like some changed their clothes. But he loved her, and she him, and they had managed to build a very successful and happy life together.

Trevor, their son, walked into the kitchen and said, "Good morning, Mom and Dad."

"Good morning," they said.

"Son, will you go to morning worship with us?" his mother asked.

"Mom, you must not have had your morning coffee. You know I'm not going with you. Please stop asking me. I don't know why you guys keep asking me the same question Sunday after Sunday."

"Trevor, it's because we care for you and we want you to be saved through the precious blood of Jesus Christ."

"Mom and Dad, I understand, but right now I don't want to hear this stuff. So," he said, changing the subject, "Are you having company over?"

"Yes," his father replied.

"Oh yeah," Trevor said. "Church folks." He chuckled.

"You know that we alternate hosting dinner," his mother said. "It's our turn."

"Oh, so is Lisa coming?"

"Yes, with her husband," his father replied.

"Okay, Dad, I just think she is so fine, that's all I am saying."

Mr. Tananka cut his eye at him.

"Whatever, Dad, whatever." Trevor got so irritated that he just left the kitchen; Mr. and Mrs. Tananka shook their heads.

"Sometimes," Mr. Tananka said, "I wonder where we went wrong with him."

"What do you mean, sweetie? We did nothing wrong."

"That is a grown man there. He's 30, but the way he acts and talks, you would think he's half his age."

"I know." Mrs. Tananka sighed. "We can only keep praying and hope our Heavenly Father intercedes and helps Trevor change."

The couple held hands and offered a prayer for their son.

Marco and his family arrived at Solid Rock Missionary Baptist Church and he became so agitated because there was no hospitality committee just a lame Usher Board that looked as if they all were standing on one leg.

"Oh no! The choir is about to sing, he thought. *Why is the pianist looking and playing like Little Richard? Doesn't he know he's Asian and there's no resemblance in there looks? I don't even think he knows the key he's playing in. Oh know he's feeling excited he better not say it,* before Marco could finish his thought the pianist yelled *"Good Golly".* Marco leaned forward in his chair bent over into his lap and cupped his hands covering his ears and shook his head in frustration. He then looked up took inventory of everything around him, finding something negative to say about it all. The lead singer sounded like a cat that had its tail stepped on trying to hit

high notes. *If the drummer hits those cymbals one more time I am going to take those drumsticks and stick them where he will never want to use them ever again.*

The choir; to him, the ten sopranos sounded like a 91-year-old granny, the seven altos he gave a reprieve to, and the three tenors were as loud as 30 people. Marco didn't expect the choir to cut an album anytime soon, unless the album was for deaf people.

As he looked around the place of worship, he became sick and tired of seeing the same old things. The worship building needed to be upgraded; they needed young new people in the church. He was so tired of seeing the same old families every Sunday. Since the mega church had moved into the neighborhood, he really wanted this church to move in the same direction as the mega churches. Inside, Marco raged with jealousy and envy. He truly believed this church could move in this new direction if Juan was not the senior pastor.

I know if I was the senior pastor, I could make this church into a mega church.

Instead of listening to Juan preach, he daydreamed. He couldn't digest the sermon because his heart and mind were solely concentrating on moving this congregation to a whole new level. He was determined to address this issue after morning worship. He couldn't sit there and listen to this mess anymore.

Morning worship had ended and Juan stood down by the altar, meeting and greeting the visitors and members, enjoying his time of fellowshipping with the saints of God.

Marco approached him and said, "I need to speak with you."

Juan smiled and said, "Later."

"Why not now?" He yelled.

"Don't you see I am fellowshipping with the parishioners?" The people standing around looked at Marco with perplexity on their faces. In a softer voice, Juan added, "Did you make the appointment with the secretary?"

Marco ignored the question and said, "You see these people all the time. I need to speak with you." He tried to say it in a joking manner, but he knew it came off wrong.

Marco saw the revulsion in Juan's eyes before turning and walking away. He sat in the back of the sanctuary until Juan finished his meet and greets.

He began to imagine himself as the pastor, but as soon as he got deeper into his thoughts, Lisa and the kids approached him.

"Marco," she said, "I called your name three times."

Marco was jostled from his thoughts and jumped a bit when he saw his family before him.

"Oh?" he managed to say.

"What are you thinking about so hard that you didn't realize that we were here?"

"Oh nothing. So what's going on?"

"I'm ready to go eat," Lisa replied. "Don't forget the kids are going over Sister Cook's house for dinner."

"I remember."

"I wonder what the Tanankas are serving for dinner."

Marco sighed. "I don't know and I don't care! I just need to speak to Pastor Cortez, that's all I am concerned about right now."

"Whatever you need to say must be very important because this is all you can focus on."

"Yes, it's very important," Marco said, looking up at his wife. At the moment, everyone that wasn't the pastor irritated him. "Lisa, just go now," he added, more aggravation in his voice than he intended.

Lisa looked at him and rolled her eyes.

"Watch yourself, boy," she said. "I don't know *what* your problem is, but you will *not* be disrespecting me."

She spun on her heels and escorted the children away.

Marco looked at Pastor Cortez and said with a bitter tone, "Hurry up." He rolled his eyes and shook his head. "I really hate being here pretending I like this whole atmosphere."

Marco glanced back toward the pastor and found him smiling and approaching. "I am ready to see you, son."

Marco followed behind, his bitterness growing with each step. "I got your son," he muttered.

Before Marco stepped fully into Juan's office, he said, "Don't you think we should be moving in the same direction as the mega churches? This is the way to go and we need to move in a new direction, don't you agree?"

Juan leaned against his desk and eyed Marco. Marco couldn't read the look.

"Oh," Juan said, "You think that we should run the house of God like a corporation?"

Marco nodded. "Yes, if it gets the people in here and we can build and do the big things like they do, such as daycares and big recreation centers. You are really holding us back, pastor." Marco leaped in front of Juan and pointed his finger at him. "You need to step down and let me move this place to a whole new level."

"Marco, leave my office right now. You really need to ask the Lord to change your heart."

"Nothing is wrong with my heart. You just upset because I don't let people walk all over me the way that you do!"

Juan said, "What do you mean by this, Marco?"

"When the older women and the widows of the church come to you needing something, you say it would not be in our best interest at this time. Then when they start crying and saying things like what are we going to do? Or would God be pleased with your response, you give in."

"You are a wimp, pastor, a silly old wimp. Just tell those old folks no! I don't care what they need. They better be glad they're living. Or what about the time the members came to you saying that the church needed a new bus? You said we didn't have the funds at the time and when the members started crying and whining once again you gave in."

Juan crossed his arms. "Marco, I don't know where..."

"Listen, No means No! Step down, old man. You are doing us a disservice. It's time for bigger and better things. We have overcome! Didn't you get the memo? You are in charge. You need to put your foot down and let them know who is in charge. Man, you are really killing me with your soft leadership skills."

Marco walked out and slammed the office door.

Juan looked up and said, "Lord, this young man doesn't understand that it's not about moving to a new level, it's about your Son Jesus Christ who died on Calvary's cross, and rose on the third day so that mankind can have eternal life though Christ, Jesus our Lord and Savior."

He looked down and shook his head. "You said in your word in the last days these things would happen, that Christians must be very careful with false teachers who want to tickle the ears of the people, and lead them on the road to destruction, thinking that material pleasures and vain words and large crowds would be pleasing to God. I just hope we can correct the wrongs before it's too late."

The heavenly angels were all gathered inside and outside of the Tananka's house. There were 25 angels surrounding their house.

Ashshod told Hunter, Deoriel, El, Enu, and Alexander to go and transform into humans to walk up and down the street to watch over the Tananka's house.

Hunter transformed into a Black male in his twenties, Deoriel and El transformed into two white males in their forties, Alexander transformed into a seven -year-old child playing with his remote-controlled truck on the sidewalk, and Enu transformed as a father figure watching Alexander play with his remote-controlled truck. The ten other angels stayed close to them.

Inside the home, the Tanankas, Cortezs, Weinbergs and Pablos were at the dining table as Trevor walked in.

"Ooh, dinner is ready and I am starved," replied Trevor.

"Hello to you to son," his father said.

"I'm so sorry for not speaking. I just smelled food and I am so starved," Trevor said.

They waited until Trevor said grace for his food before speaking with him.

"I missed you at morning worship today," said Juan.

"Pastor, I know you want to see me at the place of worship. I just don't see myself there. I like doing what I do and I am just a ladies' man. Do you know what I mean, reverend?"

Marco laughed and his wife hit him. "There is nothing funny about what he just said!" answered Lisa.

Marco just continued to eat.

"Trevor, you better get yourself together and repent and give your life to Jesus Christ," Juan replied.

"Rev, I'm just not ready to hear this right now. Can I just eat? I don't want to be preached to. Let me eat in peace, please."

"Son, watch your mouth and your tone, especially speaking to the pastor like that," his father John said.

Trevor looked up from his plate and rolled his eyes.

Everyone around the table was quiet in awkward silence before Juan asked Forest how things were going on with him.

"Things are okay, but some things I just can't put my finger on. Something is not right to me," Forest replied.

"Can you try to tell us?" Juan asked.

"I can't explain it, I'm sorry."

"We will all pray for you, Forest, so the Lord can reveal to you what's going on," Juan said.

"Thank you, Sir," Forest said.

Juan turned to Rachael. "How are things with you, sweetheart?" Juan asked her.

"Well I can't complain. I heard that they are building a new complex around my property," Rachael replied.

"That sounds great," Juan said.

"Pastor, do you have any new plans on building a new place of worship so you can get some new and exciting members?" Trevor asked. "I'm sorry to say, pastor, but the last time I went to church I was ready to fall on my face and go to sleep. The inside of the place is so outdated I thought I was in the '70s" Trevor shook his head. "Come on up with the times, pastor. If there are some good looking honeys up in there, I will definitely be up in there."

Trevor laughed and Marco followed suit. Lisa kicked his leg underneath the table.

"Aw Lisa, it was funny to me. I just had the same conversation with Pastor after morning worship," Marco said.

"I will not have this conversation and especially with you, Marco," Juan said, agitated.

Insulted, Marco got up from the dinner table. The whole table became quiet, yet again. They had never seen Juan become so irritated. Joyce got up and rubbed her husband's back.

"Honey, please don't get yourself so worked up. He's young," stated Joyce.

"I'm so sorry, pastor," said Lisa.

"Sweetie, it's all right. I'm okay," Juan said.

Lisa smiled with caution; she was so embarrassed. She could not believe the nerve of her husband acting like he had no common sense.

In and outside of the house, the angels sensed trouble but nothing had appeared or occurred.

Marco returned back to the dining room table and sat down. They all looked at Marco, waiting to see if he was going to start some more trouble. A couple of minutes passed by and Marco remained silent.

"I really feel my spirit being bothered," Juan said.

"Honey, what do you mean?" asked Joyce.

"I see a big spiritual battle about to approach."

"Maybe it's just gas," Marco commented.

"I need for you to stop speaking," Juan said.

"I was just joking. Can't you just take a joke?" Marco said.

"Marco, will you please keep your comments to yourself, enough already," replied Lisa.

"Marco, you are entitled to your own opinion, but I think we need to calm things down." Jane Tananka said.

"Everybody is so sensitive about me expressing my views and opinion on Pastor Cortez's statement. I'm a grown man. I can express myself," stated Marco.

"You sure can, but you need to understand that this is my house, and I need for you to act as if you're grown and now it's time for you to stifle your behavior," stated John.

Marco gave John a look of disgust and underneath his breath, he said, "This man don't know me. I will get up and knock him into the middle of next week. Telling me to stifle myself. Who does he think he is?"

Everyone knew that Marco still had a chip on his shoulders. Joyce jumped in and started to talk about the church service and how the Lord's presence was in the house of worship.

3

The Mission Begins

Juan could not sleep; he just could not shake the eerie feeling he was having. Friday night in bed, Joyce noticed that her husband kept going to the bathroom then would turn on the television in the bedroom a couple of times and continuously looked out the bedroom window.

"Honey," Joyce said, "What is wrong with you?"

"Baby, I don't know," Juan answered. "My spirit is restless, and I can't put my finger on it. Whatever it is, it's really shaking me."

"I see. Have you prayed about this and asked the Lord to give you some answers?"

"Yes I have, but God hasn't responded. It must be something really major because the Lord always gives me an answer or a clue. This time I am getting nothing."

"Honey, come on back to bed. I will hold you real tight and keep you safe from all the ghosts and goblins that are keeping you up."

Even in the dimly lit room, she could see his smile.

"Thank you, baby," he said. "I love you. This is why I married you."

They both laughed, then went to bed.

Saturday morning Juan had his breakfast and read his newspaper.

He informed his wife Joyce that he would be spending his entire day in prayer. "Don't disturb me, and take all my phone calls for me, please."

All Joyce could do was nod. She knew that something major must be pressing upon her husband's heart and mind for him to pray all day.

Sunday morning had arrived. The Tanankas were in the kitchen eating breakfast before they attended morning worship and their son Trevor walked in with his typical good morning. They tried constantly to bring him to church, to Christ, and this day was no exception. Before they could get the question out, Trevor moaned and said, "No, I will not go to worship with you today. Mom and Dad, I love you guys, but this religious stuff is not for me. I want to go out and enjoy this beautiful day by playing basketball with the guys. You guys enjoy yourselves, sing a song for me."

He chuckled and left the room.

The Tanankas prayed endlessly to bring their son to Christ; they loved him dearly, but they knew that he was living his life recklessly. They wanted to see him come to Christ and stop using and abusing women and their trust.

During Sunday service, Juan walked into the sanctuary. He noticed that his hands were clammy, but he blew it off. He thought it was his nerves. He listened to the choir and sat through the entire order of service. He began perspiring heavily. When it was time for him to speak, he sat in the pastor's chair. He was slow to get up. The congregation noticed this. Joyce looked perplexed and said, "What is wrong with him?"

Juan got up in slow motion and walked to the podium very carefully.

Marco looked at Juan and said, "What is his problem?"

Juan stood quietly for a moment and then began to speak, but he was very careful how he spoke. He began by reciting 1 Peter 5:8 "Stay sober, stay alert! Your enemy, the Adversary, stalks about like a roaring lion looking for someone to devour." Clearing his throat, he added, "Today's topic is on "'Delusional Saints'." Juan was into his sermon about five minutes, informing the parishioners to watch out for demonic beings that appear to be helpful but in actuality are very harmful. He informed them to read their Bibles because it was the most essential tool to show them these wicked beings.

With each sentence he spoke, he felt fervently that the message had to be conveyed, and quickly. He grabbed the microphone, intent on adding more fire to his words, but his speech slurred and before he could blink or wonder what was going on, he passed out. The congregation exploded with shouts of concern as his body thudded to the floor.

Joyce stood to her feet and screamed. She moved lickety-split from the pew she was sitting in, ran up into the pulpit, and stood over her husband. The ministerial staff stood back; Marco pulled out his cell phone and dialed 911. Some of the parishioners were yelling and screaming. The Tanankas and the Weinbergs ran up into the pulpit to be by their friend's side. Marco was just stunned. He could not believe his eyes. Could this finally be his opportunity? He wondered.

In an instant, Ashshod and all the heavenly angels surrounded the pastor and the entire congregation. They began to move very quickly around them; they knew that the demons were soon to come to stand their ground and cause havoc.

Juan laid lifeless on the pulpit floor, not responding to anyone's cries. Joyce kneeled down next to Juan hugging him tightly screaming in his ear, "Juan speak to me. Can you hear me honey?"

The congregation panicked not believing what they had just witnessed.

Finally, after ten minutes passed, the emergency medical service arrived rushing through the crowded sanctuary. The female EMS worker lifted Joyce off of Juan shoving her out of her way. She took his vitals and rushed him off to the hospital.

Joyce was in a daze not believing that her beloved husband was being rushed to the hospital in an ambulance.

Rachael grabbed her arm, "I'll drive you Joyce," she said.

"We'll follow you," replied the Tananka's.

Joyce arrived at the hospital, the Weinberg's and Tananka's at her side. They all waited frantically in the waiting room.

A young African-American woman dressed in scrubs came into the room and asked, "Who is here for Mr. Juan Cortez?"

Joyce stood. "I am. I'm his wife." Rachael stood alongside her and placed a hand on Joyce's shoulder.

The woman smiled warmly. "I'm Dr. Casper, chief doctor in the ER."

"Doctor, what has happened to my husband?"

Dr. Casper informed Joyce that Juan had suffered a hemorrhagic stroke, which was caused by bleeding on the brain. "We have run numerous tests," she added, "And something remarkable has happened."

Joyce glanced at her friends, their expressions as confused as her own, then returned her gaze to the doctor. "What happened?" she asked.

"Your husband cannot move his body, but he is still in his right mind and he can speak. This normally does not happen with stroke victims. Trust me, I have seen some things in my life, but this is amazing, Mrs. Cortez."

4

Friends with Issues

Monday morning, the imps Racism, Bully and Hatred circled the hallways of Forest's school. They went into Mrs. Roberts's classroom discussing how to cause trouble. Mrs. Roberts noticed that the students in the hallway were causing too much noise. She stepped out into the hallway, and she noticed Forest and Piper were holding hands and interacting with their friends. Mrs. Roberts had a look on her face as if she was sucking on a lemon and it captured Hatred's attention.

"What is she looking at that's making her so frustrated? Let's go see what has captured her attention," he said.

The bell rang as everyone was going to their classrooms. Mrs. Roberts summoned Piper. Racism blurted out, "There is something wrong with this picture, missy, and you know what that is? If not, there is only one superior race and that's yours."

"Yes, Mrs. Roberts," Piper said as she walked over to her.

"I see that you are very close to Forest," replied Mrs. Roberts.

"He's my boyfriend."

"How do your parents feel about you dating him?"

"Mrs. Roberts, why are you asking me this question? I have class to go to, and I don't want to talk with you about this. I am starting to feel very uncomfortable." Piper walked away.

"Who does she thinks she is walking away from you without answering the question?" Racism said.

Hatred blew furious fire from his nostrils. "I just hate it when young children act so stupid. She could have answered the question. This has me so worked up, I'm outta here. I'll see you all later." Hatred vanished.

Mrs. Roberts stood in the hallway with her mouth dropped to the floor, not accepting how Piper just walked away from her elder, treating her as if she was her equal. She stood there until she saw Piper vanish around the corner.

After class Piper went to Forest's locker; he was chatting with Turquoise, Lil' Audrey and another kid, and she told them what happened between her and Mrs. Roberts.

Bully moved toward Piper. "So you think you are telling on us?" he asked. "I don't think so."

"Stay far away from her, Piper, do you hear me?" Forest said.

"I knew it was something weird about her," Turquoise said. "I don't think she approves of interracial dating."

"Yep," said Lil' Audrey.

"I'm kind of freaked out by her," Piper said.

"Don't worry. I won't let her hurt you," Forest said. He embraced her. The bell rung and it was time for them to go to their next class.

Forest was 'chillin' and hanging with Piper and other friends before their next class began. Mrs. Roberts came out of her classroom, and looked up and down the hall as if someone had taken something from her.

"What is her problem?" Turquoise asked.

"I don't know, but whatever it is she needs to fix it," Lil' Audrey replied. "I don't like her. She is really strange."

Mrs. Roberts looked at Forest and Piper and gave them the "stink eye." All of them noticed it, and they just responded by shaking their heads and giggling. Mrs. Roberts became really agitated and saw three of her students in the hallway and summoned them into her classroom. She stood in front of her classroom door and when all the boys walked in she slammed the door. Everyone in the hallway just looked like she was from outterspace. The bell rung and Forest kissed and hugged Piper. "I'll see you later," he said.

"Okay," Piper said.

The rest of the gang said bye in unison.

■ ■ ■

Hunter, Rafael and Sebastian were in the gymnasium awaiting Forest's arrival. As they were waiting for him, Racism and Bully appeared in the gym.

"Look who's here, Bully, I guess "The Calvary" has arrived," Racism said.

"Yes, I guess we can go now," Bully replied.

"Not!" said Racism. "What are you bumbling idiots doing here? We don't want to see your happy faces and your spread love attitude around here. Go back to happyland where you belong."

Hunter, Rafael, and Sebastian overlooked the silly imps. They saw Forest enter the gym room and flew toward him.

Bully flew over in the direction of Forest and yelled, "I don't care how many of you 'goody two shoes' angels surround him, I'm going to get him, mark my words," he said.

Sebastian looked over at Bully "You will do no such thing," he said.

"What do you think you are going to accomplish by thinking you can stop me?"

"Oh, nothing because you dingbats can't stop me," explained Bully.

Hunter looked over at Bully. "You don't want to mess with me today, Bully. I am not in the mood."

"Hey Racism," Bully said, "Did you hear him he said he is not in the mood?"

"Well, stupid angel, I am in the mood and you better just get out of my way," said Bully.

Rafael looked at Bully and flew right in front of him and slapped him in the face. Bully looked at Rafael and said, "You will definitely pay for that."

The students were playing basketball in the gym and everyone was having fun.

Forest was playing basketball and accidently hit Steward. He apologized as Steward went to get the ball.

Racism saw Steward, one of Mrs. Roberts' students, and jumped on his left shoulder. Steward became outraged and jumped in Forest's face and pushed and shoved him.

Racism said, "Steward, this is the way you do this. Hit him."

As Steward was aimed to knock Forest out, Hunter jumped in and pushed Steward back, making it look like Forest had hit him.

Bully said, "Oh, if you are fighting his battles, then I will join in."

Forest apologized over and over, but Racism kept instigating Steward to harm Forest. But Bully continued to make sure that the boys kept fighting. The boys just shoved each other around for a little bit until the coach broke it up.

Steward was so bitter and angry that he started to throw out racist language: "You coon, you black spade, ghetto trash." The whole gym became silent. No one could believe the horrible things that were coming out of Steward's mouth.

"Steward, if you don't calm down, I will send you to the principal's office," replied Coach Reynolds.

Steward looked at Mr. Reynolds. "You don't tell me what to do. I can say whatever I want. I have freedom of speech."

"You do but not in my classroom."

"I don't care about your class, you coon lover."

"Well, I need for you to get yourself together, Steward, and calm down," Coach Reynolds said.

"No, you get yourself together, Coach, loving and protecting this coon."

Coach Reynolds sent Steward to the principal's office. Steward turned back around and gave the coach a piece of his mind, "Screw you, you spade lover," before slamming the gym room door.

"You arrogant no good angels," Racism said. "This is not over." He left the gym room with foul language coming from his mouth, following Steward to the principal's office.

"It ain't over until I say it's over," Bully said, blowing smoke out of his nostrils before vanishing.

Hunter, Rafael and Sebastian all looked at each other and shook their heads.

"What a mess," Sebastian said. "At least we know we have to protect Forest at *all* times."

Ashshod, Zaso, Gabe, and Enu were at Rachael's commercial property awaiting her arrival.

Zaso and the others were giving Ashshod their reports.

Zaso, Gabe and Enu were assigned to this case even though Ashshod was the leader; they still reported to him for all instructions.

"Zaso," Ashshod said, pointing at Rachael as she stepped from her car, "you watch over her at all times."

Rachael owned a piece of commercial property that housed the mentally ill and those who were ex-cons. On the ground level of the building, were ten storefronts, in which she allowed individuals to start their own businesses. Rachael and Forest lived in a well-to-do neighborhood, and Rachael worked tirelessly to make sure that her son got the best education in life.

As soon as she arrived at the building, one of the tenants raced towards her.

"Ms. Weinberg, Ms. Weinberg, I need to speak with you," the tenant said. When she reached Rachael, the tenant added, slightly out of breath, "I want to talk with you. I'm planning to leave the complex."

"Oh, I am so sorry that you want to leave," Rachael said.

"Me too. I heard about all the rebuilding they are doing around here, and I don't want to be around all this mess and noise. I also heard that the community development team can take over your property, so..."

"This is not true," Rachael replied.

"Well, all I know is what I heard, and if this is true, I don't want to be put out on the streets. Besides, I don't want to deal with any politics."

"I understand your concerns, but you don't need to worry."

"I thank you, but I am going to go with my first instincts, and I must say my goodbyes."

With a sad smile, the tenant handed Rachael her thirty-day notice.

"Well, you know what's best for you," Rachael replied, sighing. They looked at each other and smiled before the tenant turned and walked away.

When other tenants learned of the development news and possible purchase of the building, they grew scared and concerned about the new project. Several of them approached her and voiced their concerns.

"There is no need to worry," Rachael said, attempting to calm them. "They will not take over my property."

"We heard that they can take away your property because of eminent domain," one tenant said.

"No," Rachael said, "They cannot. I have spoken with my attorney, trust me."

After Rachael had spoken with her tenants, trying to reassure them that she had rights, she was exhausted. But she was determined to regain her energy; she had a meeting with the development company in thirty minutes, and she told her tenants that she would get to the bottom of this and have information for them soon.

Greed, Covet, Hate, Lust, and Lie appeared at the developing company that wanted Rachael's property. There were three people that were over the project and they were going to do everything in their power to get Rachael's building.

Greed became irritated and began to hiss.

Covet, [the head imp of this project], was eager to capture Rachael's property, and he used Gary Grabber to do this.

"Here is what I want you to do," Covet said to Lie. "I want you to have Gary lie to Rachael's tenants and tell them the company will give them $10,000 to move out of Rachael's building."

Lust was much irritated because he could taste the building in their possession. "Why can't we just take it?" he asked.

They all watched as Rachael entered the expansive conference room and the group went into formalities. Once introductions were finished everyone was seated, Mr. Grabber, one of the members of the board, said, "I am just coming straight to the point. We want your property. It is hindering us from building a drug store there."

Rachael looked at the man as if every word he said was going in one ear and out the other. She had no intention of giving up her property.

"You have two options," Grabber continued. "You can sell us the building or you can work with us on fixing up your building."

"I will work with the development company to fix up my building," Rachael replied.

Mr. Grabber's face turned red. Rachael's response was not the one he wanted to hear.

Hatred flew near Rachael and blew fire from his nostrils. Zaso stood even closer to Rachael.

Hatred said, "No, this will not be acceptable."

The rest of the team was silent and looked at each other knowingly.

Mrs. Betty Smith, another board member, asked, "What if we offer you $300,000 for it?"

"That would not be enough because I would still owe on the mortgage," Rachael replied.

"Do you have *any* intentions on selling your building?"

"No, I don't. The Lord has blessed me with this property, and I'm going to keep it."

"I see."

"Zaso, you better get her before I do," Covet said.

"Or what, Covet?" Zaso asked.

"Your idiotic human seems not to understand that I am on a mission and she is interfering with something that is more powerful and has much more worth than her existence."

"What you are failing to realize is that Rachael is worth more than what you are trying to accomplish."

Covet huddled near Hatred as the two began to think of a plan to get Rachael. The others watched as impatience grew upon Mr. Grabber's face. Fury could be seen in the red splotches that appeared on his face.

Hatred said to Covet, "Rachael is going to make me hurt her. We want that property."

"Not to worry," Covet said. "Something is going to happen to her or her son or with the building—whichever comes first."

"I like that."

The room became silent and everyone from the development company just looked at one another. Almost as soon as it began the meeting concluded.

"We would like to thank you for your time," said Mr. Grabber.

Rachael shook everyone's hands and exited the room. After leaving the meeting, Rachael was very perplexed; she thought she would have the backing of the development company, but that was not it at all.

Zaso walked extremely close to Rachael, especially since the other imps were looking on; they knew not to touch her.

Rachael went home, and as soon as she saw her son, she smiled. He always had that effect on her. Out of all the decisions she'd ever made, adopting Forest had been the best and most rewarding. Years ago, when she learned she could not conceive, she decided to adopt. When she saw Forest and his beautiful brown baby face, she knew he would be her son. Others had questioned early on what a white woman could provide for a black child, but throughout the years, she had proven that she could raise her son to be tolerant, to be loving to others, to know about where he came from and be a good young man. She was beyond proud of all of his accomplishments and it did her heart good to know that he was saved, friendly, popular and in two years would be graduating high school and going to The New York Conservatory For Dramatic Arts.

At the dinner table, she filled him in on her day, and Forest was as surprised about the turn of events as she was.

Behind Forest at the dinner table stood angels Sebastian, Rafael, and Hunter; they watched as Forest informed his mother of Mrs. Roberts' antics at school. The story nearly floored Rachael, and she could barely believe it or Steward's reaction toward Forest while in gym.

"He was really going off, Mom," Forest said, concluding his story. "Steward called Mr. Reynolds a coon lover before heading to the principal's office. We could only stare at him. We were too surprised."

Rachael was so stunned over what she had heard. She did not know what to say or think besides, *What in the world is my baby boy going through?* "Forest, you just let me know if you need for me to come up to the school."

"Mom, this is being handled. Don't worry. I'm a big boy."

She looked at him and said, "All right my big boy." They both chuckled.

■ ■ ■

Trevor was in his bedroom getting ready for his date for the evening with Monique. He was dating multiple women at one time. Trevor was the kind of man that had to dress to impress, from his watches and rings to his outfits and shoes. The imps loved Trevor because he was the man that got the job done. Lust, Fornication, Covet, and Greed hung around Trevor all the time. Greed had the chance to move more freely; whereas, the other imps stayed close to Trevor.

Trevor received a phone call from Sade' and was excited to hear from her.

"Hi sweetie, what's up with you?" he asked.

"We need to talk," she replied.

"Okay I was just about to call you."

"Whatever. Let's meet in an hour at our spot in the parking lot."

"Yes," Trevor replied.

Fornication appeared when Trevor met Sade' at the parking lot. He wondered what she wanted to discuss. "This should be interesting," he said.

Trevor kissed Sade' as if she was the only woman in his life.

"What do you want to talk to me about?" he asked.

Sade' didn't beat around the bush. "I'm pregnant."

Trevor's eyes widened. "What? How did this happen?"

She gave him a look like he was crazy.

"I *know* how this can happen," he said, "But you said that you were using protection."

Fornication said, "Oh that's not your child and no way will you give up on sleeping around with multiple women."

"I know it's not mine," Trevor said, anger and aggravation in his voice. "You better go talk to the guy you've really been seeing."

"The only person I've been seeing is you!"

"That baby is not mine. What you are going to do is keep moving. I'm not the father of that child. And don't think about calling me, Sade'. It's over. I don't have any time to deal with children. I'm a ladies' man, do you hear me?"

Sade' could not believe the arrogance that came out of Trevor's mouth. She tried to gather her thoughts.

"Oh you must get rid of her," Covet said. "We don't need to deal with nonsense like this."

Trevor looked at Sade' then turned and walked away. After taking a few steps, he stopped, turned, and went right up to her and reached into his pocket, pulled out his wallet, and gave her ten hundred dollar bills and said, "Here, this is for you, do whatever you need to do."

She took the money and started to cry.

"Be an adult about it." That was his favorite phrase. He looked at Sade', gave her a gentle smile, and walked away. Sade' just watched him walk away from her, get into his car, and drive off.

As soon as Trevor got into his car, he called Monique on his car phone. When she answered, he said, "Hi honey, can't wait to see you tonight."

"Same here. I'll see you soon."

Lust, Greed, and Fornication smiled and drooled.

Lust said, "Boy, you are really handling your business, my little mini me."

Trevor went home before meeting up with Monique. He saw that his parents were in their sitting room just talking and spending time with each other.

Mr. Tananka said, "Son, what's going on?"

Trevor said, "Mom and Dad, don't be alarmed, but this dumb girl came up to me and told me that she was pregnant with my child."

"What?" his parents yelled together.

"That's what I said." Trevor laughed.

"What have you done, Trevor?" his mother asked.

"Calm down. I know it's not my child because she sleeps with everybody."

"So you just go out and sleep with loose women?"

"Mom, it's not like that, and she said she was using protection."

"Oh, that's just great," his father said. "You have it all figured out. So what did you say to her?"

"I told her that I did not want to see her anymore, and I gave her a thousand dollars to handle anything she needs to handle."

Mrs. Tananka could barely speak, but her flustered face and the red in her eyes showed just how she felt.

"Mom," Trevor said as if he was a kid talking about not doing his homework, "it's just a way of life."

Mrs. Tananka got up out of her chair and punched Trevor in the arm and said, "No, that is not the way of life, son."

"Oh Mom, don't act this way. She was wrong not me."

"What?" his father said. "What were you thinking, Trevor?"

"Why are you so upset? I gave her money. I made a grown up decision."

"In whose world, Trevor?" Mrs. Tananka asked. "Oh I forgot, your world."

Trevor stomped out the room and Frisky, their dog followed him. He went up into his room and slammed the door.

A short time later, Lust stood very closely to Trevor as he met up with Monique in a big parking lot. Little did Trevor know that Monique was followed by her husband to the parking lot. Her husband watched how his wife was being kissed and groped upon. He got out of his car, bent down, and maneuvered through parked cars and snuck up on Trevor and pushed him away from his wife before punching Trevor in the face.

"Man," Trevor yelled, "What is wrong with you?"

"Why are you on my wife?"

"Wife? She did not tell me she was married."

Lust just smiled and said, "Ooh, Trevor, you bad boy, messing with a married woman. Shame on you."

Greed showed up and said, "What's going on here? I see our boy has to have everything he wants. Oh, how I love this young man."

Lust said, "Me too".

"Hey Lust," Greed said. "You have any popcorn because I just love this show." They both laughed hysterically.

"Terry, what are you doing here?" Monique asked, exasperated.

"I should be asking the questions not you. Monique, did you tell this man you were married?"

"I don't know, Terry I can't remember if I did or not," she replied.

Terry shoved her away. "Get in your car and go," he said.

"Man, I didn't know that she was married," Trevor said again.

Terry threw another punch at Trevor; this time Trevor blocked it.

"Now you know." They began to fight.

Monique hesitated on returning to her car. She turned and softly said, "I'm so sorry, Trevor."

"Monique, just go. Now!" Terry said.

Monique left the parking lot screaming and crying loud and hard. Someone who was walking to their car saw the fight and called the police; the police arrived and broke up the fight. Trevor and Terry both got cited and received tickets for disturbing the peace. Trevor got in his car, beyond angry.

"That silly female could have told me that she was married," he said.

Saturday afternoon found Satan's imps at Rachael's commercial property causing havoc. If she wouldn't give into the development company's demands, then it was their duty to damage her property.

Zaso, Rafael, Sebastian, and Hunter were in Rachael's bedroom watching over Rachael and Forest.

Greed appeared and said, "Aw, just look at them just having mother and son time. Isn't this lovely?" He paused before adding, "Not."

"Greed, I think it's time for you to leave," Zaso said. "Why are you here?"

"I'm just here to check on this stubborn subject of yours," Greed replied.

"Greed, take your nonsense and go," said Hunter.

"Well since you all are in a great mood, it's time for me to wipe those dumb smiles off all of your faces."

When her cell phone rang, Rachael picked up and found one of her tenants on the other line; none of the tenants in the building had hot water. Rachael was puzzled by this, so she called her maintenance man to meet her at her commercial property.

"What in the world is going on?" Rachael said after she got off the phone.

"Well, that's my cue. Got to go, ta ta," Greed said before vanishing from the room.

"Annoying imp," said Zaso.

"Mom, what happened?" Forest asked.

"Tenants have no hot water."

"Dag Mom, you want me to go to the building with you?"

"No son, you stay here and start your homework project."

When Rachael left, Zaso was right by her side.

Rachael and her maintenance man met at the building and found that someone had vandalized the property; they had broken into the boiler room and burst the hot water tanks and pipes. Rachael was appalled, but it had to be fixed because the tenants needed hot water.

"What is going on around here?" asked Zaso.

"Greed and these bothersome imps are in full force," Gabe replied, "And they are starting to make their presence known. They are very angry because of Rachael's decision concerning her property."

"Thanks for this information. I need to stand real close to Rachael now."

"Stay away from my territory," replied Covet.

"I have the freedom to go anywhere I want at any time," said Zaso.

"Once again you dumb angels think you can protect your subjects from Satan's warriors? I don't so. You all can leave now."

"We will leave when we are ready," said Zaso.

It pained Zaso and the rest of the angels to see discouragement as it washed over Rachael.

Covet and Hatred were very angry because she was getting these things fixed. God sent more angels to assist Gabe and Enu. Gabe told them where to stand guard and to watch over the property.

Rachael called the police, but none showed up until 8:00 p.m. She had been there since three.

She had been calling the police all day and said, "No one ever showed up."

The dispatcher said, "What, no one came by yet?"

She said, "Why is he acting so surprised? He knows that they are so lazy. What jackasses." Then she said, "Excuse me, Lord!" She quickly added as a way of explaining, "This is the only curse word I use when I am so frustrated." When the cops showed up, they were apologetic. She was so aggravated; all she wanted to do was go home from sitting at the building all day.

5

Who's Going to Be

Our Pastor?

During Wednesday night prayer meeting, the congregation came in full form to pray for their pastor; even pastors from in and out of the city joined in. Everyone came to show their support and Joyce was truly pleased. Juan even received a large donation to help with medical and household expenses.

A month had gone by, and there were no changes in Juan's condition; the congregation was informed through the grapevine that his condition was not going to change anytime soon. So the members became restless because they were missing their pastor. They knew that his medical bills were going to be costly, so they felt that it was in their best interest, [especially] the ones who wanted him gone, to get a new pastor. Very few parishioners felt this way. The ones who wanted him gone felt they shouldn't have to pay for someone's medical bills when they were not getting any services in return.

The chairman of the deacon board had a small meeting before Sunday school with the deacons and trustee board and informed them that he would have a mandatory church meeting after morning worship to induct Minister Marco Pablo as their new pastor. He went on to explain that they needed someone now instead of later.

"We really need to form a committee," said one deacon.

"No, we do not," replied Chairman Smith.

The chairman continued to explain to the boards that the ramifications of not having a pastor as well as the finances depleting because of no leadership. The membership was dropping, so he reiterated why they needed to do this. Some of the members showed some signs of hesitation but went along with it. He led them in prayer and they adjourned.

After Sunday morning worship, the chairman of the deacon board called an emergency meeting. It was a prime time to do so considering Joyce opted not to come to church so that she could visit her husband in the hospital.

The congregation felt it was in the best interest of the church to remove Juan as their Senior Pastor due to his medical condition. The chairman of the deacon board said, "How can we hear the word without a preacher?"

Even though the congregation knew of the other associate ministers, Marco had the most experience and he was the most popular.

They quickly accepted Marco Pablo because they knew him and they did not want to go through all the rigor of finding a new pastor. Finally this young enthusiastic associate minister would get his chance to be pastor.

"This is not right," Rachael said, the Bible says, "Who among you is wise and understanding?" "The person who fits this position must show moral responsibilities, he should be able to instruct, guide, and have the wisdom in all of these areas."

"This position takes years of experience and Minister Marco Pablo is in no position to handle this heavy responsibility. I think you all are making a very bad decision. You all are being lazy instead of forming a pulpit committee. This congregation is going to suffer in the long run."

"We don't want to hear all that," someone blurted out. "We are trying to pick a new pastor. Sit down. You are getting on our nerves."

Rachael looked around the building and said, "Who said that?"

The same person replied, "Your momma." The congregation started to laugh.

"This place is about to go down the wrong path," Rachael said.

"So are you. Sit down and shut your mouth. We don't want to hear you."

Rachael finally located the member and looked at him. "I was here before you," she said, "And the only way I'll be leaving is in a hearse. Do you hear me?"

The congregation chuckled. The chairman of the deacon board said, "Order, order."

The congregation overlooked Rachael and voted Marco in anyway. Marco was stunned and speechless, yet very proud to finally get the break he had been longing for. He bent over and put his head in his hands and started to weep profusely. The parishioners looked on and someone blurted out, "God bless his sweet precious little heart."

They noticed how overwhelmed he was. Then the members started to give a round of applause to Marco. One of the other ministers just patted him on his back and said, "Congratulations, Marco, well done."

Rachael jumped up. "Listen, you don't want to do this. He is not ready," she said. "You all are making an emotional decision that can hurt you in the long run."

"How dare she try and stop my dream," Marco muttered to himself. *Who does she think she is?* Marco looked at Rachael with disgust. *I want her to get it.*

Mr. Tananka jumped up and said, "You all are out of order here." He was furious.

Another member jumped up and said, "You guys can just leave, we don't need you all here. You can go, too, Rachael."

After the church meeting, Rachael and the Tanankas were talking in the church parking lot.

"I really have a bad feeling on what's going on around here," Mr. Tananka said.

"I'm going to go see Joyce and inform her of what just happened," Rachael said, "but let's have a word of prayer first."

Church members looked on as they formed a circle of prayer.

As they were in prayer, someone in a car that was passing by yelled, "You all need prayer. You should be ashamed of yourselves trying to stop us from getting a pastor."

They all held each other's hands tighter.

Then another car passed by with someone screaming, "Leave, we don't need you here, you troublemakers."

Mr. Tananka held his head up and opened his eyes and someone threw an open pop can and just missed Jane.

"What in the world? Who threw that?" she asked.

"I don't know, but they better be glad they're in a car right now," said John Tananka.

"See," Rachael said, sighing, "Things are starting already."

The same church member that yelled at Rachael saw them in the church parking lot praying and went inside and told Marco what they were doing.

"Pastor, you need to watch out for them. They are going to do whatever it takes to get rid of you."

"Thank you my dear brother for informing me."

"No problem, Pastor, but be very careful. They already informed you of how they feel about you in this position."

After the church member left, Marco became even angrier. He wasn't about to relinquish the control that was just given to him. He left the church with Lisa and the children.

Nate, one of Marco's old neighborhood buddies, came up to Marco while standing in the parking lot and congratulated him. "Hey man, I have a little something for you to say well done." Nate handed Marco a small bag with a white powdery substance in it.

Lisa looked on, furious.

"Man, I'll see you around," Marco said, offering Nate a short hug.

As Nate walked away, Lisa continued to stare at Marco in disbelief.

Marco told his wife to get into the car.

Lisa got into the car with a ferocious attitude and slammed the car door. Marco was standing outside of the car and he began to wave at the parishioners who were lollygagging around before he left. Marco finally got into the car.

Lisa looked at her husband and said, "You should be ashamed of yourself. What did Nate hand you?"

"Just a little something. You act like I'm going to use this. I just took it because I didn't want him to think I was trying to be a 'goody two shoes' okay."

She looked at him and rolled her eyes and turned and looked out of her window.

He said, "Oh honey, don't be like that, don't act that way."

Lisa flinched. "Don't touch or talk to me."

"Okay be like that. I'm still the new pastor." He did a little dance move while driving the car.

His children in the back seat said, "Dad, you're crazy. Stop embarrassing us."

Satan's imps took a rare opportunity to rejoice. With Marco in place, they knew their plan to take over the congregation was in effect. They would use this young man to get the joy of sending people straight to Hell. The imps smiled and drooled because they could taste and see their evil deeds about to fall into place.

Marco took his family out to dinner to celebrate, but Lisa was not in the mood, especially after what she saw between Marco and Nate.

Greed, False Doctrine and Hatred appeared at the restaurant.

At the dinner table Marco said, "Lisa, I'm going into work tomorrow, and I'm going to quit."

"I don't think that would be the best thing to do," she said. "You should put in a two-week notice."

"Okay Lisa," he said, but he was only saying this to appease her. He knew she was still upset.

False Doctrine, Hatred, and Greed started to hover around Marco. False Doctrine was on his right shoulder, Hatred was on his left shoulder, and Greed hugged him around his neck. Marco grabbed his neck as if something was holding him real tight.

"I'm so proud of you, Marco," said Greed.

"The reason you are holding your neck, Marco, is we are showing our gratitude toward you. If you just keep following our lead, you will go far, our dear boy," said False Doctrine.

Rachael called Joyce from her car phone and said, "I need to speak with you. It's very important."

"Rachael, what's going on?" Joyce asked.

"I'll explain when I get there."

Rachael tried to obey the traffic signals as she raced to the hospital. For the first time since arriving at church, she managed to smile when she saw Joyce sitting upon Juan's bed, smiling lovingly at him.

Juan smiled as he caught Rachael peeping into the room. She walked through the door and she returned a bigger smile. She hugged him and said, "How are you doing?"

"I'm okay," he replied. "I would be better if I could move." Rachael and Joyce just looked at him with no words to respond to his statement. Juan asked Rachael, "So what's going on at the church?"

She gave him a look as if Juan was speaking Chinese. "Why do you ask?"

"Just keeping a conversation," Juan responded.

"Oh nothing, the same old stuff."

"Is there something I need to know?"

"No," Rachael said. "I just wanted to say hi before I headed home. I'll be back to see you later this week."

"Okay."

Rachael hugged and kissed him and said goodbye. Turning to Joyce, she said, "May I see you for a moment?"

"Sure," Joyce said. "Honey, I'll be right back."

"Okay baby," Juan said, smilingly.

Out in the hallway, Joyce wasted no time. "Rachael, what is wrong with you, girl, that you need to speak to me so urgently?"

"Joyce, they had a secret church meeting after morning service and voted Juan out as senior pastor."

"What?" Joyce said, grabbing her chest. "Oh no!"

"There's more, Joyce."

"What else could there be?"

"They voted Marco in as the new senior pastor."

Joyce fell against the wall and wept profusely, and Rachael just held her as she began to cry herself.

"We are now in grave danger," Joyce said. "Poor Solid Rock."

"I know the Tanankas and I were standing up against this monstrosity," Rachael said. "We were praying in the church parking lot. You should have heard the things they said to us."

"What did they say?"

"You don't even want to know." Rachael gave her friend another hug before saying, "Go and tell your husband before someone else does."

"Okay."

Joyce watched Rachael disappear around the corner and hugged herself.

"Lord," she whispered, placing her hand on Juan's door room. "Please protect us all from what's going on."

She entered into the room very slowly.

"Baby," Juan said when he looked up and saw her wet eyes, "What's wrong with you?"

"I don't know how to tell you this…"

"Tell me what? Come here and talk to me."

Inch by inch, Joyce's emotionally-weighted legs carried her to the bed where she sat beside Juan.

"The church had a secret meeting today," she said.

"About?"

"They voted you out as senior pastor and voted Marco in."

"Thank you for telling me this," he whispered.

He closed his eyes and became silent while Joyce took his hands in hers and wept.

6

Trevor Meets Monica

Trevor could not take his eyes off his temp. When he entered his office, he learned that his personal secretary would be out for two weeks: entered the beautiful, young temp that had attracted Trevor's eyes.

Lust appeared in Trevor's office. He felt Trevor summoning him. He noticed Trevor looking at a gorgeous woman. "Oh she's nice," stated Lust.

Lust called upon Fornication to come into Trevor's office. Lust filled Fornication in on what Trevor was thinking and planning with Monica.

She entered into his office and said, "Can I get you some coffee? Or some water? Is there just some juice you would like?"

"What is your name?" Trevor asked.

"Monica Swartz."

"Okay Monica, so tell me a little about yourself."

"Like what?"

"I know I should not ask you this, but are you married? Or are you in a relationship?"

"You are asking me too many personal questions," Monica said, offended. "You do know that this is not ethical, right?"

Lust smiled before he entered Trevor.

Monica turned and left the office and went back to her desk. When she looked up, she noticed that Trevor was looking at her with lust in his eyes.

Monica had an angel standing around her at all times; it was big in stature and very powerful. No one knew whose side this angel was on, nor did anyone know its name. His sole job was to protect her.

Lust began to speak to Trevor, "Look, you gotta to get that girl, she is so fine. Ooh, she smells so good. You better find a way to get some alone time with her, you hear me?"

Trevor looked perplexed; he was trying so hard to find a way to get Monica's attention.

As the day progressed, Trevor approached Monica and said, "Can I take you out to lunch?"

Monica responded and said, "No, I have other plans for lunch."

"Why are you playing so hard to get?"

"Mr. Tananka, trust me, you are way out of your league! Sometimes it's better to leave well enough alone."

"Maybe I like to live on the edge."

"Well that is not good because you never know what you are getting yourself into. I wish that you would stop bothering me!"

"I am so sorry. I can't do that."

"Well, I am going to say goodbye. It's my lunch time." Monica left the office.

Trevor grew frustrated and angry as rejection set in. He had an attitude and took it out on his staff.

Monica arrived back from lunch and noticed Trevor's attitude.

The staff noticed how belligerent Trevor was. He was snapping at them when they asked questions about projects they were working on. He was very short with them. One employee asked, "Is everything all right, boss?"

"I'm just fine. Get back to work," Trevor replied.

The employee walked back to his desk with frustration because he needed questions answered about his project and Trevor had no time for him as he dwelled in his negative attitude.

Monica began to smile but overlooked Trevor's hard looks at her. But to Trevor's imagination, he felt that she was prancing around the office with her short business skirt on and her blouse which was unbuttoned from the top. Monica was totally focusing on doing an exceptional job for the temp agency as well as for Mr. John Tananka.

Fornication was in Trevor's office, bothered that Trevor was not moving fast enough.

"Trevor," he said, "Why are you letting her tease you? Go after her and ask her out."

Trevor ordered lunch in, but he could not enjoy his lunch because he was not used to rejection. He had the looks, money, the car, and lived in his parents' big mansion and no woman ever said no to him. Trevor had no problem getting women to overlook the fact that he was a grown man living at home with his parents. When the ladies saw his parents' home, all they saw was money and lots of cha-ching.

"What's wrong with this woman?" he said to himself.

He summoned Monica to come to his office.

"Yes," she said. "May I help you?"

"I need for you to type up this document for me," he said, "And I need for it to be finished by the end of the day."

"No problem. It will be done for you by the end of the day."

Trevor handed her the papers and she looked at them and said, "This is already typed."

"I know this. You just need to type these 300 pages again, and I want them finished by the end of the day. Do I make myself clear?"

"Yes sir." Monica smiled and as she turned toward the door. Softly she said, "You jerk."

"Excuse me, did you say something?" Trevor asked.

"No."

Trevor looked on with disgust; he gazed at Monica as she walked with a sexual tone with all her tight fitting clothes. "I don't know who she thinks she is, but I am going to break her down. She doesn't know who she is messing with."

All day Monica irritated him, so he needed to let her know who was boss. He called Monica into his office.

"Monica, there may be other things that I would like for you to do. But please keep in mind that everything that I want you to do for me must be finished by the end of the day."

Monica just looked at him and smiled.

He watched her like a hawk and she did not flinch.

Lust said, "Oh, she is playing you. She's in trouble. We are going to get you, Monica."

While Monica sat at her desk, she was not bothered by Trevor's demands. He kept trying to distract Monica from completing her assignments, but she would do as she was told and get right back to what he needed her to handle.

Monica approached Trevor at the end of the day, and handed him the three hundred page paper that he wanted her to type and all the other assignments that he bestowed upon her.

He looked at Monica and said, "You seem to have everything in order so thank you."

Monica said, "Well it's quitting time." She walked out of Trevor's office.

He watched Monica as she left his office. "If she thinks she has beaten me," he said, "Then she has another thing coming."

He continued to watch her, peering out his window. As she got into her car and pulled off, he seethed. "I'm going to make her pay for her actions."

He sat at his office desk and tried to figure out why she was not into him.

He got up and looked around his secretary's desk to see if she had left anything behind that would indicate that she had been slacking off; he found absolutely nothing. He had to leave and go get a drink because this was troubling him. He didn't know why, but he could not shake this.

He walked inside his favorite upscale night club and sat at the bar. The club set him up a tab and he ordered a drink. The bartender Bruce noticed that something was seriously troubling him.

He said, "What's wrong, man?"

"Nothing."

"It's something because you are not your usual self."

"Man, this female. She is fine and she wouldn't give me the time of day, go figure."

"That's females for you." They both chuckled.

Trevor just sipped on his drink and listened to the music. There were a lot of nice looking women there, but no one matched Monica to him.

One young lady walked over to him, trying to have small talk, but he was just not interested; he said, "Sorry no thanks."

She walked away and all you could hear her say was "It's your loss."

He turned around and finished sipping on his drink and then he said, "Bruce, I'm going now, man."

"Already?" Bruce said. "The night is young, man."

"Yeah, but not for me."

He left the club. On his way home he received a phone call from this chick he'd been trying to get with, but he did not answer the phone. He was just not in the mood to be bothered.

When he arrived home he heard his parents talking at the dinner table; they were having a late dinner.

"Hello Mom and Dad."

"Hello son," they both said.

"How was your day?" his father asked.

"It was one of the most interesting days for me in a long while. I had a temp secretary, and she is something else."

"What do you mean by this, son?" his father asked.

"Well, she is so fine. Dad, she had me to my knees. I asked could I take her to lunch and she said no."

Mr. Tananka said, "Good for her."

"Dad, why are you saying that?"

"Son, don't you know that we can have a lawsuit against us? All you think about is you. Cut it out, Trevor. She is there to work for us, not to fool around with you, and make this the very last time I mention this to you!"

"Okay Dad, why do you always make so much out of things?"

"Because you don't take responsibility seriously. It's not your company, but mine. Grow up, Trevor, grow up."

Trevor did not want to hear that right now. He had other things on his mind. So he just went to bed early that night.

The next day Trevor came into the office and stayed his distance from Monica, strictly because of his father's scolding. Although he kept his distance, he watched her every move with a sharp eye.

Monica heard about how Trevor treated women as if they were rag dolls he'd just used them then discarded when bored. He'd bragged to some of his employees that thought he was such a great guy.

Monica just watched as Trevor spoke with his employees telling them how big of a ladies' man he was.

Monica said, "What a scum bag ugh."

While working and taking in the scene of the office, Monica received a call from the agency that she worked for. She would have to stay at the office longer than she had expected.

"That's not a problem," she said, nodding. "I can stay on. Need the extra money."

All through the day, Trevor was furious because he was unable to have social conversations with Monica. He felt that he was going to lose his mind when other male employees would stop at Monica's desk to have small talk. Trevor thought if he had shut his door to his office and closed his blinds, the view of her from his office would erase her image from his mind. But that did not work at all. The silence and the closed office space gave his mind more time to think of her because of no interruptions. Trevor could not focus at all on his work. The phone rang and it startled him; it was his father on the other end and this made him even more bothered because his father was the one who was messing with his livelihood. The conversation ended quickly since Trevor had to inform his father that he was busy working on a business proposal. The very last thing Trevor wanted to do was speak with his father who was keeping him from something he felt that was meant for him.

The day ended quickly and Trevor heard the staff leaving the office. He jumped up from behind his desk and watched Monica through a space through the blinds as she finished her last-minute tasks then left the office.

He slowly walked over to his big office window and watched her walk to her car and drive off into rush-hour traffic.

The next day Trevor arrived at work and he was frustrated; Monica was not there.

It was just about 8:00 a.m., and he walked around the office and found no sign of her. He asked some of the workers and they hadn't seen her either.

He went back into his office and worked on some projects that he needed to finish. He heard some whistling and he looked up and saw Monica walking to her desk. He looked at his watch and it was 9:00 a.m. He waited until she was situated at her desk and then called her into his office. When she got up, he watched her every move.

All he could say was "Lord, when you put her together, you did it perfectly."

Lust said, "Now Trevor, you really have to have her. Stop delaying. Retrieve her phone number from your files and call her already. Start somewhere."

Lust started to grow, and he grabbed Trevor by his shoulders as he was standing behind him, then the imp whispered in Trevor's left ear, "Go get her, tiger."

"Monica," he said, "Why are you late to work?"

"I'm not late," she replied. "The agency that I work for said my working hours are 9 to 5." She handed him the papers.

With his wounded pride, he read the papers, and said, "Monica, as of tomorrow your schedule would be from 7:00 a.m. to 7:00 p.m. I will call the agency and inform them of this."

She stood, emotionless, which infuriated Trevor.

"Now this is what you need to do, retype these papers, this whole 500 page policy and procedure manual. It must be completed by the end of the day."

"Will do," she said, smiling.

Monica turned to leave Trevor's office, but he called her back and handed her some more papers and said, "These papers also must be completed by the end of the day."

Monica left his office and Hatred appeared and said, "Good job, Trevor. Let her pay for her actions. She should have not rejected you."

"Yes," Trevor said, smiling. "You get what you pay for."

Monica was working on the policy and procedures manual when John Tananka walked into the building, talking with the staff. Trevor looked up and heard some commotion, and it was the staff laughing and kidding around with his dad.

"What does he want?" Trevor muttered.

He watched his father walk over to Monica's desk and said, "Just leave, Dad. Why are you here?"

"Hello there," Mr. Tananka said, "Let me introduce myself. I'm Mr. John Tananka."

Monica smiled. "Hello, my name is Monica. Nice to meet you."

"Same here."

Mr. Tananka looked at Trevor in his office; their eyes connected. He returned his gaze to Monica and her desk, finding it swamped with paperwork.

"Monica, what are you working on?"

"Mr. Tananka has me retyping this entire policy and procedure manual."

"What? Stop it right now. What else does he have you doing?" He saw the other work, which was already corrected. But John had someone else previously do the work. He didn't know why, but he felt led to ask, "What time does the agency have you coming into work?"

"Well sir, they said from 9 to 5, but Trevor changed it to 7 to 7."

"Thank you for informing me."

Mr. Tananka stormed into Trevor's office, slammed the door, and pinned him against the wall.

"Trevor, what do you think you're doing?"

"What are you talking about, Dad?"

"Why do you have Monica retyping the policy and procedure manual? One, it doesn't need to be retyped, and two, you don't even adhere to it."

"And why do you have her coming in at seven when half of the time you don't even come in at all?"

Before Trevor could respond, his father answered for him: "You are making her pay because she rejected you."

Hatred leaned in close and whispered in Trevor's ear, "Get rid of your father."

Lust said, "Trevor, don't allow him to mess things up for us." They both shrunk and jumped on his shoulders before saying in unison, "Get rid of him."

"Dad, I asked her to type the manual because I was just trying to save the company some money."

"Trevor, how is her retyping it saving the company money?" The imps pressed harder on Trevor's shoulders and said, "Get rid of him."

"Dad, it's all under control."

"Trevor, you are going to leave that woman alone. You better not let me see a lawsuit pertaining to this, do you hear me, Trevor?"

"Yes, Dad. I hear you."

Hatred said, "Trevor, you better get rid of him. You are pissing me off. Tell your dad to leave now!" Hatred became so bothered that he bit Trevor on the neck.

"Ouch," Trevor said, rubbing his neck.

"Son, what's wrong with you?"

"Something bit me on the neck."

"Yes, it's a little swollen and red. Go and get some rubbing alcohol and some Cortaid. You'll be all right."

"Yeah, Dad."

"But Trevor, you are to leave that woman alone, and I am not telling you this again."

Mr. Tananka stormed out of Trevor's office and walked over to Monica's desk and asked her to have lunch with him. Then he asked three other individuals to join them. Trevor watched how his father talked with the staff, and it made him so angry. The bite he just got didn't make things any better.

Mr. Tananka walked back to Trevor's office and said, "I'm taking Monica and the three new hires to lunch and no you are not invited."

Hatred said, "Who does he think he is?"

Lust said, "We could have gone to lunch with Monica, Trevor. We could have asked Monica some personal questions at lunch. Your father really is making me sick."

Trevor watched his father escort the quartet out of the building. He grabbed his neck and said, "What in the world bit my neck?"

He sat at his desk pondering how to get back at Monica for telling his dad about what he was doing to her.

He stood from his desk and said, "Screw him. I'm going to lunch."

Hatred said, "Well let's go."

Lust said, "Will get her yet."

Mr. Tananka took the new employees out to the country club for lunch. He was going over the history and the foundation of the company and it humored them. They each shared stories about themselves and laughed. As they were sharing stories, Trevor walked over to the table and invited himself and he made sure he sat right next to Monica.

Lust said, "That's it. We love this view."

"Trevor," his father said, irritated, "What are you doing here?"

"Well Dad, I finished what I was doing. I was starving, so I decided to get some lunch."

He knew they would be there; this was where his father took all new employees. Everyone was finished with their meals.

Mr. Tananka said, "Trevor, is the Eagle account finished?"

"Yes, Dad, it is."

"Did Monica type it up?"

"Yes, she sent them before you all left for lunch."

"Well, thank you, Monica, and on that note you all are excused for the rest of the day."

Everyone was very grateful and Trevor was livid.

Monica said, "May I go now?"

"Sure Monica," Mr. Tananka replied. "I'll take you all back so you can get to your cars." They all got up from the table; Monica did not even glance Trevor's way.

Trevor looked at his Dad and said, "Why did you dismiss them while I'm sitting at the table?"

"Trevor, I can do this because I'm the boss, remember that. Also, I told you that you were not invited to lunch. Since you want to play games, I will beat you at yours."

"How dare he," Lust said.

Trevor smelled Monica's perfume. She really looked nice and that walk of hers was killing him.

Lust said, "Trevor, if your dad doesn't stop interfering in our business, then I will have to hurt him. I will allow nothing to get in my way. I have an itch and it needs scratching, do you hear me, Trevor?"

"Maybe he did not hear you," Hatred said. "Maybe I need to bite him again."

"Have at it."

Trevor yelped as he felt a stinging sensation on his neck. He sat, watching his father walk away with the employees. He watched the way Monica's hips swayed beneath her skirt.

"His dad is really annoying me," Hatred told Lust.

Trevor got up, and his face was red with embarrassment. He was not returning back to work since he was giving people time off.

He was in the parking lot when his cell phone rang.

"Who is this?"

"It's your dad."

"Yeah Dad?"

"I need you to get back to the office and finish that big overseas deal. And make sure that all your paperwork is handed to me by the end of the day."

Once again he just ruined my day, Trevor thought as he cursed all the way back to the office.

Trevor went back into the office with an attitude, and he did not want to be bothered and he let everyone know this by the way he slammed the door. He finished up all the documents his father asked for. It was about 5:30 p.m. when he finished making the copies to give to his dad when he got home.

Trevor arrived home, and his parents were sitting at the dining room table having dinner, and his mom said, "Clean up for dinner, Trevor, it's your favorite, soul food. I picked it up from your favorite restaurant Big Momma's Home Cooking."

He sat down at the table and said, "I'm not hungry."

"You're not hungry?"

"No Mom, I'm not."

"What's wrong?"

"Ask Dad."

"Ask me what?" his father replied.

"Dad, you humiliated me in front of the workers today then you undermined me in front of our new staff and you left me sitting at the restaurant looking foolish."

Mr. Tananka said, "Trevor, shut up. Lord, give me the strength from knocking him down. First of all, let's get this straight Trevor, this is my company not yours. You just carry my last name. God allowed me to build this company from the ground up. Also, I've seen Monica and yes she is a very good looking young woman, but you need to know this is dangerous."

"John."

Mr. Tananka looked over at his wife. "Yes, dear."

"She must be very attractive because you normally don't give people compliments. You watch yourself, John."

"Aw sweetheart, the only one for me is you." Looking back at his son, John said, "Now Trevor, who do you think you are to have this woman type up a three hundred page manual on top of five other projects that you wanted by the end of the day?"

"Are you out of your mind?" his mother asked.

"What?" came Trevor's reply.

"Trevor, who does that?"

"Honey," John said, "He did this because she rejected him."

"Trevor, please tell me you did not try to punish someone because they rejected you."

"Mom, she made me angry. I'm Trevor, she needs to understand this."

"Boy, I'm about to knock some sense into you."

"And how dare you show up at the country club?" his mother berated. "Your father told me about your little stunt. He told you not to come because of how you've been treating Monica, you show up anyway and deliberately sat next to her."

"Jane, you should have seen Trevor. He looked like a predator on the prowl, and we will not tolerate this type of behavior, do you hear me?"

"You left yourself sitting there looking foolish," his mother said. "The Bible says that it is better to be invited to the table than to invite yourself."

"Mom, please no Bible lectures right now, thank you."

"Trevor, the only reason I would not fire you or move you to another location is because you are good at what you do—*only* when it comes to work," said Mr. Tananka. "You need to change your attitude before you get yourself into something that you can't get out of."

"Dad, thanks for the advice, but no thanks. Mom, I'll eat my food in my room, alone. Goodnight to the both of you."

He looked at Trevor as he left the room and said, "Jane, he is too old to be acting so immature."

"John, all we can do is pray for his soul. I know our prayers keep him from a lot of danger that he nor we are aware of."

7

Cortez's First Visit

from the New Pastor

Monday morning Marco left for work at 8:00 a.m. then he returned home at 9:30. Lisa was at home. Lisa said, "Marco, why are you home so early?"

Marco sighed. He had hoped Lisa wouldn't be home when he returned.

"Lisa, I quit, I just quit. There is no need for me to do things properly. I have a new job now. Don't worry, we will still eat."

Lisa pushed Marco out of her way and walked off; she did not want to deal with his mess.

"Lisa, what's wrong with you?" He was angry because she walked out and didn't want to listen to him.

Greed, False Doctrine, and Hatred crowded around him.

"You don't need her," Greed said. "I know what will make you feel better." Greed made him think of the small bag that Nate had given him. He reached into his suit jacket pocket that he wore yesterday and took it out. While in the bathroom, Marco locked the door and began to use the drug.

"We will get so far with this young man," Greed said, smiling. False Doctrine and Hatred began to hiss and drool.

Sunday, Marco stood in front of the congregation for the very first time as their pastor. As he looked around the congregation, the pews were nearly empty. Some of the members left because they were not happy about the changes, and some were not involved with the negative process that had occurred. Marco made it through his first sermon as pastor and received some congratulations. His wife and kids kissed him and said, "Great job."

Marco was so excited that he took Lisa and the kids out to a very fancy restaurant. He took them to *The Green Block*, one of the best in the city. Lisa was impressed and she could not wait to sit down and eat. As they were driving to their destination Marco and Lisa were describing the order of service and how well it went. Marco was explaining how nervous he was and the children began to laugh. They arrived to their destination and they had a real good time fellowshipping as a family. When the children became restless, Marco said, "Lisa, I'm going to drop you and the children off at home and go visit Pastor Cortez."

"Okay, don't forget to tell him we said Hello," answered Lisa.

"Will do."

Marco was very eager to visit Juan to tell him that he would have been very proud of him with the great job that he did with his first sermon.

As soon as he walked into Juan's room, Marco smiled and asked, "How are you?"

Juan looked at Marco and replied, "God's blessing me."

"Yeah He is still in control. I have some news to tell you."

"I already know what you want to tell me, you are now the new pastor."

"Yes, how did you find this out?"

"Joyce informed me of these new changes." He eyed Marco incredulously. "Did you think I would not have found out such important information?"

"No, I just felt that it was my job to inform you of the new changes since I am the new pastor."

"Oh I see," said Juan.

"Well I am glad to see that you are doing ok. I know that you need your rest and I'm not going to hold you. I'll come and visit you from time to time. Take care."

"Yeah," said Juan.

As Marco was walking back to his car, he was very disappointed by the character of Juan's behavior. Marco went to receive Juan's blessings, but instead it was as if he got a tongue lashing just with the few words that came out of Juan's mouth. Marco shook his head in anger, got in his car, and drove off.

Two Sundays later, Marco was at home sitting in his study watching television. The imp False Doctrine appeared in the room. Since Marco had become the pastor, he wanted to bring in his new flavor; the imp False Doctrine informed

Marco to slowly get rid of Juan's present format of how service was being conducted.

False Doctrine jumped on Marco's shoulder, egging him on to change the order of service at the church. False Doctrine whispered in Marco's ear, "Get rid of reading the Scriptures, that's just so outdated. No one wants to hear it."

Marco began to smile, agreeing with his new idea.

"Put this into action next Sunday," False Doctrine said.

Marco nodded in agreement as if someone was speaking to him. After which, he became tired, and decided to take a nap.

"Yes rest, Marco, you will need it because we have a lot of work to accomplish. We will start on this project in the next couple of days," False Doctrine added.

Tuesday morning arrived and Marco was at home sitting at the breakfast table. False Doctrine whispered repeatedly over and over, "Make up your own ten commandments and you make the members read this after you start this Sunday. This is what you are going to write down, put this in play. Have the associate minister read the lead and the members must repeat their responses."

Marco continued to eat as False Doctrine whispered the commandments into his ear.

1. *I will only be loyal to my pastor.*
   Response: I will do.
2. *I will only pray for those who have the best interest of my pastor.*
   Response: I will do.
3. *I will only do my Christian service at my own place of worship.*
   Response: I will do.

4. *I will not send my tithes or give my offering to another place of worship. If I am visiting out of town, I will mail my tithes and offering, or I will hold them in my possession until I get back and place it in the basket when I return to my place of worship.*
   Response: I will do.

5. *I will attend Bible study and Sunday school so the pastor can teach me the right way to go, because he is the only one who knows what's right.*
   Response: I will do.

False Doctrine drooled. "Marco, this sounds so great. Look at the authority you will be establishing, young man." He hugged and kissed Marco. Marco felt a nice, warm, fuzzy feeling. On the side of Marco's face, False Doctrine said, "Keep on writing. I have more for you to put on paper. Let's finish these Ten Commandments."

Marco felt this urge to laugh then he started to laugh.

"Good boy," False Doctrine said.

6. *I will only do what my pastor commands me to do.*
   Response: I will do.

7. *I will only pray for my church members.*
   Response: I will do.

8. *I will only be concerned about my pastor because he is our leader.*
   Response: I will do.

9. *If I have a Christian product to sell like a book or video or CD, then I will give my pastor 50 percent of the profit so he can move forward in his ministry.*
   Response: I will do.

10. *When I am ready to date, I will introduce my mate to my pastor first before my family so he can inform me if this person is right for me.*
Response: I will do.

Marco looked at his commandments and said, "This is just what they need to hear. I am their pastor and they must follow me."

Lisa entered into the room and asked, "What are you working on?"

He smiled and replied, "You will see Sunday."

Sunday morning, Marco asked all the associate ministers to meet him in his office before service began.

False Doctrine and Hatred appeared in the pastor's office; they felt that they needed to attend the meeting.

Marco handed each of them a piece of paper and informed them that there were going to be changes such as getting rid of the Scripture reading and replacing it with what was on the paper.

All the ministers looked at the paper. They were all in shock because of the interesting statements that were on the paper. The ministers looked on with amazement and were at a loss for words.

"Pastor, are you sure you want to replace Scripture with this?" one of the ministers asked.

"Yes, I do, Minister Hall. If you do not like this, you can leave, but from now on this is how we are going to do this here."

False Doctrine began to hiss. "Why does he have a problem with what we are doing? We can get rid of him you know."

Marco looked at the ministers in the room. None of the other ministers wanted to reply to any of Marco's new suggestions since they saw the negative response Minister Hall received. They kept their mouth shut and went with the flow. He repeated how service would now be done, and that his authority was all that they needed; what he said went, and for them to remember that.

Marco adjourned the meeting and appointed the minister he wanted to lead the congregation with the new format.

Greed and the rest of the imps were in the sanctuary. False Doctrine and Hatred joined them.

The associate minister stood up and announced the new format. The imps were in full force, looking around to see who had a problem with the new layout. The angels stood their ground. When the minister finished his reading, the congregation was still because they did not know how to take in the new format as well as the information that was given to them.

"What kind of mess is this?" asked Rachael. "This is self-righteous, narcissistic gobbledygook. Who does he think he is, introducing this garbage to us? We are not ignorant in the word of God!"

False Doctrine heard what Rachael said and flew right in front of her face and said, "Oh you are going to get it, Rachael, and your pretty little son, too." He laughed. "You don't mess with my great ideas."

Rachael felt a strong wind in front of her and she just swatted her hand as if she saw a fly.

"Mom, what's wrong?" Forest asked.

"I felt like something was right in front of me."

Zaso stood close and False Doctrine just looked at him and hissed before flying away.

Joyce looked on with surprise. Jane and John were stunned; they could not say anything, they just could not believe it.

Then Sallie Cooper blurted, "Changes, this is what we need, not all this old dreaded stuff."

Marco loved that he had the attention of the crowd and that they did not fight what he introduced. He smiled on the inside because he had the authority. Service ended and he greeted everyone. He saw Joyce talking with some members and he needed to speak with her.

Marco approached Joyce after morning worship. "Sister Cortez, I would like to ask you a question."

"Yes, Marco," answered Joyce.

"I would like to know if I can call you my spiritual mother now. You don't have to worry about anything. I will take you under my wings and just love you."

Joyce just gave him a smile and said nothing.

Marco was being very deceitful; he just wanted her near him because he was going to get rid of everything that remotely reminded him of her husband and his traditions.

Marco left to speak to other members as Rachael and the Tanankas approached Joyce.

"What did he have to say?" Rachael asked.

Joyce said, "He wants to call me his spiritual mother."

"What?" Jane nearly shouted. "Where is that coming from?"

"He got his nerves," Rachael said. "What is up with this rubbish he is throwing out at us?"

Joyce said, "Rachael, I was going to ball it up in a knot and throw it at him because that's all it's worth."

John said, "I just ripped it up and opened my Bible and read Scripture the way I am used to. It's just nonsense."

Jane just shook her head.

Greed, Hatred and Covet were all talking in the sanctuary.

Hatred said, "Let's just jump inside of Marco."

"We can't possess saved individuals," Greed said. "We can only mess with their minds. We may not have their souls, but we sure can use them for our purpose."

Greed, Hatred and False Doctrine noticed Rachael, Joyce, Jane and John talking. The busybody of the church Mrs. Sallie Cooper, was standing in the back of the church all by herself watching Joyce, Rachael, Jane, and John. Greed, Hatred and Covet jumped inside of her and took over her body and mind.

Mrs. Cooper walked up to them and said, "What are you all talking about over here?"

They all said Hello.

Sallie said, "Hello. So what's going on over here? Boy, do I like this pastor. He is so full of energy and talent. I just love the way he is doing things. I love the new changes. It gives it a new twist. Pretty soon we will be competing against the mega churches. I am so happy about this."

They all looked at her and smiled. "Well," Rachael said, "You are entitled to your own opinion."

"Yes I am," said Sallie.

The imps were angry at their responses so they made Sallie ask more intense questions.

"So Joyce," she said, "What are you thinking about the new changes?"

Joyce took a step back and asked, "So when did I become Joyce to you?"

"When your husband lost his position as pastor. I can call you by your first name."

Joyce just smiled and said, "It's too early to tell."

Mrs. Cooper said, "Well that young boy just came right in and took over. I really like when a real man takes charge."

The imps laughed, and Rachael looked on with resentment.

"Oh and Rachael, I hear you are having some problems at your property? What's going on over there?" Sallie asked.

"I don't care to discuss that with you," answered Rachael.

"Whatever," Sallie replied. She rolled her eyes at Rachael. Then she said to the Tanankas, "I see your son just hitting the streets and grabbing any woman he can get his hands on. If you were smart, you would try to bring him to church."

Jane gave Sallie a look of frustration and said, "If you were smart, Sallie, you would just shut your big fat mouth."

"Well, that is our cue to go," John said. "You all take care."

John and Jane went up the aisle. Joyce and Rachael said their goodbyes to Sallie and walked away from her.

While Rachael was preoccupied, Marco had the opportunity to approach Forest. "So what's up, Forest?"

"Nothing," replied Forest.

Marco noticed how distant Forest was. "Oh your mother told you to watch out for me?" Forest did not respond. "Forest, I'm your new pastor. You can come to me and talk about anything, okay? I heard that you said you were going through something at school. Have you figured it out yet?"

Forest said, "I'm still working on it."

Marco said, "Or you figured it out and you choose not to tell me."

Forest looked at him and said, "I'm still trying to figure it out."

Rachael was talking to some church members and noticed that her son was getting irritated by Marco so she called him and said, "Let's go."

Marco looked at Rachael as if he smelled raw sewage. Rachael hugged Forest and asked him, "What did he want?"

"If I ever wanted to talk to come to him, I could. He also asked about my situation at school".

"Don't you tell that man anything," said Rachael.

"I hear you, Mother," replied Forest.

Forest asked his mother in the car, "Mom, why don't we move our membership because Marco is getting out of hand."

"No that's what he wants. You don't just leave because something is broken. You stay to try and fix it."

"What is broken?"

"Marco's not preaching God's unadulterated word. He is putting his own twist in God's holy divine word and that's the worst thing you can do because you are not to add or take away from God's holy divine word. We are not leaving. Someone has to stay and that will be me."

"Okay Mom, I'm staying with you."

Rachael squeezed Forest's hand. "I love you, son," she said.

"I love you, too, Mom."

Hatred showed up in Marco's and Lisa's kitchen, waiting to see how Marco was going to handle the events of the day.

Marco sidled up to his wife and asked, "Why doesn't Rachael like me?"

"I can't answer that question," Lisa replied, fixing herself a cup of coffee. "You must ask her."

"Mommy, come here," Marion and Lanice called from another room. "Mommy, please come here."

"You don't have to be sassy about it, Lisa," replied Marco.

"I'm not trying to be sassy."

Lisa was leaving the kitchen and Marco said, "Where are you going?"

"Don't you hear the girls calling me?" Lisa went to see what the girls wanted because they wouldn't stop calling her.

"Since Rachael wanted to make some trouble for our boy Marco," Hatred said, "We will kindly do the same thing for her. Go ahead and make the call, Marco."

Marco really did not care for Rachael; he knew she was against everything he was doing. If she could be against him, then he would be against her.

He made the call to the community development company and they led him to Mr. Gary Grabber. He spoke with him and told him about some concerns and to see what he could do about them.

Mr. Grabber said, "I'll have this handled."

Covet, the head imp of this project, was eager to capture Rachael's property. He and Lie settled around Mr. Grabber as he hung up the phone.

"Lie," Covet said, "Jump in Gary Grabber and tell him to get one of these workers to go to Rachael's property. We need to get going on our plan to inform the tenants that they will each be given $10,000 dollars if they move out of the building."

Lust was much irritated because he could taste the building in their possession. "Why can't we just take it?"

Lust was so bothered by this that he smacked Gary right in the face.

"Ouch," Mr. Grabber said, feeling the sting to his face. He stood for several minutes, wondering what caused the painful sting.

Anger built in Lust. "Do I have to *make* you leave?" he yelled at Mr. Grabber.

Finally, he saw Grabber walk toward the door. While Grabber walked, Lust looked at a stress ball atop Grabber's desk and pushed it onto the floor. Walking straight ahead, Mr. Grabber didn't see the ball and slipped on it. He came crashing to the ground, hitting his head on the side of his desk.

Lust guffawed as he saw streams of blood pour down the side of Mr. Grabber's face. "This will teach you a lesson making me wait on something I want so badly," he said.

Rachael was flabbergasted. She looked at the phone, surprised at what one of her tenants had just told her.

"Someone from the community development company came out and said they would give each tenant $10,000 if they left the building."

"Thank you for informing me," she had told the tenant. "I will call you later, but they cannot do this, trust me."

Rachael immediately called her attorney and was told what she already knew: the company could not do this to her.

"Check with your tenants," the attorney said. "See if the company gave them any type of documentation."

She called her tenant back and learned that no documentation was given. "They just told us our rights," the tenant said.

"They cannot do this," Rachael said emphatically. "I will handle this."

"Okay, Mrs. Weinberg."

Anger and irritation grew in Rachael as she hung up the phone.

"Why are they doing this?" she asked to no one. "Is this because I will not sell to them? They need to stop because I'm staying."

Zaso stood close to Rachael. The imps were around, hissing.

Rachael was bothered by this all day. *The nerve of that company*, she thought. She would call them tomorrow and see who was behind all of this. She was so sure that they would give her the runaround. But she was going to make herself clear that she was not moving.

False Doctrine loved to appear after Marco finished preaching because it gave him the opportunity to look around the sanctuary and figure out what this sad congregation needed.

He found Marco at home, sitting in his den. He crowded before him and said, "You need to share all of your wonderful ideas with Juan because it's the right thing to do. Juan needs to see how things are done correctly."

Marco always smiled after he received these Hellish notions as he believed they were brilliant and came straight from his own mind.

Marco was happy to tell Juan his great ideas, but he prepared himself because most of the time he and Juan didn't see eye to eye on Marco's changes. This time Marco felt bold and grounded on his decision.

And he felt the need to rub his new idea in the former pastor's face.

When he stepped into Juan's room, he was full of arrogance.

Juan looked none too happy to see him. "Nice to see you, Marco," he said though Marco didn't believe him. "Why the visit?"

"I just wanted to inform you of my new idea."

"Don't come in here with any confusion," stated Juan.

"It's not confusion. I have my own ten commandments."

Marco could see the irritation on Juan's face. "What and why?" Juan asked.

"So that the congregation can be aware of the new changes that are going on in the mega churches," Marco answered.

"Boy, its official. 'You have really lost your cotton pickin' mind!"

"I knew you would not understand. I don't know why I even came to see you."

"Me either. You could have saved yourself a trip with the mess you just shared with me. You replaced Scripture with false doctrine. Just leave my room."

"Why are you dismissing me like this? I did not do anything to you. I am just sharing with you my new ideas."

Juan stared at Marco, not saying another word.

Angry, Marco spun on his heels and left the room.

Marco arrived at the church for a meeting with the finance committee. Members who served on the finance committee were concerned that the money in the offering was dropping and the bills needed to be paid and the new pastor's salary would have to decrease if the congregation did not grow.

"Thank you for informing me of this predicament," Marco said. "I will have an answer for you Sunday morning."

"Okay," one of the committee members said. "We look forward to seeing what you will come up with." They left the meeting and everyone went home except for the custodian.

False Doctrine appeared in the same room with Marco.

Marco started to think about how he could bring people into the congregation. False Doctrine stood tall over Marco and said, "You don't have to worry about a thing. I will bring the people in for you." Then False Doctrine shrunk and landed right on Marco's shoulder and said, "This is what you are going to announce on Sunday. I got your back so you can get paid. This Sunday, you will announce that whichever member brings in the most people within the year will win a brand new luxury car and free gas for a full year."

"What a fantastic idea I just thought of," Marco said. "I am very pleased with this. Now I can go home. Didn't have to think about this as long as I thought I would have to."

Sunday Morning arrived and Marco addressed the flock before he started his sermon and informed them of his new project.

"We are having a contest," he began. "As you can see, some of the pews are empty, so we need to fill them so this is what the contest is going to be. The member who brings in the most people to fill up these pews will receive a brand new luxury car with free gas for a year."

The worshippers stood to their feet and applauded while Lisa sat there in astonishment.

After morning worship, the members were so excited they hugged and kissed their pastor. Lisa saw Joyce, Rachael and The Tanankas and said, "Don't even ask me. I do not know where this nonsense is coming from."

Rachael coughed in her hands and said, "Ego, that's where it is coming from."

"I'm concerned this position is really getting to his mind," Lisa said. "I'm finding out this stuff when you guys find out. I am so humiliated."

"We are so sorry to see you have to deal with this," said Joyce.

They all turned and watched Marco, his eyes shining and his smile big and bright as his congregation surrounded him.

Marco was sitting in his office at the church when False Doctrine jumped on his shoulder and said, "You need to show old Juan that sometimes you have to think outside of the box to bring people to fill up the pews." Marco just smiled because he knew that his new idea was a great one.

False Doctrine put it in Marco's mind to inform Juan of his new plans.

Marco thought that he would go visit Juan and tell him about his new changes. He jumped up from behind his desk and went to tell Juan of his wonderful news. As Marco was driving to the hospital, all he could say to himself was, *Why didn't I think of this great idea before?*

Marco arrived at the hospital, but all he could think of was trying not to get into an argument with Juan, so he said a little prayer before walking in.

Marco walked into Juan's room and said, "Good day to you my dear sir."

The angels were in full force in Juan's room.

"Why are you here, Marco?" asked Juan.

"Now Pastor, why do you greet me this way?"

"Because every time you show up, nothing good comes out of your mouth."

Marco squelched his anger and smiled. "Perhaps this time, things will be different."

Juan huffed.

"I've presented a new idea to the congregation," Marco continued. "The member who brings in the most people to fill up the pews will receive a brand new luxury car with free gas for a year."

"Don't you know that you are playing with the souls of men?" Juan said, working hard not to yell. "Their eternal destination! Who do you think you are? If Jesus was here, he would turn over the money changing tables. The Bible does not say that Jesus said, James, John, Peter or Andrew if you bring me the most people I will give you 500 oxen and 600 goats. Jesus said he would make them fishers of men."

Juan closed his eyes sadly before Marco could get a word in, he continued with, "What are you doing? Marco, listen, people will not be bringing people to Christ sincerely. All they want is a prize not caring about their eternal security. You better repent as in 1 John 1:9. Boy, get on your knees and approach the throne of Grace with a humble heart and with a bowed down head, and stop all this nonsense!"

The imps gathered together and began to stir up the anger inside of Marco.

Marco looked at Juan, got close to his face, and said, "Listen, here, you just listen and shut your mouth. I know what I am doing. The membership will grow, my salary will be way bigger than yours ever was. You were just an old stupid man just working for peanuts, but me I will be rolling with the big dogs.

"I'm so sick and tired of you telling me that what I'm doing is so wrong. Why aren't you standing up there from

Sunday to Sunday? Oh I forgot, you can't. You're just a dumb invalid, so shut your stupid mouth.

"Juan, do you know why I keep coming here to see you? If not I'm going to tell you why. It's because I need for you to see that everything I told you that would be good for Solid Rock is happening. See nothing is wrong with what I'm doing."

"Oh, yes it is," Juan said. "You just can't see it."

"I don't want to hear you Juan," replied Marco.

"Then stop coming to see me. I didn't ask you to come. I'm in this hospital for healing, not to be stressed out by a young man who can't see the forest for the trees."

Around the two men, angels and imps stood their ground.

The imps looked at the heavenly angels and shook their fingers. "Don't mess with us or you will pay."

"We are not scared of you," Ashshod said. "I think you are misunderstanding this entire situation."

Juan looked at Marco and said, "Now you listen to me, you better watch your step. God does not like ugly and He is not too particular about pretty either. If you keep playing with God, He will lay you flat on your back, son. Repent and turn away from your sins or you will be punished."

"I think you got a taste of your own medicine. You are the one who is lying flat on his back. What happened, old man, your sins caught up with you, you old goat!"

Marco threw a pillow at Juan, and Ashshod blocked it. Marco turned back and looked at him and said, "I will not waste my time on you because you are not worth it."

The next Sunday, Marco arrived at the worship building, Greed and False Doctrine; circling him. He looked around the congregation and made a statement that there was going to be another change.

"Starting tomorrow," he began, "I need for all members to give or send in your paycheck stubs so you may receive your ID so we can keep track of what you give. We need to know if you are tithing correctly. We should not beg for money. There will be no problem if you say that you cannot make it to the bank. The finance committee will be placing four ATM machines in the building.

"Two will go in the front lobby, one will go into the ladies' lounge because you know you women know why you are fixing yourself up you can get your money before you come out of the ladies' room." Marco started to laugh. "And the last machine will be placed in the annex. The men can use this one because you guys are always over there talking and shooting the breeze so now you can talk about money."

Someone shouted, "I love my pastor."

"I love you, too," Marco said. "With this method of using the ID system, we will know who is giving so if you are giving correctly we can help you out. The ones who are not giving properly we can pray about your situation. Give now."

Greed began to smile and get stronger. The angels of the Heavenly host shoved Greed and Greed pushed back and called on some more of the imps. The imps gathered around Greed.

"Get out of here," Greed said. "You don't belong here, leave." Greed let out a great roar, a sound that came out as a screech from the microphone.

Lisa approached Marco after morning worship in his office.

Shutting and locking the door, she said, "Have you lost your mind Who do you think you are? You know that this is not Scriptural for you to get people's IDs and for them to send you their paycheck stubs and to put ATMs in the Lord's house, the place of worship! I see this position has really gone to your head!"

Marco slammed Lisa against the wall and told her, "Women, no, have *you* lost your mind? You better not approach me like this ever again. I am your superior! You will do as I tell you. I see you are not complaining when you are enjoying this luxurious lifestyle."

"You are hurting my arm," she said.

"That's not the only thing that's going to hurt if you don't get your act together." He slapped her in the face and walked over to his desk and sat in his chair and opened the locked drawer. As he pulled out a big bag of cocaine, she began to scream. "You better shut your mouth. Don't let me get up. I'll really shut you up."

Then he put the cocaine on his sermon notes and looked at Lisa and said, "See, this is good for more than one thing." He laughed with a devilish grin.

As Lisa was getting herself together, he said, "You can't judge me, just shut your mouth and walk with me, but you know you can be replaced. I see some real good looking sistas looking at me real hard, so you better watch yourself. Go get the kids and go to the car so we can go get something to eat. I worked real hard today. Now you gave me a real workout, there is no need for me to go to the gym."

Lisa left, slamming the office door.

Joyce left morning service, on her way to go see Juan, and many times she just asked herself why she continued attending Solid Rock. Marco had changed the dynamics of worship service so badly she felt as if she was at a basketball game with all the action going on.

Joyce walked into the hospital room and said, "Hi honey, what's wrong with you?" Juan had a frustrated look on his face and it concerned Joyce.

"Baby, that boy is teaching false doctrine. He will lead people straight to Hell," replied Juan.

"Honey, just calm down. I see this is making you so upset. I have been attending the services for a couple of months now."

"Why didn't you tell me?"

"Because I knew you would get worked up. That's why I told you that I was going to a different place of worship. Sorry for keeping this from you. I heard and saw something that disturbed me."

"What, baby?"

"Well you know how you feel about tithing. Marco has now changed this process."

Juan sighed. "How?"

"Everyone has to give him a copy of their paystub so the trustees will know if you are giving correctly and they will track you with a new ID system. And he is putting ATM machines in the place of worship."

"What! You know the Bible says bring ye all the tithes into the storehouse. The Bible did not say force the people, you teach them how to tithe. If he wanted people to pay their tithes, he needs to teach people how to tithe. You teach the people, baby, you just teach them. This boy is something else, and I don't mean in a good way. He wasn't taught this way...what is he doing?"

The heart monitor began to beep and Nurse Glynda and Dr. Casper came into the room and asked Joyce to leave.

After a few minutes, Dr. Casper came out into the hallway and found Joyce leaning against the wall, tears staining her face.

"Is everything okay?" she asked.

"Yes," Dr. Casper replied. "He just had a little scare, nothing serious. You can go in and see him now but try not to get him too excited." She patted Joyce's shoulder before walking down the hall.

Quickly, Joyce bowed her head to pray. She knew things would get a lot worse before they got better and prayed Juan would make it through it all.

Later in the evening, Marco was in his den at home. False Doctrine jumped on Marco's shoulder and told him, "I am going to really pack the church. I want you to inform the members of this great concept. It's used in the Christian churches, but I want you to lead the way because you are very popular, and I know that you can get the message across."

Marco began to write; he just loved all the information that was running through his mind.

The angels and the imps were in attendance at morning service.

Marco approached the congregation.

"Good morning," he began, smiling out at the congregation.

"Good morning," the majority replied.

"Today, I want to tell you that there are many ways to Heaven other than Jesus Christ. You can be good, sweet and kind—helping your fellow man gets you into Heaven. Works really get you in. I will also be preaching that just having faith not only in God but to focus on believing that things can just happen gets you into the pearly gates."

False Doctrine looked directly at all the angels and said, "I'm going to take you and your so-called believers down. I'm going to teach you, Ashshod, that you don't bother me, do you hear me?"

"I just want you to know that I don't want anyone to feel any heaviness at all," Marco said, "So I will be taking down all crosses, and the church covenant in the lobby. I don't want to pressure anyone. I just want people to feel free and move at their own pace."

The imps smiled and enjoyed the expressions on the angels' faces.

The imps circled around the building inside and out, laughing and singing and hissing at the heavenly angels.

The imps started singing:

"To Hell they will go, to Hell they will go,

We are taking them by the hundreds, the thousands, the millions to Hell they will go.

Oh we've got their souls going to Hell. They will be with us forever and ever in Hell.

To Hell they will be, to Hell they will be.

At the end, the imps raised their arms and said, "Yea."

The heavenly angels stood around some of the church members, especially Joyce.

Ashshod said, "Hunter and Deoriel, go guard Joyce. They are going after her, go quickly."

Hunter stood in front of Joyce and Hunter swung his arm back and knocked two imps out of the sanctuary. They kept trying to attack Joyce because they knew that she was a prayer warrior. The imps started hissing all over the sanctuary and the microphones started screeching.

Marco told Minister Hall after morning worship, "Sometimes you must do what you need to do in order to stay on top."

The associate minster just gave Marco a strange look before walking away and whispering, "Lord, we really need your help."

Lisa approached Marco in his office and said, "Marco, do you know what you are doing? You are defeating the purpose. It's about Jesus Christ. What in the world are you doing?"

"Lisa, I need for you to leave my office right now, do you hear me?" He shoved her out the door.

Saturday morning, Lisa got up and started cleaning around the house and was just flustered about the ludicrous changes Marco was making. She was so hurt by it she had to go see the only man that she still considered her pastor, Juan Cortez. Lisa arrived at the hospital and peeked inside Juan's room to make sure it was okay to come inside his room. She noticed that he was in the room all by himself. She walked in.

"Good morning, sweetheart," Juan said, happy to see Lisa.

She hugged him and kissed him on the cheek.

"Pastor, I need to talk with you. This position is going to Marco's head."

"Sweetheart, I know. Just keep on praying," Juan said, sighing. "Something's got a hold of him and it won't let him go."

"I can't take these new changes. They're not biblical."

"God is going to do just what He needs to do."

Marco was at the hospital visiting some other members from the church that he needed to see. Since he was there he thought it would be no harm in visiting Juan.

When he walked into Juan's room and found Lisa there, anger rose quickly within him.

"What are you doing here, Lisa?" he asked.

"I'm just visiting my pastor," she replied.

"*I'm* your pastor and don't you forget that," Marco said. He became very serious when he said this. Both Lisa and Juan looked at him strangely.

The angels became very guarded.

"The Almighty has something planned, just wait," Ashshod said. "He is going to do something real big, just hold on."

Ignoring Marco's presence, Lisa took Juan's hand and said, "The mother's board misses you." Lisa grew up under Juan as a child; she loved him dearly. "I really miss you." She looked into his eyes and began to cry.

"Okay, that's enough of this mushy stuff," Marco said. "It's time for us to leave, Cortez. We know you need your rest."

Juan just closed his eyes and said, "Lord, he really needs your help."

"Man, stop saying that. I'm *okay*." Looking at Lisa with hard eyes, Marco said, "It's time to go...now."

He grabbed Lisa by the arm tightly and escorted her out of the room. There in the hallway, Marco said, "Don't you come back here unless I tell you to."

She looked at him and said, "You are not my father." As she began to walk away, he snatched her back.

"Don't you ever defy me. I said don't you ever come back here."

She snatched her arm back and walked away from him.

When they got home, he approached Lisa again and said, "You are under my authority."

"No, I am not," Lisa said. Marco grabbed her hard, and she yelled, "What are you going to do? Beat me all around the house until I agree to your lunacy?"

The children ran into the room.

"What's going on?" they asked in unison.

Marco said, "Go back to your room."

"Mom, are you ok?" asked Marion.

He said, "Go."

Lisa began to speak, and he slapped her hard in the face. Blood ran from her mouth. She wiped her mouth and looked at the blood.

Marco looked at her with disgust and walked away. Before he left the house, he said, "You serve me like everybody else."

"He is doing such a great job," several of the imps said. "He is doing just what we want him to do."

False Doctrine jumped on Marco's shoulders and said, "I need for you to go visit Juan. I need for you to inform him of what you are doing." So Marco went to visit Juan, who was not happy to see him.

"Hello there, Pastor." Juan gave him a strange look. "What is wrong with you?"

"I want to know why you are here, Marco," Juan said. Ashshod was standing very close to Juan because he was not going to allow anything to happen to him.

"Ashshod, I told you that I was going to pay you back, and I'm going to get you through the souls of men," False Doctrine said.

"I just wanted to go over the new changes that I have made," said Marco.

"Marco, I cannot hear the hot air you are blowing out."

"I'm not blowing out any hot air. This is real."

"I don't want to get my blood pressure up. Marco, you can just go."

"I will not be going anywhere. You will listen to what I have to say."

False Doctrine became huge and he stood over Marco to make sure that none of the angels would bother him.

Marco grabbed the nurse button. "Here are my new changes. I need for you to know that this week I have gotten rid of all the crosses in the church," Marco said.

"Marco, listen to how ridiculous you sound. It was at the Cross where Jesus paid our sin debt and you mean to tell me that you are getting rid of it in the sanctuary and from in and outside of the House of God?"

"I got rid of the church covenant, and especially those old tired hymn books and any other items that is associated with this aspect of Calvary."

"You are acting like a spoiled child, just trying to do things your own way. Boy it is the Covenant that God has for mankind that bond that shows His love for us and you want to just do away with it how dare you. The Hymnals we sing the songs to reflect our appreciations of who God is. You are really a sick young man."

"Listen Juan, just because you are like a walking Bible that means absolutely nothing to me. Impress those who actually care because I don't care, Juan!" Marco yelled.

Juan looked toward the wall opposite his bed. Looking at a blank wall was far better than listening to the drivel Marco spoke.

"Juan," Marco said, seething. Juan remained silent. "Juan, listen to me!"

After a few minutes of silence, Juan said. "I am Pastor Cortez to you...not Juan."

"No, you are Juan. We are equal. Don't *you* forget that."

Again, Juan went silent. Just before Marco was about to go into a tirade, Juan said, "I didn't invite you here. You came here as if I wanted to hear you speak when that's the last thing I would ever want to do."

"Shut this old man up. He doesn't mean anything to you," Hatred said.

"Hatred, take your hate and leave. You will not touch him," said Ashshod.

"Marco, now you listen to me. You better pick up your Bible and read it," Juan said. "What you are doing is an abomination to the mighty will of God! All you care about is making that place of worship a mega church."

"Juan, I don't care how you feel because what you are forgetting is that you had your turn; and it's my turn now."

"You tell him, Marco. Let him know that you are in charge," False Doctrine said.

"Marco, you can lead people straight to Hell because of your greed."

Greed said, "Now what is wrong with that? I don't see a problem with being greedy and leading people straight to Hell." Greed began to laugh.

"Marco, Jesus saith unto him, I am the way, the truth, and the life: no man cometh unto the Father, but by me. That's John 14:6; in case you don't know."

"Old man I know where that is, but it does not pertain to me, do you understand? See the problem with you Juan is that you are stuck in traditions so let me put it in your terms you are 'old school'."

"Marco, I need for you to stop calling me by my first name."

"I will not. You are no better than me, Juan. What are you going to do about it, slug me? I don't think so." Marco laughed.

"Marco, so what does Romans 10:9-10 mean to you?" asked Juan.

"It means to me just what it says, but I am not going to follow the entire Bible."

"Boy what?"

"I just think society needs to think about more prosperity and don't you call me boy. I might end up putting my hands on you, old man. I run this show, do you hear me, Juan?"

Greed, Hatred and False Doctrine loved every moment. Slowly, they moved toward Juan.

Ashshod just stood his ground and said, "Back away."

Greed said, "Oh don't worry. We are going to get rid of Juan. You just watch."

Marco made Juan so upset that the monitor started to beep and Marco began to smile.

"Wait old man, stop getting yourself all worked up. Everything is going to be just all right," Marco said, smiling. Marco politely walked over to Juan and just gave him a kiss on the forehead. "I just thought that you needed this, Juan." He smiled right in Juan's face.

Nurse Glynda walked in Juan's room and noticed that Marco was in there. "I need for you to leave. You are putting pressure on my patient, and I won't allow this."

"Oh, I was just leaving." Marco winked at Juan and left.

False Doctrine said, "Ashshod what's wrong with Juan? Why is he so choked up? Aw, look at him having to get all medicated up. Look at Juan, oh he's crying, boo hoo, hand him some tissue."

Hatred said, "Good, I hope he has another stroke for picking on our friend Marco. He didn't need to hear about the Bible. We are giving him our Bible." The other imps in the room just flew in the faces of the angels and said, "One for us and zero for you." Then they started to hiss.

Marco walked back to his car with excitement, saying, "I finally defeated that old man." He received a phone call from Chairman Smith of the Deacon Board.

"The construction company came by and they finished taking all the crosses down in and out of the church."

Marco said, "Thank you and is everything gone like the hymnals?"

"Yes pastor, they are. No one will see any of this on Sunday," replied Deacon Smith.

"Great Smith. I will see you later. Hey man, I want to get rid of prayer service because nobody ever comes out to it anyway. We waste money. We can do it on Sunday until I find a way to revamp it so that the people will be coming out in crowds. Man, I will see you at dinner. Don't forget, see you at seven."

"Okay Pastor, I will see you then."

Nurse Glynda paged Dr. Casper and informed her of what happened. She'd told the doctor all of Juan's vitals and was instructed to give Juan a sedative. Within 30 minutes Juan was asleep. Joyce walked into Juan's room and was so surprised to see him asleep she called for the nurse.

Nurse Glynda walked into the room and Joyce said, "Hello, I'm surprised to see my husband is asleep."

"Hello Mrs. Cortez," Glynda said. "Some young gentleman came in here and really got under his skin. I was at the station and I heard the monitor go off and I came in here and found his blood pressure was very high. I called the doctor and she informed me to sedate him so I could get his blood pressure down."

Concern grew in Joyce's eyes. "What? So, how is he doing? Is his blood pressure still up?"

"It's going down but not as quickly as I want it to, but the doctor is checking in every 15 minutes." Joyce got herself worked up. "I need for you to calm down. I don't want you to end up in a room."

Joyce said, "I'll try." Joyce felt so helpless. She didn't know what to tell Juan and what to keep from him. She couldn't tell when his health might decline because of stress.

Quickly, she knelt beside Juan's bed, needing to release the tension and pain that dwelled in her heart.

"Dear Heavenly Father," she began.

8

Juan's Heartaches

Ashshod and the angels were stationed in Juan's room and the imps stood by, Greed before them, looking at him. All Juan could do was lie in bed and think. What was going on in his mind was the utter destruction of Marco's behavior. The power was making him into a monster. He constantly thought about what Marco said about taking the crosses out of the place of worship, which was very ridiculous. He never thought he would ever see the day. *But Lord*, he thought, *what gets me is that he does not care about the souls of men, just his status.*

"Guess that's what power can do to a person," he whispered.

After lunch, Joyce walked in and said, "Hi honey, how are you?"

"I'm fine," he replied. They kissed.

"Why are you looking a little flush?" Joyce asked.

"Do I?"

Joyce nodded.

"Just lying here, thinking about the destruction Marco is causing. I'm thinking about what Rachael and Forest is going through as well as John and Jane with Trevor." He felt so helpless.

"That's because you are helpless," Greed said. "See, Juan, you are so helpful to me and useless to God. Your friends need you and what kind of friend are you?"

Ashshod said to Greed, "Your words can only go so far."

"Maybe to you, Ashshod, but to Juan my point is getting across." Greed pointed at Juan and said, "Look how helpless he is." Greed just stared intensely as Juan. "*I'll get to you*, dear *Juan. In fact, I'm already doing so.* Look at dear sweet Joyce just thinking that she can console him in his time of need. I don't think so."

Looking at Ashshod, Greed smiled and said, "We are creating Satan's house now because we are going to get these souls so you can just stop imagining that it's a house of…" Greed couldn't say his name.

"God," Ashshod said. "See you tremble at the sound of His name, Greed. God is His name, God and don't you ever forget it."

"I'm not going to stand here and listen to your mumble jumble, I'm outta here." The imps stationed in Juan's room hissed.

"Honey," Joyce said, "You must realize that God is in control."

"Yes baby, but it is so hard to watch the obnoxious things he is doing. Joyce, you know what's so amazing is how people follow the nonsense. It's just so sad."

"Juan, I'm always telling you, you never know why people go to the worship building. People go for many reasons—to find a mate, to socialize, political reasons and to be popular."

One of the imps jumped in and said, "To hold positions that they know that they would not hold in the real world because they are social misfits. Have you ever noticed that there are people who can't fit in the popular cliques but at church they do? And that's why they want to come. Salvation is the last thing on their mind. They are getting what they want."

Juan said, "Joyce, you're right. One will never know why people come to church. God only knows."

The same imp said, "I know."

"Juan, we may not have had all the bells and whistles like Marco, but we sure have the presence of the Lord in His house! So Juan all we can do is pray."

"Yes Joyce that's all we can do."

Discouragement settled in Juan's spirit after hearing the baloney that came out of Marco's mouth. He felt defeated because he had no control over what Marco was doing to the children and the house of God. Juan understood exactly what Joyce was conveying to him, but it still did not soothe his soul because he could not stop what was happening to the parishioners at Solid Rock.

"It is a test we are facing," Joyce said. Juan nodded. "All of us. Look at what Rachael is dealing with, Forest, too. The Tanankas and their son. It's as if everything is falling apart all around us."

"It does, feel that way." Juan agreed.

"But honey, there is one thing that we know about Rachael and the Tanankas; they fear the Lord and they believe in the power of prayer. They will pray and talk to God to let Him know that they need Him. This is all a test, a trial that we're facing. We need to stick with our Heavenly Father and face it."

"Joyce, you are so right, baby, so right. Let's pray for them right now."

The same imp that had been giving his opinion said, "Not prayer. You don't need to do this. Nothing's working for you guys."

At the end of their prayer, Juan and Joyce concluded with, "In Jesus' name we pray, amen."

"Prayer...stupid humans." The imp began to drool and hiss.

"Good night honey," Joyce said, kissing Juan. "I'm going to go home and call Rachael, Jane and the kids."

"Okay baby."

"I'll call you before I go to bed."

Juan smiled. "I'll have the nurse hold the phone to my ear like I normally do."

Joyce kissed him on the lips and left.

9

Rachael Meets Mrs.

Roberts

Mrs. Roberts was getting ready for her next class and she was so ready to address Forest about his grades. The bell rang and all the students arrived into the classroom. Mrs. Roberts waited until she gave her daily instructions before she addressed Forest. She addressed him in front of the class to show that she held all authority.

Bully, Racism and Hatred were in Mrs. Roberts' classroom waiting to start some trouble. Sebastian, Rafael and Ethan were there watching over Forest.

Mrs. Roberts said, "Forest, I notice that your behavior is changing for the worse. I need to schedule a parent meeting with your mother."

"Why do you need to call a parent meeting?" Forest asked.

"Your grades are dropping, and you are getting in confrontations with classmates."

"What?" Forest looked at Mrs. Roberts, perplexed. "When did my grades start slipping? Just recently, I was an A student in this class. We just received our progress reports last week. You mean to tell me that I am getting a failing grade within one week?"

Mrs. Roberts started smiling. "I will be calling your mother."

"Do what you must."

"Oh we will," said Bully.

The bell rang.

Forest, Piper, Turquoise, and Lil' Audrey were all standing on the outside of the school building.

"I'm telling you," Forest said, "Mrs. Roberts is acting so strange."

"She acts if she doesn't like black people," Turquoise said.

"I think she has a problem with you guys dating, and because we all hang together." Lil' Audrey added.

Bully started hissing at Sebastian. Sebastian brushed him off, but Bully started hissing louder.

"Listen you dumb angel, you do not brush me off. You have no authority over me you nitwit, so if I look your way, you better acknowledge me," Bully said.

"Why would I waste my valuable time dealing with you? Be gone you silly little imp," Sebastian said.

Bully flew toward Sebastian ready to knock his block off, but Sebastian gave him a look that stopped him dead in his tracks. Bully backed away and said, "Oh, we will finish this later."

"Oh yes we will," replied Sebastian.

Ashshod and Zaso were in Mrs. Roberts's classroom. Racism was also in the room as well as other imps.

Rachael walked to Mrs. Roberts' classroom. Mrs. Roberts was alone in the room when Rachael walked into the room and said, "Excuse me I'm looking for Mrs. Roberts."

"I am she," answered Mrs. Roberts.

"Hi, I'm Ms. Weinberg, Forest's mother."

Mrs. Roberts stood to her feet and began to stutter. "Maybe I didn't hear you correctly. Who are you?"

Racism looked at Zaso with seeping eyes and turned back to watch what was going on.

"I said I'm Forest's mother," repeated Rachael.

Mrs. Roberts's face turned red. "The reason I scheduled this meeting is I am concerned about Forest. He is not staying focused, he is easily distracted, and he is not completing his homework assignments and classwork."

"How could this be?" Rachael asked. "You are the only teacher that seems to have a problem with my son. He has informed me of how you have been treating him. We just received his progress report last week and now you are saying that he is failing when he just received an A? I don't understand this, Mrs. Roberts."

"I've noticed that he is dating Piper. How do you feel about this?" asked Mrs. Roberts.

"What does this have to do with his grades?"

"Well I was just wondering how you felt about it."

"You mean a boy and a girl dating?"

Mrs. Roberts started to get flustered. "You know what I mean."

Racism started hissing, and Ashshod moved very close to Rachael.

"Ashshod, who does she think she is by having her son date out of his race? You know the Bible says be not unequally yoked" Racism said sarcastically. "Mrs. Roberts has the right to address this problematic issue, Ashshod. What are you guys thinking?"

"Racism, you are as foolish as you look," said Ashshod. "Being unequally yoked has nothing to do with race, stop acting stupid. You know what the Lord meant."

Racism said, "You have your opinion and I have mine." He laughed. "It's my job to make sure that it's only one superior race. Now if you want to get political, Ashshod, you are on your own."

Ashshod said, "Be gone, Racism."

"You don't rule me, Ashshod."

"I said leave, Racism, right now, or you will wish you had." Ashshod's eyes began to glow.

"You better be glad I have to leave. I think I'm being summoned in the principal's office. Oh I'm so sure that I'll see your silly face there. See you soon, bye bye." He vanished.

"This meeting and conversation is now over, good day," Rachael said, leaving the room in disgust.

Rachael stormed down the hallway toward the principal's office, Zaso right by her side. Rachael arrived at the office, went inside, and yelled, "Where is Principal Griffin?"

The school secretary was sitting behind her desk; she jumped up from her chair and asked Rachael to calm down because there were parents and students in the office. Rachael was making such a big ruckus that Principal Griffin stormed out of her office. When Principal Griffin reached the secretary's desk, Rachael was yelling, "Your teacher is a racist." Everyone was looking at Rachael.

Principal Griffin said, "Calm down. Let's go into my office where we can talk like calm, rational adults."

Rachael agreed and they walked back to her office.

Zaso and Racism were already there.

"Oh," Racism said, "She's telling on me to the other one that can identify with Forest. Oh how cute. Now Zaso, let's hold hands and sing 'We Shall Overcome'. Oh no, wait, let us sing 'Kumbaya', yes, that's it." He laughed.

"I don't have time for your shenanigans," Zaso said.

Rachael followed the principal into her office.

Principal Griffin said, "Now, Ms. Weinberg what seems to be the problem?" "I think," Rachael said, shaking her head. "No, I *know* that my son's math teacher is a racist."

"What makes you think this?" Principal Griffin asked once the two were seated.

"Well Forest is doing great in all his classes, including hers, and now she's telling me he's failing and asking about his relationship with Piper Rodgers."

"How can this be?" Principal Griffin asked. "I just checked his grades. I'm puzzled."

"She is upset that Forest and Piper are dating. I just walked out of the room where she was asking me how I felt about them dating." Rachael stood. "You better handle this or I will." She left the room and stomped out of the school.

Ashshod and Zaso followed Rachael as she walked to her car.

She was baffled by the blatant racism from Mrs. Roberts. "Isn't it 2009? Feels more like 1911."

Forest, Piper, Lil' Audrey, and Turquoise were standing in the hallway by Piper's locker between classes. George walked by and grabbed Piper on the buttocks inappropriately. Piper yelled and Forest grabbed George.

George held on to Piper and said, "You need to stick with your kind. This monkey needs to go back to that inner-city jungle where he came from."

Bully flew down and gave George some extra strength. George then grabbed Forest and slammed him against the locker. "I hate you black people." Then he looked at Turquoise and Lil' Audrey.

The kids in the hallway started chanting, "Fight Fight Fight."

Principal Griffin and Mrs. Roberts ran into the hallway and broke up the fight. Principal Griffin told all of the students to get to their classes. She looked up at Mrs. Roberts who smiled.

Ashshod told Hunter to transform into a human male and to pass by the principal and Forest. Hunter and Forest connected with their eyes and Hunter said to Forest, "It's going to be all right."

Principal Griffin looked at the man; she thought it was a parent Forest knew. "Forest, do you know him?" she asked.

"No, never seen him before in my life," Forest responded.

The man just disappeared.

When Forest arrived home, he told his mother what happened, and she immediately suggested they go to see Juan.

The pair arrived at the hospital and entered Juan's room. Juan was talking to Joyce and Glynda. Juan looked up and saw them both standing right in front of him; he was so surprised and excited at the same time. Joyce smiled as well, not knowing that they were coming for a visit.

"Come in come have a seat," said Juan. "Son, you are getting so big and tall."

Forest said, "Thank you" and smiled.

Joyce said, "Yes he is, so handsome."

Forest began to blush and smile. "How are you doing, sir?"

"Joyce, do you hear him saying *how are you doing, sir?*"

"Just look at those wonderful manners," Joyce said. They all burst out laughing.

"So what's going on? Or should I say what you youngsters say and say what it do?" asked Juan.

Forest looked at his pastor. "Sir, please don't say that. Just say how are things."

"Why?" asked Juan

"Because you don't sound right saying that stuff," answered Forest. They all looked at Forest and began to laugh.

"Okay so what is really going on?" asked Juan.

"I'll be back in an hour to check your vitals," Glynda said.

"Okay," "Thank you." said Juan. Once Glynda left the room, Juan again asked, "So tell me what's happening."

"I'm dealing with racism and bullying," Forest said.

"My God, please help this young man," said Juan.

"My math teacher hates the fact that I'm dating out of my race. Piper Rodgers is white, and when she found out Mommy was white, she had a hissy fit. You would have thought somebody said something about her mother or stole her car," Forest said.

All Juan could do was pray; he closed his eyes. Bully entered the room as well as Racism; they heard that they were being talked about. They both laughed. "What is this little boy think he's doing telling on us," Bully said. "He should be ashamed of himself thinking that this paralyzed man can help him."

"Look he's praying," Racism said. "He can't even get his own prayers answered, how can he pray for someone else?" They began to drool heavily. They saw Ashshod, but they were not worried about him nor he them.

"Go on, son," said Juan.

"Sir, I have already laid a lot on you. Can you just continue to pray for me please? It is difficult to talk about," Forest said.

"All right, son."

"Thank you both for listening," said Rachael. "We have already taken enough of your time. I will call you, Joyce, real soon." They said their goodbyes and left the room.

Juan was lying in bed feeling so useless.

Joyce said, "Honey, with God's help, Rachael will handle this."

"That's what she thinks," said Bully.

"Stop right now," answered Zaso.

Bully just hissed.

10

Apostle Marco Pablo

Marco was sitting at home in his office before getting ready for Sunday morning service. The imp Arrogance jumped on Marco's shoulder and said, "It's time for you to be worshipped. You will tell the congregation this morning to start calling you Apostle Pablo, it has more meaning. You need to expose this information to Pastor Cortez first."

Marco said, "Yes it's done."

Then he says to Lisa, "We are going to visit Juan before we go to morning service. I know you want to see him, so we will go today."

"Oh gee thanks, Marco, whatever," Lisa stated.

Joyce walked out of the bathroom connected to Juan's room.

"Honey, you can't let this young man work you up like this."

"I understand," Juan said, "But I think about the souls of men who are so dear and precious in the sight of the Lord. This is about man's eternal destination. He is toying with their lives. This is why I am so concerned."

While they spent their morning together, Marco and Lisa walked into the room.

"Lisa wanted to come and see you," Marco said. "She misses you."

"Hello Pastor," Lisa said. Marco cut his eyes at her.

"Hi Sweetheart, how are you?"

"I'm all right, and you?"

"Well, I can't complain."

There was an awkward silence in the room.

"I have some interesting news," Marco said, smiling. "I am now calling myself Apostle Marco Pablo. I'll be announcing this when we go to the worship building after we leave here."

Juan laughed hysterically and everybody in the room looked at him as if he had lost his mind.

"Honey," Joyce said, "Why are you laughing so hard?"

"Well, I cannot believe that this man is doing this."

Marco looked disgusted and asked the question again, "Why are you laughing?"

Juan said, "This is not Biblical. How can you make a statement like this? In order for a person to fit this description of an Apostle, you had to be called by Jesus as he started His ministry. Matthew chapter ten verse one through fifteen. Walked with Him for all three years of His ministry, Hebrews 2:1-4 and eyewitness the death burial and resurrection of Jesus Christ! John 20:19-20. The Apostle Paul saw the Resurrected Lord on the road to Damascus. This is the only way an individual can fit this particular qualification and no one today fits this position in today's society. Don't let this status fool you. It's only going to last for just a little while."

"Once again, the Bible and everything you say means absolutely nothing to me. The Bible does say some will be apostles just like evangelist and other offices, Juan."

Lisa and Joyce looked at Marco when he called Juan by his first name.

"Marco," Lisa said, "When did you start calling Pastor Cortez by his first name?"

"When I became pastor. We are equals. I can call him by his first name, and I will not stop this."

"Marco, you are dead wrong."

"Lisa, I need for you to just hush. I'm a grown man."

"In whose eyes? You are acting very childish," Lisa said.

"Juan, why do you always stay on my case?" Marco asked.

"Because you are making some of the most serious mistakes. The Apostle Paul was making reference to these different offices of the ministry of Jesus Christ. The Holy Spirit used and called individuals into their different types of ministry because the Bible was not written in its entirety. The Apostles were used to form the church. Those 13, do I need to name them for you boy? Wake up, son. These demons have a great hold on you."

"Juan, you don't know what you are talking about. Nothing's got a hold of me."

Arrogance started to circle around Marco and he said, "Hit him, tell him to shut up. This man does not know what he is talking about." The imps stationed in the room started circling around the room; everyone felt a cold draft.

"Is there a window open?" Joyce asked. "It's cold in here."

Everyone looked toward the windows; they were all closed. Ashshod told the imps to leave.

They looked at Ashshod and said, "You don't tell us what to do."

Arrogance was so powerful now, but Ashshod did not care. He simply looked at him and said, "Leave right now."

Arrogance said, "NO."

Ashshod knocked him out of the room. The other imps followed Arrogance, shaking as they did so.

"Greed and Covet," Arrogance said, "We are going to get these angels. We are going to take them down. They may think they have won this battle, but this is not going to happen again."

"Let's go," Greed said. "We must plan for our next battle. Arrogance, you must go to the church. You know what to do."

The imps returned back to the abandoned building.

Ashshod told the other angels, Hunter, Ethan, Mickel, El, Deoriel, and Wade, "We must be ready for the real battle. It's about to begin. "Hunter, get ready for the mission. Ethan, stand guard and Mickel, you stay here and watch over Pastor Cortez. Wade, stand in front of the hospital room. El and Deoriel, you know where to go and you know what to do. I must go and get more instructions from the Almighty and bring some more angels back with me."

Marco was happy. He was at Sunday morning worship service and just loved how the congregation put him on a pedestal. The choir was in full force and they sounded so great; like they could make a CD. He looked out from the pulpit and the pews were full. Things were going just the way he wanted them to go.

Arrogance jumped on Marco's shoulder and said, "It's time to make your special announcement to the congregation."

Marco approached the podium and said, "I would like to make a statement. Starting today, you will call me Apostle Pablo."

The parishioners became quiet; Lisa held her head down.

Mrs. Sallie Cooper stood on her feet and said, "Apostle Pablo, you want to be called Apostle? It shall be." She began to clap and the rest of the congregation followed right behind her.

Marco was so full of arrogance and so energized that he did not want to speak to anyone unless they were worshipping him.

Arrogance held up Marco's head and said, "You are doing this correctly. This is what you are to do. They are beneath you. Hold your head up. They are to pay homage to you. You are their leader."

As the thought went through Marco's mind, he began to smile. When Marco sat down in his chair in the pulpit, he had ordered the congregation to rise and give him a big round of applause because of his presence.

Lisa, Rachael, and the Tanankas just looked at each other, and Forest said, "Oh brother."

Out of this group, Lisa was the only one standing although she was about to be sick to her stomach because her husband was acting foolishly. Rachael and Forest as well as the Tanankas would not stand.

Marco's morning message was on prosperity. He informed the congregation that they were to get whatever they wanted.

"Don't listen to what people try to tell you, especially if they try to tell you that you cannot," he said. "Those are the kinds of people that you leave alone because they walk in darkness."

The congregation was excited.

"So stay away from them, you hear me, stay away."

"Amen Pastor," the congregation said in unison.

Rachael, Forest, and the Tanankas just held their heads down in shame. Since Rachael and the Tanankas did not stand, Marco decided to pay them back. Marco looked over at them.

"I am talking about you guys, you hear me Rachael and the Tanankas," Marco shouted.

"What?" Rachael yelled. The congregation looked at her. "I have never been so embarrassed in my entire life."

Forest grabbed her hand and said, "Please Mom, it will be okay."

John and Jane focused their gaze on Marco, their eyes full of revenge.

After the commotion, Marco said, "I am just kidding with you."

"Joking my behind," Rachael said. "You meant that."

Lisa slid down in her seat.

The Tanankas, Rachael, and Forest got up and left. Lisa just put her head down and said a little prayer after she had noticed that her friends left.

Ashshod and Greed showed up at the morning service.

The imps were smiling then they looked at Ashshod.

"See," Greed said, "We told you there is no room in here for you."

"You don't rule this house," Ashshod said calmly. "There is a higher power. His name is God, you are nothing. This is not going to last long."

"You just shut up, Ashshod," Greed said. "You have no power here. We are going to get these souls. As you can see, from service to service, we are teaching false doctrine and people are joining all the time because they are too stupid to pick up the Bible and read it for themselves. They just take the word of a good looking man. They don't search the Scriptures. How ignorant and stupid can man be? Even us imps know Scripture. This is why we know how to fool people."

They all laughed hysterically.
"The imps sang:
"To Hell they will go, to Hell they will go,
"We'll knock them down and take their Heavenly crowns,
"To Hell they will go ha ha ha ha ha ha, to Hell they will go."

Screeching sounds went throughout the worship building. People began to grab their ears as the microphones in the building started screeching all at one time.

"It's so sad that they are so right," Hunter said. "Why is it so hard for humans to pick up the Bible, God's holy divine word, to read and follow as well as to study? It's even sadder when you see these devilish imps know God's Word. Humans like to follow the crowd most of the time without searching information for themselves. Reading to them at times is like pulling a tooth, but if it's something emotional, they will follow it until it leads them to their death. God shows them the truth!"

"Since we see that these stupid humans are under our control," Greed said, "We have such a great advantage of getting as many people as we want, so just leave and let us just capture all the many souls we can get. They don't need you to help protect them. Get over it. Really get over it."

Then the imps started singing again.

11

Rachael's Turn

nu was stationed at Rachael's building; it was his job to circle around the area. He and Gabe worked the building. The imps were enraged because the angels were protecting the building and the tenants. They knew who was trying to destroy the property. They just waited until the right time to handle everything. There were thirty imps housed at the building because a lot of them were following the tenants. But it only took half of the angels to handle them.

Gary went into the neighborhood and gathered up some drug addicts and discussed that he needed their services to stir up trouble for Rachael.

"You listen to me," he said. "Do not tell anyone that we had this talk."

"Alright," they replied.

Gary gave them ten dollars each. They took it and Gary left.

Two days later Gary met up with the drug addicts in the area again and told them to cause more damage to Rachael's building. Greed, Hatred and Covet came over to Rachael's property and told the imps to vandalize Rachael's property. The imps just looked at the angels and started hissing. The angels' eyes started to glow. The imps jumped inside of the addicts and busted a glass door to one of the storefronts. They could not get in because of the bars. Glass was all over the sidewalk, and one of the building's residents noticed it the next morning while leaving for work. He called Rachael.

"Oh just look at Rachael sleeping so peacefully," Greed said.

"Back off, Greed," replied Zaso.

"Oh you ignorant angel, I'm not going to harm her physically, so shut up."

Zaso ignored Greed and continued to guard Rachael. The phone rang.

Rachael glanced at the clock—it read 7:30 a.m.—before answering the phone. She put the phone down away from her ears and screamed. She then answered; listened with a keen ear and said, "Thank you." She immediately called her handyman and told him what happened.

"Rachael, I told you to give me your building," said Greed before he threw a ball of fire at Rachael. Zaso jumped right in front of her. His eyes glowed and knocked Greed right out of the house. The rest of the imps vanished.

Rachael's handyman had to put plywood on the door until the door could be replaced. When Rachael arrived at the building, she could not believe her eyes. The imps around the building began to hiss.

"Oh she's disturbed about this mess, you guys, boo hoo," said one imp. The imps saw the drug addicts that caused the damage and smirk.

Gabe circled around Rachael, watching the moves of the addicts. Rachael stood in awe and some of the tenants offered to help her clean up the mess. Rachael thanked them for their help. Rachael informed them that she would get to the bottom of this.

"Are you sure?" one of the tenants asked.

"Yes." She nodded her head; they looked at her as if she knew who had caused this mess. The imps at Rachael's property were becoming restless, especially seeing those dumb angels that were housed at the building. Zaso appeared and Enu and Gabe came and stood right by him. Greed showed up with Lie as well as Covet. The imps that were stationed at Rachael's property began to chant "Take Rachael's property" over and over again.

The imps around the building hissed in disgust.

Covet did not appreciate Enu's response, so he charged right after Enu.

Zaso, Enu, and Gabe rumbled with Lie, Covet, and Greed.

"It's only a matter of time," Greed said.

Rachael's screaming and waving down a police squad car got the attention of Zaso. Zaso knocked Lie way across the street and Greed looked up and saw Lie fly across the sky; he blew fire out of his nostrils and halted the fight. Greed had to see what Rachael was up to.

Rachael spotted a police car coming down the street and flagged it down and filed a report right then and there.

Wow, she thought, *quickest response ever. But I had to stand in the middle of the street and act like a lunatic in order to get serviced.*

"Jackasses," she muttered, then quickly sighed. "Please forgive me, God. Please. Lord, I really need your help everything is falling down around me."

Two weeks had gone by and the neighborhood development company continued to come by to see how well-kept Rachael's property was. None of the tenants had even *tried* to leave.

At a staff meeting, Mr. Grabber was daydreaming on how to get Rachael's property. He was so flustered because nothing was coming together for him. Instead it looked as if things were going really well for Rachael.

"Rachael is really keeping her property area clean," Mrs. Betty Smith said. "The tenants are staying, too. They love her as a landlord."

"We need to step up our game," Mr. Grabber said.

"What shall we do?"

"Don't worry. I'll handle this."

Mr. Grabber went into the neighborhood and gathered up some of the neighborhood drug addicts again to come and vandalize the building.

He paid them and said, "Don't you dare mention this to anyone. If you open up your mouth, you will have a price to pay. Here's some money, go get you some liquor. You smell, too. Go and take a bath."

After saying their thank yous, the addicts walked away from Mr. Grabber.

"He is a special man," one of them said sarcastically.

Enu and Zaso watched everything.

"We must keep doing what we were sent to do," Zaso said. "We must be patient. It will all work itself out. We just need to watch and make sure nobody gets harmed."

Three days later, Rachael received a phone call from a hysterical tenant.

"Ms. Weinberg," the tenant began, "Someone broke into my home; and I can no longer stay here. I don't feel safe." After trying to calm her tenant down, Rachael hung up and sighed.

"I can't believe this," she said, exasperated. "Lord, what is going on here? What am I doing that I deserve this kind of treatment?"

Zaso stood right next to Rachael as Greed and other imps appeared.

"Because you are useless and worthless," Greed said. "I'm so glad you are suffering, Rachael, and I will make sure you and Forest suffer badly." Greed looked at the imps that were around and said, "Step up your game and hurt Rachael and Forest and their friends."

Hatred suddenly appeared and said, "I hate her. I'm glad she is suffering."

Hatred and Greed watched how Rachael became discombobulated with her situation.

Rachael could not think straight; staying focused was not even an option. She was fumbling over her thoughts, trying to catch her breath, trying to stay focused on how to handle everything that was going on around her.

They laughed, saw what they needed, and they left.

Mr. Grabber, ever diligent in his goal to acquire Rachael's property, hired an informant, someone from the building to be his eyes and ears.

When Grabber learned that not only one, but two residents had left the property, he was beside himself with joy.

"You are going to pay me for my services?" asked the informant.

"Yes, later on today," replied Mr. Grabber.

"Thanks" replied, the informant.

"Don't call me again unless you have something really great for me," explained Mr. Grabber.

"Yes Sir," said the informant.

Mr. Grabber abruptly hung up and made a call downtown and said that he wanted the city of Cleveland to send an inspector over to Rachael's property. "I don't think the owner is paying her right taxes. Go check this out. I'm just a concerned businessman."

Before her bed, Rachael knelt and clasped her hands together.

"Lord," she began, "Tenants aren't paying their rent, and now I have a couple of vacancies. Bills are piling up and I have already had to replace items."

Zaso just watched over her, surrounding her, as she was in prayer.

Greed appeared in Rachael's home and hearing her prayer, he began to hiss.

Zaso and Greed looked at each other before Greed fled.

Greed, Covet and Lie were in Gary Grabber's office with the rest of the imps that were housed in Gary's office waiting for him to arrive to work.

"What's taking him so long to get to work?" Covet asked.

"Patience, my dear friend, he'll arrive in due time," replied Greed.

"The problem I have with this pawn is that he moves entirely too slow for me."

Gary finally arrived to work fifteen minutes late, fumbling over paperwork around the office. He was sitting in his office before his meeting with the board, thinking of numerous ways of stripping Rachael of her property.

Later that afternoon, he sat with the board as they talked about many building projects and when they came to Rachael's property, Gary blurted out "I think we may be on our way to getting Rachael's property."

"What do you know that we don't?" asked Betty.

"Let's just wait."

"Do you see what I mean? He just says things without any actions that support his statements. How annoying," said Covet.

"Just hold on, Covet," Lie said. "Things will work itself out."

"Look, I'm so sick and tired of this man moving so slowly. I'm going to take matters into my own hands."

"Betty," Covet said "While leaning in and whispering in her ear", "I need you to work. You are taking your time, and Gary is moving slow. I need you to move."

All the imps present in the room started to hiss.

Gary and Betty looked at each other and said, "We really need to get rid of Rachael. Not only is she stopping our project, but she has some popularity in the community. We really must stop this."

Rachael was home, crying out to the Lord, asking for His assistance concerning her property as well as what was going on with Forest at school. Even though Rachael felt helpless, all she could do was trust in the Lord because He always knew what was best for her.

"Lord," she said, exasperated, "What is going on?"

Zaso watched over Rachael as the imps tried to get real close to her. The imps were allowed to come in from time to time to see what Rachael was up to; these were weak imps. Their jobs were to report back to Greed. The imps did not need to report to Greed because all Rachael was doing was praying and crying and neither of these actions were getting her anywhere.

12

Gary Grabber Goes to

Church

Gary got up Sunday morning and got ready for church, something he hadn't done since a child. He was quite nervous actually, hoping that the building wouldn't collapse on him. He was only going because a friend had been begging him to visit, so he decided to go. As he was getting ready for service, he found his attention focused on Rachael and getting her building. He could not understand why Rachael was so stubborn. For her to be a Christian, she should give it to the community freely, thought Gary. That's what Christians were supposed to do.

Gary got into his car and drove to Solid Rock. As he walked into the worship building, he saw Rachael. Solid

Rock was jammed packed. He had a hard time finding a seat. He found one and sat there as if he was in a foreign land. Gary listened to the choir and then it was prayer time. Minister Hall asked those who needed a special prayer to come down.

Leaning over, Gary asked the person sitting next to him, while pointing at Rachael "Is she a member here?"

"Yes." The young lady said.

Gary just watched Rachael with a keen eye. After prayer he followed her with his eyes to her seat. Gary could not concentrate on the service he was just so fixated on Rachael. When service was over, he watched how Rachael talked with other individuals, but he made sure she did not see him. Gary slipped out the sanctuary without Rachael ever seeing him.

■ ■ ■

Monday morning arrived and the mortgage company called Rachael and informed her that she was falling behind on her mortgage bill. She scheduled a payment plan and felt great about it despite the fact that anger and stressed infiltrated her. It upset her to have to deal with such heavy issues before she could have her morning coffee.

Out on her morning errands, Rachael went to the post office to check for her mail in her post office box. In there, she found a note regarding a certified letter she had to sign for.

She nearly went through the roof when she read the letter from the Department of Taxations. They were raising her taxes.

"You got to be kidding me," she said.

She immediately called them and asked for an explanation on why her taxes went up.

"We went by your property," the person on the other line said, "And based on the building size you are not paying the right taxes. Plus, the school district's, taxes went up as well. You can appear in court, but first you must send a letter explaining why your taxes should not be raised."

"Thanks," Rachael said before hanging up. "Lord, why am I always the target?"

Zaso moved very closely because Covet came close to her and said, "I told you I was going to get you."

After running her errands, Rachael went home and there, she found yet another certified letter in the mail—this one from the Building and Housing department. Since she would not give them her building, Betty called downtown to the department and told them to inspect the building and make Rachael fix all the flaws.

"Lord," Rachael said, on the verge of tears, "You know what's best for me. Please help me, Jesus!"

Ashshod, Zaso and Gabe surrounded Rachael, for they knew she was hurting.

Greed, Covet and Doubt came close to her and said, "Oh, this is getting good."

"Rachael, where is your God now?" Doubt said. "You are the one who is suffering."

"Lord, do you even care about what I'm going through?" Rachael asked.

Doubt approached her and replied, "No, he doesn't care."

"I guess you don't care." Rachael sniffed. "You won't answer me." Rachael began to cry. She looked at the letter and it explained what she needed done and what the estimate came out to be; they totaled up to $50,000. All she could do was fall on her knees and cry.

Greed, Covet and Doubt clapped their hands and started to hiss.

"See," Greed said. "She wanted to get in our way, and now she must pay for it."

The imps were excited; they knew they had her now. Gabe knocked Greed away and Covet fled. But Doubt stayed around.

As she wallowed in defeat, Rachael decided that she would try and sell them the building. When she called the community development company, she noticed that they were acting as if they were neither excited nor interested. So she backed off.

"Let me make her doubt God more," Doubt said. "This will be even greater to watch."

Rachael was never one to ask, "Could things get any worse?" But the question didn't matter because in her life, the more she prayed, the more she saw things getting much, much worse. Tenants started paying their rent late or not at all. Rachael was a strong Christian woman. She helped those that needed assistance. She even allowed a homeless man to have a place to stay. The homeless man decided to sell drugs and have a prostitution ring on her property. They did not care at all. The imps were taking over and the holy angels just stood their ground.

Rachael tried to pray; it was something she had always done, but her bleak situation made it difficult for her to do anything.

"Wow, this is so perfect," Greed said. "Keep working on her, Doubt."

"To the imps standing around," Doubt said, "We need to get stronger."

■ ■ ■

Mr. Grabber's informant knew the building because he lived on the property, so he told the committee about the security system. They hired a pro to come and take down the system.

Once again Rachael called the police and nothing happened in response to this incident.

"Can I just get a break here?" Rachael asked. "Lord please?"

In the meantime, more tenants started complaining about how bad the building was. Then someone came and took the door off the boiler room, laid it down on the ground, and turned the lighting system off to the building.

Rachael called a plumber, and he said, "Rachael, someone is deliberately trying to send you a message. The only reason they can't blow up this building is because there are people living there. Trust me, if no one was living there, they would have set your property on fire."

"They are playing a game they are not ready for," Ashshod said. "The Bible says, Touch not mine anointed, and do my prophets no harm. Not only will the imps get it, but the humans as well."

"Lord," Rachael prayed, "I need your help".

"I told you, Ashshod, that I was going to get her," Greed said. "Oh by the way, Ashshod, where is God? I don't see Him here helping her. And what is your job exactly? How are you helping when she is suffering? Well, I must say I am very happy, can't you tell?

Rachael got on her knees and asked the Lord, "Why is this happening to me?"

"Zaso," Ashshod said, "Just keep watching out."

Doubt was laughing so hard he could barely contain himself. "God, where are you, hmm?" he asked sarcastically.

13

Turquoise and Lil'

Audrey

Mrs. Roberts was in her classroom plotting her master plan before her first period class. Her first step was taking down those two little troublemakers, Turquoise and India better known as Lil' Audrey. Those little girls irritated the very depth of her soul because of what she thought was their disrespectful mouths and their lack of respect for adults. She got up from her desk, walked over to her classroom window to give herself a little break from thinking so hard, and looked down from her classroom window. She saw Forest, Piper, Turquoise, India and a black student she didn't recognize below, talking. Mrs. Roberts became so furious just seeing all of their faces. She stormed out of her classroom into the hallway, searching for George. Mrs. Roberts spotted him in the hallway and waved her hands, summoning him to come to her. George was so busy talking and hanging around other kids in the hallway that he did not notice her trying to get his attention.

One student said, "George, Mrs. Roberts is trying to get your attention."

George looked up and saw her waving her hands; he walked quickly down the hallway toward Mrs. Roberts and she grabbed him by the arm and they walked to her classroom.

"It's time to take everybody down," Hatred, Bully and Racism said in unison.

Mrs. Roberts wanted something more drastic to happen, so she instructed George to set up Turquoise and Lil' Audrey.

"It is done," said George.

Bully and Racism were very pleased; they both started to hiss and wiggle, and then they started to chant, "We are going to get them" over and over again.

George noticed that he left his bookbag, iPod and his money at home. He was in a rush that morning because he wanted to make sure that he got to basketball practice on time.

"I got them where I want them," stated George. He began to laugh.

Mrs. Roberts looked at him with perplexity on her face; George looked straight into her eyes and nodded his head as if to say it's handled.

The bell rang and it was time for math class. George was already in his seat before the other students came into the classroom. He was so delighted to see Turquoise and Lil'

Audrey walk into the classroom. They both noticed that George was looking at them with a weird look on his face.

"Boy, if you don't take that sick look off your face I will," stated Turquoise.

"George, you are nothing but a stupid, ignorant dog face. You really give me the creeps," replied Lil' Audrey.

George just sat there and looked at them even more weirdly.

"There's nothing that we can do," Turquoise said to Lil' Audrey. "We can't tell the teacher. She is just as sick as he is."

"Yeah you're right. We have to handle this ourselves. There's nothing like taking matters into your own hands."

The bell rang and class was dismissed; everyone left the classroom except Turquoise and Lil' Audrey. They ran their mouths instead of heading to their next class.

Not too long after, Mrs. Roberts returned to her classroom as did George; the girls were still in the class talking.

George walked to where he was sitting previously and spun around, anger etched onto his face.

"Where is my bookbag?" he yelled. "Who took it?"

Lil' Audrey and Turquoise both looked at him, uninterested. They watched as he ran up to Mrs. Roberts' desk. "Mrs. Roberts," he said, "They took my stuff. They were the only ones left in the classroom. I just stepped out of the classroom to go to my locker. They took my bookbag. I had $200 and my iPod in there."

The girls looked at each other.

"We did not take anything out of here," Turquoise said.

"He is lying, Mrs. Roberts," Lil' Audrey added. "We did not do any of this."

"Yeah right," George shouted, whipping his cell phone out of his jeans back pocket. As he dialed, he added, "Don't think you're going to get away with this."

George called his parents immediately and told them what had happened to him. His parents thought the sun rose and set on him; in their eyes, he could do no wrong.

The girls gathered close, staring at the smirk on Mrs. Roberts' face as George rattled off the girls' names on the phone.

When he got off the phone, George sneered at the girls before turning to Mrs. Roberts and winking.

Principal Griffin was in her office when she received a phone call from George's father. He informed her of what happened and that he was pressing charges against the girls.

"Don't you think that's a little harsh?" Principal Griffin asked. "We don't know what truly went on."

"No, it's not harsh. I'm going to teach those kids a lesson."

"Sir, I understand your concerns, but I think we can handle this situation another way."

"I see no other way. This is my decision and I'm sticking with my decision."

"To the principal's office you go, now," Mrs. Roberts said. "Call me crazy, will you? Now who's crazy? You are!" Mrs. Roberts laughed. "I am going to get rid of all you little spooks, do you hear me? One at a time if I have to. You are bringing down this area, but not for long. Not as long as I have something to do with it. Come on and stop yapping, you little nappy headed jungle bunnies."

Turquoise and Lil' Audrey were ready to knock Mrs. Roberts out. Ashshod, Hunter, Rafael and the imps Racism and Bully followed the girls and Mrs. Roberts to the office.

Mrs. Roberts shoved the girls into the principal's office.

Principal Griffin looked up, her eyebrow raised.

"These two girls stole George Keen's bookbag with his money and personal items in it," Mrs. Roberts said.

"No we did not, Principal Griffin," Turquoise said. "We don't want that stupid boy's crap."

"Look," Lil' Audrey said. "We were in the room, but we did not take anything."

George rushed into the office and said, "They took my stuff. Where is my bookbag? You spooks don't have to steal because your parents can't afford nice things."

Turquoise tried to leap and choke George, but Principal Griffin stopped her and pulled her back.

"You redneck, hillbilly punk," Turquoise said. "If I'm going to be blamed for something, blame me for calling you these names, you jerk."

"Punch him in the face," Lil' Audrey said.

Everyone in the main office looked on with amazement.

Ashshod moved close to the principal. Bully and Racism hissed and landed on George's shoulders. "Keep calling them names."

Rafael protected the girls.

Principal Griffin talked to the girls and said, "Since neither one of you want to admit to this, I'm going to have to suspend you both until we figure this out. George's parents plan to press charges. I've already called your parents." The phone rang and Principal Griffin answered and listened grimly. She hung up without saying a word to who called. "That was George's father. He called the police. Said they were headed here. I'm going to call your parents and have them meet you here."

Turquoise and Lil' Audrey started to cry.

Ashshod just watched.

"Nothing like seeing these monkeys in cages where they belong," Racism said.

Then Bully said, "We told ya'll we will get you."

Ashshod looked at Racism and Bully then turned his back on them.

"Ashshod," Racism said, "Don't turn your back on me."

Ashshod said, "Be gone, imp."

"I got your imp." Racism dashed toward Ashshod and Ashshod pierced Racism with his sword and it put a cut in his shoulder.

"I said be gone, imp," Ashshod yelled. With that, Racism left.

Principal Griffin looked up just in time to see a smirk on George's face. "And since you like to throw racial slurs, you *too* will be suspended for your action…and until this matter is resolved."

George's face turned red. So did Mrs. Roberts'. Principal Griffin eyed her wearily.

"But I didn't…" George began, but Principal Griffin lifted her hand and yelled, "Enough. I don't want to hear another word from anyone." She gave a glare at each person. "And I mean this."

The bell rang and Forest left his French class. All the students were in the hallway getting ready for their next classes. One of the students that was in the office that saw everything ran into Forest and told him everything that happened between George, Turquoise, and Lil' Audrey. Forest immediately ran to find Turquoise and Lil' Audrey and ran into them being escorted to the police cars by two officers.

"My parents aren't here!" Turquoise yelled. "This is not right."

Forest ran to Turquoise and asked, "What happened?"

"George told Mrs. Roberts that we stole his bookbag," Turquoise replied.

"Now his parents filed charges against us," Lil' Audrey added.

"What?" Forest exclaimed.

"That's enough talking," one of the officers said. He eyed Forest. "*You* can leave."

The girls were crying; they didn't want to get in the car. The cops shoved them both in the back seat. They were screaming and hollering.

Lil' Audrey said, "Not all black people are criminals."

Mrs. Roberts looked out of her classroom window. Forest looked up at her standing in the window, and she looked at Forest with a devilish grin on her face. Then Mrs. Roberts turned and walked away from the window.

Racism said, "Bye you little black people." He waved. "Oh yeah, at least some of the stench is gone." After a satisfying sigh, Racism returned to Mrs. Roberts' classroom and sat above her.

Mrs. Roberts had a free class period, so she sat in her room, reading through some notes and smiling. So far, her day was going splendidly. She heard footsteps in the hallway about to pass her door. She saw Piper pass by. Mrs. Roberts jumped up from her chair and ran after Piper. She caught up with Piper in the hallway and grabbed her by the arm.

Piper looked at her and yanked her arm back. "Are you out of your mind, Mrs. Roberts?"

"Listen, you need to leave Forest alone. Do you hear me?" Mrs. Roberts reclaimed Piper's arm and squeezed it hard.

"Mrs. Roberts, you are hurting me."

"You haven't seen anything yet."

Piper snatched her arm away and ran. She saw Forest in the hallway and ran to him.

"What's wrong, Piper?" he asked, hugging her.

"Mrs. Roberts grabbed me," she replied. "She said for me to leave you alone."

Forest said, "What, why?

Mrs. Roberts peeped out into the hallway and saw Forest holding Piper. Anger slowly rose within her.

Forest escorted Piper to the principal's office and explained what happened between her and Mrs. Roberts.

"I'm so sick and tired of hearing things about this woman," said Principal Griffin.

Principal Griffin said, "I will handle this, calm down. I will call your mother to come and pick you up, Piper."

Principal Griffin hesitated to call Piper's mother but she knew that she had to. After dealing with a livid Mrs. Rodgers, she hung up and said, "What is wrong with this woman? Whatever it is I'm going to stop it."

An hour later, Mrs. Roberts arrived back at the school from taking a short lunch. Principal Griffin came out of her office and saw Mrs. Roberts standing at the counter and said she needed to see her right now.

Mrs. Roberts had a surprised look on her face. Principal Griffin led the way to her office and shut the door.

Ashshod, Racism and Bully were in the office as well.

Principal Griffin wasted no time. "Why did you grab, Piper?"

Mrs. Roberts looked surprised. "Whatever do you mean?"

"Piper said you grabbed her. You have no business putting your hands on a student."

"I did not touch her. I am a professional person," Mrs. Roberts said calmly.

"Mrs. Rodgers wanted to come after you, but I informed her that the school board would handle this first," explained Principal Griffin.

"There is nothing to explain. I did nothing wrong," answered Mrs. Roberts.

"Oh and you are so sure of yourself?" asked Principal Griffin.

"Yes," replied Mrs. Roberts.

Principal Griffin looked at Mrs. Roberts suspiciously.

"Well this brings me to my next question," said Principal Griffin. "I'm still confused about what happened with Turquoise and India."

"How dare you take the sides of two children over an adult," said Mrs. Roberts.

"No how dare you take the side of a spoiled brat."

"Whatever do you mean?"

"Oh you know what I mean, don't act stupid. You waltzed in this office like you were floating in the air. It's like you wanted to get these girls in trouble, and look at you with that silly smirk on your face. I must remember to stay professional at all times," stated Principal Griffin.

"Oh, should I watch myself? Do you want to put on the gloves Principal Griffin? I get to see your true colors? So this is how you black folks handle your business, with fist fights?"

"No, us black folks handle things with common sense. How do you white folks handle things? Oh I know by hiding behind racism."

"How dare you call me a racist."

"If the shoe fits, wear it."

"Listen Principal Griffin, you may rule these kids but not me. I don't like your accusations implying, that I'm a racist. Those girls took things that did not belong to them and now they are facing the consequences," explained Mrs. Roberts.

"I don't know what you are doing, but your sins will find you out," answered Principal Griffin.

"Thanks for the sermon, but no thanks," Mrs. Roberts said before smiling and leaving Principal Griffin's office.

14

Marco's New Plans

Early Saturday morning, Marco was sitting in his study at the house, thinking about how he was going to add the finishing touches at the church.

False Doctrine stood over Marco and said, "I know what you need to do. You need to get rid of the invitation to Jesus Christ. It puts pressure on people to give their lives to Christ. I think you should explain to them that they have all the time in the world to do this."

Marco suddenly wrote everything down that was going through his mind and said, "I think that this will be good for the congregation."

False Doctrine shrunk down and jumped on Marco's shoulder. "Also, I want you to stop preaching about sin. I want you to stop preaching on marriage, sexual conduct and anything else that would stir up a conflict. I just want you to speak on things that are soothing to the soul. Make the people feel good, make them feel comfortable. It's just the Christian way."

All Marco could do was smile.

Lisa peeked into the study and eyed Marco.

"What are you up to?" she asked.

"Nothing," he replied.

"Oh yes you are. You look like the cat that ate the canary. So what are you up to?"

"Lisa, you will find out on Sunday just like everybody else."

"Look Marco, don't let me walk into some nonsense. I just don't want to hear this crap at the last minute."

"Lisa, watch how you talk to me. I am doing the right thing, you just watch."

Solid Rock was full to the maximum on Sunday morning. The choir was singing dynamically, and suddenly everyone stood up as Marco walked down the aisle with his new golden robe. The congregation applauded and he began to smile. He took his seat and the congregation applauded again, this time with shouts.

Lisa looked on with bitterness; it's was so hard for her to pretend that she agreed with the false doctrine that he was making the congregation accept.

Marco got up out of his seat, approached the microphone, and said, "Greetings everyone. This is your leader, Apostle Marco Pablo." The parishioners applauded again. "I have some more news for you today."

Ashshod was there as was Greed and the other devilish imps.

Mrs. Sallie Cooper said, "Go ahead, Apostle. We are listening."

False Doctrine stood firm and tall behind Marco. "Go ahead tell them."

"As of today," Marco began, "I will no longer extend the invitation to Jesus Christ during service."

Rachael's eyes widened. "What?"

Quietly, the Tanankas dropped their heads. Lisa looked around and she noticed their reactions.

"Let me explain," Marco said. "I don't want anybody to feel any pressure on giving their lives to Jesus Christ. When one makes a decision such as this, one must not feel forced. So from now on, the parishioners will know how and when I will end the order of service. If one decides to give their life to Jesus Christ, then they need to speak to one of the ministers or deacons after service. Will the ministers please stand'. Now the deacons. These are the individuals you are to see that will help you on your new journey."

False Doctrine flew right in front of Ashshod and said, "I told you to stop interfering with my business. But since you want to interfere, then you must pay the price. Ashshod, you just don't understand it's their souls we want and if you won't allow us to take them freely and easily, we must do it the hard way and our way. Listen to me, you dumb stupid angel, I am going to take Christ out of this place. I took out the cross, the covenant and the invitation to Jesus Christ."

The imps started to sing:
"To Hell they will go, to Hell they will go,
We will knock them down and take their heavenly crowns to Hell they will go.
To Hell they will go, to Hell they will go."

"Listen to this wonderful music to my ears," False Doctrine said. "

Ashshod, you and the other angels need to leave. This is no longer 'The Man Upstairs' house. It's Satan's palace. Just accept it." The imps in the background continued to sing.

Greed flew over to Ashshod and said, "Are you tired, Ashshod? You really look it. Just throw in the towel and let us just finish what we need to do. You have no power here." Greed blew smoke out of his nostrils.

Ashshod's eyes began to glow and he raised his right hand. All of the angels rushed near him and formed a long line.

"What is this nonsense that you are doing?" Greed asked.

"Why Greed?" Ashshod asked. "Are you scared?"

"Certainly not."

Ashshod's eyes started to glow real bright as well as the other angels; they stood together and slowly turned in a circled as their eyes glowed like sun rays beaming onto a silver coin—leaving a blinding glare.

The imps stopped dead in their tracks; they looked at the angels and tried to figure out what they were doing.

Then immediately the angels stopped.

"What is this nonsense that you have displayed?" Greed asked.

"You will understand real soon, Greed." He looked at the angels and said, "Back to your post."

The imps flew around Greed and asked, "What is going on?"

"I don't know," he replied. "I don't know what these crazy angels are doing, just look out and watch your backs."

The imps hissed at the angels.

Marco stood behind the microphone and the entire congregation stood. He smiled and enjoyed the applause and told them to sit. He looked around and was very pleased. He preached on prosperity, leaving Jesus Christ out of the sermon.

"Just look at him so handsome and speaking with such great pleasure," Greed said. "I am so proud of him."

At the end of the sermon, Marco did not speak of Jesus Christ, and he didn't open the doors of the church. Marco went on to end service with a song and closed the service without prayer. Lisa was distraught by this whole situation. Marco greeted the visitors and he looked at Lisa and she rolled her eyes at him.

I will be addressing her after I finish greeting everybody, he thought, irritation growing.

After Marco finished greeting the congregation, he walked into his office so furious with his wife. He was so angry he had to get a quick fix before he spoke to her. Marco reached into his pants pocket and got his keys so he could unlock the desk drawer where he kept a stash of cocaine. He began to snort to give him the strength to handle Lisa in the way she needed to be delt with.

Not too long after, Lisa arrived at his office, and as soon as the door was shut, Marco lit into her.

"What is wrong with you? Why aren't you supportive?"

"Marco, do you really want me to answer that question?" she asked.

"Yes."

"You are taking Jesus right out of here. Where is Jesus in this place? I feel as if we are at a social event. You have great loud music in which you are hand selecting with words like *Him* with no names of God, Jesus, or the Holy Spirit and secular music, bringing it in the place of worship. What is this?"

"Handle her, Marco," Hatred said. "She is out of order."

Marco slapped Lisa and said, "This is insubordination, and I will not have this, do you hear me?" Lisa held her face. "Stop it. I love you. I'm doing this for you and the kids."

"That's how you do it," Hatred said. "Put Lisa in her place. We don't need anybody to try and stop what we are doing."

Lisa stared at Marco long and hard without saying a word before she walked out the door. He tried to say that he was sorry. She was not having it.

Lisa got into the car. "Lord, I just don't know what this man is trying to accomplish, but I can say this, he is going to self-destruct, and I know I will not be able to do anything about it."

"I can't believe the people here love this baloney. They don't challenge this and they don't seem to care as long as they hear great stuff with no substance. And here I am having to stand by my husband's side. All I can say right now is help. Please come back into your place of worship."

Marco and the kids came up to the car and Lisa had nothing to say.

Once they got onto the road, Marco said, "Lisa, I'm so sorry. I love you."

She turned toward the window and was quiet all the way to the restaurant.

Marco didn't let Lisa's silent treatment bother him on the way to the restaurant, in the restaurant, nor on the way home from the restaurant.

When they arrived home, Marco said, "I'm going to be working and I don't want to be interrupted." He went into his office and closed the door. He turned on the television set; the Browns were playing the Giants, and he sat behind his desk and watched.

He felt so good about how he changed the order of service and about his sermon.

"I think I had a pretty great day today," he said to himself. "Lisa just needed to understand that I'm not doing anything wrong. I'm not on some path to destruction like she thinks. I'm doing things right. I will not change my behavior. If anybody needs to change, it's Lisa."

If he needed any further confirmation of his great day, he got it: the Browns won in overtime.

Lisa was in the family room with the children, watching television

Marco stood at the door jamb and looked at her. "Are you all right?" he asked.

Lisa's response was silent.

"I love you," he said, and again, Lisa remained silent. "I'm going to bed. I'm tired. Goodnight."

"Goodnight Dad," the kids said.

Lisa said nothing to Marco; she could not understand how this man could sleep with all the demonic babble he threw out to people. She could not rest; he really took Jesus Christ out of Solid Rock Missionary Baptist Church. She put the kids to bed and went back into the family room and watched television; she would not sleep in the same room with Marco.

Monday morning Marco was sitting in his study, and he felt the need to make one last change.

It's time to change the name of Solid Rock, he thought. *I need to change it to give it a new style, a new flavor.* He needed for the parishioners to understand that this was a new era and they needed to move this way.

Sunday morning at service the format was in place and he stepped up to the microphone behind the podium and the congregation stood and applauded him just as they should. He told them he needed to make the very last change of their new way of doing things. He had everyone's attention.

Greed, False Doctrine, and Hatred said, "Don't worry, we have your back. They can't touch you."

"This is the last and final change of our new structure," Marco began. "We will be changing Solid Rock's name. It will now be called The Comfort Zone. We are changing the name because we want to let everyone know that we want them to feel comfortable when they enter into service. We don't want anyone to feel any pressure as I've been stating."

Mrs. Sallie Cooper stood to her feet and said, "Apostle Pablo, I love it" before applauding hysterically.

The rest of the congregation started to applaud and he smiled. After all the applauding ceased, he informed the parishioners that the church sign would be going down the following day. He asked the musicians to play some great upbeat music before he gave his sermon and did a little dance.

After service, his family went out to dinner. Marco took them home and he decided to go see the old man; he hadn't seen him in a couple of weeks and thought it was his place to inform him of the new change. Greed, False Doctrine and Hatred were in Juan's room before Marco arrived. They knew Ashshod was going to be there, so they knew they had to be ready for anything that might occur.

Marco arrived at the hospital, and Joyce, Rachael, and the Tanankas were there.

"Hello," he said.

Juan said, "Marco, what do you want?"

Marco said, "Now is this the way you treat a visitor?"

"No. Just you. What do you want, Marco?"

"I wanted to tell you the good news."

"Marco, the stuff that comes out of your mouth is not good news. It's hot air."

Ignoring Juan, Marco went on with his news. "There are two pieces of wonderful news, actually," he said. "First, I took the invitation to Jesus Christ out of the service."

Juan turned red, and Joyce had to catch her breath. Rachael and the Tanankas, already knowing, just shook their heads.

"Listen, you guys, I just don't want to pressure people about the way they give their lives to Jesus Christ. Also I wanted to let you know I've changed the name of Solid Rock Missionary Baptist Church. It will now be called The Comfort Zone. I want people to feel comfortable when they come into service."

Juan yelled, "Marco!"

"Yes Juan," answered Marco

Rachael asked, "When did Marco start calling Juan by his first name?"

"When he became pastor," Joyce replied.

"I see. I just don't know what to say."

"I do," said Juan. "For God so loved the world, that he gave his only begotten Son, that whosoever believeth in him should not perish, but have everlasting life".

"I just don't get you. The foundation of the worship building, you are going to get rid of it just like that, huh? How dare you."

"Juan," Marco said in a stern voice, "Shut up and listen to me. It's my turn to speak. I changed the name of the building and you must remember that you have no say so in anything I do."

"Marco, leave now," Juan said.

John escorted Marco out of the room.

"I don't need for you to walk me out," Marco said.

"What you need," Rachael said under her breath, "Is for someone to walk you into some deliverance."

Ashshod and Greed was in the hospital hallway with the others. Greed was smiling the whole time as things were falling into place just as he had hoped. Greed watched how Joyce and the others got so worked up because Juan's blood pressure became elevated; it was music to his ears to hear them complain about Marco's visit and to see them suffer with worry. Ashshod just looked on as he watched Joyce and the others express their concerns.

Greed said to Ashshod, "This is a great day, don't you think? I must go now. I must get my beauty rest. I'll see you real soon, tah' tah talk to you later." He hissed and blew smoke out of his nostrils. Before vanishing, he laughed and winked.

15

Trevor Visits Pastor

Cortez

John and Jane went to visit their pastor once again. Joyce was there; they said their greetings.

The Tanankas were so concerned about what Trevor was doing they just wanted to bend Juan's ear. Juan was very happy to see them.

John looked at Juan and said, "Man, I just don't want to lay this entire heavy burden on you."

"Listen," Juan said. "I might be in this condition, but I can still be a spiritual advisor. You act like I can't handle what you need to tell me."

"Trevor was or is messing with a married woman and the husband called our house threatening us as well as him, wanting to kill our son," said John.

"I just can't take this irresponsible behavior anymore," replied Jane. She began to cry.

"I'm so sorry," Joyce said.

Greed and Fornication came into the room because they sensed something going on with John and Jane. They looked at each other, and Fornication said, "Why are they here? Trevor is only doing what we want him to do. These are some silly people."

"Let's have a word of prayer," said Juan.

Greed and Fornication said, "There is no time for prayer. You better shut your mouth, Juan."

Ashshod said, "You silly foolish imps. You shut your mouths."

They rolled their eyes at Ashshod and said, "You will pay."

Ashshod just smiled and they became angry.

After prayer and fellowship, Juan said, "Can you have Trevor to come and see me please?"

John said, "We will try, but I can't promise you that he will come and see you."

"All we can do is pray that he will," Juan said.

A day later, Trevor sat in his car, beyond frustrated. He had spent the last day fussing and arguing with his parents. They wanted him to see Pastor Cortez, and try as he might, he could not get them to understand his point of view. He was a ladies' man; that wasn't going to change. He couldn't, however, deal with the flood of tears that fell from his mother's eyes.

Begrudgingly, he went into the hospital, stopping at the gift shop first to pick up a card, balloons, and some flowers to take to the reverend.

Man, he thought, *he cost me some of my drinking change.* He had to chuckle a little.

"Hello Pastor."

Juan turned his eyes toward the open door and smiled broadly. "Trevor," Juan said, "Come in. How are things with you, son?"

"This is for you, pastor," said Trevor, showing Juan the card and placing the vase with the flowers and the balloons on the table beside the bed.

"How thoughtful of you," replied Juan.

Trevor was so agitated that he could not pay attention to what Juan was saying to him. He just went with the flow.

"The same 'ole same ole'. I am the ladies' man," said Trevor.

Juan laughed. "So are you now?"

"Yes, don't you know? And if you don't know, now you know."

Juan laughed again and said, "Son, the reason I asked you to come is that you need to change your ways. It's not pleasing to God and your parents are worried sick about you."

"Pastor Cortez, my parents are okay. They know who I am, and as for God He knows that I want to enjoy my youth. Besides, I love the ladies. I don't want to be in church all the time. I don't want to be tied down in marriage. I want to have fun. I see that your mind is in great shape. I just don't want to hear you right now. I'm not trying to be rude, but you just take care."

"If that's all you had to say, then why did you bother to come?"

For a moment, Trevor was surprised by Juan's question and tone. He never heard Juan sound very angry, and he could tell that his words irritated Juan.

"You know why," he replied. "My parents."

"Well, before you leave, can we have a word of prayer together?" asked Juan.

Trevor gritted his teeth and said, "Okay."

As Juan was praying, Trevor had his eyes open. He was not sincere about the prayer; in his mind, he was saying hurry up. The prayer ended and Trevor said, "I must go. Pastor, you take care and I'll see you real soon." Under his breath, he said, "Not too soon."

Fornication followed Trevor to his home.

Trevor arrived home and Jane and John said, "Hello Trevor." They were in the sitting room reading their newspapers.

Trevor entered the room and said sarcastically, "Well parents, I went to see the pastor as you asked."

"So what did he say?" Jane asked.

"You know, the usual stuff: God, change from your wicked ways...like I said, the usual stuff." Trevor laughed.

"Well are you?" asked John.

"I'm not ready to change because I don't think I am doing anything wrong." Again, Trevor laughed.

Jane and John looked at each other Jane wanted to cry.

"Mom," Trevor said, "Don't be no drama queen, okay? Everything will be all right. Just trust me." Trevor hugged and kissed his mom on the cheek.

"Yes, Mom, everything will be all right, okay?" stated Fornication as he laughed and drooled.

16

Mrs· Roberts' Big Plan

All the imps and Mrs. Roberts were ready to set up Forest. Forest arrived at the school just as it began to rain. The imps hissed; Mrs. Roberts smiled. Forest entered the hallway.

"Forest," Mrs. Roberts said, "I need to see you."

"I need to go to History class," Forest said.

All the students heard as Mrs. Roberts yelled, "I said now!"

She followed Forest as he went into her classroom. She waited until the students saw Forest go into the classroom and then she shut the door. She allowed him to stay in for ten minutes just having small talk with him and Forest was puzzled by this. Mrs. Roberts told Forest to help her with paperwork; when he finished. he quietly opened the door and left. A student saw him leave the classroom and go to another room.

"It is done," Racism said. "Our plan is about to work."

After Forest left Mrs. Roberts' room, she put her plan into action. She waited five minutes and then she called the police. She knew who she wanted to handle her case.

The police showed up unannounced to the main office. Principal Griffin was speaking with the office secretary when they walked in.

"May I help you officers?" she asked.

The lead detective said, "We received a phone call from a Mrs. Roberts that one of her students beat her up."

"What?" Principal Griffin shouted, her eyes widening.

"She stated that a Forest Weinberg assaulted her."

"This is impossible," said Principal Griffin.

"We must see him and Mrs. Roberts," replied the lead detective.

Principal Griffin asked the school secretary to check on Forest's schedule to see what class he had. As the secretary was looking up Forest's class, Principal Griffin went into her office and phoned Rachael. She explained all that she knew which was next to nothing.

Principal Griffin said, "Miss Weinberg. get here now!"

"Rachael replied, "I am on my way as we speak."

"Officers," Principal Griffin said, "follow me. I will escort you to Mrs. Roberts' classroom."

Forest was sitting in his History class when the principal came into the class and informed his teacher that she needed to see Forest. Forest went down to the office escorted by the principal. There was a detective and four police officers in the office.

The detective slammed Forest down in the chair and said, "Why did you do it, Forest?"

"Hey, you can't manhandle him like that," said Principal Griffin. Quickly, she moved to Forest's side and glared at the detective, daring him to touch Forest again.

"I did nothing wrong but help him to his seat," replied, the detective.

"Yes…and I will make sure that you have limited contact with your…*help*, Detective."

The detective went to reach for a frightened Forest again, but Principal Griffin stepped in the way.

"You don't want to do that," the detective said, seething.

"And you don't want to do whatever you think you're going to do. If you have questions, ask them, but you will not manhandle this child."

"I think you better keep your comments to yourself. You are no better than him to me."

"Ask your questions, detective."

For five seconds, there was nothing but heavy breathing before the detective mean-mugged Forest and asked, "Why did you do it?"

"Do what?" Forest asked.

"You know what I am talking about…Mrs. Roberts."

"What about Mrs. Roberts?"

"You physically assaulted her," replied the detective.

"What man, that's crazy," explained Forest.

"You beat her up, you ripped her blouse. She has a black eye, a bloody nose, and maybe a broken arm," said the detective.

Forest was in a daze; he began to weep and say, "I didn't do it."

"Oh, yes you did. She just didn't make it up. You should see how this lady looks. Go look at her."

Principal Griffin eyed Forest thoroughly then looked at the detective. "Interesting," she said. "All this happened to her, yet there is no scratch, no mark, no blood, no anything on Forest."

"What are you," the detective gritted out through clenched teeth, "CSI?" He looked at Forest and shouted, "You will see what you did to her." He went to grab for Forest, but once again, Principal Griffin stood in the way. She helped a shaken Forest up and glared at the detective.

"Seems you are hard of hearing, detective," she said as she ignored the detective and other officers and guided Forest toward Mrs. Roberts' classroom.

The scene for her was like something from a horror movie. She could not believe her eyes.

Forest looked at Mrs. Roberts. His eyes widened. "I did not do this." He saw her all bloody.

Before Principal Griffin could respond, the detective slammed the cuffs on Forest and shoved him to the front door entrance and down the stairs; all the students saw everything. Forest kept pleading his case.

"Shut your mouth, boy," the lead detective said. "You Negroes just think ya'll can have it all with basketball, golf, music. Y'all need to all go back to Africa and swing on trees. Oh I hate you spooks."

"I will be reporting you, detective, with your racist rants. What, have you all gone crazy, spouting racial slurs like it's the in thing to do?"

Bully swirled around in the air, Racism laughed and Hatred drooled.

Ashshod looked at Hunter, Sebastian and Rafael and said, "Hunter go to Forest's home. Rafael, this time you transform and go down to the police station. You know what we must do."

They all said, "Yes Ashshod" and nodded.

■ ■ ■

Rachael franticly drove on the highway, trying to get to Forest's high school. She was so nervous and frustrated at the same time because she was on the other side of town. As she was driving, Principal Griffin called her and informed her that Forest was taken to the Westlake police station. Now Rachael was even more upset because Forest was not in the presence of his parent or an attorney. *How could they make an unethical decision such as this?* Rachael thought.

"Lord," Rachael said, "Please don't let those idiots hurt my son. Baby, Mommy is coming to get you."

At the police station, Rachael ran up to the first person she saw. It was the lead detective. He eyed her and said politely, "May I help you?

Rachael said, "Yes, my name is Rachael Weinberg and you have my son Forest Weinberg."

The formalities ended there. The detective sneered. He stared at her, disgusted, before asking, "How is this boy your son?

"First of all, you don't address me and say how is this boy my son. Forest is my son. That's all you need to know. I don't have to answer to you."

"Oh yes you do. You answer to me. I run this here. Ms. Weinberg, the charges against your son are very serious, and I want you to know that we are not going to let Forest out on bail."

"What do you mean that he can't get out on bail? That is a *right*. I have that right to get my son out of jail."

"Listen lady. I have all the authority here, and I said he will not be going home, not today anyway"

Ashshod just looked on.

Piper was panicking; she had to catch her breath. She was trying to figure out just what to do. She called her parents, and in a frightened voice whispered for them to come to the school immediately. She waited until all the ruckus was over. Principal Griffin had to go into Mrs. Roberts's room so some of the police officers could take pictures and collect evidence. Principal Griffin heard a noise; she looked around and saw Piper hidden in the closet, scared and confused.

"Piper, what's wrong?" she asked.

"I saw and heard some things that I can't believe," Piper replied.

Piper said, "You just have to hear and see this stuff for yourself."

As the officers asked Principal Griffin some questions, the time allowed Piper to forward the information from her phone to her e-mail and to another person. She erased everything then she slipped the phone into her pants.

One of the police officers looked at Piper and said, "What are you doing in here?"

"I was just picking up something from the back room," replied Piper.

The officer gave her a strange look. "Well, we need to see what you have in your book bag."

"Why?"

"Yes," Principal Griffin said, "Why?"

The angels El and Alexander stood watch over Piper.

The officer called a female officer into the room to search Piper completely.

"You cannot do this," Principal Griffin said. "She is a minor and her parents or her attorney has this right to grant this. She is not a suspect."

This made the officer angry. "We are taking her in."

Principal Griffin said, "For what?"

"She might have something to do with this."

"You are out of your mind. What is going on here?"

Greed showed up. "I like where this is going."

Principal Griffin was determined to keep Piper near her until her parents came; she'd had to get to a phone quick enough to call them first.

Before she could whip out her phone, Piper's parents rushed into the school, yelling Piper's name.

"Mom, Dad!" Piper screamed.

When they came into the room, she rushed into their arms.

The officer's anger rose. "How did they get here so quickly?" he asked.

"Mom and Dad," Piper said, "It's a lot of crazy things going on here. Mrs. Roberts is a racist and she set Forest up."

"Shut up young lady," said the officer.

"You don't talk to my daughter like this," Piper's father said. "Do you know who I am?"

The officer looked uninterested. "No, who are you?"

"I'm the District Attorney. And you have no right to treat my daughter this way." Wrapping his arms around his daughter and wife, he added, "You can follow us to the station."

The police officer followed behind them and made a phone call to the lead detective and said, "The young fellow you have in custody...his girlfriend is going to give us trouble."

The detective said, "Why do you say that?"

"Well, her father is the DA and boy is he mad."

"Dang blasted, ugh!"

"What now?" asked the officer.

"How long will it be before you get here?" asked the detective.

"We will be there in 15 minutes."

The detective called his sister Mrs. Roberts's hospital room.

"What do you know about the girl Piper?" he asked, his voice flustered.

"What do you mean?" she asked.

"Don't you know that she is the daughter of the district attorney?"

"No," she said. "Crap."

"Now, we have trouble, but I see what I am going to do. Next time make sure you know what you are doing. Make sure you know who their parents are."

"Shut up."

He hung up on her.

"Jerk."

Imps were in Mrs. Roberts's hospital room. They were just imps without names. They were informed by Greed just to hang near her because Mrs. Roberts was a valuable piece to the puzzle in Satan's plan.

Mrs. Roberts laid in her hospital bed in pain, frustrated for not researching who she was dealing with.

Piper arrived with her parents at the station, her father hot.

But her mother was even hotter.

"What's going on here?" she yelled the minute she was placed in the lead detective's path. "We see that this is your doing, trying to charge my daughter as a co-conspirator of hurting an adult. You are out of your mind. I will have your job!"

"Ma'am, you won't have anything," the detective said. "Hush."

She looked at him and said, "Watch me, you will not mess with my child!"

Ashshod smiled as the imps began to hiss.

"You will not get away with this, Ashshod," the imps said. "We will stop your plans."

Marco said before the ending of service that he could not see anyone. He had things that he must attend to, but he needed to see Lisa in his office right after morning service.

Lisa rolled her eyes and then she nodded politely and said, "Okay."

Marco watched her every move. Lisa met Marco in his office; he had a very nasty attitude.

"Lisa."

"What Marco?" Lisa replied.

"What have I told you about 'Whattin' me?" replied Marco.

"What boy?" she said again. He cut his eyes at her; she did the same and said, "I'm not scared of you. What do you want, Marco?"

"Lisa, what is wrong with those people that you are friends with?" asked Marco.

"What do you mean?"

"They will not honor me."

"I will not respond to your stupid question."

"What is wrong with the Wongs?" asked Marco, being sarcastic.

"I don't know the Wongs," answered, Lisa.

"You know, your Asian friends."

"You mean the Tanankas. When did they become the Wongs to you, Marco?" asked Lisa.

"Well you know Asians…they all look alike."

"I see that you want to crack jokes today. Boy, you are out of your mind."

Marco looked at Lisa again and said, "You got one more time to call me boy. And the white lady, I don't like her."

"You mean Rachael?" asked Lisa.

"Yes, she gets on my everlasting nerves. I heard that she is losing her property. This is good because she causes too much problems, miss 'goody two shoes'."

"You are really full of yourself."

"Watch your mouth, Lisa," he said. "I'm one step from putting my hands on you."

"Try it," Lisa said.

"I need for you to speak to your friends and tell them to stop defying me and follow me or they must leave because I'm the leader here at The Comfort Zone. There are many other places they can go. I don't have room for them here being insubordinate."

Lisa looked at him and said, "You got some nerves." Marco got angry; Lisa said, "Mrs. Cortez doesn't follow you, Marco."

"She is okay for right now because I have pity on her because of her sick husband."

"Boy, I'm leaving. I'll meet you at the car. I cannot listen to this garbage that you are throwing out at me." Lisa slammed the office door. Marco got up from his desk and locked the door.

He went into his locked desk drawer, pulled out his very expensive letter opener and his bag of cocaine, and used the letter opener as a tool to help him not to spill the drugs. There was a knock on the door; he threw the bag into his desk and said, "What did Lisa forget?"

After another knock on the door, he said, "Hold on, I'm coming." As he opened the door, he said, "Lisa, what do you want," but he found Mrs. Jennings on the other side.

"Mrs. Jennings," he said. "Well Hello, come in." He locked the door behind her, and she waited until he came close to her and groped her bottom. They began to kiss and he shared some cocaine with her. They both were enjoying the moment. She was giggling and he was really enjoying touching her and kissing her.

Lust and Fornication enjoyed the moment as well.

"You might as well just have your way with her," Fornication said. "She is all yours. I have your back."

Suddenly, Marco felt real lucky. Before he could get comfortable, there was a knock on the door; they both looked at each other.

"Who is it?" he asked. No one answered.

Fornication became angry and said, "Who is messing up my work?"

Again they heard another knock on the door; Marco yelled again and it was his son saying, "Dad open the door."

"What do you want, boy?"

"Can I come in?"

"What do you want?"

"Dad, let me in."

"Hold on."

He and Mrs. Jennings fixed their clothing and got themselves together. Marco locked his cocaine stash up before opening the door and cutting his eyes at his son.

Mrs. Jennings said, "I'll see you later. Thank you, Apostle Pablo."

His son watched her leave the office and gave his Dad a peculiar look.

"Boy, why are you looking at me like that?" Marco asked.

"No reason," replied Bryant.

"Don't let me smack you into the middle of next week."

Bryant turned, looking confidently at his father and said, "Mom said come on."

"Tell your mother don't rush me. She doesn't run anything. Now go back to the car. I'll be there in five minutes."

Bryant left the office.

Fornication and Lust were so angry

"That boy needs to be slapped," Lust said. "He messed up our plans."

Marco got into the car and said, "Son, I'm going to tear your behind up for interrupting my private session."

"Dad, I was only doing what Mom told me to do," pleaded Bryant.

"I don't care."

"You better slow your roll, Marco," Lisa said. "And who was your session with?"

"I don't need to tell you that," he replied.

Bryant blurted out, "I told you, Mommy, Mrs. Jennings."

Marco turned around and slapped Bryant in the face.

"Stop that," Lisa said.

"I'm not a child," Marco said. "He doesn't tell my information."

"You must have been doing something wrong because you are so upset," replied Lisa.

"I wasn't doing anything wrong. Shut up, Lisa."

"Watch your tone with me, boy. Why did you need to see her? You said you could not see anybody today. Oh, is this the business you had to handle?"

Marco looked at Lisa, cut his eyes at her, and said, "Shut your mouth. You have one more time before I hit you."

The girls said, "Mommy, just leave Daddy alone, please."

The children were crying in the back seat. Lisa looked at them and said, "It's going to be okay."

Marco didn't say a word and just drove them to the restaurant.

After they went out to dinner, Marco was going to take a nap and Lisa said she had to run an errand.

"Whatever," Marco said. "Don't be gone long."

Lisa paid him no attention. She went to visit Pastor Cortez. She found him alone in his room.

He was so delighted to see her, but he asked her, "Do you think it's right for you to come here, young lady?"

She said, "That she would be okay," and she smiled gently.

The minute Juan asked her, "What's wrong?" Lisa burst into tears.

"He's so gone now," she said. "He is using drugs and he's seeing Mrs. Jennings. He slapped our son today because he told me that he was in the office with her with the doors locked and he told me he had to bang on the door many times before Marco would open it."

"Baby girl," Juan said, "This is what you need to do. You and the kids get on your knees, rebuke the devil in Jesus' name all together, and pray that the Lord's will be done in his life. Trust me, this will make a difference."

Lisa hugged and kissed him and he said, "Now go. I don't want you to get into any trouble with your husband."

17

The Coffee Shop

Sunday evening Lisa called Rachael and asked could she meet her on Monday morning at the coffee shop. Rachael agreed but was very hesitant.

After the phone conversation, Rachael said, "I wonder what she wants."

Lisa also called the Tanankas. Jane answered the phone and Lisa asked could she meet with them the next day at the coffee shop as well. Like Rachael, Mrs. Tananka was hesitant but said yes.

Jane informed her husband about the phone call, and he said, "I wonder what she has to say. Poor woman has to live with that idiot."

Jane called Rachael and asked did she receive a phone call from Lisa.

"Yes and she wanted to meet with me tomorrow," answered Rachael.

"She asked us as well," replied Jane.

"Let's just see what she has to say."

Monday morning Lisa made it to the coffee shop. Lisa was waiting patiently for her guests. She ordered all of their favorite coffees and some blueberry and chocolate chip muffins; it was all at the table ready when they arrived.

Rachael and the Tanankas walked in together. They saw Lisa sitting at the table in the corner far from the window. Lisa hugged and kissed all of them, but she noticed some hesitancy from them all.

"I'm so sorry for what happened yesterday, you guys," she said. "I just wanted you to know I just don't like his attitude myself."

They all looked at Lisa and noticed tears coming to her eyes. Rachael grabbed her hand and said, "It's going to be okay."

"You guys don't understand. My husband is becoming more violent, and he wants to be in control over everything. I wanted you to have fair warning. He told me to tell you guys if you don't start paying homage to him that he will ask you guys to leave the place of worship."

"What?" they all said together.

"Your husband is out of his mind," said John.

"Tell me about it," replied Lisa.

Rachael just shook her head. "Lisa, is your husband at the church right now?" she asked.

"Yes."

Rachael took her cell phone out of her purse and called him. As she was waiting for Marco to pick up, the Tanankas said they wanted to join her in the meeting. The secretary got him on the phone and she requested that they meet within the hour and she said the Tanankas would be joining her.

"That will be okay," Marco said.

Lisa was concerned. They said she had nothing to worry about, but she sensed trouble.

Rachael, Jane and John arrived at the church and Marco was waiting eagerly for them.

He knew they never wanted him as their pastor over their precious little Juan. Marco just felt like they never gave him a chance to prove himself. So he was so looking forward to this meeting so he could give them a piece of his mind. He wanted to let John know that this was his house.

Arrogance and Greed were in the room with Marco.

Arrogance said, "Marco, don't let these people come in here thinking that they run anything. This is our territory and I need for you to stand your ground."

Greed said, "He is right. We need people to follow you, Marco. Christ is so outdated. You can do much more for these people than He ever could."

Marco took the stash of cocaine out of his locked desk drawer and began to snort.

"That's right," Arrogance said. "Get some of your motivating power."

"What do you mean by telling your wife if we do not pay homage to you that you are going to kick us out of the place of worship?"

Marco's eyes blazed fury at Rachael. *Someone needs to shut her mouth*, he thought.

"Oh, you met with Lisa?" he asked.

"Yes, we just left her."

"Was she with you when you made the phone call to me?"

"Yes," said Jane.

Marco became more irritated. "I will deal with her later."

"There is nothing to deal with. You told her to tell us this crazy mess."

"Watch your tone when you are speaking to me, Rachael!" replied Marco.

"What! You are neither my Heavenly Father nor my earthly father, so you watch your tone when you are speaking to *me*."

"Slavery is dead. I don't have to respect you because you are white," said Marco.

"You are a sick man," Rachael said. "How dare you tell your wife that you will kick us out of church? The Bible says…"

Marco stopped her. "I don't want to hear nothing else coming out of your mouth. If you guys don't straighten up and follow me, I will ban you from coming in."

John stood up and said, "Over my dead body. You are wrong, and I will get my attorney to fight you."

"You arrogant son of a gun," said Jane.

John stepped in and said, "Sweetheart, no he's not worth it. You better be glad that these ladies are in this room."

"What ladies?" replied Marco sarcastically.

John was about to take a swing at Marco, but he stopped and said, "You are not worth it."

"You are not worth it," Marco said. Marco called three of his armor bearers to escort them off the premises. Before they left, Marco was smiling as he said, "Goodbye, have a great day you losers."

Rachael heard him and said, "You're the loser."

"No Rachael, you are. You are the one that is losing your property, or have you lost it already?"

Rachael turned around and one of the men grabbed her arm real tight and yanked her and said, "You do not speak to our superior like that."

Marco said, "See Rachael, if you were on board, you would not have to go through this."

"This is ridiculous," John stated. As they are being escorted down the hallway and out to their cars, the three men took them to their cars and pushed them all and said, "Don't come back. If you do, there will be trouble for you."

The Tanankas yelled at Rachael before she got into her car and said, "Meet us at our house."

Rachael said, "Okay." They got into their cars and drove off. The three men were still watching them as they pulled off, making sure that they would not return.

Marco was heated after what took place with Rachael and the Tananka's. All he could do was think about tearing into Lisa when he got the chance. He was so irritated that he had to calm himself down by taking the edge away. Marco went into his desk drawer where he kept his stash of cocaine and he started to snort.

Marco called Lisa on the phone and when she picked up, he yelled at her and said, "Where are you at?"

"Calm down. I'm at home," Lisa said.

"I will be home in thirty minutes. You make sure that you are there."

As Marco was driving home, all he could think about was how Lisa had betrayed him. He could not believe how Lisa sold him out to the traitors.

"Lisa should have kept her big mouth shut," he said, seemingly forgetting that he told her to tell her friends the very things that she did. "She did not have to tell them how I felt toward them."

Marco arrived home, got out of his car, and saw Lisa just walking inside from retrieving the mail. Marco met up with Lisa in the kitchen. He pushed Lisa against the refrigerator door.

"What is wrong with you?" Lisa asked.

"Why did you tell your friends that they must obey me?" said Marco.

"You told me to talk to them!" answered Lisa.

"They had very nasty attitudes."

"I cannot be responsible for somebody else's actions."

"You are right."

"Put her in her place," stated Arrogance.

"Yes, because we hate her attitude," said Hatred.

Both imps were on his shoulders. Marco balled his hand into a fist and punched Lisa right in her right jaw. Lisa bent over in pain and began to cry.

"You are right, you have no control over my actions," he said.

Lisa got up and kicked him in his testicles and he bent down. Then he stood up and slammed her against the wall and start beating her. Lisa defended herself the best way she could, but he was more powerful than she was.

Arrogance and Hatred both said, "You are a good boy. I know that you feel better after teaching her a lesson."

Marco sat down at the kitchen table and said, "Lisa, you are going to learn that I am better than you. You better watch yourself. You can be replaced." He got up and noticed some blood on him and that his lips was bleeding, so he got angry and spit on Lisa and left the room.

He heard her as she said, "Then replace me. You think I want to continue to put up with a man like you?"

The words angered him. He was determined to make her think as he did. She infuriated him that even while down, she still spoke her mind.

An hour later, Lisa got herself together and called Rachael and asked could she meet with her.

"I'm over at the Tanankas," Rachael said. They told her to come on over.

Lisa arrived at the Tanankas' house and John answered the door. Lisa fell right into his arms.

"Honey," he yelled. "Come here."

They rushed to the front door and saw Lisa in disarray.

"Oh my Lord," Joyce said. "Please help this child."

John carried Lisa into the living room, Rachael ran to get some water, and Jane ran and got a blanket and some medicine and bandages.

"What happened, Lisa?" Joyce asked.

"Marco beat me because you all came up against him at the church today," Lisa replied.

Joyce started to cry as did Rachael and Jane.

"It's my fault," Rachael said, sighing. "I should not have said anything."

"We should not have gone," said Jane.

"It's nobody fault," John said. "This man is just out of control. As you can see, he was waiting for this. This is anger and self-willed behavior. He wanted to put his hands on her."

"Lisa, let's get you to the hospital," said Joyce.

"No, I will get it even harder. I will be okay. May I just rest here for a little while before I go home please?"

"Sure, as long as you like," Jane said. "You may need to be checked out to make sure that you have no broken bones okay, dear."

"Thanks but no thanks," answered Lisa.

They all left the living room so Lisa could rest.

In the kitchen, the ladies wept.

"God is not pleased," Joyce said. "Marco may think he has the upper hand, but the Lord is not done here. I must go to Juan. I must leave now. Please keep me informed of what is going on with Lisa."

"We sure will," Jane said. They hugged and said their goodbyes.

Joyce left and went to the hospital to be with her husband and to inform him of what was going on. She entered into her husband's hospital room, and Juan immediately noticed that Joyce wasn't herself.

"Joyce," he said, calling her by her first name because he knew that something serious was bothering her.

Joyce said, "Juan" then paused. "He beat her," she added in a whisper.

Juan said, "What? Who beat who?"

Joyce tried to speak and she started to cry.

"Joyce, please tell me what's wrong."

"Marco beat up Lisa. He beat her up very badly. Oh Juan, you should have seen her. I think she may have broken bones or at the very least severely bruised ribs."

"Oh my goodness gracious, what for, Joyce?" asked Juan. "Lord," he yelled, "I wish I could move right now so I could whip his tail."

"She has two black eyes. She nearly passed out when she got to us over at the Tanankas," Joyce said.

"Did you guys take her to the hospital?"

"No, she wouldn't go," Joyce said. "Lisa said if we would take her, he would beat her more severely."

Juan just looked with disgust and anger in his eyes.

Ashshod was in the room. Hatred entered and said, "Oh, I see that Joyce is informing Juan about what Lisa deserved. She had no business stepping out of line." He laughed. Hatred started to mock Juan: "Oh I can't believe that boy put his hands on her, boo hoo. So what is he going to do? Nothing now. What is this stupid little invalid think he's going to do? It's not like he can get up and walk, oh how stupid of him."

Juan asked, "Joyce, what made him act so unholy?"

"Lisa said he beat her because of the way Rachael and the Tananka's responded to him at their meeting."

"I don't understand."

"He told Lisa to tell them that if they didn't serve him, he would kick them out the church."

"No he didn't," Juan said.

"He did, and so Lisa told them, and they were angry and confronted him. He retaliated by beating Lisa."

Juan became so upset with the news his blood pressure went up. The monitor began to beep and Glynda walked in and said, "What's going on here? Why are you so upset now?"

"Nothing, I can just handle this," answered Juan.

"Apparently not. The monitor is beeping," stated Glynda.

"I'll be okay," said Juan.

Glynda gave him a look and said, "Stop letting these people get to you. You won't be any good to them if you get any sicker."

"I'm trying to tell him," replied Joyce.

"You just want to make me work harder than I already am. They don't pay me enough, my dear sir, so please stop making me work." Glynda smiled and said, "Oh, I get it. You just want to see my pretty face, is that what it is?"

She and Joyce laughed.

"If this is the case," she added, "Then I can give you one of my glamour shots."

Joyce playfully hit Glynda in the arm, and they started laughing again.

"That's what it is," he said. "Baby, I have now found me a new love."

Joyce smiled and said, "That's my honey. He is back to his old self."

18

Trevor's New Leaf

Since Monica did not want to give Trevor the time of day, Trevor thought he would call up one of the chicks that was really into him. He called Katherine and asked her out and boy was she willing to hang out with him. Trevor told her that he would meet her at the club, and she was fine with that. He looked out of his office window and he could see Monica working at her desk.

Fornication came and jumped on Trevor's left shoulder and whispered in Trevor's ear, "Doesn't she look fine? Look how she is wearing that tight fitted blouse and skirt. I think you need to go after her. The other girls you are trying to get with don't compare to Monica. You need to stop trying to occupy your mind with useless and worthless women and try to figure out how to get Monica."

Okay, I know that she is only one woman, but if you could just see her and smell the sweet smelling perfume that she wears it's enough to light your nose on fire, Trevor thought. *Then there's that walk that just makes you want to fall on your knees. I think a very big part of me loves the challenge, but when is she going to give in?*

The very next day, Trevor sat behind his desk, longing to get with Monica. He kept repeating over and over, "Monica, oh sweet Monica, oh how I long for thee." Then he would start to giggle because he felt that he was acting as if he was Shakespeare. Trevor began to daydream about him and Monica becoming a couple.

The phone rang, distracting him. Trevor gather himself together; it was his father on the other end making sure that Trevor closed all his business deals that were required of him.

Trevor became so agitated at the sound of his father's voice. It seemed as if every time Trevor thought of Monica, his father always seemed to come into the picture.

Trevor gathered his things together so he could go home. He turned off the lights to his office, closed and locked his office door, and walked to the elevator. The doors opened, and he found Monica on the other side. He looked at her as if he had seen a ghost. Monica stepped off the elevator and walked right by him as if he was not there. Trevor was so bothered by it that he let the elevator door close and turned the same direction as Monica and said, "Why are you back here?"

"I forgot something that I need," responded Monica.

"Do you need any assistance?"

"No thank you."

Trevor was waiting on Monica to ride down in the elevator to get the opportunity to escort her to her car.

Monica looked up and noticed how Trevor was lingering around; she was annoyed by this a little, feeling as if she was being watched. Monica's angel just kept flying around the room, watching over her as if he could sense something. Sure enough Fornication and Lust showed up.

"Um, what do we have here?" asked Lust.

"I don't know, Lust, but what I do see is that Trevor and Monica are alone. This is a great sign," commented Fornication. "Look at that angel near Monica. Who is that?"

"I don't know who that is, but he sure doesn't seem friendly," answered Lust.

Monica's nameless angel flew around Fornication and Lust and would not say a word.

Both of the imps looked on with amazement trying to figure out what this nameless angel was up to.

Monica lingered around a little longer. *I would take the stairs if it wasn't ten flights down*, she thought. *But definitely won't do that in heels.*

Trevor watched her from a distance, hoping that she would hurry up. There was nothing like having some alone time in the elevator where Monica could not escape.

Monica's angel kept flying around the room without making any sounds, confusing Lust and Fornication.

"I'm not so sure about this angel, so I'm going to leave. I think Trevor has this under control," said Lust.

"I'm right behind you," replied Fornication.

Then they vanished.

Monica's angel noticed that they had disappeared; he flew over to Monica and stood right by her side. Monica walked slowly toward the elevator because Trevor was there. He pushed the button just waiting for them to get inside to be alone. Monica got to the elevator and the doors opened immediately. Trevor had the biggest smile on his face. The doors shut and Trevor tried to hold his composure.

"So, do you have big plans for the evening?" asked Trevor.

Monica gave him a look, rolled her eyes, and smacked her lips. The doors opened on the seventh floor and five people came into the elevator, giving Monica a chance to move to another spot away from Trevor.

Monica was so perplexed. *Why is he so hungry for me?* she thought. *He is my boss, it's not that serious for me. A grown man still living at home with his parents? How manly is that? I don't care if he lives in a mansion, it's his parents, ugh.*

I can hurt each and every one of these individuals who got on this elevator and messed up my play, thought Trevor. He was heated.

The elevator made it to the ground floor and Monica sprinted out of there, not looking back at Trevor. She held her head down, hoping that no one would ask her anything.

Trevor walked slowly to his car, feeling as if he was just hit by a Mac truck.

"Monica, oh my sweet Monica," he said sarcastically before getting into his car and driving off into the sunset.

19

The Big Secret

Ashshod, Gabe, as well as some other angels were at the police station. Greed, Bully and Racism and other imps were there as well.

The detective was very confident because the evidence that was against Mrs. Roberts was now gone. Bully was smiling. Racism and Bully were hissing and having a great time.

Ashshod, Zaso and Gabe were at the police station with Rachael; they would not let anything happen to Rachael, Forest and Piper.

Rachael ran into Mr. And Mrs. Rodgers at the police station.

"What are you doing here?" asked Rachael.

"They are charging Piper with co-conspiring with your son Forest," replied Mrs. Rodgers.

"What? I can tell you both this. They are prejudice, and I am trying to figure out how they are connected," stated Rachael.

Piper tried to get Rachael's attention; the police officer summoned the detective and said, "She is trying to get Ms. Weinberg's attention."

Rachael looked at Piper and immediately, the detective said, "Ms. Weinberg, we need for you to come with us."

"She wants to tell me something," Rachael commented.

"That can wait." He kept on insisting that Rachael go along with him. Piper looked discouraged.

The imps were laughing. They started to do backflips and jumps.

This had been a very long day. Rachael and the Rodgers were finding out that their children could not be released on bail. They were devastated. Both of the children were in a state of shock when they heard the news.

The lead detective was determined to have probable cause to keep Piper; he suspected that she knew something and it was legal to keep her for at least 24 hours. He was going to do just that. She was at the crime scene and they had to confiscate her cell phone for any evidence. The Rodgers argued up and down that the lead detective let their daughter go. The lead detective refused and they were asked to leave.

"My daughter is not a criminal," Mrs. Rodgers screamed. "You guys are animals down here."

The detective grinned and Rachael noticed this. Zaso stood right next to Rachael.

"Well I'm going to go," said Rachael.

"Okay, we will talk to you later," replied the Rodgers.

They hugged each other and said their goodbyes.

The detective looked at Rachael, smiled, and wave. "Bye Ms. Weinberg."

Rachael looked at the detective and said, "You son..."

The detective jumped in and said, "Not you, Ms. Weinberg...the Christian" and laughed. "See I told you that I'm in charge."

Rachael went home; she was distraught about all that was going on. She made herself some tea then took a bath to relax herself. Her dog Sparky, a Westland Highland Terrier, followed her around.

"Spark, what is going on? We both know that Forest is not capable of harming another human being, not cleaning up his room yes, not assault. What am I missing here, Sparky?"

Back at the police station, the detective called Mrs. Roberts to see how she was doing.

"I'm great. I have so much morphine in my system I can't feel a thing. So what is going on with you?"

"Did you know that Piper was hiding in the back of your classroom in that closet and she saw how you beat yourself up?"

"What?" answered Mrs. Roberts. "So how are we going to fix this?"

"It's already done. She sent a copy of the video through her phone to her e-mail, but the computer specialist got rid of it."

"Are you sure?"

"I'm so sure," he said.

"Great. I need to get some rest. They are going to keep me overnight."

"Okay. I will talk to you in the morning. It's been a long day for the both of us."

Rachael began to pray. Ashshod stood right beside her; Zaso was also in the room.

After the prayer, Ashshod made the computer make a sound.

"I haven't checked my e-mails today," Rachael said. "Let me just check this before I go try to get some sleep."

She looked at her e-mails and saw nothing new, but she noticed her junk mail was overflowing. "Let me look at it. I know I will be deleting this anyway."

She looked at it, and all of it looked like junk. She saw one that had no subject, so she put them all in the trash, and then looked at Sparky and said, "Well Spark, I guess I will try to go to sleep." She laid on the bed and Sparky jumped on the bed next to her; she began to cry.

"Lord, why my son? Why? Why? Why?" As she laid down, she could not have any peace; she was trying to figure out what was bothering her. She heard a noise at the computer.

She thought about Forest and Piper and remembered that Piper had been trying to get her attention at the police station. *What was Piper trying to tell me*, Rachael thought. *What did you want to tell me?*

Ashshod once again hit the computer. Rachael sat up in her bed and looked at the computer. Her eyes widened.

"OK, what is going on, computer?" She trudged back to the computer and sighed before sitting down at it. "Not like I can sleep." She shifted through her inbox again, and something pulled her to her trash bin. The one with no subject had the following e-mail: *Babygirl@snappy.com.*

"Oh my gosh," she said, smacking her forehead. "Baby Girl. Yes, that's what her father calls her. Shouldn't have been so quick to throw things away."

In the e-mail, there was a link to click to play a video. After clicking the link, Rachael saw the most horrific sight she had ever seen. She was stunned; she could not move. Before she knew it, she began to cry and scream.

Racism tried to enter Rachael's house, but Ashshod would not allow it; he knocked Racism clear across the street.

Rachael composed herself then she called the Rodgers. She told them to get over to her house immediately.

Ashshod called the other angels to help because they were protecting Rachael at full force.

Racism returned to the police station and put thoughts in the detective's head go check on Rachael.

It was 11:00 p.m. when the Rodgers arrived over Rachael's house.

"What's so urgent?" asked Mr. Rodgers.

"What I'm about to show you will blow your mind. Brace yourselves," answered Rachael.

She played the video and Mrs. Rodgers began to cry profusely. "What kind of sick monster is she? Why would they do this?"

For a moment, they sat in silence before Mr. Patrick Rodgers's eyes widened. "Siblings," he said.

His wife and Rachael looked up at him.

"What?" his wife asked.

"So blind by rage that we didn't see what was in front of us," he said, shaking his head. "Lead detective is Thomas Roberts. Teacher attacked, Miss. Roberts. I would bet that they are related somehow. Siblings. Maybe cousins."

Patrick asked to use Rachael's computer; Ashshod smiled and nodded. Patrick searched Mrs. Roberts and the detective up by their names and he came to a dead end.

"Do you know where Thomas Roberts and Mrs. Roberta Roberts came from?" he asked the ladies.

"No," his wife Maria said.

"I think somewhere from the South," replied Rachael.

They continued searching, and while looking up information on Mississippi, they found an article on the detective involving foul play. Thomas Roberts and Mrs. Roberts are a brother and sister from Mississippi. They were angry because they both were bid out of positions by African Americans because of affirmative action; they made it their promise that all African Americans would pay for taking job opportunities away from the superior race it stated in the *Mississippi State Journal*.

Patrick stood, determination in his eyes. "May Maria stay here until I get back from my office?"

"Sure," Rachael said. "Let's get us some coffee, Maria."

Maria stood, smiling sadly. "Let's." She kissed her husband before he raced from the house.

DA Patrick Rodgers was now at his office. He called the mayor, Chief of Police, and the superintendent of the school district Mrs. Roberts worked for and had them all meet at his office ASAP.

When they arrived, he showed them the video, and all were floored.

"Thomas Roberts was highly recommended to the force," the chief of police said. "He has a stellar performance. I would not have had any idea about this. He passed all the tests and background checks."

"Well, what we are going to do?" asked the mayor.

Patrick read something else in the *Mississippi State Journal* on a short article titled *Siblings Working Together*. "Hey," he said. "There is a third sibling, and who is this? They work for the mayor. It's the Community Development Organization. "Then who is this?"

"It's Mrs. Betty Smith," answered Mayor Marshall Crane.

They were all perplexed because they all looked at each other. "How long have they been in these positions?"

They all looked at their files to see how long and when they began to work for them. After they looked through their records, they found out that they were all hired around the same time. And they were all highly recommended. They all noticed that they have interesting information in their files.

The superintendent looked closely at Mrs. Roberta Roberts's files and found that there were numerous occasions in which she was accused of racial misconduct; it stated that there was not enough evidence for her to be charged for anything, but there was a lot of suspicion. The person that was investigating these allegations was the same lead detective dealing with Forest and Piper. So of course he covered up everything because he was in control. Patrick also noticed that there were a lot of minorities that had been convicted because of him.

The police chief said, "We must go back and view all his cases so that we can see if they planted evidence and accused minorities because of personal vendettas. Mayor, I see a lot of lawsuits coming our way."

The mayor shook his head in shame.

"We are looking at so many charges," DA Rodgers said, "And they will all be felonies."

"He was known for cleaning up the South," the police chief said. "At the time, we didn't really pay any attention to the color. I was just trying to have crime at an all-time low."

They all looked at the police chief; his cheeks turned red.

"You keep telling yourself that if that makes you feel good," Patrick said. "Betty Smith works for the mayor. They made sure that minority owners lost their property. Rachael is white, but she has a black son, and this just doesn't suit them."

"No it has to be more than this," said the mayor.

"Rachael is being targeted," stated Patrick. "We must handle this the right way. We will take care of this in the morning."

Excusing himself, Patrick called Rachael and filled her and his wife Maria in on everything he'd learned. At the sounds of their cries, he said, "Keep calm. We are going to take care of this in the morning."

The imps came and they heard what was going on; they went right to the chief of police and told him to handle it.

"I'll see you all in the morning," the chief of police said before leaving out of the DA's office. Immediately, he called Thomas and informed him of what was going on.

After Chief Shawn Cumming left the meeting he drove back to the police station.

Since the District Attorney was getting mighty close to the truth he needed some leverage. He walked into the police station some of the officers greeted him.

The chief walked into his office and retrieved his keys to the jail cells and left out of his office and walked toward the cells. The chief was focused he was at the station with a purpose. He walked over to Piper's jail cell and yanked her out of there.

"Ouch, you're hurting me" said Piper.

"Shut your face you coon lover" the chief answered.

Piper said nothing. She saw the anger all in the chief's face.

The chief then walked over to Forest's cell with Piper and said, "Get up boy."

Forest gave him a look as if he could have slit the chief's throat.

"Who do you think you are by looking at me with a look of disgust? You have no right you black scum," stated the chief.

Forest walked out of the jail cell and he moved toward Piper and the chief snatched him and move him to the other side.

"It will be none of that unethical behavior around me. Young lady stay with your own kind, leave that nappy headed Oreo alone," he said.

The kids just looked at each other scared to death not knowing what was going on.

"Are you taking us to our parents?" asked Piper.

"Shut up! You are in no position to ask questions," replied the Chief.

They walked up to the front of the station. One of the officers said, "Chief, what's going on? Why do you have them?"

"I must take them to another location for their safety," answered the chief. The officer did not question the chief he just agreed with him.

The chief just held their arms tightly. Another officer said, "Oh Chief, where are you taking them?"

"To one of my vacation spots," he replied. They walked out of the station and the chief shoved them in the back seat of his car and drove to the hiding place.

The detective then called his sister and told her about what he learned.

"We have to leave tonight," he told her.

"What?" Mrs. Roberts said, surprised. "How did they find out?"

"I don't have long, but your student Piper taped everything and sent it to Forest's mother."

"That little cow," replied Roberta.

"Well enough of the love words, we must vacate."

"Did you call Betty and tell her to come on?"

"About to. Our dear step brother, 'good ole' police chief, is going to get us all out of here tonight, so meet me at the hangout spot," said Thomas. Quickly, he hung up then called his sister, Betty, and informed her of all the information and told her to meet him at the secret spot.

With coffee in hand, Rachael and Maria sat and talked about the current events going on. Rachael got on the internet and looked at the article that Patrick pulled up. Rachael looked up at the small print on the article and it led her to another newspaper article. She read something that almost made her vomit.

"Rachael, what is wrong?" Maria asked. "What do you see?"

"Look at this and tell me what you see."

"Isn't this the police chief?"

"Yes, the police chief is their half-brother. This is how they got their jobs. He just looks younger in this photo. It's Shawn Cumming. That's why we did not recognize him. There was no name, just a picture of all four of them together."

"I must call my husband and tell him what's going on," replied Maria. Mrs. Rodgers called her husband and gave him all of the details. Although he was disturbed, he couldn't sit and think about that. He called for backup and the mayor went with him down to the police station.

The imps were angry and they followed them. The angels were right behind, beside and in front of them.

Patrick was driving to the police station; he was so perplexed because he could not believe all the nonsense that was going on right under his nose. He was more concerned because his daughter was caught in the midst of it all, and he had no clue that it was even going on. He said to himself that he was going to do a thorough background check on all the employees after he cleaned up this big mess. Since his daughter was involved in such a terrible situation.

Patrick walked inside of the Westlake police station fuming. The officers at the station looked at him as if they made sure they did not want to be on his bad side. He told all the officers at the station to gather around because he had some information to disclose. "Listen everyone, I have some news. The police chief needs to be apprehended because of unlawful acts against minorities."

"What?" said Officer Pearson.

The officers in the room had bewildered looks on their faces.

The chief came back here and took the children to a safe place" said Officer Pearson.

"When did this happen?" asked Patrick.

"About 40 minutes ago," answered Officer Pearson.

"I must get those kids back or it could lead up to a tragic situation" shouted Patrick.

The D.A. asked Officer Pearson if he knew where Shawn, Thomas, Roberta, and Betty would meet.

"You know," the office replied, "I think he has a place he takes his family on vacation. Cartwright," he called out to an officer across from him, "What's the name of his vacation spot?"

"You mean, Lake Tikie?"

"Yeah, that's where it is."

"I need an APB out on the chief and his siblings." The officers looked on with surprise. "Let's go! I don't want anyone trying to warn them that we are coming after them."

Little did they know that the chief had his walkie talkie with him and he heard everything.

Patrick Rodger called his wife and told her of his findings.

"Rachael and I will meet you there," Maria said.

"No, let us handle this, do you hear me?"

"Yes, I hear you." Maria told Rachael everything.

"Well that's your husband," Rachael said. "I am not paying attention. I am going to the lake, are you coming?"

Maria sighed. "Yes."

Rachael locked up her house and they drove off to the lake.

Shawn was not happy about using Forest and Piper as hostages but sometimes you have to do things you don't want to he said to himself. He arrived at the hideout and all the siblings were there waiting for him. "What are they doing here?" asked Roberta.

"They are our leverage" answered, Shawn.

"What a big mess all of this is turning out to be" screamed Betty.

"Get yourself together" said Roberta.

"What's next" asked Thomas.

"Take the kids into the bedroom and I'll think of something," replied Shawn.

After Betty got the children settled in the bedroom she tied them to a chair. Shawn called a meeting with the siblings.

"Listen we are going to do whatever we need to do to survive. Do you hear me? It's either us or them. Do you hear me?" shouted Shawn.

"Yes we do," they said all together.

Shawn, Roberta, Thomas and Betty were in the house, panicking, but they were also armed and willing to fight this battle.

The FBI agents and the police showed up. There were road blocks set up as well. The officers surrounded the house and they said, "Come out all of you. Come out with your hands up."

Police Chief Shawn Cumming yelled, "No, we have demands."

"You are in no position to have demands," an FBI agent replied.

The angels and the demons were in the air, the demons circling to and fro.

Rachael and Mrs. Rodgers arrived at the scene. They heard someone yelling for them to come out the house. Rachael and Mrs. Rodgers grabbed a hold of each other.

"We have demands," the police chief yelled.

The FBI and the Westlake police officers all looked at each other and Rachael said, "Who are they to ask for something? Give me that bullhorn. I'll get them out of there."

The FBI agent looked at her and said, "Can you please hush?" Rachael rolled her eyes at him.

"Get her out of here, this is official police business. Get these civilians out of here," said the FBI agent.

"What are you guys doing here?" Patrick said, angrily. "I asked you both to stay put. It's dangerous out here."

"Seriously did you think I was going to stay put when my baby has been kidnapped by these racist freaks?" replied Rachael.

"Honey, there was no way I was not going to come when our baby girl is in trouble," answered Maria.

"Hush her up," said the agent closest to them. "I can't hear what they're saying."

One of the female police officers pushed Rachael and Maria back so she could quiet them down.

The police chief, Shawn Cumming came out onto the porch and said, "This is what we want—a private plane to South America and we don't want anyone to follow us or someone will have to pay."

The imps hissed and chanted, "Someone will pay."

The FBI agent calling the shots yelled, "What do you mean by this?"

"We have hostages."

"We know, Let us see them."

"We will show you when our plane is ready."

"We must give into their demands until we come up with a plan to take them down," Patrick said.

"No," said the FBI agent. "We need to know what we are working with. We can't just take their word for it." The FBI agent got on the bullhorn and said, "How do we know if you have hostages? We need for you to show us your leverage before we give in to your demands."

It was silent for a little while. They saw movement in the house then the police chief came to the door. They saw a figure, but they could not see who it was because the majority of the lights were off. They had enough light to see when he reached a certain point to identify the person. The chief had a gun to Forest's head.

Rachael started to scream.

"Someone keep her quiet," the FBI agent said.

"That's her son," Patrick said.

"That's not my problem. If we are going to handle this, then she needs to keep quiet. She shouldn't even be here."

"Yeah," Patrick said, wearily eyeing both his wife and Rachael. "I know."

Ashshod moved closer to Forest and the imps became perplexed.

"What is he doing?" one imp asked.

Forest saw his mother and said, "Mom, I'm all right, don't worry."

The police chief hit Forest upside the head with his pistol and said, "Shut your mouth. You are not in control here, I am."

Blood flowed down the side of Forest's face. In a flash, Forest was pushed into the house and another person was drawn out: Piper.

"Piper," Patrick whispered.

"My baby," his wife screamed.

"Daddy," Piper cried out.

"Now give me what I want," the police chief said, "and shut up talking to me. Get that plane here right now." He slammed the door.

The imps circled inside and outside of the house.

Rachael said, "Get my son out of there right now."

"You better come up with a plan right now to get these kids out of there," Patrick said.

The FBI agent lowered the bullhorn. "Look," he said, "we know how to do our jobs. We do not need your hysterics." Rachael opened her mouth to talk, but he cut her off with, "Let us do our job—*ma'am*."

He spun from her and faced the other agents that worked feverishly to get their gear together. Quickly, he laid out the plan.

"This will not hurt them, will it?" Rachael asked.

"A little with breathing," the agent replied.

"A little with breathing?" Mrs. Rodgers said, exasperated. "What does that…"

"Do you want your children back or not?" the agent asked, irritated. With no response, he added, "Let's do this."

Ashshod and the other angels looked on.

With any other culprit, the tear gas would have worked, but the police chief was prepared.

"They are going to throw in tear gas," he said. "Put on your masks so we won't inhale this crap." They did and watched as the tear gas was thrown in through the window. Two minutes passed and no one came out. Those outside drew concerned. Five minutes went by and nothing happened. Suddenly, they heard shots fired from the inside and a FBI agent was hit by a bullet.

"Get our kids out of there," Rachael and Mrs. Rodgers screamed.

"Let's get in my SUV," the chief said. He pointed a gun toward Forest's head; the lead detective had Piper. Mrs. Roberts was moving very slowly; she had to get help from her sister Betty.

"Listen," Ashshod said to the angels, "I wish the saints of God could see what they look like when they are armored up. Because of Rachael's faith she allows us to fight for her. Gear up. Get ready for battle."

All the angels appeared in their garments.

Ashshod said, "It's time for battle."

Quickly the angels changed into spiritual garments on behalf of the humans. They wore the breastplate of righteousness, shoes of the gospel of peace, the shield of faith, the helmet of salvation, and the sword of the spirit.

Brilliant colors glowed from each angel's armor, from Ashshod in scarlet red, gold, and chrysolyte to Enu's sapphire and gold.

Racism tried to attack Ashshod, but Hunter came and attacked Racism with a heavy blow. Racism gathered himself together and said, "What's wrong, Ashshod, you can't fight your own battles?"

"Shut up, Racism, you only single out what's around you," replied Hunter. "This battle is not about you. This battle is about not accepting the fact that God planted all different races on this earth and it is for all of them to live amongst each other in unity."

"Boo hoo, I'm going to cry. Where are my tissues?" said Racism. "You destroyed the perfectness of our god. This is our job and our purpose."

"It's my job to get rid of you!" said Hunter.

The other imps hissed as they began to wrestle with the angels.

"Just let us be," the imps said in chorus.

"No," Rafael said, "You have no peace, you have no authority, you have nothing."

"No weapons that is formed against us shall prosper," the angels chanted.

Bully looked and said, "Angels, your chants don't mean anything to us."

Hunter put a big gash in Bully's shoulder with his blazing sword. Dark red blood streamed down Bully's arm.

Bully said, "You are out of your mind."

Hunter said, "No, you are out of your mind." He took his sword and slashed one imp and he just vaporized and smoke appeared. Bully let out a loud screech.

Rafael turned and looked at Racism; he went toward the imp, but two imps appeared from out of nowhere to attack him. Seeing this, Rafael extended his arms and grabbed them both, going right into their chests. The two imps vaporized and smoke came out with the stench of sulfur.

Racism tried to flee, but Hunter went right after him. Bully was injured, but he tried to stay close to Racism. Racism summoned up three more imps who came toward Hunter, but Rafael took out his sword and knocked the life out of all three of them at one time. Bully summoned a handful of imps to come and assist him in the fight against the angels. He looked at Racism and they nodded and tried to escape, leaving the weaker imps to battle Ashshod and the rest of the angels.

Ashshod appeared right in front of them.

"You want a fight, Ashshod?" Bully asked. "Then you've got one."

Ashshod quoted from the Scripture, "For we are not struggling against human beings, but against the rulers, authorities and cosmic powers governing this darkness, against the spiritual forces of evil in the heavenly realm."

The imps became stronger because the police chief's family members were all together.

"Sebastian!" Ashshod yelled.

Sebastian looked up, took his sword, and cut off Racism's head. A big poof of smoke appeared as well a large, high-pitched screech. The imps looked at each other.

"I'm tired of playing games," Bully said.

"Hunter, Rafael, and Sebastian," Ashshod said, "It is time to finish them off."

The imps all formed together, the angels gathered themselves, and they all began to wrestle and tumble. Smoke came from everywhere.

Ashshod said, "Bully, now it's one on one. It's time to fight."

"You think this will be over?" Bully asked. "You know I will come back."

"You don't think I know this? You have been here for a very long time, and every time you think you've got it made, we come back in full force. Slavery in many forms died, Civil Rights came then affirmative action."

"That's nothing. There is still slavery. You have human trafficking, a form of slavery. You have drug trafficking. There is always someone weaker that is made to do things. Don't you understand we go after the weak, the arrogant, the proud and those who think they have the answers?

"Right now it's bullying. Do you know how many children I have gotten under my control because parents don't pay any attention to their own children? We've got the teachers, too. They don't care. They feel that they don't get paid enough, so it's whatever goes with them their just dummies."

Bully started hissing very loud. "Kids killing themselves and other kids over nothing." He laughed. "We have kids killing over their appearance, or who's dating who. We even have kids killing and bullying just off of pure lies. So you think this is going to change anything, Ashshod? I'm going to always exist because people are stupid. They choose not to act upon what is right."

He hissed again before saying, "The problem with Rachael is she would not waiver on her beliefs. There are not many people like her and we were determined to get her. She reminded us of Job. We took everything from him and he still wouldn't budge, just like her. She would not turn her back on God. Dumb wench.

"Not only did she have God, she had peace in the midst of her storm. Do you know how many people we've got to commit suicide because they lost their jobs, homes, and money? We even got people to lose their minds." The imps started hissing again. "Humans don't see us, they don't know what impact we have on them." Bully started circling around Ashshod, but Ashshod did not move. "You have nothing to say because you know it's all true, don't you, Ashshod?" he asked. "It was our job to put Rachael through this trial especially since she is close friends with Juan."

"The Lord giveth, the Lord taketh away. Blessed be the name of the Lord!" Ashshod said. "Rachael fears the Lord. Not only does she fear Him, but also she respects God's decisions. She knows the Lord knows what's best for her. Rachael also knows that handling circumstances herself would make things worse. Rachael fights her battles on her knees. She applies the word of God to her everyday life.

"Bully, since the beginning of time, you have tried to succeed in overpowering people. You were kicked out of heaven when you tried to overthrow God from His thrown. In Hell you lifted up your eyes, you and those other imps. You become weak when knowledge prevails. You hiss and you laugh about destruction, but you don't laugh about being overthrown by the power of GOD!"

The imps started to hiss and screech.

Ashshod turned his head and made an unexpected move before taking his sword and ramming it down Bully's throat, killing him. The remaining weaker imps were killed by the other angels.

Greed showed up with Covet and Lie and said, "Ashshod, you are not going anywhere."

Gabe said, "You don't give out orders."

Zaso and Enu appeared, and Enu sliced right into Lie, killing him.

"We don't want to hear it," Enu said.

"I'm so sick and tired of you all interfering in our matters," Greed said. "It's time for me and Lust and the other imps to put you all in your place. See you don't understand it is our job to keep humans from concentrating on the truth." Greed's screech, on the human ear, could shatter their ear drum. With the angels, they only stared, unimpressed. "Ashshod, I want you dead!"

"Greed, I really think that's impossible for you to do," replied Ashshod.

As Greed was arguing with Ashshod, Covet grew furious with Ashshod's responses.

"Oh, yes, I want this, too," Covet said. "I want to take Zaso out. As I was trying to get Rachael, you stopped me from succeeding. You just had to protect her. So since you were so 'Hell bent' on watching over her, 'I'm Hell bent' on taking you out of here."

"Be gone, Covet," Zaso said. "You can't have what's not yours. The earth is the Lord's and the Fullness thereof. You don't own anything. You cannot claim anything. Rachael is God's child."

Covet hissed and moved toward Zaso, and they fought. Covet blew smoke out of his nostrils and summoned imps to come and assist him. While Zaso was fighting with Covet, hundreds of imps came attacking Zaso. As soon as Covet knew that Zaso was preoccupied, he made his best move. Covet came up from behind while some imps were distracting Mickel; and Covet took Mickel's life.

Covet looked up and hissed. "Zaso, you're next." Enu looked with hurt in his eyes; he smirked at Covet and let out a loud yell before taking his sword, swinging it around like the speed of light chopping Covet into pieces. It happened so fast that the whole area got quiet. Greed saw the look in the angels' eyes, and he knew that they were serious because Mickel lost his existence. Greed let out a big roar and said, "Let's go; meet at our hiding place."

Ashshod and the angels could not believe their eyes. "How did we let this happen to Mickel?" asked Gabe.

"Listen," Ashshod began, "Things happen for a reason, but everything is not always as it seems. Now we can't sit here on the pity pot. We must continue to do the job our Heavenly Father sent us to do."

The police chief and his family sat in the SUV with Forest and Piper. Thomas drove the car and he knew what strategy the Westlake police might come up with. He started driving faster, the police and FBI right behind them.

"We must get away from here," Thomas said.

Mrs. Roberts yelled, "Get us out of here."

"What do you think I'm trying to do?" Thomas asked.

"Go down this road," said the chief of police.

As soon as Thomas started down the road, the SUV swerved as an officer from the force shot the right front tire. A second later, the left front tire was hit. Everyone in the car screamed as the car flipped over. The cops went to the car with their weapons out."

"Suspects down," the agent said.

Thomas was bloody, but the FBI agents managed to pull him from the car. Four EMS's arrived. The police chief was badly hurt but would live. Forest could not walk on one of his legs. Piper could not move her arm. Mrs. Roberts was complaining about her ribs; Betty could not move at all.

Rachael pulled her car over to the side of the road. Mrs. Rodgers hopped out of the car as soon as Rachael parked. The pair raced toward the flipped car and upon seeing their children, began to weep.

"Thank you, Lord," Rachael prayed, "For watching over our children and getting them back to us alive."

At the hospital, both Rachael and Maria asked if they could see their children; the nurse said, "You must wait until the doctor sees them first."

The ER doctor on call came out and spoke with the families.

"Who is here for Forest Weinberg?" she asked.

Rachael quickly stood and replied, "I am."

"Forest has a broken leg, so we are going to send him to x-ray to make sure there is nothing else wrong with his leg. If nothing is wrong, we will then get him in a cast. You can see him after he comes back from his x-ray."

Patrick and Maria jumped up and stood alongside Rachael. "Do you have news on our daughter, Piper?" Maria asked.

"Piper has a broken arm, and we've sent her to be x-rayed, too. You can see her once we've done that."

"Thank you, Lord," Patrick said as he hugged his wife.

"What about the others?" the lead FBI agent asked as he stood and walked toward them.

"Mrs. Roberts has broken ribs and internal bleeding," the ER doctor replied, "And Mrs. Betty Smith, for now, doesn't have sensations from the waist down. The police chief's spleen is gone, and Detective Roberts had to have his left leg amputated. They will not be going anywhere anytime soon."

20

Trevor's Destiny

Fornication and Lust were at the office ready to make Trevor move quickly on their demand for him to start dating Monica.

Monica watched as Trevor spoke with his employees, telling them how big of a ladies' man he was.

"What a self-absorbed creep," said Monica.

Since she had to stay longer than expected, she had to sit and listen to Trevor's nonsense. But she didn't complain. She was so happy to have employment.

"You know," Fornication began as he whispered in Trevor's ear, "Perhaps we need to change your tactics. Maybe you need to impress Monica but, oh, I don't know, seeming to be a good man who doesn't use women."

Lust laughed. "Brilliant. Let her see that Trevor, old boy, can be good, and then he can have his way with her."

It didn't take long for Monica to change her tune. As the next few days rolled along, she saw a change in Trevor. He wasn't bragging to employees anymore. He buried himself in his work. He didn't joke and kid around. He didn't even bother her. He came into the office, did his work, addressed who needed to be addressed, and returned home.

It threw Trevor for a loop when Monica approached him with small talk.

This is all I had to do? He thought as he saw her smile, in his direction no less, for the first time ever.

He worked hard not to come on too strongly; if playing the kind, quiet guy got points with her, then he would definitely keep his cool and let Monica lead. He did not care about going at her pace as long as this opportunity was happening. Plus Trevor knew how his father would react if he had approached Monica. All his dad could think was lawsuit.

Despite the openness that seemed to blossom from Monica toward Trevor, the big angel who watched over Monica stood very close to her when Trevor came around.

A month and a half had gone by and Monica noticed that Trevor was turning a new leaf. Monica seemed impressed, so she decided to go on a date with Trevor.

He picked her up at her house, and the minute she opened her door, he said, "You look just so scrumptious that I could just eat you up."

Monica looked at him with a little concern, but she let that dumb comment go.

She smiled and said, "Thank you. I see that you are back to your old ways."

"I'm sorry I'll watch my behavior from now on. Remember I'm not perfect," said Trevor.

At the car, Trevor opened the car door for Monica.

"Thank you," she said, smiling.

"You're more than welcome."

Monica felt her mind spinning. She watched Trevor as he drove them to a nice fancy restaurant. She watched him as they ate and talked, smiled, and laughed. She even stole glances while they were dancing after dinner. He held her close and made no advances to seduce her on the dance floor. His mannerisms and the way he held her so close clicked a switch on in her that startled her.

She wanted him. Now!

In the middle of the dance floor, she stopped dancing, stared into Trevor's eyes, and whispered, "Want to take this some place more...private?"

She watched Trevor's eyes widen as she took his hand and led him outside.

The big angel watched over Monica, but made no move to intervene as she told Trevor to drive back to her home.

"Monica," Trevor said, excitement lacing his words, "You know how long I have been waiting for this wonderful day to come along. I wished you would not have played hard to get. I had to punish you for punishing me. I'm so sorry."

"I know," she said as they sat in his car. "But I promise to make it up to you tonight."

Come morning, Trevor stood to get dressed. His bright smile and swagger were definitely back.

Monica slipped from her bed and tied a robe around her body.

"Want some breakfast?" she asked as she dropped a kiss on his cheek.

"I have to go," Trevor replied. "I have an appointment I must get to."

"Oh, you got what you wanted and now you're just going to leave me?" said Monica, crossing her arms.

"Please don't act this way, but you were the one who suggested this, right?"

She pushed him away from her.

Before Trevor left, Monica said, "I'll see you at work Monday."

"Yes," he said. He gave her a kiss on the lips and left. Trevor went home; it was Sunday morning and he wanted to speak to his parents before they went to Sunday morning worship.

After Trevor left Monica's house he began to feel a little under the weather. He sneezed a little and said to himself that he needed to stop leaving his shirt unbuttoned. It could be what's causing him to feel under the weather.

"Trevor, you look bad," Jane said. "Let's go to the worship building and pray."

"Mom, I have a cold."

"Well, we can pray about getting rid of this cold," said John.

Trevor sneezed and coughed. "I am on my way to work," he said.

"No, you need to go to the doctor," said Jane.

"Mom I'll be just fine. What I'll do is take some medicine then go to bed," replied Trevor.

Hours went by and Trevor woke up from his nap feeling a lot better. He went downstairs and his parents were in the sitting room watching television. "Are you feeling any better"? asked, Jane. "Yeah Mom I'm alright," Trevor, replied as he walked by them to go to the kitchen.

Trevor walked into the sitting room where his parents and Frisky were and watched some television and he became tired. "Dinner will be ready in an hour Trevor" said, Jane.

"I don't want any" responded, Trevor. He just went back to bed. He remained there all night.

Jane went and checked on him every once in a while. He was sound asleep.

Monday morning arrived, and Trevor was on cloud nine; he finally got what he wanted and that was Monica.

Monica looked at Trevor through his office window. Trevor just smiled. Fornication and Lust were bigger and stronger. Now that Trevor got what he wanted, he decided to brush Monica off.

Monica was watching Trevor as he walked around his office talking on the telephone. She needed to speak with him. Monica waited until Trevor got off the phone then she jumped up from her chair and walked into Trevor's office.

"Can we talk?" Monica asked.

"There is nothing that we need to say to each other," Trevor said. "I got what I wanted. You are no longer any use to me." He touched her on her shoulder and said, "Don't cry or say why, we are both adults, you know how to handle this. I'll send you some flowers and a bottle of wine. You just keep on working and stay beautiful, but girl, I just wanted you to know it was really worth the wait."

"What a good boy. We showed her that we get what we want." said Fornication.

A week went by and Trevor still showed signs of a cold, which he thought he had gotten rid of. Trevor showed up at the office and one the employees said, "Boss, you might need to go to the doctor because you look 'under the weather'."

Fornication and Lust were at the office, trying to see what mischief they could get Trevor involved in. They saw that Trevor was sneezing and trying to get rid of the cold he had for over a week. Trevor kept putting off going to the doctor, but when he saw blood in his mucus, he reluctantly decided to go; he was tired of putting it off.

"Trevor, you don't need to go to the doctor," said Lust.

"Just keep taking the cold medicine, Trevor," said Fornication.

They saw Trevor asking Monica to call the doctor's office. The big angel that stood around Monica looked at the imps and gave them a gesture of disgust. Fornication and Lust looked at each other and went after Trevor.

Trevor walked into his office and Fornication and Lust followed him in. The big angel that followed Monica flew over to Trevor's office window and looked in; he had a very furious look on his face, and it startled Fornication. Lust looked at the big angel from the other side of the room.

"What is his problem?" said Lust.

"I don't know, but whatever it is he needs to fix it," replied Fornication.

Fornication looked at Trevor, trying to distract him from leaving the office. He made the phone ring and it was a client from Hong Kong trying to discuss business. Trevor could only talk for fifteen minutes because he had to excuse himself from the call. Trevor got off the phone and got a glass of water and sat behind his desk.

That didn't work, so Lust jumped in and made the telephone ring; it was a young lady that he had been trying to get with Trevor for quite sometime. He tried to talk with her, but he had to tell her that he had a cold but will get with her soon as possible. He got another glass of water immediately after getting off the phone.

The big angel looked at both Fornication and Lust then he began to ball up his fist and looked at them with rage. At one point it looked as if he was banging on the window. Fornication looked over at Lust with concern on his face. The big angel would not say a word; he only kept making gestures of rage.

"Wow, he is really angry," said Lust.

"I know," replied Fornication.

Then the big angel appeared in the room and flew quickly toward Fornication and Lust and knocked them across the room. He said not a word as Fornication and Lust were trying to gather themselves together; he knocked them across the other side of the room. Then he turned around and left the room. The big angel stood in the position where he stood all the time and that was right by the side of Monica.

Monica noticed a big draft of wind come right near her. "Whew, it's cold in here," she said. She looked around the room and nobody else felt the strong wind.

As Trevor left the office for his doctor appointment, he stopped by Monica's desk and said, "Monica, hold all my calls and meetings until further notice because I need to know what the doctor is going to tell me."

"Okay, I'll wait for your call and good luck," Monica said sarcastically.

Trevor sat in the examination room, waiting for Dr. Writz to show up. Although Dr. Writz was a few years older, he and Trevor had grown up in the same neighborhood and socialized together several times. If anyone could tell him what was wrong, Trevor knew the good doc could.

Dr. Writz knocked on the door before peeking in.

Trevor said, "What's up, doc?"

"Trevor, what's up, man?" asked Dr. Writz.

"You know me, man, the same 'ole same ole'."

"When will you ever slow down?"

"Never man, I am the man. I can't slow down; then I will be nothing."

"Stop the madness. What brings you here today?"

"Man, I think I have a bad cold. Just feeling a little bit under the weather."

"Ok, let's take a look. The nurse is going to do some blood work. It will take an hour, so you just wait here until I get the results."

"I hope I don't have that H1N1," said Trevor.

Dr. Writz shook his head and Trevor started to laugh.

An hour and a half passed. Dr. Writz knocked on the door, and Trevor said, "Come in."

Trevor was lying down on the bed. He looked up and asked, "So do I have H1N1?"

"No," Dr. Writz said, his tone serious. "It is serious. What you have is an STD and another serious matter."

"Well, do I have Chlamydia or Herpes? You can just give me some pills or a shot or some cream, and I know get lots of rest." Trevor chuckled. Dr. Writz looked at Trevor. "Doc, why are you so serious?"

"Trevor, I had the lab run these test three times. I'm so sorry to have to tell you this, but you have Human Immunodeficiency Virus which is in full effect. It's at the advanced stages, full blown AIDS.

Trevor went into a daze as Dr. Writz spoke to him; he couldn't comprehend anything being said. Slowly, he blinked, looked at Dr. Writz, and asked, "So, all I have is a cold, right?"

"Trevor," Dr. Writz said, sadness filling his eyes, "The reason why you are experiencing cold symptoms is your immune system is breaking down, and it seems as if you have a cold—but you don't."

Trevor grabbed the doctor and started yelling and screaming, "No, No, No!"

"Trevor, you must tell me, do you know who gave this to you? Trevor, do you hear me?"

Trevor responded softly, "Monica."

"What?"

"Monica."

"You must inform this person that she is carrying the AIDS virus. We can slow the process with some medication, but it won't stop the pain and suffering much. Man, I am so sorry."

The nurse knocked on the door and came into the room with medication in her hands. Dr. Writz administered medication to Trevor then handed him the prescription. "Trevor, you need to come see me in a couple of days."

"I hear you, man, but I can't focus on what you are asking of me right now," replied Trevor.

"I understand, Trevor, but you really need to come in. I need to see you in a couple days. Please call me, you have my number," said Dr. Writz.

"I can't take this right now," said Trevor.

Trevor's mother called him as he was leaving the examining room and asked him if he went to the doctor and what did he have to say. She could tell by his one-word responses that something was wrong. "You *did* go. What did he say? Tell me, baby."

Sobbing, Trevor said, "Mom, I really messed up. I can't talk to you right now. I will tell you guys later when I get home."

"Trevor, I'm worried."

"Mom, I can't talk right now," said Trevor. He staggered out of the doctor's office. Passerbyers watched as he stumbled to his car.

He drove to the lake and looked out at the water as he began to cry. He gathered himself together then he drove over to Monica's house. He got out of the car and knocked on Monica's door three times, and then he rang the doorbell recklessly.

Monica finally answered the door. "Trevor," she said, surprised, "Hello. What are you doing here?"

"Do you have AIDS?"

"What?" Monica replied.

"Do you have AIDS?"

"Trevor, whatever do you mean?" replied Monica.

"You gave me AIDS, you nasty wench," said Trevor.

Monica looked at Trevor and began to laugh profusely. "Yes, I know I have AIDS," she said.

Trevor looked at her, surprised. "What?"

"Oh sweet dear Trevor, the man that uses women and takes advantage of them, the one who says he gets what he wants all the time…well I got what I wanted and that was to get you back, you dirty dog.

"You wanted to play with the devil, well you just did. Now you are going to die. You are going to die in your sins. You are nothing but a user. Well how does it feel to be used? What, cat got your tongue? This isn't the Trevor I know. Are you suffering? It looks like it. Oh what did you say to me? Oh you are no use to me now. You were so full of lust and greed, you were only thinking with your…" she paused before adding, "*other* head". This is what you get for playing with deception."

"You are so cruel, you crazy wicked beast. I hope you drop dead," Trevor yelled.

"Oh by the way, I will not be in to work tomorrow," Monica said. "My job is finished."

She slammed the door in Trevor's face.

Monica was actually a fallen angel who bred with humans, which was a sin before God. Her sole mission as a fallen angel was to spread diseases in their advanced stages.

The angel that swarmed about her, the entity *pretending* to be an angel that is, was Deception. He helped a fallen angel that transformed into a human to destroy God's people. Monica's sole purpose was to get Trevor's soul so he could die in his sins and spend eternity in Hell with Satan and the rest of the lost souls.

Deception went to meet up with Fornication, Lust, and Greed at Trevor's home; they knew he'd be headed there soon. Deception then transformed into his original being, as an imp.

"I was so sick and tired of looking like a 'goody two shoes'," Deception said. "It's so nice to be in my real form. So what's going on?"

"What was your problem at the office, Deception?" Fornication said. "All that throwing us across the room."

"Yeah," said Lust.

"I was doing my stellar performance you dingbats. Can't you take a joke?"

"Listen you idiots. It was your job to stop him from going to the doctor. If he would have held out, he could have been dead in two weeks."

Ashshod and the angels appeared at Trevor's parents' home. "I see that you are here for the show," said Greed.

"Why, are you ready to entertain us today?" asked Ashshod. Greed became infuriated and blew fire out of his nostrils. "What's wrong, Greed, can't stand the truth?"

Trevor arrived home, and both of his parents noticed how incoherent he was.

"Trevor, son, what is going on with you?" John asked.

"I have full blown AIDS he screamed. "I'm going to die. I'm going to die. Oh Mom, I'm so scared. What am I going to do?"

Jane fell right into her husband's arms as she looked at her precious baby boy and just bawled.

"Oh look at Trevor," Greed said. "He's just a big mess. I don't understand why he's so upset. He got everything he ever wanted. He received the desires of his own lust, what's so bad about that? Now he gets to die in his sins and boy I'm loving it."

"You are just full of nonsense," said Ashshod.

"Why thank you very much, Ashshod, I didn't know you cared." Greed began to laugh. "See you guys, Ashshod is not as dumb as he looks. Hey look at Trevor's dad. What does he think he's doing? Oh it's too late, John, we have his soul he's going to Hell. Oh how sad for you guys but it's great for us. You know, Ashshod, I'm truly going to look forward watching him burn in his sins."

All of the imps just laughed and blew smoke out of their nostrils.

John looked up toward the ceiling and said, "Dear Heavenly Father, please have mercy on our son." John felt so helpless he could not help his son. He began to cry profusely.

"Hey Ashshod, it was so great posing as a good angel, but I just could not stand doing this all the time," Deception said. "Don't you ever get bored?"

"You know you miss paradise. Don't try to persuade yourself otherwise," stated Ashshod.

"Don't mock me, Ashshod," replied Deception.

"Trust me, that's not very hard to do," answered Ashshod

"I really detest you, Ashshod," stated Deception.

Ashshod laughed. "Oh, how sad, Deception."

Trevor laid his head down on the kitchen counter and his parents went over to console him.

"I need to be left alone, please understand," said Trevor.

"Let's follow poor little Trevor," Greed said.

Ashshod and Deception stayed in the kitchen with Trevor's parents. The rest of the angels and imps left when Greed left.

Trevor went into the den, sat in his favorite chair, then turned on the television. He flipped through the channels and ran across a television evangelist; he looked at the last ten minutes of the program. The preacher was giving the invitation to accept Jesus Christ as one's personal Savior.

Trevor looked on and said, "Nobody can save me. I am a useless person. I have sinned so badly, Lord, you just don't understand. I have full blown AIDS. I really screwed up." Trevor looked on then started talking out loud, trying to figure out just what to do.

The television evangelist said, "There is nothing that God cannot do. Look, you may not have tomorrow. Now is the time. If the Lord God can save me, He can surely save you!"

Ashshod entered into the room as well as Deception.

Deception said, "He doesn't need you, Ashshod."

Deception entered into Trevor's mind and told him repeatedly, "Nobody can save you, your life is over, it's over, just turn off the television set, you don't need it on."

Deception became furious because Trevor was not moving fast enough to turn the television off.

Ashshod rushed over to the television set and turned it up, and the preacher was going more in-depth on Jesus Christ and how he could save one from their sins. Deception tried to push Ashshod from in front of the television set. But he could not move Ashshod; he stood firm.

"Deception, you forgot about God's Grace," Ashshod said. "It's so sufficient and God's Mercy is everlasting. Here they come."

Grace and Mercy's presence entered into the room, and the imps panicked.

Deception yelled in a loud pitch voice and said, "No!" All the imps started to tremble and fly around the room frantically. They began to hiss loudly.

Ashshod shouted to the other angels, "The saints are praying. Put on the body armor of God for the praying saints which are Trevor's parents."

All the angels put on body armor.

Trevor put his head down as he grabbed his hair and started to tug it. The pastor said something and Trevor looked up.

And the pastor said it again: "You don't have to go to a place of worship to be saved. You can be saved in your home even in your living room watching this program. Just say this prayer: Lord Jesus, come into my heart. I am a sinner that need you to save me. I accept that your precious blood, that you Jesus, shed on Calvary's Cross was for me now I can have eternal life. You rose, Lord Jesus, on the third day with all power in your hands. Just say yes Lord Jesus, I believe in you."

After hearing the television evangelist say those words, Deception became furious; he noticed how Trevor began to clearly think and was becoming receptive of what he was hearing.

Deception became so bitter he rushed toward Ashshod and moved him away from the television set; they began to wrestle.

Ashshod's eyes started to glow extremely bright, summoning all the other angels to come and assist him.

Hunter appeared as well as the other angels and imps they all start to wrestle heavily.

The stench of sulfur filled the room as Ashshod and the rest of the angels defeated the weak imps. Greed shouted at Deception, False Doctrine, Hatred and some of the other imps he said, "Retreat. This battle is over. I'll meet up with you all later." Greed stayed behind with the weaker imps.

"Listen," the pastor said. "Please, just repeat after me."

Trevor struggled as he said, "Lord, can you really save me?" Then Trevor looked up and the pastor began to say the invitation again, and Trevor begins to repeat after him.

Deception and the other imps screamed as God's Grace and Mercy surrounded Trevor.

The imps yelled, "No, God can't do this to us."

Trevor fell on his face and apologized to God for being such a sinner and asked the Lord to forgive him.

The angel Change showed up, and Trevor had a sense of peace come upon him.

"Lord," he said, "I feel your presence inside of me. Thank you, Lord."

Trevor stayed on the floor, worshipping the Lord God for saving his life. Cries of joy escaped his mouth.

"All of this time, I could've had all of this peace of mind and joy. Thank you, Jesus. Thank you, Lord."

Trevor's parents rushed into the den and noticed Trevor on the floor thanking God and they noticed that he was watching a religious program. Trevor looked up and noticed that his parents were in the room and said, "Mom and Dad, I gave my life to Jesus Christ."

They rushed over to Trevor and they all cried together. John looked up and said, "Thank you, Lord, for answering our prayer."

Ashshod said to Change, "Now this is your post."

God said, "Therefore, if anyone *is* in Christ, *he is* a new creation; old things have passed away; behold, all things have become new. I'll be around him, and he'll be just fine," quoted Change.

"Trevor's name is now in the book of life where nobody or nothing can erase it," Ashshod said. "Our assignment is over here."

"You think you won this battle, Ashshod," Greed said, "But you have another thing coming. He was just a pea in a pod. We have bigger fish to fry. He is not our only mission, you son of a——."

Ashshod lifted a hand, silencing Greed. "Watch your mouth and be gone."

"Don't worry. I must go since you put a dent in these plans. How can The Man Upstairs just come in and make a big decision like this? He wonders why we do what we do."

"It's time for us to go," Ashshod said. "We must be ready for their next assignment."

All angels except for Change left to fight the next battle.

21

Rejoicing and Mourning

W hen Joyce arrived at the hospital later in the afternoon, she found Juan looking different. She couldn't pinpoint how, but she knew her husband. Something was different.

"Honey," Joyce said, "What is going on?"

"Baby," he managed to get out before crying.

"What's wrong?"

"Look." He started to move his legs and hands.

Joyce screamed, "Thank you, Jesus!"

They both said, "Hallelujah, Hallelujah, Hallelujah!"

Marco finished his sermon and the worship service had ended. He was outside greeting the congregation. He told his wife and kids that he would meet them at the restaurant before kissing them.

"Bye Daddy," the kids said.

Ashshod and the other angels hovered over Marco as well as the imps.

The imps were very angry. They shouted, "Leave him alone. He's ours." Their eyes turned red, and they started to blow fire out of their noses and mouths before pulling out their swords.

Ashshod said, "Get ready for battle," and all the angels appeared in their garments.

The angels and demons fought heavily. The sounds of hissing and screeching were heard all through the air.

"He is ours," Ashshod said.

"He is ours," Greed said. "Let him alone. You don't need him."

"You are correct. God needs him," answered Ashshod.

"Stop interfering in our matters," said Greed.

"This matter is strictly the Lord's," stated Ashshod.

"I hate you meddling angels," said Hatred.

Imps were everywhere—jumping on cars, trucks and buses, screaming and hollering.

The angels and the imps started to push and shove each other.

As Marco drove, he had to get on the highway in order to get to the restaurant. He got on the highway and began to sing to some gospel music, bobbing his head and tapping his fingers on the steering wheel. He noticed up the road that there was an accident on the median and some of the cars were slowing down to view the accident. Marco began to slow down to view the accident.

The Death Angel was lurking at the accident scene. He looked up as Marco passed the accident scene, and Death passed right through Marco.

A semi-truck, unable to slow down, rammed in the back of Marco's luxury car, sending him toward the dashboard, his seat belt snatched him back, but the impact of the collision released his seat belt throwing him through the windshield and onto the highway face first. After skidding twenty feet, his lifeless body came to a lumped halt.

Ashshod and the imps circled over the automobile.

"Ashshod," Greed said, "Leave us alone. This is our business."

"No, this is our business," Ashshod said. "You all have no power over this situation."

They began to battle, punching each other while the imps yelled profanity.

"We want these humans' souls," Greed said. "We needed him. He was leading people straight to Hell."

"Not anymore," replied Ashshod.

Ashshod and the angels gathered around the terrible sight.

Ashshod said, "Humans just don't understand that in God's Word He states that you have three chances to repent of your sins. The first chance is confessing of one's sins. Two, if you do not change your ways God will lay you flat on your back to get your attention. And thirdly, because He loves His creation so much and if you keep on sinning He will eventually take you out through physical death! All of the angels just shook their heads.

Ashshod looked at all the angels and said, "Our mission is over here".

Joyce and Juan were in the room, worshipping and praising the Lord for what He had allowed to happen in their lives.

Dr. Casper, who was also in the room along with Glynda, turned to the nurse and said, "I want you to order up a CAT scan and a MRI. We need to get more blood work done."

"Doctor," Joyce said, "So what's going on?"

"Well someone upstairs has a better plan for your husband. Now I need for you to leave the room so I can examine your husband right now," answered Dr. Casper.

"Joyce," Juan said, smiling, "I'm going to be all right. I tell you everything is going to be just fine, and don't you worry about a thing. I love you."

"I love you, too, Juan," replied Joyce. She stepped out in the hallway and walked into the waiting room; it was empty and she went into the corner and got on her knees and thanked God for what He had already done.

Joyce gathered herself together and called Rachael to tell her what happened. "God is good all the time," she said. "Slowly, slowly, he is working it all out."

"What's going on, Joyce?" Rachael asked.

"Juan," Joyce said, tears choking her, "He can move his arms and legs, girl."

Rachael screamed, shouted, "Thank you, Lord," and rushed to get off the phone to call the Tanankas.

Lisa and the children made it to the restaurant; they were seated and Lisa was wondering what was taking Marco so long. Marion, their youngest, wanted to eat; she was nagging Lisa asking if she could eat then the rest of them started asking.

"We will order," Lisa said. "I'll just order what your father normally gets and it will be at the table by the time he gets here."

By the time the food arrived, Marco still hadn't shown up.

"I'm going to call him and see what is taking him so long," she said. There was no answer. "I'm going to call him again he might be playing his music loudly."

"True," Bryant said. "Or someone from the church might have called him. You know Dad."

The girls said, "Yes, you know, Dad." They all laughed.

"Well he better answer the phone so I'll know what is taking him so long," answered Lisa.

Dr. Casper walked into the waiting room and told Joyce that they were going to take Juan up for some tests.

"Can I see him before he goes?" she asked.

"That will be fine."

Joyce walked into Juan's room, and he was sitting up smiling. He looked so like his old self.

"Joyce, watch this," he said, excited. "I can lift my arms." He lifted his arms so he could hug his lovely wife. Joyce embraced him tightly; she didn't want to let him go.

"Joyce, it's all right," he said.

Joyce just kept crying on his shoulder, saying "Thank you, Lord, thank you."

Glynda came into the room and said, "Okay you love birds, break it up. I must take him to get some tests done."

Zaso, Gabe, Enu, Sebastian, Deoriel, Rafael, and Hunter were all in the hospital room. Enu looked around and saw that there were imps all over the place.

Deoriel said, "Don't worry, they are weak. They can't defeat us."

The imps were hissing and drooling all over the place; one of the imps jumped from one side to the other and as it was moving, it dropped a puddle of drool on the floor.

Joyce stood, hugging herself as Glynda rolled Juan out of the room. She smiled brightly when Rachael and Forest walked into the room. Rachael gave Joyce a huge hug.

Joyce said, "Girl, ooh, you just don't know."

Forest, standing at a distance, waved and smiled.

"Forest how are you doing with that broken leg?" asked, Joyce.

"I'm handling it allright I guess," replied Forest.

"Young man," Joyce said, "Get over here and give me a big hug." When Forest went to hop toward Joyce with his crutches, he slipped on the puddle of drool that came out the mouth of one of the imps and fell on the floor. The imps started to laugh and drool; they even started to do back flips.

"Are you okay?" Joyce said, "Where did that puddle come from?"

Rachael went to the bathroom and got some paper towels to clean the floor. One of the imps said, "Yes that's it, clean up our mess." All the imps started to hiss.

Deoriel said, "Back away."

They all said, "No, you annoying angels, leave."

All of the angels' eyes began to glow; the imps moved closer together and stood still. Joyce made sure that Forest was allright before she squeezed the life out of him.

The Tanankas walked into the room and squeezed Joyce. They both said, "Where is he?"

"They are doing loads of test on him," Joyce said.

They greeted Rachael and Forest after speaking with Joyce. "Looks like God is trying to work out things for all of us," John said.

"All of us?" Joyce asked. "What's going on with you two?"

"Trevor gave his life to Christ."

Joyce grabbed her heart and said, "Praise God." They all wept except Forest; he just smiled.

Lisa kept calling and calling Marco; it kept going straight into voice mail. "What is going on with him?" she asked no one in particular. She called again, and was told that the voice mail was full.

"Keep calling, Mommy," Bryant said. "He'll pick up."

At the end of their meal, Lisa was talking with the kids and her cell phone rang. She looked at the phone and said, "Finally it's your dad."

"Yay!" the kids yelled.

"Marco," Lisa said, "Where have you been?"

"Hello?"

Lisa looked at the phone, confused. "Who is this?"

"I am of the highway patrol from Westlake, Ohio."

"Okay but why do you have my husband's phone?"

"Ma'am, I need for you to meet me at the police station."

"For what?"

"I need to speak with you about your husband. I will not tell you over the phone. Please, get here as soon as you can."

Lisa got off of the phone.

Bryant said, "What's wrong, Mom?"

"Don't worry, sweetie. I'm going to call Sister Kimberley to see if she can watch you guys while I take care of some things."

On her way to the police station, Lisa called the chairman of the church's deacon board Hubert Smith and asked him to meet her at the station.

When she got there, he was waiting.

"Is everything all right?" he asked.

"I don't know," she said, worried. The two walked into the police station and asked for the police chief.

He arrived at the desk and asked them to follow him to his office.

Deacon Smith and Lisa walked to the back with the police chief and went into his office.

"Please have a seat," he said to the pair.

"I prefer to stand," Lisa said.

"Are you sure?"

She nodded.

Out of respect, the chief stood, too.

He said, "May I ask you your last name?"

"Pablo."

"Mrs. Pablo, I am so sorry to have to inform you of this, but your husband was killed in an automobile accident this afternoon."

Lisa crumpled to the floor and passed out. When she awakened, she was on the sofa in the office.

"What happened?" she mumbled.

"You passed out," the chief said.

"I thought you said my husband was killed."

He nodded. "Yes, ma'am. That's what I said."

"Where..." she tried to say but tears choked her voice. "Where is his body?"

It took a minute for the chief to reply, "At the morgue, ma'am. We will need for you to go down and identify the body."

Lisa broke into loud sobs. The deacon tried his best to comfort her.

"I will give you some time," the chief said before leaving his office.

"Oh Lord, why did this happen?" she asked. "Why?"

15 minutes passed by, and the chief returned.

"Here is all the information you are going to need to take down to the morgue," he said. "I am so sorry for your loss."

Lisa gathered herself together, the police chief handed her the paperwork; even though she was hesitant to take them. He told her that after the investigation he would return Marco's phone to her. Lisa said, "Thank you".

My husband is gone, she thought as Deacon Smith helped her into the car. *Marco is gone.*

As they were on their way to the morgue, you could hear a pin drop. All you saw on their faces were tears; hurt. They arrived at their destination and they both hesitated to get out of the car; but they knew it had to be done. Lisa and Deacon Smith stepped out of the car. As they walked toward the entrance it seemed as if it was the longest walk of the lives. It felt as if life itself had stopped for them. How was she going to tell the children? What about his parents? What about the church? All these thoughts were flowing through her mind. "Our children without their father; oh what am I to do?" Deacon Smith and Lisa arrived at the front desk; Lisa handed the clerk the paperwork the police chief gave to her. The clerk asked them to have a seat. The lady behind the desk looked up everything on the computer and typed all the information into the computer. The clerk summoned Lisa to come to answer some questions. Lisa answered all the questions; then prepared herself as she saw the coroner approaching. The coroner asked which one of them was going to view Marco's body. The clerk asked Lisa if she was ready. Lisa shook her head no. The clerk said she'd give her some time. Deacon Smith told Lisa he would go view the body if she wanted him to.

"No, I need to see for myself," answered Lisa.

The coroner walked up to Lisa; offered her deepest condolence. The coroner escorted them to the back. Before entering the morgue the coroner, turned to them and said, "This will be very hard to see him like this because he was brutally injured." Lisa walked into that cold room and saw a body on the slab covered up and immediately lost her footage. Deacon Smith caught her. The coroner saw that she was having difficulty and waited until Lisa could get herself together as best she could. She asked Lisa if she was ready. She said, "Okay" as the coroner lifted the white sheet, Lisa saw Marco lying on the counter; cut up and bruised. She vomited all over the floor and became lightheaded. Deacon Smith caught her and the coroner grabbed a chair to put beneath her. The coroner called for the custodian to clean up while she attended to Lisa. Deacon Smith had to leave the room. It became too much for him to handle. As he exited, he could hear Lisa screaming and crying; it was too much for her.

As Joyce and the others rejoiced, the blessings that were falling in their lives, her phone rang. She was never one to answer private calls, so she ignored it and the next call that came. When her phone rang a third time, she sighed and looked at the screen: *Hubert Smith*. She scrunched up her face.

Rachael looked at Joyce. "What's wrong?"

"It's Hubert Smith," Joyce replied.

"What does he want?"

She shrugged before answering.

"Hello," Deacon Smith said, "I'm so sorry to disturb you, Sister Cortez, but I have some devastating news." Joyce was silent, but the others saw her eyes widen and her mouth drop open. When she ended the call, she stared at them, still stunned. She fell into a chair, and they all surrounded her.

Rachael asked, "What happened, Joyce?"

"Deacon Smith informed me that Marco was killed in an automobile accident this afternoon."

John said, "Oh no."

Joyce said, "Lisa, oh sweet dear Lisa and the kids."

Everyone was numb. The imps were furious; Hatred appeared in the room as well as Greed. All the angels were in the room, keeping guard.

"You might have gotten Marco," Greed said, "But do you understand the souls we have gotten because of his recklessness?" Greed laughed profusely.

Enu said, "You have gotten nothing. Just remember it's not over. What are you all thinking?"

"Shut up you little nothing of an angel. You are not in charge."

"And neither are you," stated Enu. He charged after Greed, but Ashshod showed up and stopped him in mid-air.

"This is not the right time," replied Ashshod. The imps formed a straight line to get ready for battle. "Not now, this is not the time for battle."

Greed said, "Ashshod, what is your problem? Scared to fight your battles?"

"Greed, you are out of your league, so back away."

"No, you all just back away," Greed stated. "Don't you know that we are going to take you down?"

Ashshod's eyes began to glow. Joyce and the rest of them saw a glare of light coming from the hospital's window; they all looked and turned their faces away from the window because the light was blinding.

Joyce said, "What is going on around here?"

Ashshod said, "Greed, leave."

The imps in the room said, "Let's take them down."

Greed said, "No not right now. I must put something into play. Let's go."

Lisa thought Marco's death was the hardest thing she'd have to go through.

But she was wrong.

Telling her children proved far more devastating.

As soon as she arrived at Sister Kimberley's home, the kids ran to her, all of them asking, "What's going on? Where's Daddy?"

Lisa was barely able to make two steps into the house before she broke down and said, "Your father was killed in an automobile accident this afternoon."

Bryant stood in a daze as Marion and Lanice began to scream.

"Oh my God," Kim whispered before falling against the wall and weeping.

Lisa waited for the kids to calm down so she could take them home.

"I will go with you, "Kimberley said. "I'll drive my car."

Juan finally arrived back into his room, so pleased to see everybody. They all ran and hugged him after the orderlies put his bed back to where it needed to be.

"It is so great to see the old you but looking new," John said.

Juan said, "Yeah man, I know exactly what you mean." They both laughed.

Jane hugged him and kissed him on the cheek and said, "Good to see you."

"Pastor," John said, pulling a blushing Trevor alongside him, "Trevor has something to tell you."

Trevor, happy; yet embarrassed, "I finally did it."

"Did what?" asked Juan.

"I gave my life to Jesus Christ," answered Trevor.

Juan was so excited, he wanted to get out of the bed and do a little holy dance.

"I see you, Juan," Joyce said. "Please do not over stimulate yourself."

He chuckled. "Allright, allright you know I'm just so excited."

The imps began to hiss; the angels stood their ground.

"We are going to get you, Ashshod," Greed said, "You and your little angels."

The angels' eyes began to glow, and Greed began to hiss. But there was something different about Greed. He began to grow to an alarming size and then he began to drool. He looked over at Ashshod and said, "This is my battle and it's time to fight."

Ashshod said, "No Greed, this is not the time. Leave if you know what's best for you."

"Ashshod, you think that you are better than us because we did not retrieve Marco. He was just a drop in the bucket. We have bigger and better plans. I see that Trevor is here. He is nothing as well. He might be saved, but we sure enjoyed damaging his health." He laughed. "Oh what do we have here, Ashshod? Juan is moving around, aha, so the plot thickens. Don't worry. I have a plan for this as well, so get ready for me."

The imps started to fly around the room. The rest of the angels just stood still, watching.

"I'm about to go," Greed said, "But trust me, I will be back and the next time you see me, I am going to destroy you all."

"Oh we are shaking in our boots," Hunter said.

Greed looked at Hunter and blew fire at him and missed him by an inch. Hunter pulled out his sword and Ashshod said, "Don't even bother."

Greed and the ones he wanted to follow him vanished.

Ashshod stayed close to Juan.

Lisa was home making funeral arrangements and holding the children close when she could without breaking down. Sister Kimberley was doing her best to comfort her. Some of the congregation began to drop by after they had heard the announcement at church. Everyone was dropping by, and Sister Kimberley knew how to handle the crowd. She would not let everyone crowd Lisa and the children, so she gave them ten minutes each to pay their respects.

Of course there were individuals who wanted to be rude and take more time, and it was none other than Mrs. Sallie Cooper who walked into Lisa's house talking very loud and taking the attention away from the family. Kimberley walked up to Mrs. Cooper and asked her to calm her voice. She became indignant with Kimberley and Kim felt herself stooping down to her level and caught herself.

"You need to leave," Kim said, "And if you don't, I will help you."

Lisa jumped up from her sofa and said, "Thank you so very much, Mrs. Cooper, for coming by. The kids and I really appreciate it."

Lisa looked over at Kim and gave her a look like let me talk to her so she could leave. Kim understood her facial gestures and gave a little grin.

"You were my husband's number one fan, Mrs. Cooper," said Lisa. Although she wasn't a fan of Sallie's at all, Lisa smiled as Sallie gave her the biggest hug. "Thank you for coming."

Sallie said, "If you ever need anything, please give me a call."

"I will."

Sallie attempted to go on about how handsome and good looking Marco was.

Lisa jumped in and repeated, "Thank you for coming."

Mrs. Cooper left the room, but she left with an attitude.

Juan noticed that there was a strange mood in the room. He looked around at everyone's faces and noticed that there was something they were not telling him.

Juan said, "Joyce, honey, what is going on?"

"What do you mean?" she said.

"Joyce, you should look at all of your faces. What are you hiding from me?"

Everyone looked at Joyce. "Well baby," she said, "We just learned that Marco was killed in an automobile accident."

Juan sat straight up in the bed. Everyone looked at him, scared about what was happening.

Juan could not take in what he just heard. He looked around the room and just got sick to his stomach.

Joyce hit the call button.

"You did not have to do that," he said. "Has anyone called Lisa?"

They all shook their heads.

Glynda came into the room and said, "I was not invited to the party?" They all chuckled. Glynda looked at the monitor and noticed that Juan's blood pressure was elevated and said, "I am going to ask if everyone would leave. I need to examine him." Joyce got concerned and Glynda said, "I will let you know your husband's test results after I have examined him."

"Go check on Lisa, everybody," Juan said. "Joyce, go see her now. I'll be all right. Do you hear me? Go see Lisa."

Lisa was in the living room holding a picture of Marco in her hand. She looked up and noticed Joyce standing at the door jamb. She jumped to her feet.

Rachael, Forest, and the Tanankas followed Joyce into the room. "We didn't want to just come barging in," Joyce said.

They all surrounded her and showed their compassion..

"Lisa," Joyce said, "Is there anything we can do for you?"

"No. All I want is my husband back."

"We understand," Rachael said. "We are so sorry."

"The children and I got the opportunity to say goodbye before we left to go to the restaurant," Lisa said. They all listened to Lisa vent because they knew the devastating pain she was under.

Joyce said, "Pastor sends his love."

Lisa said, "Tell him I said thank you."

The children walked into the living room, and Jane and John hugged the girls, and Rachael hugged Bryant, and everyone started to cry all over again.

22

The Funeral

When Joyce arrived at Juan's hospital room, he gave her the biggest smile. They hugged and kissed, and she told him that she spoke with the kids and informed them of his fantastic news; they were all excited.

"I have more great news to tell you," Juan said.

"What is it?" asked Joyce.

"At therapy today I stood up on my own and I took a small step." Joyce screamed, and Juan laughed. "Quiet down, Joyce. You are going to get us kicked out of here. This is a place full of sick people."

"I'm sorry," she said, "But this is fantastic news. I think they will forgive me."

"But that's not even the great news."

"Then what is?"

"The doctor is allowing me to attend Marco's funeral."

"You've got to be kidding me."

"No, I'm not. Dr. Casper wrote the orders up. I'll be getting a wheelchair and I told her that I would ask John to help me."

"Great. Call John and ask him."

Juan smiled. "I will right after dinner."

Joyce and Juan had dinner and small talk, but Joyce could hardly contain herself. She wanted Juan to hurry up and call John. Their excitement waned briefly when John told Juan that he couldn't take him to Marco's funeral.

"I have a business meeting to attend," he explained.

"Oh," Juan said, sighing. "That's too bad."

"But don't fear, my dear pastor," John said. "I'll have Trevor take you."

"Are you sure? I don't want to impose."

"I'm more than sure. Trust me. We'll get you there, pastor."

Greed began to have a conversation with the imps about who he was going to use for his special plans; he began to look around and pointed at False Doctrine and Hatred and looked at the others imps and said, "You have big roles as well." The imps began to hiss.

The eyes of the angels stationed in the room began to glow. No words were exchanged.

The morning of Marco's funeral was quite solemn. It was a bright sunny July morning, but everything around seemed so gray. Juan got dressed and waited for Joyce and Trevor to arrive.

Dr. Casper came in, took a look at Juan in his suit, and smiled.

"Well, don't you look handsome?" the doctor asked.

In his best Elvis' voice, he said, "Well, thank you...thank you very much."

They both chuckled.

"Joyce brought me one of my black suits so I could look like a decent human being for a change. It sure feels good to have a great shave and a fresh haircut."

"I can imagine. Where is your ride?"

"They are on their way," replied Juan.

"I must go but have the nurse page me before you leave," said Dr. Casper.

"Will do."

Dr. Casper left the room, and Juan wondered what was taking Joyce and Trevor so long to get there.

As soon as the thought left his mind, Joyce and Trevor walked in.

"Look at Pastor looking all dapper," Trevor said, chuckling.

"Why thank you my good young man," Juan said, smiling.

Joyce looked at Juan, smiled, and started to cry.

"Oh, Joyce, cut that out," said Juan. He winked at her.

"Honey," Joyce said, "I miss seeing you this way. It's been so long, that's all."

Dr. Casper peeked into the room. "I thought I'd swing by again," the doctor said. "And I brought wheels."

Glynda rolled a wheelchair into the room. Dr. Casper watched how Joyce and Trevor helped Juan into the wheelchair.

"Did you administer all of his medication?" Dr. Casper asked Glynda.

"I have," Glynda replied.

"Now, Juan," the doctor said, "I need you to be back here by 1 p.m."

"Consider it done," Joyce said.

At The Comfort Zone, Joyce rolled Juan inside. She watched him carefully as he took in the new sign out front, the ATM machines, the missing crosses. All he could do was shake his head.

As she wheeled him down the aisle, Joyce smiled, proud to have Juan out and about. The majority of those in attendance went silent as they saw Juan.

When they reached the coffin, Juan viewed Marco's body. *I'm so sorry it had to end this way*, he thought. While praying, he could hear the crying of the members over the dreadful music that was being played. He looked over at Lisa, and she looked at Juan as if she had seen a ghost. Slowly, Joyce rolled Juan over to the corner where the trustees sat. Trevor followed.

Juan looked around and some of the old members smiled at him with amazement. Juan looked up at the ceiling and looked around the sanctuary and took in the massive changes Marco had made. Instead of thinking about the complete-180 transformation, Juan prayed.

Deacon Smith walked to the pulpit and asked if anyone would like to say a kind word about Pastor Pablo. Many pastors in and out of the city came with high praise of Marco. Former co-workers from the transit company also came with words.

When the chairman of the deacon board handed Juan the microphone, he said his words and Lisa was well pleased. The church applauded and some were even shouting.

Ashshod and the angels were in large numbers; they were standing at their posts. Greed and the imps were in full force; they were jumping on the pews and spitting on the saved. The imps walked up and down the aisles trying to devour all that they could. Greed started to hiss and the other imps turned and looked at him. He nodded his head, and Hatred looked toward Sallie Cooper.

The shouting died down. Hatred jumped right into Sallie. She walked up to the front, took the microphone, and started talking about how she loved and respected Marco as her pastor. Then she looked over at Juan and said angrily, "Why are you here?"

The congregation went in an uproar against Sallie for making such a hideous comment. Greed was smiling and the other imps were swarming around Sallie because she was the beginning of their plan to destroy.

"You did not even like him," she said. "You never gave him a chance to do anything."

Juan looked at Sallie Cooper and did not get upset. Chairman Smith jumped up and grabbed a hold of the microphone and escorted Sallie off the platform. She looked at Juan and said, "I hate you, I really do."

The whole congregation watched as the deacon escorted Sallie up the aisle.

Lisa looked up at one of the associate ministers and gave him a look as he stepped to the podium. He quieted the crowd, reminding them that they were in a place of worship and that there was a funeral going on. The congregation settled down and the service went back in session.

The recession to the cemetery was forming; Lisa and the family left first. Juan, Joyce and Trevor were not going to the cemetery. Juan stayed and socialized. Rachael and Forest were talking to Joyce, then Jane came over and joined them. It was a long line of people that wanted to speak to Juan. He talked to as many as he could, and told the rest that he had to get back to the hospital.

Trevor started strolling Juan up the aisle toward where Joyce was talking with Rachael, Forest and Jane.

Ashshod stood right beside Juan. Greed swooped down right in front of Juan and said, "It's not over until I say it is."

Ashshod said, "Get out of his face, Greed. Be gone."

Greed looked up and hissed at Ashshod. Ashshod's eyes began to glow. Greed laughed and he flew up toward the ceiling and went out into the lobby. There were imps all over the place. The angels stood at their posts.

Greed welcomed all the imps as he reached the lobby and he said, "Look at all these wonderful souls that are acting as if they're saved." Greed started to jump from person to person. "This person isn't saved, but she sure can sing. Oh yeah, look you guys, this one said he was called to preach, and he's not even saved. Oh and look at Big Momma, she's not saved; she just comes for the company. Hey, look at the deacon Hatred. He sure knows how to form those words in prayer, and nor is he saved. How stupid can he be? God will not hear his prayers."

Greed summoned all the imps to come around him. There was no need for him to go to the cemetery because Marco was gone.

The imps hissed and drooled and Greed led the song; he even had a new verse:

"To Hell they will be, to Hell they will be.

We jump inside and control their minds,

To Hell they will be.

We hear them say rescue us Lord Jesus we believe in you now. Satan will hear their scream asking the Lord to rescue them and hear their pleas.

God doesn't hear your cries I'll tell you why you rejected the Almighty so this is what you get!

To Hell you'll stay, to Hell you'll stay. Ha, ha, ha."

Juan looked out into the lobby and saw that Sallie was still here and she was surrounded by her clique.

"Trevor," he whispered, "Could you get me out of here as quickly as possible?"

"Yes sir," Trevor responded.

The last thing Juan wanted was to deal with Sallie's nonsense.

Trevor rolled Juan out into the church lobby, and Sallie could not wait to approach him.

She jumped in Juan's face and started pointing her finger at him and said, "How dare you show up here. You didn't even like this boy."

Joyce jumped right in the midst of the conversation and said, "I will not let you talk to my husband like this."

Sallie ignored her. She was on a mission to embarrass Juan. "You hindered Marco from doing big things like he did here. He did all the things that you were incapable of doing. You are nothing but a conniving, manipulative piece of scum. Why don't you get back to the hospital where your old tired self belongs?"

Then she spat on his pants leg.

"See that's how you do it. You go girl," said Greed. He flew right to Ashshod's face and said, "So what do you have to say about that? Nothing? Not a little something, huh, huh? What, cat got your tongue? See, I keep telling you that I'm in control here not you. Look at your subject. He's looking just like you, dumb."

Everyone looked at Juan with astonished looks on their faces. They felt helpless over the situation they just witnessed. Everyone was furious at Sallie; this was not the time nor place for this kind of nonsense. It was as if time stood still. Juan could not believe that Sallie spat on him. Joyce wiped the spit off his pants. She and Rachael went after Sallie. but her clique grabbed her and walked her out of the lobby and straight to her car.

Greed was full of laughter, and the other imps were jumping all around.

Ashshod said, "Greed, you cannot harm him."

"Oh, yes I can," said Greed. He pointed his finger in Ashshod's face.

"Greed, back away," Ashshod said.

"I'm going to get Juan and there is absolutely nothing you can do about it."

Ten imps swarmed around Greed. Ashshod looked at Greed and pulled out his sword and Greed said, "Oh you don't scare me, Ashshod."

Ashshod noticed that Greed was beginning to grow. Greed saw something that caught his eye, a vast number of angels appearing knowing that he and the other imps were outnumbered. He told the other imps, "Let's go." They flew away, and then Greed quickly returned and said, "Ashshod, this is not over." Then he vanished.

"It will be over sooner than you think, Greed," Ashshod said.

"I am livid," Joyce said. "How dare she start all of this commotion in God's house. She has nothing but the devil in her. Juan, if you were not here I would have belted her one."

"Joyce, calm down," Juan said. "Trevor, please take me back now. I really need to go."

Trevor got Juan in the car and Juan was happy to leave that place. "Where is God in that place of worship?" he asked.

On the way back to the hospital, Juan did not say a word. He could not believe what just happened. Joyce just kept talking and Trevor was scared to open his mouth. They arrived at the hospital and put Juan on the bed.

Dr. Casper and Glynda came into the room, and Dr. Casper noticed the flushed tone on Juan's face and grew concerned. She took his blood pressure herself and checked his pulse.

Joyce and Trevor looked at Dr. Casper. Joyce asked, "Is he okay?"

Dr. Casper noticed that Juan was having transient ischemic attacks, mini strokes. Dr. Casper asked if Trevor and Joyce could step out of the room so Glynda could give him his meds.

"I need for you to go home and take it easy, Joyce," Dr. Casper added. "He is going to need all the rest he can get. What happened that caused him to have his blood pressure so high?"

Joyce said, "We took him to the funeral and one of the members just acted a complete idiot, and she accused him of being a very hateful person. She caused such a show that it really got to him because he didn't say anything in the car."

Dr. Casper said, "I'm going to need for you to just go for right now. I need for him to get lots of rest and I will need to run more test. I'll tell him that I asked you to go home. Please, it will be best."

Joyce looked at Dr. Casper and was a little agitated, but she knew the doctor was right.

"Okay," she said. "Tell him that I love him."

Dr. Casper said, "I will."

Juan just laid there, staring at the ceiling. His room was silent; he didn't even have the television on. He closed his eyes and immediately went into prayer.

"Lord, what in the world did I just experience at the house of worship? It was so horrifying. First Marco takes everything that resembles You out of the church, and then people like Sallie are able to act so foolish...*in* your house, I might add. I just don't understand."

Ashshod stood around Juan. *The sphygmomanometer machine* started to beep. Glynda ran into the room and said, "Juan, I need for you to calm down."

Dr. Casper followed quickly behind and added, "I must give you a sedative so you can rest."

"No matter how much drugs you give me," Juan said, "Only God can give me the rest I need."

23

What's Next?

A month after Marco's death, The Comfort Zone was going through some lonely and uncomfortable times. They formed a pulpit committee to find someone who could lead them to bigger and better things. Sallie Cooper was on the board and she was doing everything to take charge, and she was stopping at nothing to put someone in so she could take rule. Even though there were ten people on the board, she acted as if she were the only one.

False Doctrine appeared because he had a lot invested in this area. He was there to assist Sallie in the choosing of the right leader of The Comfort Zone. He watched on with concern and made sure that things were in order.

The committee had their meetings every Wednesday night since Marco got rid of Bible study. The committee received a stack of resumes of individuals wanting to become the next leader of The Comfort Zone. Sallie was leading the group and she loved every moment of it. She was not qualified at all; and she could quote some Scriptures; this made her a leader. She handed the committee members ten resumes and they looked at each and every one of them very closely.

False Doctrine jumped inside of Sallie, and she said, "Okay, these are the ones I am going to allow us to bring in. These are the ones that fit our criteria."

One of the members on the board, Mr. Johnnie Boone said, "What criteria do we have, Mrs. Cooper? What we need is that old time religion back. All of this new age stuff is not what I want."

Sallie looked over at Johnnie and said, "Why are you here because I don't think you want what we want? Nobody wants to go backwards. Do you see the progress that we are making? We have so much more than what we had with that old dumb Cortez, so I will not go backwards."

"Sallie, the church is God's house. This is a den of thieves. I don't even know why this place is considered a place of worship. This is a gymnasium, that's what this is. It's pure damnation," Johnnie said.

"I would like to thank you for that boring speech, Brother Boone. Now let's look at these resumes."

The other committee members were a little frightened of Sallie; they knew not to get on her bad side. If one did there was a price to pay. Many of the members hated confrontation, so they went along for the ride. They were just happy to be on the board; they felt important.

There was a resume that caught False Doctrine's eye and he made Sallie pick this particular guy. Sallie said, "This is the one we need to bring in."

Greed appeared and said, "False Doctrine, I see that you are running things here."

"Yes I am," replied False Doctrine.

"Great choice because Trendon is far greater than Marco was. He will keep everything in place and make it even better than Marco."

Trendon Palmer was 35, married, and the father of four children.

The board voted to send for Trendon—everyone except for Johnnie.

Pastor Cortez had been transferred to the rehabilitation center. He was now standing on his own and doing exceptionally well for someone who had a massive stroke at his age.

While Rachael was visiting Juan she informed them that The Comfort Zone was looking for a new pastor and that a young man from California was coming in for the position.

Joyce said, "I'll go on Sunday and check him out."

Rachael said, "I will too. I'll call Jane and John to see if they will come."

■ ■ ■

Greed, False Doctrine, and Hatred arrived at The Comfort Zone looking forward to seeing this wonderful speaker do his thing. Ashshod, Zaso, Enu and Hunter appeared.

"Oh joy look who's here, the 'do gooders'," said Greed.

"Why do you dumb angels always have to mess up a good thing by showing up?" asked Hatred.

"I don't care that you annoying angels show up," False Doctrine said. "Just don't interfere with my work in progress."

"You silly little imps, just keep quiet. There are just some times you guys need to keep your big mouths shut," replied Ashshod.

Hatred became so angry that he threw a fireball over at Ashshod; Zaso blocked it.

"I don't think you are thinking clearly," said Enu.

"Look Greed, I think you need to calm your little imp down. If not, there is going to be a battle that you can't possibly win," stated Ashshod.

"We are not scared of you useless angels," replied Hatred.

"Back down you guys. We have bigger and better things to focus on," stated Greed.

The Comfort Zone was very crowded; everyone wanted to see how this new minister was going to sound and what he could bring to the table.

Joyce, Rachael, and the Tanankas were there, including Trevor.

The service was as usual; Minister Palmer's wife was sitting next to Lisa and her children; The Palmers brought their kids. The time had come and the chairman of the deacon board escorted Trendon down the aisle. Looking like a younger version of Tom Cruise, the minister had movie star good looks, a smile that could just melt through one's heart, and a body like Arnold Schwarzenegger in his prime. Even though Trendon was a married man there was no doubt that there would be women in the congregation that would try to latch on to him. His wife was gorgeous; she looked like a young Linda Carter.

He stepped up to the microphone and he sounded just like Alan Rickman. Trendon gave a formal introduction and introduced himself and his family; the congregation applauded. Then it was time for the message, but before he gave the message he sang a song and the congregation enjoyed it.

False Doctrine and Hatred stood on both sides of Trendon, and Greed stood behind him standing tall and strong. Ashshod and the rest of the angels were up in the air, watching. Trendon began to give the message; he did not come from Scripture. He just gave a quote from a popular personality from history. He came from a different angle; he was very passive aggressive on his teaching on prosperity. Trendon explained to individuals that they should tell God to work for them rather than mankind working for God. Greed moved from behind Trendon and started to circle around the sanctuary. He wanted to get a closer look to see who was agreeing with Trendon; he loved the responses. He looked at Rachael and the Tanankas and knew they were off limits, but not Lisa. Ashshod looked at Greed and said, "Don't you dare think about going after Lisa."

"She is not off limits for me," stated Greed.

"Greed, she is off limits. You will not touch her. Do I make myself clear?"

Greed flew back behind Trendon and looked at Hatred and said, "We are going to make Lisa feel as if she is not welcomed here. We are going to speed this up. They are going to accept Trendon as their new pastor."

Trendon was winding down; he looked into the audience and explained to them his beliefs. "I want you to understand I know that Pastor Pablo did not extend the invitation to Jesus Christ and I believe that he did the right thing. I want to express that I hate it when people give out false doctrine and information and it leads me to this. I want you to listen to me very closely. I do not believe in Hell. It is just a state of mind. So when people want to say otherwise you just walk away or turn the television channel. God is a loving God. He will not send His creation to Hell."

The crowd became still. "I see that I have everyone's undivided attention. Listen, how can a loving God send His creation to Hell? He just loves us so much. I know that Jesus Christ died for the sins of mankind, but you need to know that Hell does not exist. So mankind needs to stop stressing over this nonsensical idea because humans, all humans, regardless of one imperfection will go to heaven."

Sallie jumped to her feet and said, "Amen" and others started to stand to their feet. Trendon finished and sat down and they did not extend the invitation to Jesus Christ. Service had ended and everyone wanted to meet that gorgeous looking young man. Sallie was standing right beside Trendon and his family introducing him to everyone who came by to shake his hand.

Rachael, Joyce and the Tanankas were talking. Lisa came and joined them; they hugged and kissed each other. Lisa said, "I thought Marco was off the chain, but this one is way off in left field. When did Hell become non-existing?"

Rachael said, "I just don't know what people are thinking."

Joyce said, "Wait until Juan here's what is going on."

"This place is like a zoo," said Rachael.

"Tell me about it. I don't see God in here anywhere," stated Lisa.

John kissed Jane's cheek and told her he was going to the lobby to chop it up with a few of the men.

As Sallie was meeting and greeting individuals, she noticed how Joyce and the rest of them were encircled; and that made her very suspicious and angry, so she had to go see what they were up to. She grabbed Trendon and his wife by their hands and walked them up the aisle and said, "There are some people that I really want you both to meet." Sallie approached their huddle and said, "I want you to meet our new pastor and first lady, oops did I speak too soon?" She began to laugh.

"Let me introduce you to the gang," she continued. "This is Joyce, her husband is the former pastor who was stuck in tradition. He was very old fashioned. Yes, he is the one that's in the hospital." Joyce looked at her with her mouth wide open; she tried to play it off, but everyone noticed how upset she was. "Then there's Lisa. This is the late Pastor Marco Pablo wife, God rest his sweet soul. But Lisa has no power here like Joyce. They are just past first ladies. They are just regular ordinary people here." Eyeing Rachael and the Tanankas, she added, "Speaking of ordinary people, here are Rachael and the Tananka's and that's their son Trevor; who thinks that he is God's gift to women."

"It's so nice to see and meet you all," said Trendon, feeling very awkward.

Sallie was about to fix her mouth to say something, and Joyce said, "Sallie, I think you need to stop talking right about now."

"You don't rule me, Joyce," replied Sallie. "Listen Pastor Palmer, I just wanted to inform you that the late Marco Pablo banned Rachael and Mr. And Mrs. Tananka from attending here because they will not get on board with what he believed and his teaching. If I were you, I would keep this in play because all they will do is cause you great trouble."

"Sallie, who do you think you are telling this young man all of this nonsense?" Joyce asked.

"Joyce, you just shut your mouth. I am sick and tired of you coming into this building, gathering up your little friends, and looking down on us."

Rachael jumped in and said, "Sallie, this is not the time nor the place for this. Let's go, everybody. Nice to meet you both."

As they began to walk up the aisle, Sallie yelled, "Like always, Joyce, everybody fights your battles."

They all stopped dead in their tracks, and Jane turned completely around and walked back to Sallie and slapped her in the face. Sallie screamed and caused a scene, and Jane walked away and went right back up the aisle.

"You go, girl," replied Joyce.

"I didn't know she had it in her like that," said Rachael.

24

Who Put Sallie in

Charge?

Greed, Hatred and False Doctrine were in the church annex, eagerly awaiting the pulpit committee meeting to begin.

It was Wednesday evening, three months had gone by, and the pulpit committee had their weekly meeting being led by Sallie. She let the incident with her and Jane pass because she was on a very big mission. Greed, Hatred and False Doctrine had to get ready for their next mission.

Ashshod appeared and Greed became indignant.

"What in the Hell do you want?" asked Greed.

"I don't answer to you, you wasteful piece of scum," replied Ashshod.

"Oh my, name calling now, Ashshod?"

"You don't exist to me."

"Well you don't have to be so snappy."

"Shut up, Greed."

Sallie said, "Listen, we have heard enough people, I think that we should pick Trendon Palmer. His appearance is great and he is what we are looking for."

One of the committee members said, "No, he is not what we are looking for. He has nothing to offer us. I am so sick and tired of this cult behavior. It's wrong and I will not have it."

"We need him and we are going to get him, and if you don't like it, then tough. I am going to do this my way, and I will stop at nothing to get what I want and what's best for this congregation."

"Sallie works real well for us, I must say," said Greed. The other imps agreed.

"I love it when a woman takes a stand," said False Doctrine.

Ashshod just looked over at False Doctrine and shook his head.

"We don't need him," said Brother Picker. "We need someone God fearing and of course God saved, not this nonsense again."

Hatred waited until Brother Picker opened his mouth, and he threw a dagger, which turned into a bug and flew down his throat and he began to choke. The imps in the room began to laugh hysterically.

"That will teach you to keep your big mouth shut," said Hatred.

One of the committee members called the EMS, and while they waited, everyone grew in concern—except for Sallie. When EMS finally arrived and took Brother Picker to the nearest hospital, she sighed, smiled, and said, "The meeting is now back in order."

Sister Mary Gordon said, "Hey, we just went through this scary, unpleasant incident. I don't think we should go on. We just need to pick this up next week."

Hatred said, "I think someone else needs to shut their mouth." Hatred shrunk down to five inches and started jumping on Mary's head, kicking her with his feet and punching her on both sides of her head.

Mary groaned. "Oh, I have a splitting headache all of a sudden," she said.

Hatred kept hitting her in the head and saying, "I will teach you to stop interfering in our plans."

"I'm so sorry, everybody. I must go. My head is throbbing," said Mary.

"That's right you leave, stupid lady," Hatred said. "Now who's next?"

Then Sallie said, "What you all should do is let me handle this."

The rest of the committee members were so sidetracted that they didn't even think about second-guessing her decisions.

The very next morning, Sallie got involved in doing a background check on Trendon—an official one and one she conducted herself. She learned Trendon had several aggravated domestic assault charges against him pertaining to his wife and children. He also had a severe substance abuse problem with alcohol.

She did not inform Deacon Smith or the congregation of what she learned. She called Trendon and after pleasantries, stated, "I received your background check, and it said that you have a history of domestic violence. Can you explain this to me?"

"Mrs. Cooper, all these charges are misunderstandings. They were blown out of proportion, trust me," answered Trendon.

"Why would they blow it out of proportion?"

"I love my wife Kelly and there is no possible way I would severely harm her. The court is a lie and all the paperwork is a lie."

"Can you explain about your children, please?" asked Sallie.

"Really they just fell and hurt themselves and they want to blame me for how uncoordinated they all are."

"All four of them?"

"Yes all four of them," replied Trendon. "Look Mrs. Cooper, I don't know what you want me to say. All I can say is that I am a changed man."

Thursday afternoon after Sallie got off the phone with Trendon Palmer, none of her questions were answered. She didn't think he knew how to answer the questions; he just swindled his way on out of them. Sallie liked that because that was the kind of man The Comfort Zone was looking for.

Ashshod made it his business to arrive at The Comfort Zone before those mischievous imps showed up. He circled around the sanctuary just looking for any new tactics those imps were trying to incorporate into their schemes.

That morning, Trendon spoke and he had this wonderful air about himself. He spoke just the way Sallie wanted him to speak, with surety in his voice.

He would be a great spokesperson for The Comfort Zone, she thought. *He really has all the elements that I'm looking for.*

Trendon spoke with the pulpit committee after service and they just loved him except for Brother Michael Plicker and Sister Mary Gordon. They had very negative attitudes toward Trendon and you could see it in their body language; they didn't say a word to Trendon and his family. Sallie had The Comfort Zone pay for Trendon and his family to stay in a hotel for a month. This would allow The Comfort Zone to let him and his family view the community and get to know the members as well as to show the congregation his vision.

Monday morning Trendon was in the community meeting and greeting people; they all loved him. Monday evening he stood in front of the congregation and gave them his vision plan. All month Trendon spoke and the parishioners listened; he was ten times better than Marco Pablo in their eyes.

"Listen everybody," said Trendon. "As your leader, I will not talk about sin. But I will be there when the parishioners need me. And I will definitely take The Comfort Zone globally and build a bigger and better place in Westlake, Ohio."

The congregation stood to their feet and shouted with joy.

"I thank you, but there is more. We will be everywhere. You can take that to the bank."

Again everyone stood to their feet and smiled, and then Kelly and the children stood right by his side. Trendon and his family greeted the members before Sallie walked up to him and said, "I need to speak with you for a moment."

She took Trendon into the pastor's study and said, "You better just listen to me and keep quiet. I have changed your criminal report to make you look like a saint. I will make copies for the congregation so you will be in the clear. You better make sure that you are true to your words. I will make sure that you will stay true to your words." Then she pointed her finger in his face and said these words in her stern voice, "If you mess up, and don't keep your word you are going to wish that you never met me."

Trendon lowered his gaze to the ground; he believed every word Sallie said.

"Thank you for your time, Mrs. Cooper," he said. "I'm going to get back to my family." As he walked away, a slither of fear raced up his spine. He knew he had a lot to live up to.

When he returned up front, Kelly looked at him and asked, "Are you all right?"

All Trendon wanted was a stiff drink. Trying not to think of Sallie, who stood giving him the evil eye, he smiled and kissed Kelly's forehead.

Kelly looked at Trendon to see who he was looking at and she noticed how Sallie was giving him the stink eye. Kelly grabbed his arm and said, "Don't let that women intimidate you."

"Everything is under control," he said.

Greed and Hatred were very pleased with what they were looking at and the great job Sallie was doing by taking control over the whole process.

"We might have gotten further if she was the preacher," said Hatred. They all laughed.

Greed, False Doctrine, and Hatred followed Trendon and his family back to the hotel where they were staying. Kelly and the kids hugged him; they knew he was under a lot of stress.

Then he gave Kelly a look, and she knew exactly what Trendon needed. He went into that mini fridge and took any liquor he could find and drank it.

Greed, Hatred, and False Doctrine were in the room with Trendon.

"Trendon, go ahead and drink yourself into a coma," Greed said. "Enjoy yourself. You've earned it."

"Children," Kelly said, "You will not bother your father the rest of the evening. He needs time to himself and he needs his rest."

Trendon turned on the television to see what was on; he found a baseball game and left it there while he grabbed some more mini bottles of liquor out the mini fridge. He started to feel a lot better; he even ordered room service for the family. The food came as well as his two big bottles of Scotch. He then returned to the room to be by himself.

"We are going to go so far with this young man," Greed said. "Hey False Doctrine, go and talk with him, let him know that everything is going to be just fine."

"Good point, Greed," answered False Doctrine. False Doctrine shrunk down in size to an inch and got on Trendon's left shoulder to get close to his ear.

"Trendon," he said, "You are in charge. You can tell these people anything that you want and they will accept anything that you have to say. You need to understand that humans are looking to be consoled. They don't want logic, they just want emotions. Seek the ones who have your back. Knock only on the doors of influential individuals. Leave the less fortunate ones where they belong, at the bottom. You don't have time to deal with them."

Trendon rasied the glass to his lips. "That's right, you keep drinking, Trendon, keep making me proud. You just tell them your philosophy. Inform them that you don't entertain false doctrine. They would love it, but just remember that you are to win souls."

False Doctrine jumped off of Trendon's shoulder, and then Hatred jumped on Trendon's neck as if a child was holding him for a ride and said, "You are going to make sure that all the people that try to get in your way are stopped."

Trendon just kept sipping on his Scotch; it was so good to him. He finished one bottle then Kelly walked in and said, "How are you doing?" He gave her a look and she knew he was lit up like a Christmas tree. "Trendon honey that's enough. You know you have to go to The Comfort Zone in the morning."

"Kelly, I know. I just needed a little something to get rid of the edge," replied Trendon.

"I'm going to bed. The children are asleep, and it's 1:30 in the morning. You need to get up by 7:30 am."

"I know, I know, I know."

"Goodnight Trendon."

"Good night, and I love you, Kelly."

The imps chuckled and said goodnight. Trendon cleaned up behind himself before going to bed.

Ashshod, Zaso, Hunter, and Enu were at The Comfort Zone. Greed, False Doctrine, Hatred, and Arrogance appeared.

"Ashshod, why are you and your fairies polluting the atmosphere?

Why don't you guys just fly somewhere else?" asked Arrogance.

"That's because you need us here to show you what real work looks like, Arrogance, so I guess we will be staying," answered Ashshod.

"Oh how comical, Ashshod, Not."

"Well I see you can't take the heat, Arrogance. Oh that's because you are so full of yourself, isn't that right?" said Hunter.

"You bullheaded no good son of a gun," replied Arrogance.

"Oh I see you have some manners, you didn't curse," said Zaso.

"I really can't stand you no good want to be holy angels," replied Arrogance.

"Aw, were your feelings hurt, you narcissistic jerk?" replied Enu. "Dealing with these imps is like a human having their teeth pulled without using any form of anesthetics."

"Why are you whining, Enu, we did not ask you here. You ornery angels keep coming into our territory. So stop complaining and just leave," said Greed.

"Oh that's not going to happen," replied Ashshod.

The Palmer family arrived at The Comfort Zone before 9:00 am; Trendon was to teach a seminar. He spoke on science and how the Big Bang Theory made a lot of sense and how he was connecting it with the Bible. He had everyone's attention just like he should. Greed, False Doctrine, Arrogance, and Hatred were smiling and gloating standing there with their chests stuck out on the success of Trendon's teaching. After the seminar was over, Sallie came over to Trendon. Greed stood behind Trendon and whispered in his ear, "She is the one you truly want on your side." Then Greed touched Trendon.

Something overwhelmed him and he smiled. Sallie gave him the biggest hug. He received her well, as well as the rest of his family.

Sallie said, "I need for you all to meet me for lunch on Saturday."

"Alright," Trendon said. "We will."

Sallie called a meeting with the pulpit committee on Friday evening. Greed, False Doctrine, and Hatred were in attendance.

"I would like to thank everyone for coming," Sallie said. "The reason why I summoned you all here today is to inform you that we are going to put Trendon Palmer in as our new pastor."

"Don't you think we need the congregation to vote on this?" Mary asked. "What about the committee? You did not ask if we wanted him."

Hatred said, "I know she does not want another beating. If she doesn't shut her mouth she is going to get one."

"Mary, I don't need the congregation's or the committee's approval. I run this and if you or they don't like it tough stuff, but I am going to put him in Sunday—not Deacon Smith. I am."

Greed said, "That's it Sallie. You tell them. We've got your back."

"You are out of order," replied Mary.

Hatred shrunk down and pounced on Mary's head. "You haven't seen a splitting headache yet."

Mary said, "Why is it that every time I speak here, I get a splitting headache? Only when I am around you all."

Hatred said, "If you keep your big mouth shut, you could keep your good health." Hatred kept hitting her in the head, and he hit her between her eyes, and he punched her in the nose. Her nose started to bleed.

Mary got up and said, "I'm gone. This is mess here. I feel as if I am getting a beat down for nothing."

Sallie gave Mary a devilish grin and everyone noticed it and became very nervous. Sallie said, "May I continue? Like I said, I will introduce our new pastor and then we will go from there."

The meeting was adjourned, everyone left, and Sallie was left with a big smile on her face. Come Saturday morning, she would be having lunch with the new pastor of The Comfort Zone.

Sunday morning at The Comfort Zone, everyone was there, including the imps, Ashshod and the angels.

Greed said, "Are you here for the show? Because this is what this is."

Ashshod said, "A show is exactly what this is, but it is a sad show."

"To each its own. It's good for us."

Sallie walked up to the pulpit and stood behind the podium and announced that Trendon Palmer was their new pastor. The congregation was very surprised and Greed jumped inside of Sallie and spoke through her.

"Listen, I know what I am doing. He has a great reputation and an excellent background so you don't have to worry. I have all his information to give to you after service. You will not be disappointed."

The congregation was puzzled at how Sallie had the power to do this.

Sallie took her seat and Trendon stood up and said, "My people, I will be the best leader you've ever had." He spoke on prosperity and explained how they could be bigger and better and the parishioners had no complaints after listening to a topic they longed for. After service the parishioners came and hugged Trendon and his family.

Sallie grabbed Trendon's hand and took him back into the pastor's study. She noticed the special ring he was wearing. "That's an interesting ring you're wearing. Does it represent anything?" asked Sallie.

Trendon said not a mumbling word. Sallie rolled her eyes at Trendon and said, "You better not make one mistake or I will take you out myself. I put you in here. I will take you out."

Sallie walked out and left Trendon standing there in awe.

25

Trendon's Preparations

Trendon got up out of bed after his alarm clock woke him up at 5 o'clock a.m. He wanted to get a head start on preparing for the new position of being the new pastor of The Comfort Zone. Trying not to wake up his wife Kelly he tiptoed to the bathroom. As he went into the bathroom Greed, False Doctrine and Arrogance appeared in the den. The imps were delighted to be there to prepare Trendon for his new adventure. Trendon walked into the den. Trendon walked over to his navy blue duffle bag and pulled out ten candles and a black book, pen and paper and set them on the coffee table. After he lit the ten candles he knelt down in front of the candles. Greed moved and stood behind Trendon. Then he placed both of his hands on his shoulders and pressed down on them. Trendon felt this intense pressure on both of his shoulders and placed his left hand on his right shoulder to massage it. Unknowingly Trendon put his hand on top of Greed's hand. Greed smiled.

False Doctrine flew over to Trendon and stood on the right of him. Trendon felt this chill come all over his entire body. Greed led him to turn to the first chapter. He opened the book to the beginning and he began to read the first paragraph.

"To be a part of the Lither organization one must promise to adhere by the rules and regulations that are governed by the founding members of so said organization."

Trendon smiled.

"It is your sole purpose to enlightened mankind to believe that there is only one true god and all other religious teachings are false."

"The human race only needs one god, one true religious leader, one ecumenical system and one government economic system in place. It is your job as a member to recruit the elite and the ignorant. Also as a member of so said organization it is your responsibility to hold all power in the position that you possess. And with so said power you are only to dictate orders. You do not take orders. If the world would just embrace this concept the world would be a better place. It is your duty as a member of this great organization to implement all so said teachings that were mentioned above to see this theory reach the world."

All of the imps smiled and breathed fire from their nostrils.

Greed pressed down even harder on Trendon's shoulders and whispered in his left ear, "It is your job to stress the importance of a one world order," demanded Greed.

"Ouch," yelled Trendon. "Why are my shoulders killing me?" he wondered.

Then Greed stood back behind Trendon and False Doctrine shrunk down to the size of a pinky finger and grabbed Trendon's right ear and he began to speak.

"These are the things you will be executing at The Comfort Zone." Trendon felt some great ideas come to his mind. He began to write these things down.

1. I will be their dictator not their pastor.

2. I will only surround myself with the elite and the ignorant. I must stay away from confrontation. Do not let anyone challenge me. If I come to a situation such as this ignore, fight back or obliterate the one causing me discomfort.

"Perfect," stated False Doctrine squeezing Trendon's ear. The other imps nodded in agreement.

"Don't worry Trendon, our boss will give us the strength to see those things through," said Greed.

Trendon picked up his pen and started writing again.

3. I am only to focus on unity. Don't let anyone think for themselves. *"You know the saying if two individuals are thinking exactly alike someone is not thinking."* Trendon said to himself. Good because this is what I am trying to accomplish. The parishioners should not think but only to worship me. I'll think for them.

4. Go after the people's money so you can support the Lither organization, and live the lavish lifestyle you want to live.

Trendon looked down on the page and he especially liked reading what he saw next. Then he paraphrased it for his new position.

5. Don't talk about the God of the Bible; this will put a strain on your leadership. It is my sole purpose to deprogram my new congregation, to only listen to me.

False Doctrine was so excited that he bit Trendon's ear in excitement. "Awe, S***," yelled Trendon holding his ear.

Greed blew fire from his nostrils and Arrogance's chest puffed out with pride.

Trendon looked down at the bottom of the page and saw the organizations symbol. Then he smiled. There were stars surrounded by the crescent moon that were at the bottom of the page showing the authenticity of the book. Trendon got off of his knees and walked back over to his duffel bag and pulled out his ring box. He opened it and pulled out his ring symbolizing that he was a member of the Lither organization. Then he put the ring on his pinky finger next to his wedding ring on his left hand.

"That's it wear the ring proudly," commanded Greed.

False Doctrine grabbed Trendon's ear and pinched it real hard. Trendon yelled.

False Doctrine yelled in Trendon's ear, "Say the chant."

"Wait," said Arrogance.

Arrogance jumped inside of Trendon.

Trendon had the urge to chant so he began to say, "One true god, one dictator, one religious leader, one ecumenical system and one economic system, this is all we need," he kept saying over and over for a straight hour without taking a breather.

The imps in the room grew bigger and stronger.

After he finished chanting he blew out the candles, and placed the black book back into his duffle bag. He was feeling a little on edge. He knew exactly what to do in order to get rid of this feeling that was making him feel so uncomfortable. He walked over to the mini fridge and removed five small bottles of Scotch walked over to the sofa and drank them straight. Trendon still felt on edge. So he went back to the mini fridge. He noticed that all of the

Scotch bottles were gone so he pulled out five small bottles of Vodka and drank them. He turned on the television to the news and fell asleep on the sofa.

"This young man is certainly going to get the job done," stated Greed.

"Yes he will. Since Arrogance is inside of him nothing will stop him," answered False Doctrine.

"Greed keep in mind that I will surround them at all times. I must make sure that he fulfills our master's plan. As you know we don't want to disappoint him," stated False Doctrine.

Ashshod appeared in the room.

"What are you doing here? This is no place for holiness," demanded Greed.

"I can come and go whenever I want. You have no control over me," replied Ashshod.

Greed yelled and Ashshod drew his sword. Greed blew fire from his nostrils and Ashshod blocked the flames with his sword. False Doctrine grew in size and snuck up behind Ashshod. Ashshod turned around swiftly after smelling the stench of sulfur from behind him. He saw False Doctrine in his peripheral vision trying to side swipe him. Ashshod knocked him out of the room with the smack of his might and sword.

"Aww", yelled False Doctrine.

"How dare you come in here and hurt False Doctrine," screamed Greed.

"How dare you plan this unthinkable scheme," yelled Ashshod.

"Ashshod listen to me and you listen to me very clearly, I will get you and your little puppet Juan that you are overseeing. Trust me. Trendon will get the many souls that we are wanting," demanded Greed.

Ashshod said not a word.

Greed looked over towards Trendon and said, "My job is accomplished here." Then he vanished from the room.

Ashshod shook his head and flew over towards Trendon shook his head again and left.

Hours later Greed appeared in the room. He noticed Trendon was still knocked out on the sofa. Greed took the opportunity to use subliminal messages while he was asleep.

"I need for you to go see Juan Cortez," Greed kept repeating to Trendon.

Trendon began to toss and turn on the sofa. A loud commercial came on and awakened Trendon from his sleep.

Trendon said to himself, *"I must go see Pastor Juan Cortez."*

Greed smiled and said, "Oh you must," then he vanished from the room.

Trendon spent the rest of his day with his family.

26

Juan Meets Trendon

Juan was sitting in his room watching television, finishing his lunch, and enjoying the bright sunny day. He was waiting for Joyce. He knew she went shopping but did not know how soon she would arrive. Ashshod and Greed appeared in the room. As Juan was watching a religious program, a young man walked into his room. He walked up to Juan's bed and said, "Hello."

"Hello," Juan replied.

"I'm Trendon Palmer the new pastor of The Comfort Zone. I wanted to meet you. Deacon Smith told me that at one time you were the greatest and it's very nice to finally meet you."

Juan looked Trendon up and down as if he were a robot scanning him. He noticed that Trendon was well dressed and that he wore a strange ring on his pinky finger next to his wedding ring. It was silver trimmed in gold with a crescent moon surrounded by diamond stars. Trendon noticed Juan looking at him hard as if he had stolen the ring. He politely placed both of his hands in his pockets.

"Don't let him start any trouble, Ashshod," Greed said.

"What's wrong, Greed? You can't handle the action?" asked Ashshod.

"I'm not worried you nincompoop," replied Greed.

"Then shut up and listen to what Juan has to say."

Greed blew fire from his mouth and the imps in the room started to jump and hiss.

Juan said, "So, young man, do you agree with the former pastor's tactics?"

"Yes sir I do. I believe that the late Pastor Marco Pablo had some of the most outstanding ideas."

"Trendon is your name, correct?"

"Yes, you are correct."

"Since you believe in the late Marco Pablo's theology what will you be bringing to the table may I ask?"

"I'm glad that you asked. Well I'll take some of that 'Old Time Religion' and mix it up with the 'New Age Movement' and put it all together and you get what one will call 'Freedom of Religion'."

"Did you actually make a ridiculous statement like that?"

"I don't know about *ridiculous* but I just made that *profound* statement." Trendon smiled.

Juan just shook his head in disgust.

"You know nowadays pastor, people just want to feel good on the inside and all I need to do is just motivate them. It is my job just to inspire them. They don't go to the place of worship to learn about God or grow in Him so I don't deal with those areas. The very last thing people want is to feel convicted for their actions or wrongdoings. But if I were to deal with the issues of growing in God or making individuals feel convicted of their actions the pews of my mega church would be empty, and I want be able to afford the gorgeous house I want to live in. So I don't teach it, and I want allow it. You get what I'm saying?" Trendon winked his eye and let out a chuckle.

I can see that this is going to be a visit that should not have happened. Juan said to himself.

"Young man why did you feel the need to meet me?"

"Like I said, I wanted to meet one of the greats."

"Trendon there are so many questions I need for you to answer for me."

"Go ahead Pastor. Just ask me."

"So young man are you on this prosperity kick as well?" asked Juan.

"Yes, I believe it's the only way to go."

"Why is it always the pastors and preachers with the money and expensive material possessions always telling the underprivileged to obtain farfetched unrealistic desires?" asked Juan. "Why are you setting people up?"

"How and why would you say I am doing this prosperity thing? It could mean numerous things. What makes you think I'm setting people up?" asked Trendon.

"Because prosperity in the Bible is completely different than what is being taught in today's society. Prosperity biblically means to walk in the will of God and allowing God to give the person the desires of their heart based on their walk in Him. Prosperity today means challenging God to prove Himself by being a genie and giving individuals the desires of their hearts even if it's against His will."

"Well son, if a person is walking it might not be in God's permissive will for him to have a luxury car. They can go from walking everywhere then God can allow them to afford an express bus pass. This is prosperity; they went from walking to riding the city bus. But you won't teach this because it makes too much sense." "Like I stated earlier it's just a setup."

"Now pastor why do you keep making such a statement?" asked Trendon sarcastically.

"That's because people are too stupid to realize that this is a tactic that pastors use to keep the pews filled. I can't help it that people are too stupid to figure this out." *"This is why I love to deal with individual's emotions* Trendon said to himself underneath his breath." Then he chuckled to himself.

Juan looked right through Trendon. He knew Trendon was caught like a deer in headlights. Trendon remained silent. He would not answer Juan.

"That's right Trendon. You don't answer to him. Who does he think he is? That piece of trash," yelled Greed.

"That's right. You will use any gimmick to draw in the crowd and if you could you would pull a rabbit out of a hat just to amaze the people to keep them running to those seats," stated Juan.

"He is so right, Trendon said to himself, because at times I might get a tough crowd." He started giggling to himself.

"He knows I'm right, Juan said to himself."

"You are one that will tell the people that the Lord told you to tell them to take their McDonald's paycheck and go to a Maserati car dealership and get that car. What a ridiculous setup and there are people like yourself that do this all over the world. And you wonder why people lose their faith and hope in God. God is no genie. You don't rub the Bible and think you get your wish granted," explained Juan.

"Well pastor it works for me and no one is getting hurt by it. The Bible does say ask," replied Trendon.

Juan turned and looked at the wall.

"Why are you looking at the wall pastor?" asked Trendon.

"Because I will have a better conversation with it rather then what's coming out of your mouth. Boy you are the most conceited, cocky, and arrogant individual I have ever meet."

"I am none of those things. I'm just sure of myself."

"That's what you call it?"

"Yes, it's called confidence."

"No, it's called stop it. It's not a good look on you. Oh you also teach name it and claim it too, right?"

"Why yes I do."

"Stop it. It is not biblical. There is nothing in the Bible that teaches on this subject matter, name it and claim it, but the Bible teaches us The Ten Commandments which will certainly destroy this sort of teaching," stated Juan.

"How would the Ten Commandments destroy this sort of teaching?" asked Trendon.

"Whenever a person considers himself naming and claiming something it allows the person to place a person, place, or object in the place of God. Their only focus will be what they are acquiring. And if you know anything about God you know He will never allow anyone to put Him second! Don't you know you would be coveting what you want, a person, job, money, house, or car? This is why nothing such as this is mentioned in the Bible, because it's against God's will. This is also why we are to ask for God's permissive will to be done in our lives. If we would have it our way, we will do it the way you are teaching it, the wrong way. See, I know you don't want to teach the truth because it's too sound."

"Now I know you're 'old school' talking about The Big Ten," said Trendon.

"The Big Ten?" asked Juan.

"Yes, the Ten Commandments. That's what we call them nowadays," answered Trendon.

"How ridiculous," replied Juan.

"As you know pastor no one even considers The Big Ten to have any validity today. Better yet the concept is a complete joke. How many people do you know follows them?" asked Trendon.

"The ones who fears the Almighty God," answered Juan. "Trendon this is simply nonsense. You should think clearly before you speak," answered Juan.

"Oh I'm thinking very clearly, and I'm very levelheaded. The problem with you is that you want me to be caught up in those pre-historic, outdated relic documents you consider the truth," replied Trendon smiling devilish.

"I'm just looking at how wretched you are," stated Juan.

"No you're wretched you piece of mud," yelled Greed.

"Of course you would consider me to be wretched because I live and react to today's standards," stated Trendon.

"You can just stop right here! I certainly heard enough of your theory on this subject," demanded Juan.

"Nope. It still works for me. I will not change my theology. I will continue to teach on both of these subject matters, prosperity and name it and claim it."

"I feel so sorry for pastors and preachers such as yourself on judgment day standing in front of the Bema seat. You will certainly have to answer for this.

"The Lord will be thanking me for opening the eyes of the lost pastor," answered Trendon.

"Trendon stop," yelled Juan. "Young man, you don't need to teach false doctrine. Cut it out." "Do you believe that there is a Hell?"

"No!"

"How can you explain this?" asked Juan.

"Well sir, I know that this will be very difficult for you to understand because you are 'old school'. Where do I begin?"

"I think it's best for you to start at the beginning."

"See Hell is a place that examines the negative behaviors of human beings; it is just a state of mind. A loving God will not send His creation to Hell because we are made after His image so He will not do this."

"Pastor you do understand that this is the new trend and I'm going to take full advantage of this new trend, the nonexistence of Hell, and I really believe it's the truth," explained Trendon.

"What?"yelled Juan.

As Juan was looking at Trendon he noticed that whenever Trendon felt as if he had made a profound statement he would wear this big grin on his face.

"As the humans would say, Boy this guy is simply wonderful," stated Greed.

"Some things just doesn't require a response," answered Ashshod as he shook his head.

"Young man, do you know the serious implications of what you are doing to God's creation?"

"No because I'm not doing anything wrong."

"Trendon you are leading people straight to Hell in a hand-basket."

"You have your opinion pastor and I have mine, but please keep in mind that my opinion is more valid because it fits in society today. There are more case studies that prove that Hell does not exist."

"Man I feel my lunch about to come back up."

"Pastor that won't be necessary. I see that you have a hard

time dealing with the truth. A lot of people can't handle the truth."

"Oh I can handle the truth when I hear it."

"Hell is not real and people need to stop acting as if it's real," demanded Trendon.

Juan looked at Trendon with disgust in his eyes and underneath his breath he said, "Lord please forgive me because I'm about to lose my patience right about now. Now I know exactly what I am dealing with, a pure lunatic. I'm about to turn into Batman and knock that conniving, deceitful, hideous Joker grin right off his face!" Juan immediately repented of his sins. He waited a couple of seconds before he spoke then he took a deep breath, inhaled, exhaled, and said, "What would Jesus think about you teaching this rubbish?"

"Pastor, Jesus was not considered God to me. He was just a great leader. He led great examples that the Bible conveys to us. We are all sons and daughters of God. He was just one of them."

"You keep telling yourself that Sherlock."

"Roger that."

"I see that you disagree with Genesis1:26, Isaiah 9:6, John 1:1, John1:14, John 3:16-17 and Romans 10:9," quoted Juan.

"Pastor just stop. You're wasting your time. You tell the old folks about those old Scriptures. They don't fit my lifestyle nor my philosophy."

"These passages of Scriptures, informs of that Jesus is God," explained Juan.

"So you say," replied Trendon.

"You're acting like an idiot," stated Juan. Then he sighed loudly.

Trendon chuckled.

"Now back to the subject of Hell, since I was rudely interrupted," stated Trendon.

"You're excused," Juan replied cynically.

"You're starting to bother me pastor," said Trendon pointing his finger and shaking it.

Before Trendon could continue his thought Juan spoke out and said, "Jesus tells us of the parable of the rich man and Lazarus," stated Juan.

"When Jesus was referring to these passages of Scriptures He spoke in parables. You know that parables are earthly stories with heavenly meanings. Jesus just wanted us to stay on the righteous path, that's all. Every time He spoke it was always the same thing, cute little stories for us to stay on track with," explained Trendon.

"Hell is just something that Jesus put into our thought process to allow us to get our acts together. People say that the rich man wasn't a bad person. Was he bad because he had money? Jesus did not inform us that the rich man had malice in his heart. That he mistreated or committed a murder. He was just simply rich. So does he go to Hell because he was rich and Lazarus goes to heaven because he was poor? No! Because it makes no sense at all. So do all rich people go to Hell because they don't want to share their wealth with the poor? The poor has all the same opportunities to become rich like the rich. I can't help it if the poor might be incompetent in learning how to become rich or handle their money. Jesus is saying only the poor gets into heaven. 'No way Jose'. When the Bible talks about Hell it's just a metaphor because Satan and the fallen angels will not get punished and live in a tormented Hell. Once again pastor we are all God's creation."

Juan just looked around the room.

"Trendon you think that you are so intellectual. Parables were often used in biblical times to describe prophetic biblical truth."

"Since you want to talk philosophically Trendon the narcissism of the rich man gave himself gratification. He felt that it wasn't his responsibility to feed the poor begging Lazarus. Also it wasn't because the rich man was rich that warranted him to go to Hell. It was his narcissistic, self-absorbed, vainglorious behavior that accompanied his selfishness, greedy, judging neglectful behaviors and not following the Lord. It is apparently clear that he chose not to follow God. We see this answer because the rich man asked God if he could go back to earth and tell his brothers about God! Rejecting God is the key here with the other attributes that accompanied his characteristics. Pick up your Bible and read it son. It's all in there, the true facts," explained Juan.

Juan looked around the room. "What are you looking for?" asked Trendon.

"Rod Serling because I know that I am in the outer limits because you are saying absolutely nothing that makes any common sense," stated Juan.

"Ashshod shut your puppet up," demanded Greed.

"First of all he's not my puppet, he's God's child," answered Ashshod.

"Shut up talking about Him. He made the stupid beings. How dumb of Him," replied Greed.

"The only dumb thing here is you for making that worthless decision following Lucifer," stated Ashshod.

Greed blew fire from his nostrils and moved away from Ashshod.

"Trendon stop this nonsense before you end up in Hell," yelled Juan.

"I have the right to disagree with you pastor. I know within my precious heart I will not go to Hell," stated Trendon.

"Apparently you don't."

Trendon just smiled.

"Young man where do you get your information from?"

"I heard it from the Bible that we are made after God's own image and you know how great philosophers and scientists have confirmed that Hell is nonexistent. So you must understand that this is the real truth."

"Son so what about the Bible?"

"What about it?"

"Is it the truth to you?"

"Only in some ways not all the way because it is very outdated. See I know you can't grasp this new concept because you are very old."

"Young man I am more hip then you think I am," said Juan.

"I see you have a lot to say. What are you a walking Bible or something?"

"I just have the Word of God hidden in my heart."

"As I stated I don't believe in the Bible in its entirety."

"Well you should. All Scriptures are inspired by God, 2Timothy 3:16-17, 1Peter1:21, John 10:35, Matthew 5:18 and 1Timothy 5:18," quoted Juan.

"Look pastor, I see that you are certainly on a roll right now but this doesn't pertain to my teaching."

"It should because we as Christians need to watch out for individuals such as yourself with all this false doctrine of the wicked, 2Peter 3:17-18," quoted Juan.

"Whoa! Pastor I'm not here for Bible study."

"Oh yes you are. Because of what you just said to me you definitely need Bible study."

"It saddens me pastor that you feel this way about my teaching."

"No it saddens me that you actually believe the deceptive philosophy you are teaching."

"Listen man, I am not here to argue with you. You have your own opinion and I have mine."

"Listen young man, this is not my own opinion. This is just God's unadulterated Word. Now you will continue to listen. Hell is real. That 'wishy washy' crap you are trying to dish out to society needs to cease. Let me tell you young man; you are on the road to destruction. Trust me."

"Pastor Cortez, again I hear you but man you are just so 'old school'. You can't even hear yourself it's so old," said Trendon.

All Juan could do was shake his head while this young man kept talking to him.

"What is your theory of the Holy Spirit?"

"Well I believe it's a separate entity from God. It's a spiritual gift from God. I believe it can think."
"Wait it?" "You're calling the Holy Spirit an it?"

"Yes! It's a thing, it's not a being or an object. It's just a thing."

"Young man the Holy Spirit is God the third person of the Godhead."

"Pastor as I stated before I don't teach that old doctrine,"

"Son you must recognize the Holy Spirit is God. Look in the book of Acts 5:1-4. He is just simply God. The Holy Spirit is a He, He is not an object.

"Pastor you have your opinion and you are entitled to it."

"No! This is what the unadulterated Word of God tells us."

"Pastor, pastor, pastor."

"Trendon I'm not like those knuckleheads that teach this bumbling nonsense that you're dishing out. I'm not trying to motivate nor give out false doctrine. You're just slopping over God's people. What you're doing is serving bull crap on a shining silver tray and calling it a gourmet dish. Don't you know that people that are in godly positions will be judge on a higher standard? God makes sure of this because people such as yourself will be held accountable for their actions."

"I hate Juan," yelled Greed.

"Is that right?" said Ashshod then he smiled.

Greed hissed at Ashshod.

"I'm not slopping over God's people. I'm just telling them the facts. They don't have to live in the past. Leave those myths and fables alone and those boring Bible stories they grew up with."

"The only myth I hear is the bad terminology that's coming from your mouth. The Bible says, Men will become lovers of themselves and this is referring to you, 2Timothy 3:2. Pick up the Bible and read it," commanded Juan.

"Now pastor you are saying a lot of harsh words to me."

"No I am not. You walked into my hospital room with this nonsense doctrine and think that I'm not going to stand up for the truth which is the unadulterated Word of God!"

"I just proved my point. You are just 'old school'."

"Your entire belief system is totally against the Word, will and actions of God."

Trendon just shook his head.

"I must finish this discussion on the subject matter concerning the Holy Spirit being God. The Holy Spirit created the world and us humans if you didn't know. Genesis 1:2 and Genesis 1:26, He brings things back to our remembrance and He teaches, John 14:26 The Holy Spirit orders our steps, Romans 8:14. The problem with you is that you associate yourself with individuals that believe in false doctrine and nonsense. You're not used to hearing the truth because it's been fabricated in your ears for so long. That's why you surround yourself with ignorant gullible people and weak Christians that are too lazy to pick up the infallible Word of God for themselves. This is how you flourish because they walk in darkness."

"Now pastor, don't get yourself all worked up over my doctrine."

Juan closed his eyes for a moment. He could not stand the sight of Trendon. So he said a little prayer.

"Pastor you had your say. I will have mine. The Holy Spirit is not God. I see that you are working with the trinity doctrine. This doesn't fit my beliefs, the three in one theory. NO! Not for me. I believe that it gives out spiritual gifts but is not God as I stated earlier. I believe it works for God. That is what it does." Trendon put the biggest grin on his face.

"Ugh," said Juan. "Trendon, I am going to go out on a limb. So are you one of these people that believe one can lose and regain the Holy Spirit since He works for God?" asked Juan.

"Yes I do believe this."

"How do you explain this, young man?"

"Well it's quite simple really. When an individual sins, the Holy Spirit leaves the believer because it cannot dwell in a place full of sin. It can't work its spiritual gifts through the sinner. When the believer repents of their sins then the believer can regain the Holy Spirit because he is now cleansed. You see it is very simple, the Holy Spirit is just doing its job."

"Trendon I'm going to need for you to stop referring to the Holy Spirit as a thing," stated Juan.

"No you will not dictate to me on how I should respond to you," answered Trendon.

"Umm," said Juan then he moaned.

"Trendon, how in the world did you come up with that ridiculous nonsense?" Juan asked, exasperated. "There is not a passage of Holy Scriptures that could back that bull up. Once a believer is saved, the Holy Spirit stays inside of the believer. Even if the believer sins, the Holy Spirit would never leave the believer. The Holy Spirit would not be active as He normally is because of sin, but He is still present in the life of the believer. Once the believer repents of his sins, He would be active again. Not one time did I mention that one can lose nor regain the Holy Spirit."

"Well sir, you have your point of view, and I have mine, and mine stands for the truth," replied Trendon.

Juan caught himself becoming more annoyed with all the rubbish Trendon was saying.

"So Trendon you believe that sin does exist?"

"Of course I do. I believe that man does wrong and I agree to call it sin meaning wrong doing of an behavioral act. I also believe that man will die but I don't believe that after they die they will go to a burning Hell."

"So let me get this straight you believe that because of man's wrongdoings which is called sin leads to death?"
"Correct," replied Trendon.

"But you don't believe that sin leads people to Hell especially if they don't accept Jesus Christ as their Lord and Savior?"

"That is correct. Give this fine man a prize," Trendon said mockingly.

"If this is the case, I'll want you to stop talking preposterously; I guess this will not happen." Then Juan put a big grin on his face.

"Ha ha very funny," replied Trendon.

"See, I know just how to pick them," said Greed.

"I don't think that you do, Greed," replied Ashshod.

"Shut up, Ashshod,"

"You are one sick, sad imp."

"So I see," said Juan. "So young man, do you feel that it is in your best interest to teach this false doctrine? I have another question."

"Okay."

"I know that you said you don't believe in Jesus Christ as your personal Lord and Savior. So what do you put in place of this time of service," What do you do?

"Nothing!"

"Nothing?" asked Juan.

"Yes because it's not necessary. All are welcomed and I don't believe in Hell. So why stress individuals out with nonsense like accepting Jesus Christ as their personal Lord and Savior? It's not practical."

Juan slapped his forehead with his right hand. His mouth gapped wide opened. He was completely speechless. He could not believe how the Word of God had been diluted to fit the needs of the people today.

"Listen Trendon, you must look at John Three 3:16-17. God sent His Son so humans would not be separated from Him and live eternally in a burning Hell. Jesus is the only way to stop this from happening, 2Thessalonians 1:9."

"Oh so you say?"

"No I'm not saying this, it's in the Bible."

"Pastor please stop. Your information it's useless to me."

"Boy I will finish what I need to tell you on the subject of Hell. The only reason you don't teach the truth about the serious subject of Hell its because you enjoy living the way that you're living. Young man if your name is not written in the Lamb's Book of Life you will go to Hell stated in Revelation 20:15."

"Man my name is in that book. Just because I don't agree with your theology it doesn't mean I'm not in it."

"If Jesus Christ is not your Lord and Savior your name would not be put in the Lamb's Book of Life."

"Once again blah blah blah."

"You can mock me all you want but remember you will learn the hard way when you end up in Hell."

"I will not go to Hell pastor."

"Son you need to pick up the Bible and read Revelation chapter 21:8, Matthew 25:41. Matthew chapter 25:46 and don't forget the Bible talks about worms festering in and out of one's body when one goes to Hell, Mark 9:48. Because you are so arrogant you fall in the area of Romans 1:24-32 and Romans chapter 2:1-29. You need to watch yourself son."

"I need not to watch a thing old man."

"Wow the cockiness you display."

"Wow the old outdated theology you taught. No wonder they wanted to get rid of you."

"They chose Marco because I could not be there."

"Pastor so sorry to say this I'm so glad you're not in the pastoral position at the Comfort Zone. Because now the people can really hear the truth," said Trendon and then he smiled.

"Oh you leading people straight to Hell is what these innocent people need to hear? Hell is a very bad place. They need to hear that it does exist."

"Not under my watch. They will not hear any nonsense pertaining to Hell existence."

"You are so pathetic Trendon."

"No that's you old man.

"Once again Trendon, Jesus is the key out of Hell," stated Juan.

"No, the key is the Kingdom of God. This is why we need to stop talking about Jesus," answered Trendon.

"What delusional irrational nonsense are you spewing out of your mouth. The only way to God's Kingdom is through Jesus Christ. John 14:6 look it up," demanded Juan.

"No the Kingdom is the key! Jesus is blocking people from getting in. This is the sole purpose. I don't believe He's God and our answer to forgiveness of sin," explained Trendon.

Juan twisted up his face. Then he began to speak. "Trendon you are so farfetched with your beliefs. The things you believe and teach are pure entertainment. It has no validity and it brings no contradictions to their behaviors. This is why you love to teach it."

"No pastor, the reason why I teach it because it's the truth," answered Trendon.

"You're no different than Jim Jones, David Koresh, and the many other lunatics out there teaching false doctrine," explained Juan.

"I'm nothing like them," replied Trendon.

"You keep telling yourself that. The only difference between you and them is you look the part," stated Juan.

"I'll take that compliment; it's the only good thing that's came out of your mouth since I got here," answered Trendon. Then he smiled.

There goes that stupid smile again Juan said to himself.

"Pastor once again we will agree to disagree," stated Trendon.

"Yeah blame me for telling the truth and teaching you the truth about God the Heavenly Father, Jesus Christ, the Holy Spirit and Hell."

"Oh you're excused," Trendon said sarcastically.

Juan looked away from Trendon and said a silent prayer to himself.

"Ashshod I am going to kill Juan," stated Greed.

"I don't think so Greed," replied Ashshod.

"Oh I promise you this. I will get Juan. I really loathe this good for nothing jerk," said Greed.

"Watch yourself Greed," demanded Ashshod.

With the words barely escaping Juan lips, he said, "So baptism is out of the question?"

"No, I will perform it. It's always one lost soul who wants to do this. So we just go through the motions. I don't have any specific Sunday or a day of the week where I perform baptisms. The individual requesting this act will call and set it up, but I will not break my neck to see it through.

"I know that baptism doesn't save you. But it shows the outward obedience to the Lord and to other Christians that you have joined the Kingdom of God," stated Juan.

"Now you're getting it. Out with the old and in with the new," said Trendon then he smiled.

"No! Don't get it twisted," demanded Juan.

Trendon smiled so big that this time he was showing all of his teeth. If he opened his mouth wider you could see his tonsils.

Juan rolled his eyes.

"Now pastor I don't baptize but I will be making the parishioners brand the barcode symbol on their bodies to represent the unity of our faith and that they are members of The Comfort Zone," stated Trendon.

"What? You are totally crazy," stated Juan.

"No this barcode symbolizes the unity of god and man. This barcode will allow the world to know that Hell doesn't exists and that when you get this symbol your eternal destination will surely be in heaven," answered Trendon.

"I think not! Yahweh will not allow this. First of all the Bible describes the total opposite about the barcode in Revelation 13:18 It describes the symbols of the mark of the beast which is the antichrist. Any human being that receives this mark or symbol, depending what it would looks like, will certainly spend eternity in Hell. What you are doing is grooming them for Hell," explained Juan.

"No what I am doing is teaching my people that the old ways of following God is strictly traditional, nonsense and it needs to cease," replied Trendon.

"You have people fooled by the diluted information influenced by emotions and false doctrine," yelled Juan.

"Pastor Cortez you are getting yourself all worked up over nothing. Listen to me. Everything is going to be alright. The people are in good hands, mine." Then he put the biggest joker grin on his face.

"How are these innocent people in good hands when you are deliberately leading them straight to Hell. There is no way in the world that you have God's creation's best interest. You only have yours. You love the power, fame; and fortune and you will do whatever it takes to keep it. That includes destroying the lives of others for your gratification. You really need JESUS!" explained Juan.

"Well pastor that's not going to happen. I refuse to serve another human who can do the same things that I can do for myself," answered Trendon.

"And what is that?" asked Juan.

"Save souls," replied Trendon.

"Trendon, please stop talking because you can't save anyone. You can't even save yourself. Give your life to Jesus. Only he can save and heal a sinned sick soul," explained Juan.

"No I can do that myself," answered Trendon Seriously.

"Trendon I will certainly be praying for you. I have witnessed to you about God the Heavenly Father, Jesus Christ our Lord and Savior, and the Holy Spirit. I informed you of God's truth through His flawless Word. Jesus is the only answer to God. I am so sorry to hear that you teach this rubbish. You are like so many popular television evangelists. You teach false doctrine just to get the numbers and the popularity. The vanity in your heart saddens me. You have no room for God, just Satan's tactics."

"Now I get it." Juan snapped his fingers. "You're a part of that Lither organization. This is why you are so arrogant because those forces of evil allows you to feel empowered and they promise to protect you and make you a big star."

Trendon said to himself *"I will not entertain this subject."* Then he flinched.

"I see that I hit a nerve of yours?

Trendon slowly lifted both of his hands and grabbed his head turning it from side to side cracking it. He then at the same time cracked both of his knuckles and gritted his teeth.

Juan raised his right eyebrow.

"Are you threatening me son?"

Trendon said not a mumbling word.

Juan kept watching him closely and continued to speak.

He said to himself *"What does he think he's about to do? I know he doesn't think he's about to punch me?"* Juan placed his left foot on the floor from his bed giving him some leverage if he had to dodge a blow from Trendon. Then he continued to speak.

"Son you don't scare me. The Holy Spirit who is God in which you don't believe in is allowing me to see straight through you. You don't give a rat's behind about God, His children nor, His Word. The Lither illogical doctrine keeps God's creation in the dark. It keeps you from focusing on God's truth and allows you to focus on the devil's strategies. First, their job is to get rid of Jesus and focus just only on God! Their job is to deprogram society to focus on just one Supreme Being and this is to condition mankind to get ready to serve the antichrist. The Lither organization is making headway by getting rid of Jesus Christ on Christmas day, by substituting individual thoughts with a materialistic mind frame. Limiting Christmas programs mentioning Jesus and putting Santa Claus in the forefront, and when you unscramble those letters up it means exactly what it says Satan Claus is in the mist of it all. You notice that the majority of the horror films comes out Christmas Day."

Trendon moved closer to Juan's bed, gritting his teeth even harder. Juan slowly lifted his body off the bed leaving him with no other choice but to stand. Their eyes locked. They stood at this position for a good 15 seconds. The emergency page from the intercom asking Nurse Glynda to come to the nurse's station broke their stare. Nurse Glynda passed by Juan's room and as she was walking by she glanced into Juan's room. She noticed that Juan's demeanor was very guarded by the way he was standing as he had company in his room. She could not stop in because she had to hurry to the nurses' station.

Juan stood dead in his tracks and said, "Satan you're rebuked in Jesus's name!"

Trendon stood back, lifted up his nose to avoid the stench of righteousness.

"This conversation is beneath me," stated Trendon.

"Beneath you or not as I stated earlier you walked in here. I did not send for you but as I was saying. Good Friday used to be a time that schools and government organizations were closed for reverencing the death of Jesus Christ for the shedding of His precious holy righteous blood at Calvary on that old rugged cross. Now it's just a regular day. Get rid of Jesus and focus on just one Supreme Being. Get rid of the Trinity theory as well. Let's not forget that things were closed on Sunday. Now everything is open. You can even play the Lottery. And let's not forget to pick up a 40 ounce on the way out the door. The Lither organization that you represent thinks that they are cleverly blinding the eyes of the ignorant. Don't be mistaken. There are a few of us that the Lord is using to make us aware of what's going on. Get rid of godly morals and replace it with liberalism."

"You have well-known television evangelists that don't believe in the Trinity. They have this set up correctly by putting unbelieving so- called spiritual leaders in the driver's seat. And boy are they doing their jobs correctly by neglecting the truth and replacing it with baloney. How sad."

"Fortunately I see that the financial world is in shambles not because of our money crisis but because of that organization that you work for. It is setting things up to make sure that the world just uses one form of currency. They are very clever by using companies to take nosedives. Well you have to prepare this world for that great dictator that's coming and it's not Jesus! This one world currency is moving favorably in their way because the hardcore dictators are dead and gone and not a threat to their crafty plans. The ones that are left are in place. They are not a threat. They were put in due to politics. They are a part of this deviant plan. They are to go along with the flow."

Trendon took two giant steps towards Juan bed slapped his hand on the bed, and said, "You shut your dirty mouth" then he started to growl.

Trendon grunted louder.

"Now I think I have seen it all, a grown man growling," Juan said to himself.

"Ashshod I told you to shut that old worthless piece of dirt up," yelled Greed.

"No!" answered Ashshod.

"Well if you won't shut him up, I will." Greed blew fire from his mouth toward Juan's face. Ashshod immediately took his sword and blocked the fiery flames. He pushed Greed up against the wall, pinning him so he could not move.

Juan suddenly felt hot flashes come upon his body, especially his face. Sweat just poured down his forehead. He picked up one of his napkins off his lunch tray and started patting the sweat from his face. Trendon looked at him with a smile on his face wondering what was going on with Juan but did not ask.

The imps in the room began to hiss uncontrollably.

Juan hesitated for a moment but he wasn't going to let this young conceited control freak intimidate him. He continued to speak.

"With the fame you were offered I see that you took that ticket to Hell for the price of it. What did the Lither organization promise you? The spotlight? Your 15 minutes? Since you like to wear that big grin on your face you will certainly not have a problem smiling for the camera. Say Cheese."

Trendon shook his head in disgust.

"You better let me go Ashshod," demanded Greed.

"I will not!"

"I will make him suffer because you are playing the tough bodyguard."

Ashshod pressed Greed up against the wall harder and Greed surprised Ashshod by calling on Satan for more power. In an instance Satan gave Greed the power to grow in strength and height. Greed knocked Ashshod across the room and he became discombobulated. This allowed Greed to think quickly by blowing fire from his mouth, hitting Juan dead center in his chest. Juan grabbed his chest and let out a yell. "Ouch," he said over and over. Nurse Glynda came running into Juan's room. She heard him all the way down the hall. Sweat was just pouring down Juan's face. His entire body was drenched. She noticed that he kept holding his chest.

"It hurts Nurse Glynda Oh it hurts," Juan kept saying repetitively.

Nurse Glynda put Juan back into bed having him to lay down.

Trendon smiled as he watched Juan unpleasantly in pain.

Nurse Glynda asked Trendon to step to the side as she checked on Juan's vitals.

Greed looked at Ashshod, "I told you to stay out of my way."

Ashshod pulled out his sword but would not use it and stared at Greed.

"What's wrong Ashshod? You scared?"

Ashshod's eyes began to glow. "I was informed it's not time to deal with you."

Nurse Glynda got Juan settled down and she asked Trendon to leave.

Trendon walked over to Juan's bed.

"Well sir, I need for you to understand I am in charge now; your time has come and gone." He leaned over and patted Juan on the top of his head. "Now all you need to do is rest. It was nice meeting you, and you take care."

"See Ashshod, you know this young man is just right. He understands how to reach and teach the people. This is why we have him," said Greed.

"Greed as usual you speak out of ignorance," replied Ashshod.

"Well you view it your way Ashshod but I am correct. I must go now. I don't want to waste any more of my time here. I have already lost a lot of my brain cells like the humans would say by listening to your puppet grueling theology. Goodbye you loser," said Greed. The imp Greed left the room and shadowed Trendon.

Hours went by. Juan felt much better. He buzzed the nurses' station asking for permission to get out of bed. Dr. Casper entered into Juan's room, examined him, and gave him the okay to move around but not to overexert himself.

Joyce was smiling as she entered the rehabilitation center to see her beloved. When she walked into Juan's room, she found him on his knees beside a chair in the corner of the room.

She raced to him, fear rushing through her body. "Juan," she yelled, kneeling beside him. "What's wrong? Are you OK?"

He turned to her, his face calm, his eyebrow lifted. For a moment, he hated that he was ever placed in the hospital.

Over time, he found Joyce had turned from a strong, laughing woman to someone who grew concerned and nervous every time Juan showed a smidgen of emotion.

"I am *very* OK, honey," he said. "I'm praying. This is how we do it, remember?"

She swatted his arm, embarrassment creeping across her face. "Yes, smarty pants. I remember. Anything in particular you're praying about?"

"Trendon." Slowly, Juan stood then sat in the chair. He came to see me this afternoon. I know God brought him here."

Try as she might, Joyce could not hide the fear that evaded her. "What did *he* want?"

"Same nonsense as Marco spewed. It's like they want me to agree with their false teachings. Like having me believe their mess would somehow legitimize their beliefs. I don't ask them to come. That boy doesn't even *know* me, so I have no idea why he came. But I do know one thing."

"What's that?"

"God is stirring my spirit. All of this…it's not good. It's horrible, and God wants me in the midst of it. Somehow, I think. I'm supposed to help."

"You *are* helping, sweetie," Joyce said, rubbing Juan's hand. "You are the strongest prayer warrior I know."

"But it's bigger than prayer. I feel it, Joyce. Solid Rock is in deep trouble. These newcomers can end up in Hell if they don't receive the truth."

She sighed, troubled.

"I need some more alone time," Juan said, "If that's okay. I need to be back on these knees."

Joyce kissed Juan's cheek and stood. "I'll go get you some coffee and a doughnut."

Juan chuckled. "Like I need it."

"You look just fine," she said. "I'll see you in a little bit." She kissed Juan and left.

Juan went immediately into prayer. "Lord, please put me back on my feet like a fiery flame and with strength of a lion."

27

Trendon, the New

Leader

The angels and imps were at The Comfort Zone in full force, eagerly waiting to see what was going to transpire.

Rachael, Joyce, Lisa, and the Tanankas decided to visit The Comfort Zone. They all wanted to see the pastor and how he led service.

The service was as usual, and Trendon walked down the aisle. The entire congregation stood to their feet. He took his seat in the pulpit and everyone applauded. Trendon looked over at his wife Kelly and they smiled at each other. The choir rendered two selections and then he took the microphone.

Trendon stood behind the podium and he began to sing. "You gonna to make me love somebody else if you keep on treating me the way you do...whew." The congregation did not know how to handle this because it was a secular song.

"Just wait until you see what we have planned starting today," said Greed.

Ashshod looked at Greed and then he looked at Hunter and nodded; Hunter nodded back. Greed just looked on with perplexity on his face.

Trendon started to talk and Hunter took his sword and damaged the entire sound system.

"What is wrong with that bubbling idiot?" said Greed. He threw a flame of fire at Hunter.

Hunter dodged the fire flame. Then he turned and looked at Greed.

"Do not go after him, not now," replied Ashshod.

"What's wrong, you puppet? Why won't you fight back? You can only move on command? You sick little dog. I hate you dumb angels. You are good for nothing and you are pests," said Greed.

Trendon said, "I guess we don't have any more sound, so I'm going to do the best I can. I need to lay down the ground rules. I like the way that you receive me and I like the entire way service is done. As of today if you wish to speak to me you must submit your request and place them in the boxes that will be placed in the lobby."

Arrogance shook the inside of Trendon and said telepathy, "Go right ahead and say what you need to say."

"What I need for you to do is write down your questions, comments, and concerns, along with your name so I can address you and your questions. Every Sunday I will take five minutes to address your issue, I need for you to know as your leader I need for you to treat me as your god."

The parishioners were silent.

"Let me explain," Trendon continued. "It is a lot to handle and if you treat me with the utmost respect, I then in return can help you. How can I take you to the next level if you don't give me my proper respect?"

Sallie stood to her feet and said, "You are my god!"

Trendon said, "No, I want to be your savior. Let me specify it is still in a form of a god."

Sallie was still standing on her feet. "I understand, savior. We will follow you."

The congregation was still; some did not know what to say. Others just agreed. But Rachael, Joyce, Lisa, and the Tanankas were not amused.

"I also need to inform you; I will be needing all of you members to receive our very special symbol, which is a barcode."

Joyce yelled, "What?"

Parishioners that were sitting around her turned and looked at her as if she was in the wrong. They told her to hush.

"I know you might be asking yourselves why. It's another form of baptism. It will show the world that we are on one accord and that I'm your new savior," explained Trendon.

"This young man is wonderful," stated Greed.

"Yes, he is," replied False Doctrine.

"Just look at the arrogance," answered Arrogance internally.

"Next, because I do not believe in Hell, I will not be teaching or speaking on this issue. It was just a metaphor when it was mentioned. God is a loving God, so I don't believe He would send His creation to Hell."

Arrogance started to expand and he got too heavy for Trendon's insides. Trendon hit his chest and Arrogrance jumped out of him before he could feel the effects of the hits. "Also," Trendon added, "Please do not bring anyone here that wants to question our belief system because we are not of the world."

Then False Doctrine came and stood right beside Trendon and said, "Preach boy, you are saying the right things."

Arrogance kept growing and growing.

Greed said, "So Ashshod, he is really doing a great job, don't you think?"

Ashshod said, "Now this is what you call a puppet."

Greed blew fire from his nostrils.

Trendon said, "I'd also like to say I will not mention the 'saved and the unsaved'. We are all God's children so we are all saved. Calvary happened over two thousand years ago, so we need not to mention it any longer. We are not consumed to the past but rather to the future."

The crowd applauded. Arrogance and False Doctrine began to grow and they became stronger.

"That's it, Trendon, we need your strength and you are really giving it to them. Just stay focused," replied False Doctrine.

Trendon announced that he would be getting rid of the choir; the church only needed a 'praise team'. He knew that some of the members might be disappointed, but this was his decision.

"Also," he said, smiling at the congregation, "I will not speak on the subject of sin. Man has a sinful nature, we all know this, so there is no need to speak on the topic."

The congregation began to applaud while Joyce, Rachael, Lisa, and the Tanankas looked at Trendon as if he were an alien that just fell from the sky.

"This man is a lunatic," said Rachael.

"That's putting it lightly," answered Joyce.

"My last announcement," Trendon continued, "Is directed toward Lisa. We have appreciated her hospitality during this transition."

Lisa offered a tight smile and nod.

Arrogance grew even stronger and taller.

"Kelly," he said, "Will you please stand?" When she stood, he asked, "Doesn't my wife look fine?" The parishioners started to applaud.

"This is a hot mess right here," Joyce said, sucking her teeth.

"Lisa," Trendon said, "We don't need your assistance anymore, so you can sit in the back or the middle of the congregation like everyone else. There is a new first family, in which you are not a part of. You will not sit there starting next Sunday. You are okay for today."

Lisa just sat there with her mouth wide open. Kelly looked at Lisa and smiled.

Joyce had to hold Rachael's arm to keep her from jumping up and racing down the aisle to pummel both Trendon and his wife. Although Trendon had claimed to be nearing the end of his list of 'insanity', he went on for another 30 minutes, astonishing some of the parishioners with his absurd suggestions.

He concluded with, "Whenever there is a fifth Sunday, you will have to give me extra pay because this is not in my contract. The fifth Sunday only comes every once in a while and if I'm speaking on these Sundays I need to get paid."

Greed smiled.

Rachael and Joyce grabbed each other's hands and went into prayer.

Greed said, "Why are they praying?" He summoned imps to go stop Joyce and Rachael's prayer, and Zaso jumped in and knocked them out.

Trendon said, "Now that we have gotten through the formalities, it's time for the words of encouragement." Trendon spoke on the angle of getting what you want; he was explaining that we don't work for God, God works for us. We are to tell God what we want, and God would give us the desires of our hearts.

The congregation started to clap, but Rachael and Joyce could not move at all; they could only shake their heads.

Greed summoned four imps to attack Joyce and Rachael. Two imps jumped on both of them. One of them bit Rachael on the arm and made it swell and then the other one bit her on the leg. Rachael was sitting there itching and watching these bites get red and swollen. Two other imps attacked Joyce, biting her on the back of the neck and on her big toe. Joyce was in so much pain she had to take off her shoe. When she took off her shoe, she had a big bunion on her big toe.

Greed started to laugh.

After service ended, Lisa noticed that Joyce and Rachael were in much pain. Joyce could not walk, and Lisa had to escort Joyce to her car. As they were walking up the aisle, Sallie noticed them and hurried up over to them and said, "We don't want you all here."

Joyce did not pay her any attention. "Let us go. I need to get out of here."

Lisa said, "What happened to you guys?"

"I don't know," Rachael said. "Something bit us."

Lisa asked if they needed her to take them to the hospital, but both Joyce and Rachael insisted they could make it on their own.

"Then I will meet you both there," Lisa said.

While driving Joyce's pain increased.

The imp that bit her followed her, saying, "I will teach you a lesson for praying." He bit her on the same toe again. Joyce screamed because the pain shot up to the back of her neck. The imp was screeching and drooling and said, "Joyce, if you don't stop speaking to God, I am going to hurt you even more."

Joyce was screaming; the pain was so unbearable; she was having so much trouble getting to the hospital, but she finally made it there.

Rachael was having trouble staying focused. She felt as if she was going to lose control while driving; all she could say was, "Lord, please keep me safe." The imp that bit Rachael bit her again. She screamed and she could not move as quickly as she wanted to. It seemed as if it was taking her years to get to the hospital, but she too made it.

Lisa jumped out of her car and saw Joyce hobbling to the entrance.

"Joyce, are you okay?" she asked. "Can you make it into the emergency room?"

"No."

Lisa ran and got a wheelchair for Joyce. On her way to help Joyce, she saw Rachael.

"I'm having trouble staying focused," shouted Rachael.

Lisa ran into the ER and told some nurses to come and get both of them.

Joyce said, "I'm in so much pain."

Rachael vomited all over the parking lot.

The nurses got both of them in the examining rooms. They took their blood pressure and both of them were elevated. They summoned the ER doctor, and it was Dr. Casper and Dr. Writz.

They noticed that the women were slipping in and out of consciousness. They took blood samples and gave them some morphine.

An hour passed before their bloodwork came back. Dr. Casper walked into the examination room that Joyce and Rachael were sharing with just a curtain dividing them. She pulled the curtain back she said, "Joyce, I know you haven't been out of the country."

"I sure haven't," Joyce replied.

"Well your test results showed that you have been bitten by an exotic insect. It left its venom inside of both of you. We must get the antidote quickly and pump your abdominals."

Joyce and Rachael were surprised.

Rachael said, "I will have no problem vomiting."

The imp said, "I told you to stop relying on God. If you both don't, we are going to bite you again."

Hatred and Arrogance showed up in the ER room and Hatred said, "You should have stopped praying to the Lord to change the functions of The Comfort Zone."

Lisa was sitting in between both of them and Dr. Casper came back into the room and told Joyce and Rachael that they had the antidote for them and they would be hospitalized for a week. Dr. Casper said, "I will go up and inform your husband, Joyce. Is this okay with you?"

"Yes thank you," Joyce said in a very quiet voice.

Lisa said, "Rachael, I will call Forest for you and tell him to come up here."

"Thank you, Lisa. I really appreciate you," replied Rachael.

Glynda wheeled Juan to the emergency room. When he saw Joyce, he said, "Joyce, are you all right?"

"Juan, I feel so sick," she replied.

"Rachael, what about you?" asked Juan.

"I'm about to get sick." Rachael vomited all over the floor.

Forest ran in and said, "Mom!" The ER nurse informed Forest of what was going on with his mother and he spoke with Mrs. Cortez and thanked Lisa. Lisa stayed for a little while but she had to go pick up her kids at Sister Kim's house. She said her goodbyes and left.

Juan and Forest were sitting right by their loved ones' side.

"I can put you both in the same room," Dr. Casper said as she sidled up to the group. "It will give us a chance to watch both of you."

Ashshod appeared in the ER room and Hatred and Arrogance said, "Here comes trouble. What do you want, Ashshod?"

"Listen, this is just a little and I mean a little roadblock," stated Ashshod.

Arrogance said, "This is no roadblock. It's just part of our master plan."

"I think you all better rethink your plan because you are going to wish you were never in existence."

Rachael and Joyce were in their room, and Juan and Forest were right by their sides. After they all were situated Juan asked, "What happened?"

Joyce said, "All I can say is Rachael and I were sitting in church and we went into prayer because of all the craziness that new leader was speaking. We got bit right after we began praying."

"Oh what a spiritual warfare we are facing," Rachael said. "Pastor, this warfare is so big that Solid Rock will be going straight to Hell if it doesn't change its path. The sad thing about it is that it looks like the people love what they are going through. The congregation has changed completely."

Joyce said, "Juan, we all really need to pray. Trust me, we all need to pray."

Hatred said, "You know that prayer got you in this position in the first place. So if I were you guys, I would not suggest you do this."

Dr. Casper walked into the room. Forest asked if he could stay with his mother. Dr. Casper said it was okay. She even ordered a little couch for him to sleep on.

That evening, Glynda took Juan back to his room and all he could think about was what Joyce had told him. Glynda administered Juan's medication and made sure that he was in his bed.

Ashshod appeared in the room along with five other no named angels and stood right beside Juan. The imps in Juan's room were hanging on the walls, drooling and hissing. Juan hung his head down and went into prayer, "Dear Heavenly Father, I come to the throne of grace asking that You will please forgive those who have trespassed against me. Lord, I need for You to please step in this situation. The souls of the lost will go straight to Hell if they do not hear Your true words. We need for real leaders to step up and show that they are not afraid to tell the truth."

Greed appeared in Juan's room. "Ashshod, stop this man. Any second he'll go into Scripture."

"I will do no such thing" answered Ashshod.

Greed became so irritated that he charged after Ashshod.

Juan felt bothered in his spirit, but he continued to pray and quote the Scripture.

Greed yelled, "Stop quoting those ridiculous Scripture. They are not going to help you. Not this time."

Juan was becoming more restless, trying to stay focused on his prayer and quoting Scriptures.

Greed said, "I'm going to bring that blood pressure up so high. He hasn't seen anything yet." Greed blew fire from his mouth and he harmed three angels. "Ashshod, I told you worthless angels to stay out of my way. Annihilate these worthless angels."

Alexander's, Ethan's, and Wade's eyes began to glow when they felt Ashshod in trouble. They appeared in the room and noticed that Ashshod and the others were being outnumbered by Satan's imps. Alexander pulled out his sword, flipped in the air, and sliced ten imps in one blow.

Ethan flew fast across the room like a ray of light and blinded the imps in the room and took out twenty imps in one blow. Wade flew down to the ground and walked in slow motion with his eyes bringing forth a bright glare, taking imps out one by one; when he finished he took out thirty imps. Greed summoned Satan to send more imps.

Ashshod broke free from Greed; they both grew taller and stronger. Then Ashshod called over Alexander, Ethan, and Wade. Ashshod nodded, and they grew taller and bigger in might. They all combined their swords together and wiped all of the imps out of the room except for Greed.

Greed looked on with amazement and said, "It's not over you foolish angels." Then Greed vanished.

28

Planning the Big Plan

G reed and the rest of the imps were meeting at the abandoned building.

"It is almost time for us to put our big plan in motion," Greed said. "Now I need for you all to stay focused and to be ready to fight a very mighty battle. You all have been given your assignments, and so far, we are moving in the right direction. We need to finish what we've started."

"Greed, how long will it be?" Hatred said. "Juan Cortez is trying to recover and he is stirring things up quite a bit, so I need to know what is it that we need to do to quiet him."

"We are going to leave him alone for right now because Ashshod is protecting him very closely. But I want you all to know that we will get Juan. He is not invincible. He is already down so he can only do so much."

"What about Rachael and Joyce?" asked False Doctrine.

"There is nothing to worry about with them. After receiving those bites, they are down for the count right now.

Even if they wanted to get back on their feet, they will think twice before doing anything. Please keep in mind my little devilish friends, that they will not win. We know at times that it seems we start off winning and we are always defeated at the end, especially in Christian films, books and especially the Bible, but this time Satan has come up with a master plan that will defeat God's will and His plans."

Ashshod and the rest of the angels met at the abandoned church.

Zaso said, "Ashshod, I see that these imps are ready to make their move. They just don't understand that we know exactly what they are up to."

"Yes they do," Ashshod said, "They just don't care. How can they not know that the Great Almighty is all knowing? I need for you all to take note on what is going on. This battle is about to happen real soon and everyone needs to stay close and guard their post."

"I just want to go and tear those imps apart," said Gabe. "Sometimes people think that we are so weak or very passive."

"No Gabe, that is not the way we handle God's business," replied Ashshod. "It is not our job to be very flashy and loud. When God steps in, He does what He needs to do. At times it may seem to others that God should intervene, but He knows what He is doing. If He can create man to have function with a heart, lungs, and kidneys and make sure that their white and red blood cells are in their proper place, what makes you think that He is not in control of this?"

Ashshod smiled and concluded, "And we know that all things work together for good to them that love God, to them who are the called according to his purpose. So we

must do what we are called to do. I will go talk with the
Heavenly Father, and I will see you all a little later because
He wants me to do something, He is now summoning me.
Everyone, stand your guard and stand on your post.
Everything is going to be all right.

29

The Set Back

Rachael and Joyce were in the hospital for three weeks. Doctors had to pump their stomachs, and they were on IV's constantly. It took them two days to come out of what they both considered the 'Twilight Zone'. They were hallucinating and fading in and out. Juan and Forest were by their sides at all times. Rachael and Joyce just could not believe what had happened to them. Forest and Juan were thrown back by the whole situation. They kept asking them why they were the only ones targeted. Dr. Casper even called Trendon Palmer to see if anyone else had been attacked or bitten by a foreign insect. Trendon was so astonished to hear the news and said he'd heard nothing from other parishioners. Dr. Casper was perplexed because there was no explanation of why and where the insect came from.

Rachael was feeling a little better, so she and Forest went to visit Juan and Joyce in their room. As they were socializing, Rachael told Forest to go home and spend some time with his friends, but he kept insisting that he didn't want to leave her side.

Joyce said, "Rachael, you sure did raise a good boy."

"I thank God every day for him," replied Rachael, smiling.

Juan said, "Joyce, did you call the children?"

"No, I did not want them to get worried that both of their parents are hospitalized. You know they will try to move in and I don't want that at all."

"I see what you mean baby because they would not let us do anything."

Rachael looked over at Juan and Joyce and said, "You've gotta love "em"."

Alexander, Wade and Ethan came into the room, and then the imps that bit Rachael and Joyce appeared in the room.

One of the imps said, "Oh how sweet, they are socializing."

"You trifling imps, be gone," replied Wade.

"We can come and visit our enemies," said the other imp.

"You have no power," Ethan said. "You are a waste of space."

"We have power, if we did not, your little friends would not be in this hospital now."

"I don't have time for nonsense," Alexander said as he pulled out his sword and pointed it right in front of the imps. He swung his sword and annihilated both of the imps.

Greed immediately appeared and said, "How dare you take out Satan's warriors."

"We don't care about him...or you," stated Ethan.

"You will have to pay for that."

Greed's eyes turned red and he summoned fifty strong big imps to come and assist him. They filled the room, and the angels pulled out their swords and started to fight. Ethan did a backflip in the air; his eyes started to glow and he became bigger, then Alexander and Wade grew stronger and taller. They were fighting a brutal battle as Greed kept summoning imps.

Alexander yelled and his sword changed to the color gold and he wiped out ten imps in one blow. Greed went charging after Alexander because of what he just accomplished. Alexander was solely focused on wiping out all the imps and didn't see Greed sneaking up on him. Greed went to cut him in half and Ethan snuck up from behind and knocked Greed clear across the room. As Ethan knocked Greed across the room, Greed's sword pierced Ethan's right arm.

"This is not over. Trust me," said Greed.

"We will be ready for you," replied Alexander.

All of the angels flew down to attend to and be with Ethan as he laid on the ground holding his right arm.

"I must go back home and get mended. Let me just say humans do bear a lot of pain because this right here hurts," said Ethan.

"Stop complaining. You know you can take the pain," said Zaso.

"Whatever. You are not the ones with a messed up arm. I will see you guys later. I might stay longer than I should."

"Why?" asked Wade.

"Because I just want to be around holiness and once I get back home, the Heavenly Father is going to have to shove me back down here."

They all laughed and Ethan flew straight up through the ceiling.

Sunday morning arrived and Trendon was ready to walk into The Comfort Zone. He was more ready than ever before. Kelly told him to slow down before he burned a hole in the carpet.

Trendon said, "Kelly, I am just so excited about my new method of what the congregation has to do. I just need for everyone to be there today."

"Well whatever it is it must be real great because you are on fire."

"Yes I am, baby girl. I am on fire. Is everybody ready to go?"

"Almost, the boys just need a little more tidying up. Can you help me with them?"

"Yes I can. Boys, get yourselves together," said Trendon.

"Trendon, I could have done that myself," said Kelly.

"I know, but it just sounds better when I do it."

They laughed.

Greed and the rest of the imps were at The Comfort Zone, smiling and hissing. Ashshod was there and the other angels were with him looking on to see the atmosphere around the sanctuary. The imps were all over the place, dancing in the aisles, hanging on the ceiling, and sitting right next to many of the members who were attending service.

Kelly, the children, and Trendon had arrived at The Comfort Zone, and Trendon went into his study to prepare for service. One of the associate ministers entered into his office to inform him that the sanctuary was jammed packed and the overflow room was packed as well.

Trendon became even more excited. It had been three months since he became the overseer and he believed it was time for him to plant his foundation. Things were finally looking up for him and his family. Their new house would be finished being built at the end of the week. Now, it was time for him to make his grand entrance.

Trendon walked down the aisle with his posse behind him and the entire congregation stood to their feet. He walked up onto the pulpit and sat in his new royal chair and when he sat down he summoned the congregation to sit.

Greed had the biggest smile on his face. He cut his eye at Ashshod and blew fire out of his nostrils and said, "You'd better just leave."

The other imps stopped and all of their eyes turned red.

Ashshod said nothing and just watched how Trendon approached the podium. They all turned and watched him.

Trendon said, "Good morning, everyone."

The congregation replied, "Good morning."

"I have a very special announcement to bring to you today."

The place was quiet as a church mouse.

"I need for you to comprehend what I am trying to convey to you. Not only am I your leader or your overseer, I am now your god." The crowd was so surprised. "Let me explain, I was in my den yesterday and this very thought came upon me and I know that I am right, I will follow my instincts."

False Doctrine stood real tall and whispered in Trendon's ear, "Go ahead. I got your back. Don't be afraid of their responses. They cannot harm you."

Trendon said, "Let me tell you what I can do for you. I can forgive you of your sins. I know you all are going to say what about Jesus? Well what about Him? He is not here and

I now have been informed that I can to do it now. What you do is form a line and I will forgive you of your sins. You don't have to worry; you all will have safe passage to heaven. Like Pastor Pablo was explaining to you, God will take everybody to heaven. There is nothing to be scared of. I am now your savior.

"My new title will not be Pastor Palmer. It is Savior Palmer. Or you can just call me savior because I can save you from your sins. You will address me as your savior and you will kiss my hand because you will be showing me reverence. I will be the one to get you out of all your bad situations. I need for you all to come down and join me. Kelly will show you what I am asking you to do."

Kelly walked down the aisle and kneeled down in front of Trendon. He extended his hand and she kissed him and said, "Yes my lord." She stood to her feet and walked quietly back to her seat, then his children went down and after them Sallie came down and kissed his hand then the entire congregations followed behind.

Trendon said, "My little children, come unto me and I will give you rest."

The parishioners formed a very long line. Trendon just smiled at each individual and when he finished blessing the entire congregation, he gave on words of encouragement. The congregation all applauded and he smiled and said, "I bless you. Now when people want to go to heaven, they must go through me. When we extend the invitation, we are extending it to me only and not to Jesus."

"Now this is sad and real sick," said Hunter.

"What's so sick about this?" asked Greed.

"Shut up, Greed," said Wade.

"See you dumb angel, now you know Satan gives the humans what they want, someone that they can see and believe in."

"I just love how dumb humans are. They will take 'The Man Upstairs' true words and just screw them up and make them fit their needs," replied False Doctrine.

"But it is not our jobs to make sure they walk in the light. It is just our jobs to make sure they go to Hell and be with our lord," said Greed.

All the angels and imps listened to what Trendon said. The imps flew closer to Trendon; they did not want to miss a beat.

"All week I want you to remember that I am your god," he said. "Go in peace now. Also I need for everyone to come to The Comfort Zone this coming Wednesday because you will need to come and pay homage to me at least one day out of the week."

Sallie said, "I love you my lord, and I adore and worship you."

Trendon went back to his office, and Kelly met him there and said, "Wow, what an eventful day."

Trendon said, "Yes, now I want you to know that the things I said today are true. It was no joke. I am now your savior. I can save you from your sins. On Wednesday I am going to start baptizing in my name and my name only. No Father, Son and Holy Ghost. They have no part in this. So I will teach them how to really worship me."

"Well my lord, I am famished so let's go and feed our children," said Kelly.

Zaso said, "Ashshod, why are things going this way?"

"Watch Zaso. The Heavenly Father has a bigger plan," said Ashshod.

"I know this, Ashshod. I am just concerned about the humans. This is so miserable to watch."

"I know but we must let it run its course, Zaso."

Joyce and Juan were sitting in Juan's room when Glynda entered into Juan's room and said, "Are you guys about to watch the local news?"

"We weren't planning on it," Joyce replied.

"The new overseer of The Comfort Zone has some special announcement this afternoon," Glynda said.

"Is that right?" Juan asked. "Well can you turn on the news? Let's hear this very special announcement."

"I will only turn this on if you promise me that you will not get yourself all worked up."

Juan said, "I promise."

Dr. Casper walked into Juan's room just as the news anchor said, "We are live in front of The Comfort Zone formally known as Solid Rock Missionary Baptist Church."

Trendon cut his eye at the news anchor. He was well groomed and spoke with great pride. All of his members were there supporting their savior.

"Let me introduce myself to you," Trendon began. "I am the overseer of this congregation, but now I am their savior and if you want salvation and questions answered, please come and worship and praise me because I can forgive you of all of your sins. You don't need Jesus. You only need me. This is a new era and a new day and age, and we don't want to be stuck in traditions and the old ways. I will accept you for who and whatever you are. I will be your god, do you hear me?. I am your god."

The Comfort Zone members cheered.

I want you to understand that there is no such place called Hell, because it doesn't exist. You will not hear me teach on that baloney," stated Trendon.

The Crowd cheered even louder and harder.

Someone yelled in the background, "We love you savior." Trendon had the biggest grin on his face.

"For those of you who want to become bishops under my great leadership, even if you haven't been called by God and you want to be licensed and ordained in this state, I would do it for a price. If you want it done in a day it will cost you $100,000 but if you don't have that type of money I can get the job done for you within six months but this will cost you $10,000. Just to let you know I am not doing anything shady or underhanded there are bishops and pastors doing this all over the world charging these specific amounts, getting individuals licensed and ordained every day. The reason we are charging these amounts is to weed out the weak and the so-called called by God! Don't worry about God He doesn't mind. He doesn't need the money like I do," Trendon smiled.

The crowd cheered once again.

"Listen we are no longer in the past but in the present. This is how the world does things now," explained Trendon.

The crowd started chanting, "No longer in the past but in the present God doesn't mind," over and over again.

Dr. Casper turned off the television and looked at Juan; he was speechless. All he could do was stare off into space. Dr. Casper ran over to Juan and noticed what he was doing and said, "Glynda, give him some water" and gave her some orders to administer some medication to Juan to calm him down. "His blood pressure is slightly elevated so I need for him to get back into that bed and get some rest."

Joyce, beyond worried, was sent home so that they could assist Juan.

A few days later, a strong-willed Juan looked at Dr. Casper and said, "I need to go to The Comfort Zone this Sunday."

"Juan, do you think it is best for you?" asked Dr. Casper.

"I do. I just had a little setback I will be just fine. Just let me go, trust me."

When Joyce sauntered into the room, she sensed the conversation was a serious one.

"What's going on?" she asked, fear in her voice.

"Nothing," Juan said, sighing. "I'm fine."

Joyce gave her attention to Dr. Casper, who said, "He is. He just wants me to let him go to church this Sunday."

"Juan, why are you insisting on going over there?" she asked. It was hard for her to articulate her fear, to tell Juan or anyone really how much she feared what could happen to Juan—to any of them that seemed to be displeased with what's going on at The Comfort Zone.

"I have my reasons," replied Juan.

"What are your reasons, Juan? You just need to move on."

"Joyce, why are you speaking to me like this? You know I was called to do God's work not man's, and you are really making me very angry right now."

Hatred came into the room and said, "That's it, Joyce. Get him to change his mind. He does not need to be there Sunday or any other Sunday. I want you to make sure he does not go. If not, sweetheart, you will pay."

"Listen Joyce, if you are having difficulty accepting this, will you please leave? I do not want your negative behavior around me. What's the point of me being well if Satan is allowed to win major battles around the places near and dear to us? I would think you'd understand that."

"How dare you, Juan? I have stuck by you all these many years and went through situations I did not ask for. I ask you for one thing, just one thing, because I care about your health, and you want to make me look like the monster." Joyce stood, her anger swarming about her like a force field. "Screw you then," she said, surprising both Juan and Dr. Casper. "I don't need this."

She left without saying goodbye.

When she got home, she went into prayer. She could not for the life of her understand why she said what she said to Juan. "She said screw you. Joyce doesn't talk like that. She sounded as if she was a ghetto woman from off the streets speaking that type of language".

Joyce had a hard time shaking her negative feelings. She felt as if she had to protect a young child and as she lashed out at Juan. She paced her dining room floor for about two hours, exhausting herself to the point of needing to take a nap.

Joyce awakened from her nap still bothered by the thought of what happened between her and Juan.

She called Juan; they did not talk long. She just informed him that she would see him in the morning.

"Alright," he said. "Have a good night."

After Juan hung up from Joyce, he said, "Lord, I know that she was looking out for my best interest, but she can't grasp that this is bigger than her. Please watch out for her Lord. She will understand it later." He stayed up until midnight, reading his Bible. He prayed and went to bed.

The next day, Juan was sitting in his hospital room; it was Saturday afternoon and Joyce was right there by his side.

Doubt appeared and the imps that were in Juan's room started to hiss. Discouragement followed and said, "I'm here you guys."

Ashshod just looked at all of them and said absolutely nothing.

Juan asked Dr. Casper again if he could attend Solid Rock the next day.

She said, "I don't see why not. You are getting better and stronger."

"Thank you, Doctor."

"I'll be back in a little bit," the doctor said before leaving the room.

"Joyce," Juan said, "Do you mind getting my navy blue suit and the accessories that go with it?"

Doubt jumped on Joyce's shoulder and said, "Tell Juan he does not need to go to church."

"Are you sure that you want to do this?" asked Joyce.

"Joyce, why don't you want me to go?"

"Honey, it's not that I don't want you to go. I just don't want any nonsense to start."

"That's it, Joyce. Tell him that you are more concerned about what he might encounter," said Doubt.

"Well I'm not worried about any nonsense, Joyce. I need to go see for myself what is going on in the supposed house of God."

"Juan, I understand that you want to go, but I just don't think it would be best for you right now."

"I hear you, baby, but my decision is final. Nothing you can say will sway me. This isn't about me. And it's not about you. It's about God."

"So I have no say?"

"Is your say higher than God's?"

Joyce was silent for a moment before she said, "I rather for us just to start over somewhere else than go to that place."

"So what you are telling me is that it is okay for you to go and give me reports on what is going on, but not okay for me to see things for myself?"

"Well since you put it that way, yes!" said Joyce.

"Joyce, you are out of order. I love you, but if you do not go home and get the things I told you to, I will get John to get my things for me."

Discouragement said, "Let me work her a little." He grew stronger and stood directly behind her. "Listen, Joyce. This is what I need for you to do. Just tell Juan that he doesn't have all the necessary things to go tomorrow. Do it now." He stomped on Joyce's big toe.

Joyce let out a big scream.

Juan said, "Joyce, what's wrong?"

"My toe, it's really hurting me."

Juan called Dr. Casper into the room and she looked at Joyce's toe; it was red and bruised. Dr. Casper said, "Did you bump it, Joyce?"

"No, I haven't left my seat at all," said Joyce.

Dr. Casper said, "Do you want me to hold off on letting you leave in the morning?"

Juan said, "Absolutely not."

"Oh, we will see about this," Discouragement said. He and Doubt looked at each other and nodded, and Doubt hit Joyce in the head and she developed a splitting headache and Discouragement bit her on her toe.

Dr. Casper noticed that her toe started to bleed and sent Joyce down for an x-ray. Joyce started to groan she was in so much pain.

Doubt said, "You can help her, Juan. Do not go to The Comfort Zone tomorrow."

As they were taking Joyce down for x-rays, Juan could not for the life of him figure out what was going on.

The imps in the room started to jump from wall to wall; all five of them were very restless, and their eyes started to turn red.

Hatred appeared and the other imps filled him in on what was happening and he started to blow smoke out of his nostrils. Since Joyce was gone, Juan called John and asked him to go to the house and get his navy blue suit. Juan gave John a key years ago, so he knew just what to do.

Hatred said, "Oh, you think he is going to do this for you? I will handle this. I'll be right back."

John went to get his keys and Jane walked into the kitchen and said, "So how is my pastor?"

"He is doing great. He asked me if I would go and get a suit for him. He plans to go to The Comfort Zone in the morning."

"Wow, is he sure he wants to go to that Hellhole."

"Now Jane."

"Well it's the truth!"

"Truth or not, behave." He chuckled. "You want to ride with me?"

"Sure."

They both got into the car and John tried to start it up and the car was completely dead.

Hatred said, "I said no one will help this man get to The Comfort Zone."

John called the car dealership, and the customer service representative said it would be four hours before they could come out.

"We are backed up today, and this is very unusual."

Jane said, "John, go ahead and use my car. We can still make it back in time to meet the car people."

They walked over to Jane's car and she had all the tires slashed on her Bentley.

They were both stunned.

Jane said, "I'm calling the police."

The police came within three minutes and they wrote everything down and they took pictures. They looked at John's Ashton Martin and said, Can you please lift the hood?"

"Well somebody did not want you guys to go anywhere. The starter is missing and they completely removed the wiring.

"There was no way that you were going anywhere," said the officer.

John called his insurance company and told them what happened and they informed him that there was nothing they could do regarding a rental car until Monday morning do to paperwork processing.

Hatred said, "I told you that we are going to take all measures to stop Juan from messing with our business."

As they all were standing in the driveway, Trevor rolled up in his two-door Porsche. Trevor got out of his car and said, "What happened here, Mom and Dad?"

Police officer Vera Jackson said, "Well someone wanted to make sure that your parents could not leave."

"Mom and Dad, are you okay? Did anybody try to go into the house?"

"No we are okay. It is just the cars."

"Officer Jackson," Trevor said, "Would you take a look around the house and make sure that there were no intruders for us, please?"

"Sure, I will do that, and I will call for backup," said Officer Jackson. Officer Jackson and her partner Kenny Parker went around the house. The officers then returned to the front of the house and wrote down some notes. Then Jane went with Officer Jackson into the house and Trevor and Officer Parker stayed outside.

Hatred said, "I will teach you all a lesson for not obeying me."

As John was waiting for the officers to finish checking around the house, Juan called.

Juan said, "Did you find everything?"

John said, "Juan, you won't believe this, but somebody slashed all of Jane's tires on her car."

"What?"

"That's not all. Somebody removed my battery, engine, even took my starter and snatched out all of my wiring."

"You got to be kidding me, John."

"And I cannot get a car until Monday morning. I'm going to use Trevor's car to go get your things though. Don't worry."

As soon as John said this, they heard a gunshot in the backyard.

Everyone ran to the back to find the family dog Frisky lying dead on the ground.

"Mom," Trevor said, "There was some rambling in the bushes, and the officer asked many times for whoever it was to come out and they did not, and he shot the dog."

Jane started to yelled, "Not Frisky" as John held her in his arms.

All John could do was say, "Heavenly Father, what a day, what a day."

Office Parker said, "We are so sorry. We will get you another dog."

At the time Jane did not want to hear this. The officers left after giving them a copy of their report and a card with their badge numbers on them.

Hatred said, "I told you not to make me angry. Well someone must pay for your disobedience. Poor little Frisky. You foolish people just need to mind your own business."

After calling the vet to have someone come pick up Frisky, John said, "Trevor, lend me the keys to your car. I need to get out of here."

"Here Dad, be careful. It seems as if there is a spiritual battle going on out here," said Trevor.

"I know, son. It sure feels like it."

As John was driving, he could not believe the events that were going on. He turned the radio up because Trevor had it on the gospel radio station, and it made John smile. He remembered a time when Trevor would not even listen to gospel—calling it garbage.

One of his favorite songs, "Jesus Can Work It Out" with Albertina Walker singing the lead came on, and it made him feel so good. He needed to hear something that would soothe his soul. John made it over to Juan's house and picked up all of his things without a problem.

At the hospital, Juan was very delighted to see John finally arrive.

"It is a miracle I'm here with all you asked for," John said, chuckling.

"John, I really need your help. Please listen, there is really a big battle going on here."

"Tell me about it."

"Joyce is so scared. She tried everything she could to let me know that she would not and could not take me to Solid Rock in the morning. Can you please take me?"

"I sure will."

30

Trendon Savior?

Ashshod summoned all of the angels to meet him in Juan's room. Juan was still sleeping.

"He will be up in an hour," he said, "So I must protect him because he is going to the church today."

"We are all ready," said Hunter and Zaso.

"I hope they will try something stupid," said Enu.

"Calm down," said Ashshod.

"We are not barbaric. I just do not like those imps."

"I know. I feel the same way."

Greed, Hatred, and False Doctrine appeared.

"What, you all are having a meeting and we were not invited? Oh how naughty of you all," said Greed.

"Greed, I don't think you want to play today," said Ashshod.

"Who's playing? Ashshod, I am ready for battle and if your lackey walks into that building today, he's going to wish he hadn't."

Enu the Arch angel pulled back his sword.

"No Enu," said Ashshod.

"Imps," Greed said, "Let's go. It reeks of holiness in here."

They all vanished.

"It's time for us to do our jobs," said Ashshod.

The morning nurse came in and woke Juan up. He had his morning prayer and read his Bible. He ate breakfast and took his medication. He went down to Joyce's room to see if she was okay. She was up and she was having some discomfort in her toe, but she said that she would live. Juan stayed for an hour; he told her to rest and that he would see her later.

"Why can't you stay?" she asked.

"I need to use the bathroom," said Juan. She laughed, and he smiled, kissed her, and told her that he loved her before he left the room.

Juan went back to his room, took a shower and got dressed; he was waiting on John to come and get him. Juan got so excited. The imps in the room started to hiss and their eyes began to turn dark red and the angels in the room just stood in front of each imp. These imps were weak; the angels were not worried about them.

The Palmer family was getting ready to go to church. The imp Arrogance appeared in the room and jumped inside of Trendon.

"Where I'm worshipped...boy, doesn't that have its advantages?" Trendon said.

His wife and kids loved the way they were being treated as if they were more special than the regular parishioners.

Well, they are because I am a god, Trendon thought. *They are to get special treatment.*

"Amen to that," Arrogance said, listening to Trendon's thoughts.

As John and Juan arrived at The Comfort Zone, Ashshod and the angels saw a horde of imps all around the building. The angels that were stationed there were outnumbered but not concerned. There was a loud screeching noise outside, then the imps' eyes turned red and they began to hiss.

Ashshod said, "Be on the lookout."

"Juan," John said, "Are you okay?"

"Yes, thanks for asking." Juan took a deep breath.

The parking lot was extremely crowded. As John was ready to get out of the car, Juan noticed Trendon and his family walking into the building. Juan took a deep breath and John said, "Are you sure you're okay? Are you really up for this?"

"Let us say a word of prayer," said Juan. They bowed their heads and Juan offered a prayer and asked God to cover them.

Ashshod stood closely to Juan and Enu to John.

Dr. Casper walked into Joyce's room and said, "Are you feeling any better?"

"A little," Joyce replied.

"Do you need some more medication?"

"Yes please. Dr. Casper, what is going on with Juan?"

"What do you mean?"

"It's been over an hour and a half since he has been down here. Is he all right?"

"He is fine."

"So where is he?" asked Joyce. She looked at Dr. Casper with a lifted brow when she didn't reply fast enough. "Dr. Casper, I am speaking English, aren't I?"

"Yes, you are," replied Dr. Casper.

"So where is my husband?"

"He went to The Comfort Zone."

"Why did you allow him to leave?"

"Because I'm his doctor, and I felt that he could go."

"What kind of monster are you?" It didn't matter to Joyce that she heard Juan say his decision was final. She was sure that she had persuaded him not to go.

"Joyce, I think you better calm down," said Dr. Casper.

"I will not. Who do you think you are allowing my fragile husband to go to a place that will kill him? I will have your job for this. I am leaving. I am getting dressed, and I am going to get my husband."

Dr. Casper left the room and informed everybody that Joyce was on a rampage. Joyce got dressed and left the hospital without the doctor's consent.

John and Juan walked inside, and some of the old members were so surprised to see them there. They hugged both.

Greed said, "I thought I told you not to bring your puppet to this place."

"You have no power over me, Greed," replied Ashshod.

"You just started a war."

Juan walked in the sanctuary and sat close to the back in the middle section of the sanctuary. The praise team was singing and it was loud and everyone was cheering and clapping. In the order of service, they kept what Marco called his ten commandments. All Juan could do was shake his head.

Then the show began. Trendon walked down the aisle and everybody stood to their feet and said, "Our savior."

Juan's mouth dropped open and John whispered to Juan, "These people are idiotic, what in the world!"

"I know, John. How sad."

Trendon went up into the pulpit and sat in this big royal chair before summoning everyone to sit.

"What kind of freak show is this?" asked John.

"I don't know, but it really needs to cease," stated Juan.

Joyce was driving as fast as she could to get to Juan. "I am so furious with Dr. Casper," she said. "What was she thinking? Why is everybody driving so slowly? Move get out of my way. I better slow down before I get a ticket. It's the last thing I need right now."

Joyce called Rachael and barely allowed her to say a Hello before she said, "Girl, Dr. Casper let Juan go to The Comfort Zone, and I'm on my way there."

"What, are you kidding me? Is he ready for this?"

"No, he is not. I am so angry."

"How far are you from The Comfort Zone?"

"Where are you, Rachael?"

"I was on my way to another place of worship, but I'll meet you at The Comfort Zone. I'm just around the corner. I know that Lisa is already there. She was only going because they were going to give her something on behalf of Marco. I'll wait inside my car until you get there."

Trendon approached the microphone and said, "Your savior is here, I have risen."

The crowd jumped to their feet and cheered and shouted, "Thank you, my savior!"

They were screaming and hollering as if they were at a sporting event. The cheering died down and Juan stood to his feet and shouted, "This is blasphemy. Stop all of this nonsense."

Greed said, "Ashshod, sit your dummy down. He has no power or control in here."

"But that's where you are wrong, Greed. God gave Juan the authority to do His will," replied Ashshod.

The parishioners became silent. Trendon said, "Excuse me. What did you say?"

"This is blasphemy," stated Juan.

"Oh how delightful. Everyone, it's the old man, I mean excuse me it's the old pastor, Pastor Juan Cortez."

Sallie jumped to her feet and said, "He does not belong here. Get him out of here."

Greed said to the other imps, "Stop him."

Juan moved into the center of the aisle and started to walk down the aisle. "This man here cannot forgive you of your sins."

"Don't you dare come into my house and tell my children what I can and cannot do. You are out of line, Juan," answered Trendon.

"No, you are out of your dang blasted mind. Stop all of this bizarre behavior and get from up there," said Juan.

Greed went straight for Juan's head, throwing a fiery dart it made Juan stop in the aisle, grab his head, and moan.

Ashshod took out his sword and said, "Armor up." The angels transformed and Ashshod took his sword and hit Greed upside his head and knocked him clear across the room.

Greed said, "Attack!"

Trendon asked, "What is wrong with you, old man? Too much action for you? I see that you are having some trouble there, buddy. Do you need some help?"

Juan shook his head and said, "You better come down out of that pulpit, Trendon."

"Or what, Juan? What can you do? You can barely stand on your own."

"Boy, if you don't get down from there speaking all of these un-godly blasphemous words I will knock you down."

"You and whose army, Juan? Listen, you were just a pawn here. You were cute and little with no power but you did your job. You did what you were to do and that was to make sure that everybody understood that they had to come here from Sunday to Sunday. But what happened? You lose your touch? People were not coming here. How many people showed up at prayer meeting? What five or ten tops? With me as their leader, I can't keep them away."

"Shut up, Trendon," replied Juan. Juan kept on walking slowly down that aisle, focusing on snatching that boy down from that podium.

"You better just stop there while you know what's best for you," demanded Trendon.

"Listen everyone, Trendon is a part of that Lither organization. It's his job to keep you in the dark as well as ignorant," explained Juan.

"You shut your lying mouth, you old goat," yelled Trendon.

"I will not! I will not allow you to let these people go to a burning Hell so you can have the fame and fortune your heart desires," yelled Juan.

"Listen everybody. Get rid of the barcode on your body. This antichrist is grooming all of you for Hell," explained Juan.

"Juan shut up," yelled Trendon.

Juan looked around the sanctuary shook his head and said, "Pick up your Bibles and read it for yourselves. Revelation 13:18 tells you what that mark means," demanded Juan.

"Listen Juan, they have their barcode symbol branded on their foreheads, hands, and other parts of their body to represent me as their savior," stated Trendon.

One of the parishioners stood up and walked up to Juan and showed him his barcode as clear as day. "We are proud to wear our savior's symbol," stated the parishioner.

"Trendon this is blasphemy. Stop all of this madness. Get rid of this garbage and give your life to Jesus Christ," pleaded Juan.

"Young man you don't know how badly you walk in ignorance. It can lead you straight to Hell, and you can't even recognize the truth because you are so blinded with false doctrine. Please pick up a Holy Bible and read it and give your life to Jesus Christ. This is the only way that your life can be saved," explained Juan.

"You don't know what you are talking about old man, our savior Trendon knows all," replied the parishioner.

"Read you Bible son like I stated earlier. It can save your life," answered Juan.

"Juan enough," yelled Trendon.

"People, Juan pleaded, "Pleaded up the Bible and read it. Your life depends on it," begged Juan.

"You shut your lying mouth. They don't need to read that old nonsense. They have me. No old outdated book that deals with today's issues. So stop telling them to read it," demanded Trendon.

"Shut him up Ashshod," yelled Greed.

Joyce pulled up into the parking lot and parked right next to Rachael.

The imps were angry.

Hatred appeared and said, "I told you both to stay away, but since you both don't like to pay attention to direction, then I must take matters into my own hands." Hatred blew smoke out his nostrils, and Zaso appeared from out of nowhere and punched him in the face. Hatred was thrown for a loop; he was not expecting this and some of the imps that were stationed around the church went to help him, and the angels that were stationed around the church went to assist Zaso.

Joyce and Rachael walked inside. Zaso was out there fighting a mighty battle; they were bumping on automobiles and turning on alarms. The sky was becoming dark and lighting began to flash. The parishioners were becoming scared and nervous because the sun was shining when they arrived this morning. They were watching what was going on in the inside as well as the outside.

Joyce and Rachael looked inside and saw Juan walking down the aisle.

Greed said, "What are they doing here? What is this?"

Greed looked out the window and saw Hatred and some of the imps in battle with Zaso and some angels. Greed screamed and blew smoke out his nostrils and fire from his mouth. Rachael and Joyce were trying to get to Juan, but were grabbed.

Sallie stood and said, "Savior, we have more special guests."

Joyce said, "Close your mouth, Sallie, before I put my foot in it."

The congregation did not know how to handle the situation; they just sat there and watched the show.

"Joyce, what are you doing here?" Juan asked.

"I'm trying to get you away from this mad house," replied Joyce.

One of Trendon's servants said, "Stop moving. If you don't, I will hurt you."

Joyce looked at him as if everything was in slow motion before saying, "I would like to see you try." Joyce took her pocketbook and smacked the man in his face with it. "Don't you ever threaten me ever again."

Rachael was arguing with the people who were holding her back, and Joyce wobbled to Juan.

"Oh look everyone," Trendon said, "How sweet. A women who stands by her man."

Trendon looked over at Kelly and said, "Make note of this, Kelly. You make sure that you stand by my side always."

The congregation said, "Ooh."

Then Kelly stood and walked up into the pulpit and stood by Trendon and the parishioners said, "Aw."

"See Juan," Trendon said, "You are not the only one who has a special someone. Now where were we?"

Juan said, "Trendon, get your butt down from out of that pulpit."

A big roar of thunder came across the sky and a streak of lightning flashed, lighting up the world it seemed. The parishioners were scared; some were clinging to each other.

"Trendon," Juan said, "The Bible says, in Exodus twenty, chapter three "You are to have no other gods before me."

"Here we go again. He is like a walking Bible. How did you all sit under that stuff? Listen to me, Juan. I have my own Bible."

"No, Trendon, you have your own emotions."

Greed said, "Stop him, Ashshod, or I will."

"Repent of your sins, Trendon, or the Lord will punish you," stated Juan.

"I cannot repent to myself, Juan. That's impossible."

"Listen everyone, he is a deceiver, and the truth is not in him. The Word of God says, in 1Corinthians, 3:18-20, "Let no one fool himself. If someone among you thinks he is wise (by this world's standards), let him become "foolish," so that he may become really wise. For the wisdom of this world is nonsense, as far as God is concerned; "He traps the wise in their own cleverness. ADONAI knows that the thoughts of the wise are worthless."

"Don't listen to him," Trendon shouted. "He just wants your sympathy."

"Leave our savior alone," Sallie yelled. "He is not hurting anybody."

Joyce looked at Sallie and said, "The only reason you like it here is because you feel important. You have a little status around here and you are doing whatever it takes to keep it. You don't care if people go to Hell or not. You just care about yourself."

"Joyce, if you don't hush your mouth, I will," said Sallie.

"People, you better listen to me," said Juan.

"Shut up and leave," someone shouted in the back. "You are not our savior."

"I don't want to be your savior," Juan said. "The only one that fits this position is Jesus Christ, the son of the living God. You all better listen to me. 'Many false prophets are gone out into the world. Hereby know ye the Spirit of God: Every spirit that confesseth that Jesus Christ is come in the flesh is of God: he that is not of God heareth not us. He is an Antichrist'. Those of you that have your Bibles read it with me, First John, four, one through three," pleaded Juan.

"Juan, I do not let them bring that book in here. We don't need it," replied Trendon.

"This man is an anti-Christ," Juan shouted. "He is against our Lord and Savior Jesus Christ. He is not God. Jesus is. Just read Philippians2:5-11."

"I said shut up and leave," Trendon yelled.

"I see that I am making you very angry, Trendon," replied Juan.

Greed flew toward Ashshod in a flash and knocked Ashshod to the other side of the sanctuary and said, "Shut that man up right now."

Wade went over and fought with Discouragement, and Discouragement was not going out like Covet. Wade had his sword moving like the speed of light. Discouragement was prepared for this; he worked his sword just as quickly as Wade. Two imps tried to attack Wade as he was concentrating on getting rid of Discouragement. Wade smelled them coming upon him and he turned around so quickly they did not see this coming; Wade sent his sword piercing straight through Discouragement's heart.

Ashshod turned and looked at the rest of the angels and he made his eyes glow white. The rest of the angels started to do the same thing and they said, "We will defeat Satan and his imps!" They flew like a flash and started tearing all the imps in half and as soon as they could get rid of some Satan kept sending more imps.

"Ashshod, I'm going to take you down," said Greed. "Shut him up, Ashshod." He threw a dart to Juan's head.

"Ah," Juan screamed, "My head."

Rafael was fighting Fornication; Fornication saw how all the other imps were being annihilated and knew he was up a creek without a paddle.

Fornication looked at Rafael and said, "I'm a lover not a fighter," and Fornication took his sword and took his own life.

"I am their savior," Trendon said. "They can see me. They can call me anytime and whatever they want they can come to me. When they need their rent paid, they call on me and I pay it. When their bills are due, I can pay them, so don't tell me what I can and cannot do."

Juan grabbed his head and said, "Trendon, son…"

"I am not your son, Juan. Do not call me that."

"Well you devil then. I will call it as I see it. You are way over your head."

"No, you are, Juan. You come in here with this old theology and think we are to take it in. You are totally wrong. I give them everything that they need right here and right now."

Rain came down in sheets; the thunder was so hard it made hearts quake.

It was noon, but it sure looked as if it were midnight.

"Honey," Joyce pleaded, "Let's go."

Juan said, "No. I must say what I need to say."

"I thought you were finished, Juan," Trendon said. "You better listen to your wife. I'm getting very agitated."

Arrogance saw that Ashshod was preoccupied so he decided to take advantage of this delightful situation. He flew over to Juan and kicked him in his leg and smacked him in the back of his head and Juan lost his balance. "I will teach you for interfering with our plans."

Juan yelled and Joyce caught him the best way she could. John broke free and ran down to help her and Juan stood back to his feet and the imps were angry. Then Rachael broke free to help Joyce and John.

A great roar came from outside and everybody was scared; they saw trees falling on the cars in the parking lot.

"This is utter nonsense," Joyce said.

Arrogance flew down on Sallie and made her go to Joyce.

"Joyce, leave our savior alone. We love him here". Arrogance grew and stood behind Sallie and said, "I am so sick and tired of this woman. Do it…teach her a lesson."

"Shut up, Joyce, and stay out of this," said Sallie.

"And what are you going to do, Sallie?"

"This!"

Joyce screamed to the top of her lungs as Sallie deliberately stepped on her bitten toe then dug her heel, twisting and turning her foot.

Alexander went right after Arrogance and his glow was a blinding light that split Arrogance right in half and all that was left was the black smoke and the smell of sulfur. Greed saw the whole scene as he was fighting with Ashshod.

Zaso went right after Doubt, and Zaso did not hesitate to blind him to have the advantage, but Doubt was prepared for this. He yelled and another imp came to assist him and Doubt fought Zaso as if he had money on the fight.

Doubt fought with all his might and Wade came over and assisted Zaso by taking out the imp that was guiding Doubt. Then Zaso took his sword and cut Doubt's head right off his shoulders; smoke filled that area.

Rachael said, "Oh no you didn't hurt my best friend." Rachael drew her arm back and knocked Sallie flat on her back.

The congregation could not move; they were appalled from what was going on.

Rachael said, "I would be feeling guilty if I was in the house of the Lord, but this is not God's house. This is just an circus arena, and I am looking at all of you and you should be ashamed of yourselves for not searching the Scriptures."

The rain came pouring down harder and stronger, and the parishioners were hearing hard bumps against the windows. Satan sent more imps and God in return sent more angels. False Doctrine was pissed off, so he went after Rachael and made one of the parishioners out of the clear blue sky come and attack Rachael and he made sure she was hit on the back of the neck. Rachael went down and Ashshod looked down because he was close to the ceiling. Zaso heard Rachael's cry and flew inside the building; he saw Rachael on the ground and he took his sword and sliced ten imps at one time, spun, did a backflip and took ten more. Then when the rest of the angels saw how angry Zaso was, it boosted them and they started taking imps out left and right.

Both Joyce and Rachael were on the floor, screaming in their pains, and John was too sHell shocked to move.

"See Juan," Trendon said, "Look at what you've caused. See, I am a savior of peace. I have power to calm down this hot air, but I see that you want to keep it up."

Juan looked as Trendon moved to the middle of the pulpit.

"You have no power," Juan said. "You are no god or savior. You are just a regular human being that needs his soul saved like everyone else. If you think you're someone's savior, let us see you calm this storm."

Ashshod and the rest of the angels were still in battle.

Greed said, "You will not defeat us, Ashshod."

The congregation started to chant, "Savior, stop this storm. Show him that you have the mighty power to stop it."

"Yes, Trendon," Juan said sarcastically, "Stop this intense weather."

"Listen, everyone," Trendon said, "Stopping the weather won't prove anything."

One of the parishioners stood and said, "Prove this idiotic old man to be dead wrong."

Ashshod said to all of the angels, "It is time."

All of the Arch angels' swords made a big blinding glare inside of the building; everyone screamed and then at that very moment Trendon raised his hands up in the air as if he was *Charlton Heston playing the role of Moses in the motion picture The Ten Commandments* and said, "By the power that I possess, I demand and command this storm to cease."

And the Lord God sent a giant lightning bolt into the sanctuary; it shattered glass and pierced right through the center of Trendon's chest. His wife Kelly was thrown out of the pulpit into the deacon's corner by the force of the lightning bolt leaving her unconscious.

False Doctrine was fuming because he saw his partners lose their existence and his work being tampered with. Alexander noticed how angry False Doctrine was, so he got rid of ten imps that were right in front of him. Alexander went right over to False Doctrine and said, "It's over."

"I don't think so," replied False Doctrine. He grew real tall and started attacking Alexander. False Doctrine's might was so strong that he had Alexander up against the wall. "You were saying something about *over?*"

Alexander's eyes glowed, and False Doctrine said, "I will not allow this" before smacking Alexander so the light from his eyes would stop glowing.

Alexander was discombobulated, and False Doctrine began to laugh. Alexander heard the fighting in the background; he got himself together and looked down as

False Doctrine had him up against the wall. Alexander let out a loud scream and grew in strength and height, and False Doctrine was taken aback by this. Alexander took his sword which was by his side and cut False Doctrine in half. The top part of False Doctrine went behind him while his legs stood in place; seconds later he just vanished. All that was left was black smoke and the stench of sulfur.

Greed was furious about what was going on. He just kept summoning for more imps to come. The imps were coming by hundreds. The angels were fighting imps all around them.

Greed looked at Ashshod and said, "It's just me and you, big man."

"Yes, it is," replied Ashshod.

Twenty imps came charging after Ashshod including Greed. Ashshod got assistance from some of the angels. He was annihilating all the imps that were in his path. Greed noticed that all the imps kept dying off. So he became ten times bigger than Ashshod.

He knocked Zaso and Alexander clear across the room, and it took a while for them to gather their thoughts. Greed had hatred in his eyes just trying to focus on getting rid of Ashshod. He blew fire out of his mouth and he took his sword and swung it around and knocked Ashshod's sword right out of his hand. Ashshod went to go retrieve it by flying close to the ceiling.

Greed said, "Oh no you don't."

Ethan's head touched the ceiling; he looked down and yelled, "Ashshod!" and threw him his sword and Ashshod began to fight. Ashshod grew in height as well as strength; his eyes were glowing so strong it looked as if the moon had left the sky. Greed continued to blow smoke from his nostrils and fire from his mouth, trying to burn Ashshod to death.

Ashshod let out a big scream and he shut the glowing light out of his eyes; he grew even taller and he took his sword, swung it around three times, jumped up in the air, flew to the ground, and looked right up at Greed before taking his sword and slamming it on the floor. Greed looked on with amazement and said, "I'll be back. You can't stop me. I will come back bigger and stronger." As soon as the sword hit the ground, the vibration from the sword hit the air, and it split Greed right in half. All the imps disappeared, leaving behind smoke and the bad stench of sulfur.

Rain poured inside The Comfort Zone; people were getting wet.

Juan looked at a lifeless Trendon lying upon the pulpit. He wept because the price of fame meant so much to him and not the souls of the human race.

The angels stood all about.

The rain ceased as Juan turned to attend to Joyce.

After the storm, a big rainbow formed in the sky.

31

A New Beginning

J oyce and Juan were in the hospital for three weeks; they both had to regain their strength, and Joyce had to learn how to walk with a missing toe, which was definitely a challenge. They both were discharged at the same time. They had some help that came by the house three times a week, a sweet young girl. Their kids had been by; they all came one at a time. Joyce and Juan were very happy to see their children as well as their grandchildren, but it seemed as if they were happier to see them leave. Joyce and Juan were so happy to be back home together and slowly putting their schedules back on track. It was difficult at first, but now they were back in the swing of things.

The Comfort Zone was trying to recover from that big fiasco that they had experienced. Nobody wanted to become the pastor there; ministers were petrified that if they took on the pastor's position at The Comfort Zone they would be killed. Membership dwindled. The Comfort Zone had a membership of 8,000 and now it was down to a 1,000. But at least the likes of Sallie Cooper was a thing of the past. Dr. Casper had filed charges against her the moment she learned of what she did to Joyce.

The Comfort Zone and those left in the aftermath needed a lot of prayer and damage control.

Four months after leaving the hospital, Juan was feeling stronger, healthier, as was Joyce. She did, on occasion, get discouraged every time she saw her bare feet.

She kept telling Juan that she had to get rid of all her open toe shoes.

"You are out of your mind," Juan told her every time. "All that money I spent on designer shoes? If you don't wear them, I will."

Every time he said it, they fell out laughing.

One afternoon, while Juan sat in his sitting room doing his devotionals, the phone rang.

It was Deacon Smith from The Comfort Zone.

"We had a church meeting," Deacon began, "And we were wondering if you can do us the pleasure of preaching for us tomorrow. I know it's the last minute, but we would love it if you could come."

Juan was stunned by those words. "Can you please hold the line for a moment?" he asked.

Deacon Smith said, "Sure."

Juan walked into the kitchen where Joyce was. "Baby, it's Deacon Smith on the telephone and he is asking me if I would be their guest speaker tomorrow."

"What do you think about that?" asked Joyce.

"Should I do it?"

"Juan, do what you feel is best. They need to hear the truth, the word of the Living God versus what they are used to."

"Alright" he said, nodding. "I'll do it."

Joyce smiled. "Well you know Sallie is not there, so I'm okay."

Juan went back into the sitting room, picked up the phone, and said, "Deacon Smith, I talked it over with my wife, and it's a go."

After Juan got off the phone, he then realized that he hadn't preached for quite sometime.

"What am I going to say?" he asked himself. "What am I going to do?" His mind was all over the place. So he immediately went into prayer. After he got out of prayer, the Lord had given him everything that he needed; it was like he never skipped a beat.

Joyce called Rachael.

Rachael answered, "Girl, what's going on?"

"Juan received a phone call today from Deacon Smith, asking if he would be a guest speaker tomorrow at The Comfort Zone."

"Hush your mouth," said Rachael. "Well what did he say?"

"He said yes, so I was wondering if you and Forest would come and support him."

"We will definitely be there," Rachael said. "Of course."

Joyce received the same kind of encouraging words from the Tanankas when she called them.

When she called Lisa, Joyce found her a little hesitant, which was understandable considering the insanity that had ensued.

"Juan will be the guest speaker at The Comfort Zone tomorrow, and we were wondering if you and the kids would come to support him."

"Sure but please forgive me," Lisa said, "I'm a little apprehensive when it comes to that place. I'll make sure I'm all prayed up before walking into that place."

"I truly understand, Lisa. Believe me. It's going to be hard for all of us."

Juan was in the kitchen reading his Bible, and the Lord told him to preach on the topic of restoring one's walk in Christ. Juan saw the need because The Comfort Zone had experienced a lot of trauma and the false doctrine they were receiving was ridiculous.

Ashshod and the other angels were in the kitchen with Juan just floating about and still protecting him.

Ashshod said to Zaso, Enu and Hunter, "We will be here just for a little while longer. The others are happy to be back in the presence of The Almighty God. Our jobs are not completed yet, but they will be real soon."

Early Sunday morning Ashshod and the angels were watching Juan get ready for Sunday morning service. Ashshod told Zaso, Enu and Hunter to go to the church and wait for him and that he had everything under control at the house and that he would see them later. They left and Ashshod just watched on.

Juan was so nervous; he didn't know why he was feeling this way. Joyce noticed and told him to calm down.

"Honey," she said, "It's like riding a bike. You never forget how to do it."

"Well Joyce, it seems to have been quite a while since I've been on a bike," replied Juan. Joyce just hit Juan and they both chuckled.

At The Comfort Zone, Deacon Smith met Juan and Joyce at the door. Their friends met them in the lobby.

Ashshod appeared at the church and met up with Zaso and Hunter. "How are things here?" he asked.

"Things are going well," replied Hunter.

"Well as you know, Ashshod, there are a few imps left here, but they can't cause any harm," said Zaso.

"Yes, we will never get rid of those irritating imps until the Lord says so," said Ashshod. "I need for you all to fly up and down the aisle and make sure that things are in order."

The three imps that were left at The Comfort Zone would not cause any trouble; they had little power. They were left there to let it be known that you can't get rid of Satan easily.

Juan walked down that aisle and all he could remember was what happened to Trendon. As he walked up into the pulpit, he looked at the very spot the Lord took Trendon's life. All he could do was shake his head.

The praise team sang two songs and nothing had changed in the order of service. The congregation had about 1000 people in attendance; it was more than Juan had on any given Sunday. Juan became sick to his stomach with the order of service, but he had to remember that he was there to spread the unadulterated gospel of Jesus Christ and that he was not their pastor.

Juan saw Joyce, Rachael, Forest, Lisa, Jane, John, and Trevor; they were all in the area they normally sat in. It warmed his heart to see Trevor sitting next to his parents.

One of the associate ministers introduced Juan and he stood behind the podium. It was an experience that he never would have ever fathomed. Juan looked around and all he could do was remember when he was standing up there and had his massive stroke. He thought he would never move again let alone walk all by himself.

What a wonderful feeling, Juan thought. After he got himself together, he preached and the Lord really used him.

After service, Joyce and the gang hugged him and said, "Well done."

Joyce said, "Honey, I told you it was like riding a bike."

He hugged Joyce and loved her all the more for believing in him.

"The congregation seemed to receive me well," he said. "It was great to preach again."

Joyce and Juan visited different local congregations and it was nice to fellowship with different local churches. All during the summer, The Comfort Zone asked Juan to speak and he spoke there six times. Each time it was an experience. Every time Juan preached, the Lord always gave him a powerful message.

On Tuesday morning after Labor Day, Joyce and Juan just finished eating their breakfast when the telephone rang. Juan picked it up and it was Deacon Smith.

"Hello Deacon Smith," Juan said.

"Hello, Reverend Cortez," replied Deacon Smith.

"How can I help you?"

"Reverend Cortez, we had a very serious church meeting last night."

"Okay."

"We have voted and we would like to know if you will be our new pastor."

Juan dropped the phone; he could not believe his ears. All he heard was *Hello, Hello, Hello*, and he remembered Deacon Smith was on the other line.

"I am so sorry, deacon, I dropped the telephone. I must pray about this and talk this over with my wife."

"I understand, reverend. I also need to tell you that the salary is $2,000 a week with great benefits and four weeks of paid vacation."

"Thank you for informing me," said Juan.

"Can you give me an answer by Saturday because we would love to see you in the pulpit on Sunday," said Deacon Smith.

As soon as he got off the phone, Juan said, "Heavenly Father, oh how I adore thee. You have literally given me another chance to live and serve you. I have a great portion of my health and strength, and I am going to do your will to the fullest. Thank you, Lord, so very much for giving me the second opportunity. Lord, if this is your will, please let me know. Lord, I will wait until you speak to my spirit."

Juan walked into the kitchen and found Joyce still cleaning up from breakfast.

"Who was on the telephone?" she asked.

"Deacon Smith," Juan replied.

"What did he want? Let me guess, he wants you to be the guest speaker for this coming Sunday."

"No Joyce, the church asked if I could be their new pastor."

Joyce stopped cleaning and looked at Juan. "What?" she asked.

"You heard me. And that is not the half of it. They offered me $2,000 dollars a week, four weeks of paid vacation, and full medical benefits for us."

Joyce could not believe her ears. "Juan, what are you going to do?"

"I must wait until I hear from the Heavenly Father."

Joyce smiled and nodded. "I know, Juan, I know."

Juan left and went into the living room. He got on his knees and prayed; he was on his knees and in prayer for five hours. Joyce knew not to disturb him. She had to go pick up a few items from the grocery store and then to the cleaners and run other errands; it was great timing. He prayed quietly on his knees, waiting on the Lord to give him an answer. After prayer, Juan went into the kitchen because Joyce was preparing dinner, and he wanted to know what was smelling so good.

"Hi Honey," he said.

"How are you?" she said.

"Fine thanks, baby, for asking. What are you cooking for dinner tonight?"

"Ox tails, mac and cheese, cabbage, and cornbread," replied Joyce.

"What, is this a celebration dinner?"

"Yes it is because of your job offer."

"Wow, I should get more offers if we will eat like this," said Juan.

Friday morning Juan got up and did his morning devotion with the Lord, and the Lord led him to call Deacon Smith.

"I'm calling," Juan said, "Because I want to address some of my concerns."

Deacon Smith said, "That's fine. Go ahead."

"If I accept the pastor position, I will get rid of Marco's false ten commandments. I will put the crosses back in the church, inside and out. I will also put the church covenant back inside the church. Last but not least I will change the name of The Comfort Zone back to Solid Rock Missionary Baptist Church. The cultic brainwashing tactics that Marco and Trendon started will cease. I am led by the Spirit of God to address these issues, circumstances and categories. This is all I needed to say."

"Well, Reverend Cortez, if the Lord is leading you this way, we will accept it," replied Deacon Smith.

"Deacon Smith, I'm so surprised that you allowed these men to bring false doctrine in God's house. You knew better than that." Deacon Smith was quiet. "I will call you back with my answer on Saturday," Juan said.

"We will eagerly be awaiting your response," said Deacon Smith.

Early Saturday morning about 2:30 a.m., the Lord awakened Juan and he got up out of bed and went into the living room. He did not want to disturb Joyce. God had a talk with Juan and told him to take the position and He also gave him more direction and told Juan to get rid of individuals in positions and how he was to change a lot of other things around the church.

Juan said, "Okay Heavenly Father." After the Lord finished talking to him, it was 5:30 a.m. He had his morning devotion and went back to bed around 7:00 a.m.

When Juan awakened, it was well after 3:00p.m. in the afternoon.

He called out to Joyce, asking her why she allowed him to sleep in so late.

"Because the Lord was talking with you, and I just wanted you to rest, that's all," Joyce said.

"Joyce, the Lord told me to take the position and to get rid of people and to do a bunch of other things pertaining to putting things back in order."

"Well, you know that you were called to do what God says, and that you fear God and that you will do just what He led and commanded you to do."

"I'm going to call Deacon Smith and tell him that I'm going to accept the position." But before doing so, he went into prayer.

Juan called Deacon Smith and informed him that he was going to take the position. He was happy, but he said that a problem had occurred.

Juan asked, "What was that?"

He told Juan that someone on the pulpit committee took matters into their own hands and called our second choice and told him that he had the position. He needed for Juan to preach the next day and said everything would be handled that evening at a church meeting.

"Don't worry, reverend," Deacon Smith said. "I've got this covered."

Juan got off of the phone and immediately got on his knees and went back into prayer. After prayer Juan spoke with Joyce and he told her what happened. All she could say was, "You've got to be kidding me."

Joyce called Rachael and the rest of the gang and told them that Juan would be preaching the next day, and they all vowed to be there. After she got off the phone, Joyce told Juan that everyone would be there. He was pleased, but he would have paid anything to be a fly on the wall to see what was going on at the church meeting.

Ashshod, Zaso, Enu and Hunter arrived at The Comfort Zone, checking things out. Of course Satan's little imps were there, happy because there was some havoc going on. Ashshod paid them no mind because they had no power; they were just decoration. Their appearance was enough to cause a ripple, but not strong enough to cause waters to rage.

After the meeting was over, Deacon Smith went into the pastor's study and called their new pastor.

When the new pastor answered his phone, Deacon Smith said, "Welcome aboard, Pastor Cortez."

Sunday morning, Ashshod, Zaso, Enu, and Hunter were at the sanctuary, all smiles. The battle had been fought—small fights leading up to the ultimate battle, and for this day, God had won.

Juan stood at the podium and spoke into the microphone. "Thank God for this wonderful opportunity." He shook his head, smiled, then added, "Please don't stand when I walk down the aisle because I am not to be worshipped. Also, the order of service will be changing. This is the House of God, and it was turned into a den of thieves. If you can't accept these changes, we will pray for you."

After a moment of silence, Juan preached from the book 1Peter on the subject of false teachers. He opened the door of the church and extended the invitation to Jesus Christ. Ten people came forward. The energy among the congregation was high and palpable. The congregation welcomed Juan in so sweetly. Joyce hugged Juan so tightly and kissed him. John hugged and squeezed Juan as Jane, Rachael and Lisa sobbed.

Juan went back to his old office, an office that held decades of wonderful memories. He changed clothes and broke down and cried while doing so.

"Thank you, Lord," he said, "For this wonderful opportunity and the great portion of my health and strength." After he gathered himself together, he joined the gang, and they all went out to celebrate.

Monday morning, Juan met Deacon Smith at the church, and told Deacon Smith that as of that moment, he would be released of his duties.

"I just can't see how someone in this position could be so easily persuaded," Juan said. Deacon Smith admitted that he sensed this decision coming and understood.

Upon dismissing Deacon Smith, Juan called John and asked him to be a deacon in training; he was so honored.

As soon as that was handled, Juan picked up the phone again to order a bigger and better sign for the church that would read *Solid Rock Missionary Baptist Church...To the Utmost JESUS Saves!*

Ashshod, Zaso, Enu and Hunter looked around and nodded.

"Our mission is completed," Ashshod said. "It's time for us to return to our Heavenly Father."

With smiles upon their angelic faces, the foursome flew up into the sunny skies then vanished.